DEMONIC™

CREATED BY
ROBERT KIRKMAN & **MARC SILVESTRI**

CHRISTOPHER SEBELA
WRITER

NIKO WALTER
ARTIST

DAN BROWN
COLORIST

SAL CIPRIANO
LETTERER

SEAN MACKIEWICZ
EDITOR

ARIELLE BASICH
ASSISTANT EDITOR

NIKO WALTER & DAN BROWN
COVER

SKYBOUND

FOR SKYBOUND ENTERTAINMENT
ROBERT KIRKMAN CHAIRMAN
DAVID ALPERT CEO
SEAN MACKIEWICZ SVP, EDITOR-IN-CHIEF
SHAWN KIRKHAM SVP, BUSINESS DEVELOPMENT
BRIAN HUNTINGTON ONLINE EDITORIAL DIRECTOR
JUNE ALIAN PUBLICITY DIRECTOR
JON MOISAN EDITOR
ARIELLE BASICH ASSISTANT EDITOR
ANDRES JUAREZ GRAPHIC DESIGNER
PAUL SHIN BUSINESS DEVELOPMENT ASSISTANT
JOHNNY O'DELL ONLINE EDITORIAL ASSISTANT
DAN PETERSEN OPERATIONS MANAGER
NICK PALMER OPERATIONS COORDINATOR

INTERNATIONAL INQUIRIES:
AG@SEQUENTIALRIGHTS.COM
LICENSING INQUIRIES:
CONTACT@SKYBOUND.COM
WWW.SKYBOUND.COM

image

IMAGE COMICS, INC.
Robert Kirkman—Chief Operating Officer
Erik Larsen—Chief Financial Officer
Todd McFarlane—President
Marc Silvestri—Chief Executive Officer
Jim Valentino—Vice-President

Eric Stephenson—Publisher
Corey Murphy—Director of Sales
Jeff Boison—Director of Publishing Planning & Book Trade Sale
Chris Ross—Director of Digital Sales
Kat Salazar—Director of PR & Marketing
Branwyn Bigglestone—Controller
Susan Korpela—Accounts Manager
Drew Gill—Art Director
Brett Warnock—Production Manager
Meredith Wallace—Print Manager
Briah Skelly—Publicist
Aly Hoffman—Conventions & Events Coordinator
Sasha Head—Sales & Marketing Production Designer
David Brothers—Branding Manager
Melissa Gifford—Content Manager
Erika Schnatz—Production Artist
Ryan Brewer—Production Artist
Shanna Matuszak—Production Artist
Tricia Ramos—Production Artist
Vincent Kukua—Production Artist
Jeff Stang—Direct Market Sales Representative
Emilio Bautista—Digital Sales Associate
Leanna Caunter—Accounting Assistant
Chloe Ramos-Peterson—Library Market Sales Representative
IMAGECOMICS.COM

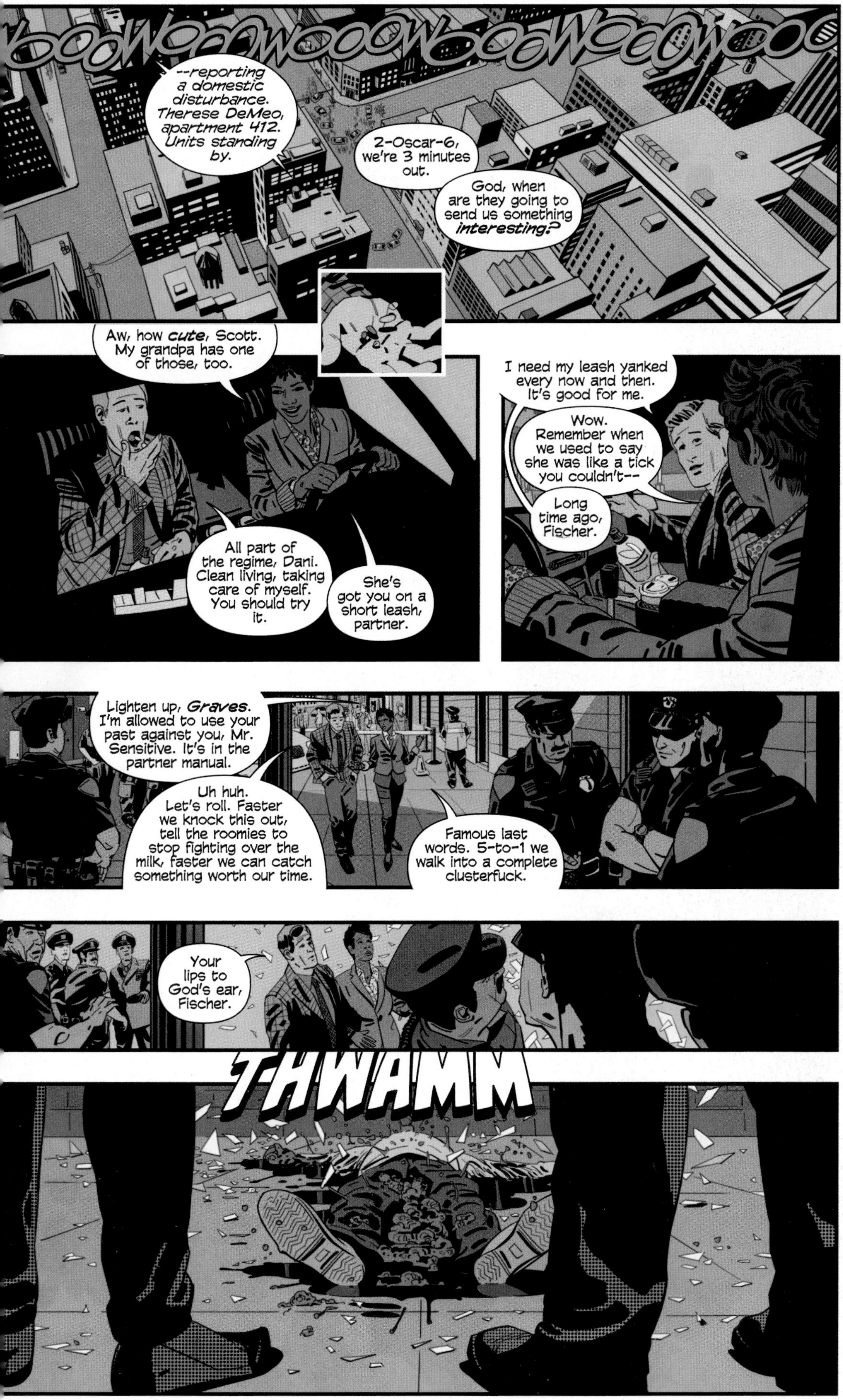

BOOOWOOOWOOOWBOOOWOOOWOOO
--reporting a domestic disturbance. Therese DeMeo, apartment 412. Units standing by.
2-Oscar-6, we're 3 minutes out.
God, when are they going to send us something *interesting?*
Aw, how *cute*, Scott. My grandpa has one of those, too.
All part of the regime, Dani. Clean living, taking care of myself. You should try it.
She's got you on a short leash, partner.
I need my leash yanked every now and then. It's good for me.
Wow. Remember when we used to say she was like a tick you couldn't--
Long time ago, Fischer.
Lighten up, *Graves*. I'm allowed to use your past against you, Mr. Sensitive. It's in the partner manual.
Uh huh. Let's roll. Faster we knock this out, tell the roomies to stop fighting over the milk, faster we can catch something worth our time.
Famous last words. 5-to-1 we walk into a complete clusterfuck.
Your lips to God's ear, Fischer.
THWAMM

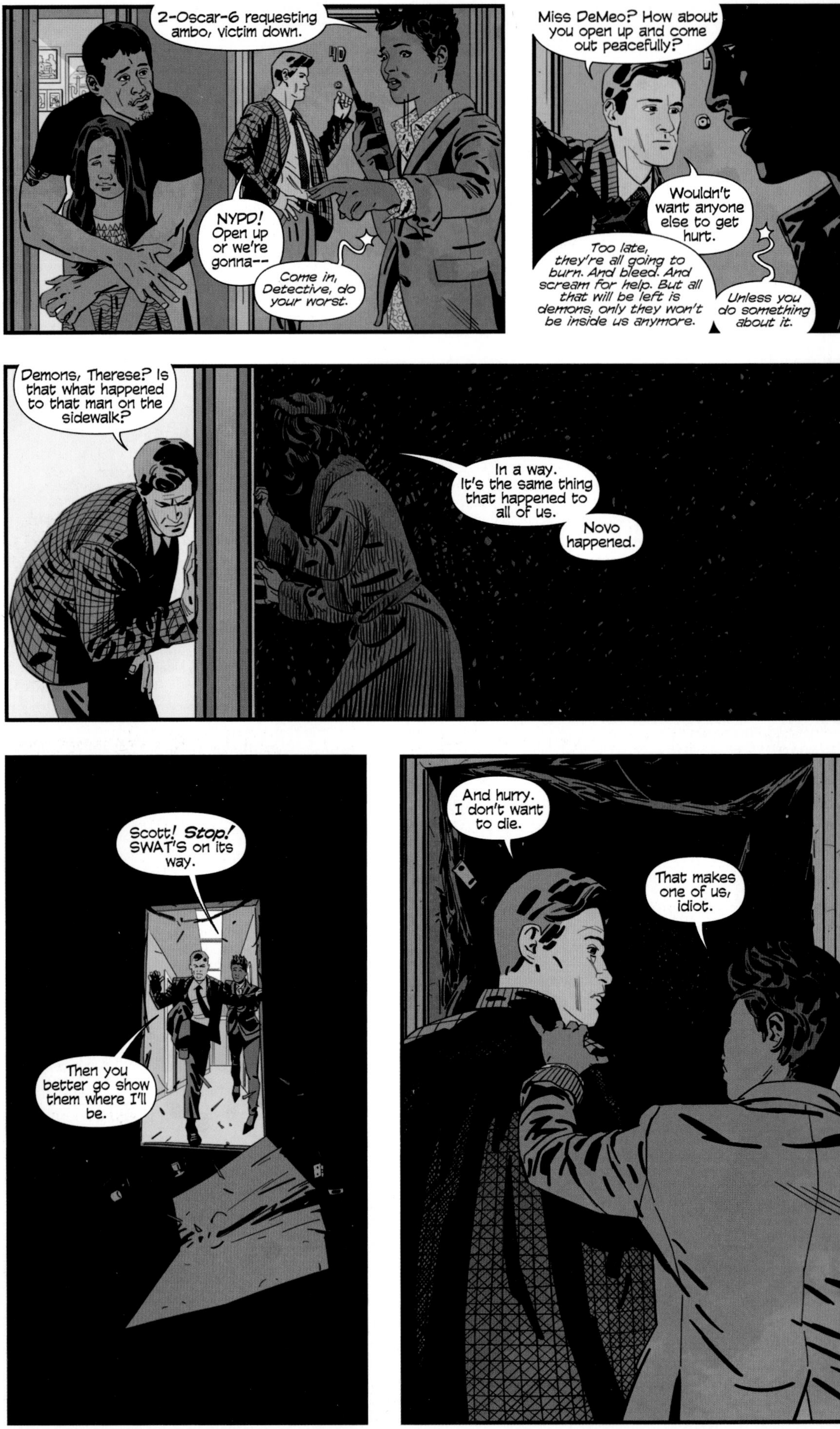
2-Oscar-6 requesting ambo, victim down.
NYPD! Open up or we're gonna--
Come in, Detective, do your worst.
Miss DeMeo? How about you open up and come out peacefully?
Wouldn't want anyone else to get hurt.
Too late, they're all going to burn. And bleed. And scream for help. But all that will be left is demons, only they won't be inside us anymore.
Unless you do something about it.
Demons, Therese? Is that what happened to that man on the sidewalk?
In a way. It's the same thing that happened to all of us.
Novo happened.
Scott! Stop! SWAT'S on its way.
Then you better go show them where I'll be.
And hurry. I don't want to die.
That makes one of us, idiot.

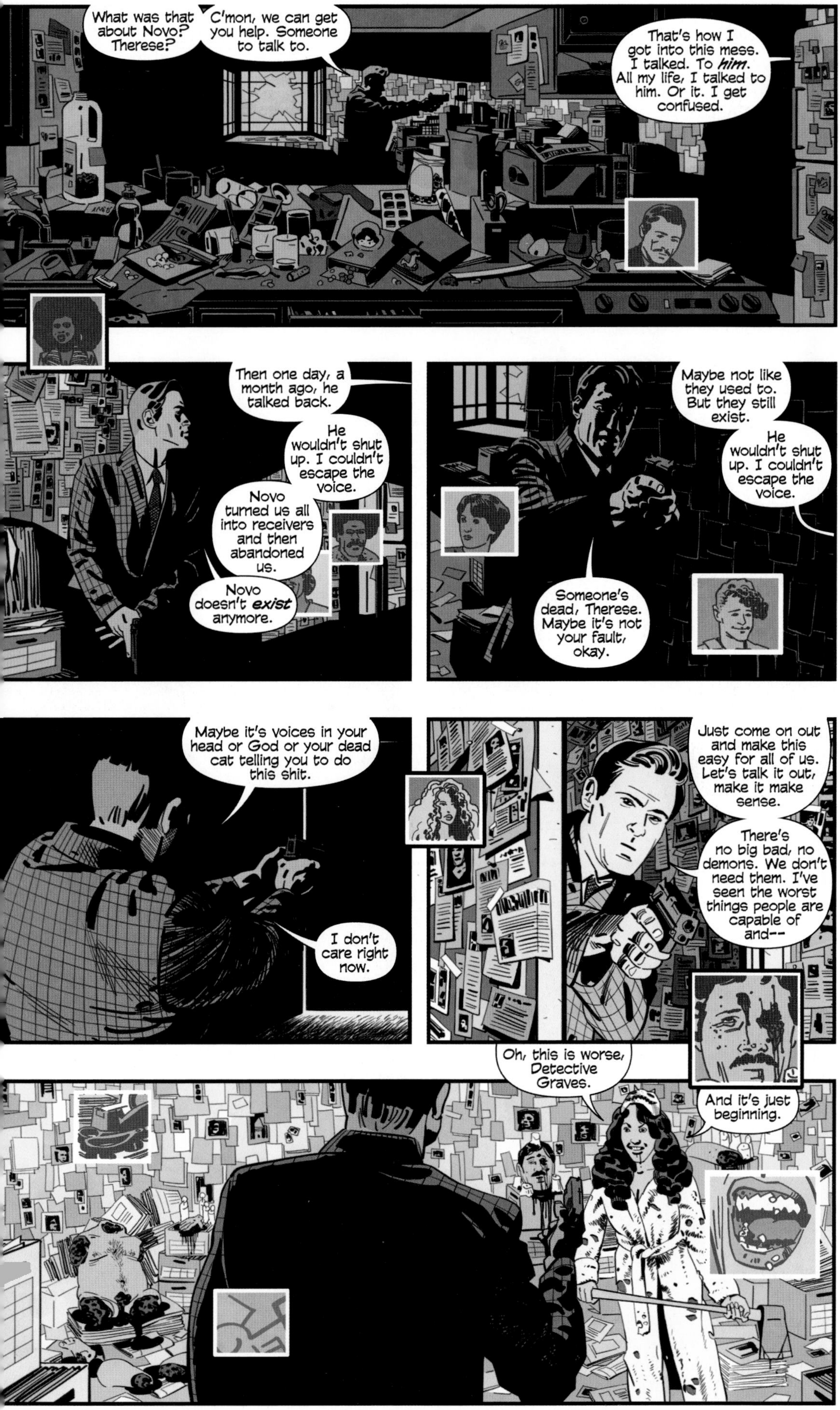
What was that about Novo? Therese?
C'mon, we can get you help. Someone to talk to.
That's how I got into this mess. I talked. To *him*. All my life, I talked to him. Or it. I get confused.
Then one day, a month ago, he talked back.
He wouldn't shut up. I couldn't escape the voice.
Novo turned us all into receivers and then abandoned us.
Novo doesn't *exist* anymore.
Maybe not like they used to. But they still exist.
He wouldn't shut up. I couldn't escape the voice.
Someone's dead, Therese. Maybe it's not your fault, okay.
Maybe it's voices in your head or God or your dead cat telling you to do this shit.
I don't care right now.
Just come on out and make this easy for all of us. Let's talk it out, make it make sense.
There's no big bad, no demons. We don't need them. I've seen the worst things people are capable of and--
Oh, this is worse, Detective Graves.
And it's just beginning.

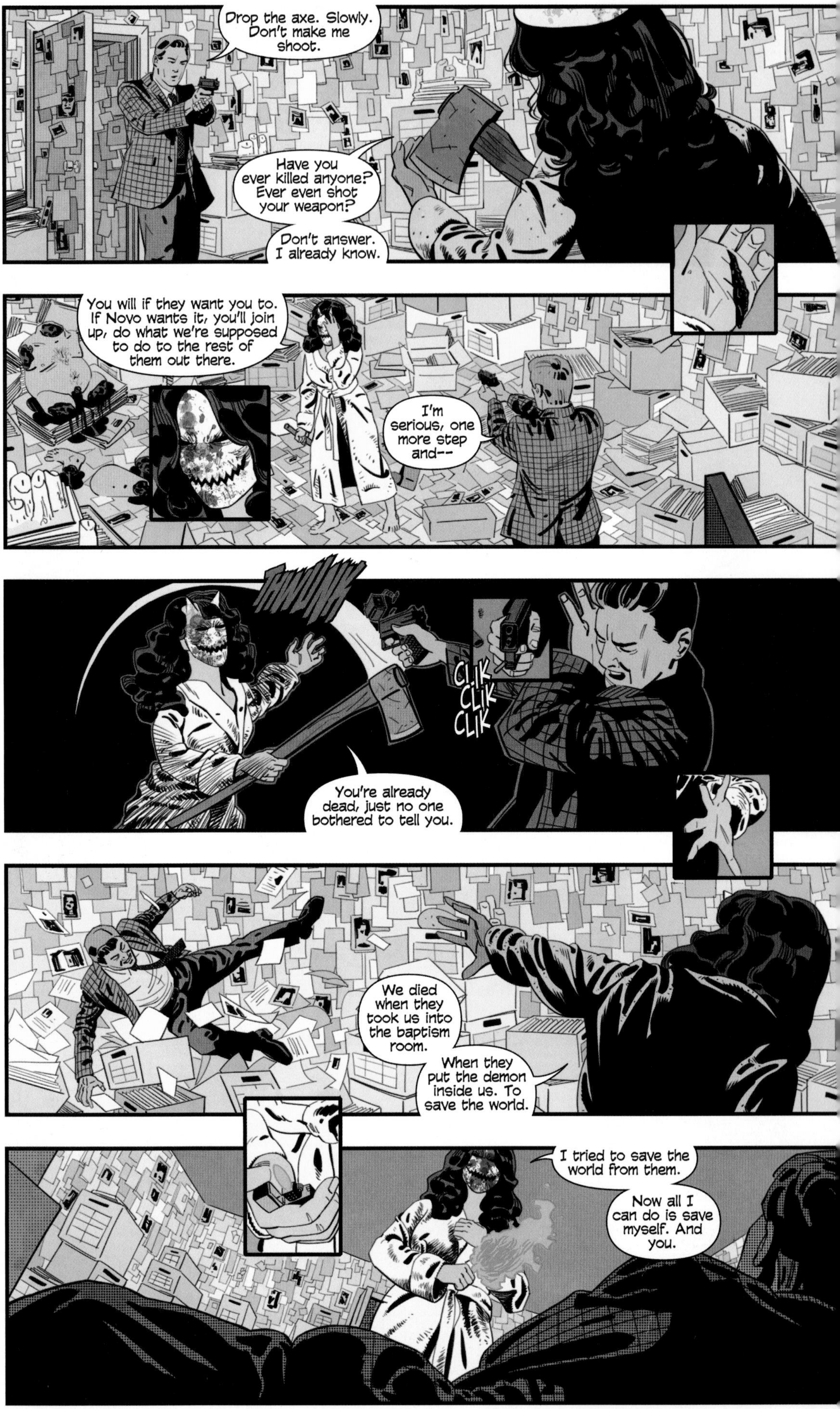
Drop the axe. Slowly. Don't make me shoot.
Have you ever killed anyone? Ever even shot your weapon?
Don't answer. I already know.
You will if they want you to. If Novo wants it, you'll join up, do what we're supposed to do to the rest of them out there.
I'm serious, one more step and--
THUNK
CLIK CLIK CLIK
You're already dead, just no one bothered to tell you.
We died when they took us into the baptism room.
When they put the demon inside us. To save the world.
I tried to save the world from them.
Now all I can do is save myself. And you.

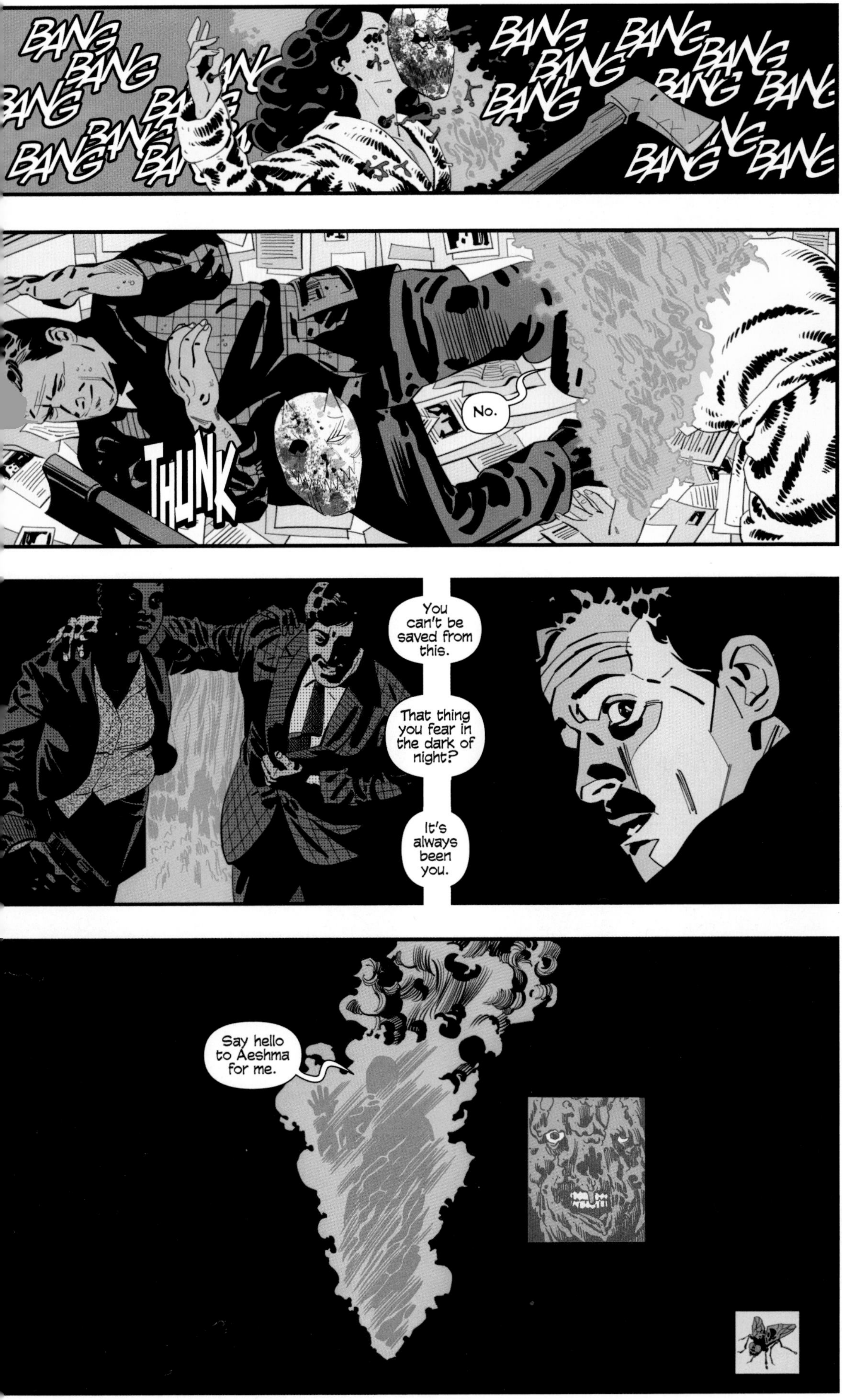
BANG BANG BANG BANG BANG BANG BANG
BANG BANG BANG BANG BANG BANG BANG BANG BANG
THUNK
No.
You can't be saved from this.
That thing you fear in the dark of night?
It's always been you.
Say hello to Aeshma for me.

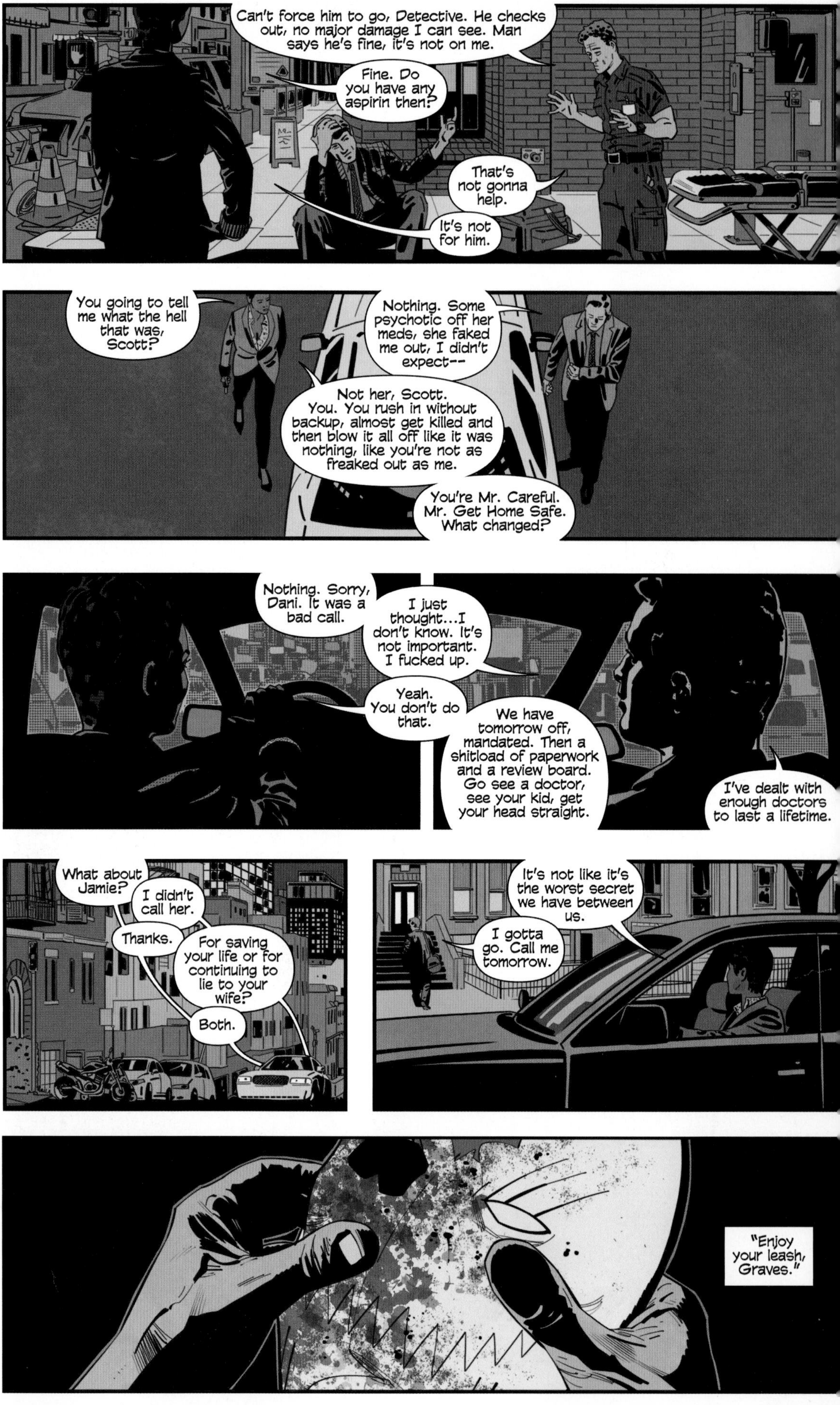

Can't force him to go, Detective. He checks out, no major damage I can see. Man says he's fine, it's not on me.
Fine. Do you have any aspirin then?
That's not gonna help.
It's not for him.
You going to tell me what the hell that was, Scott?
Nothing. Some psychotic off her meds, she faked me out, I didn't expect--
Not her, Scott. You. You rush in without backup, almost get killed and then blow it all off like it was nothing, like you're not as freaked out as me.
You're Mr. Careful. Mr. Get Home Safe. What changed?
Nothing. Sorry, Dani. It was a bad call.
I just thought...I don't know. It's not important. I fucked up.
Yeah. You don't do that.
We have tomorrow off, mandated. Then a shitload of paperwork and a review board. Go see a doctor, see your kid, get your head straight.
I've dealt with enough doctors to last a lifetime.
What about Jamie?
I didn't call her.
Thanks.
For saving your life or for continuing to lie to your wife?
Both.
It's not like it's the worst secret we have between us.
I gotta go. Call me tomorrow.
"Enjoy your leash, Graves."

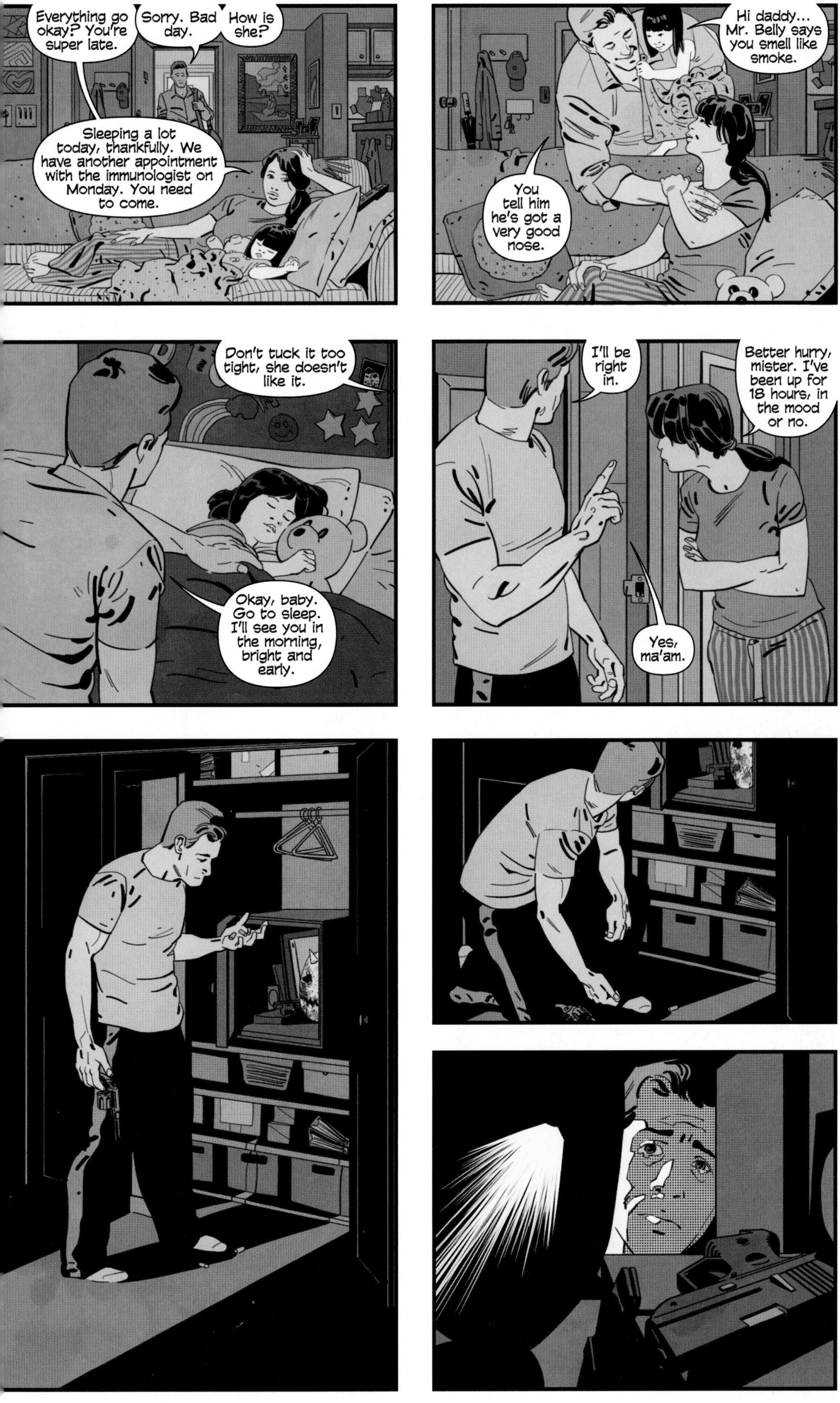
Everything go okay? You're super late.
Sorry. Bad day.
How is she?
Sleeping a lot today, thankfully. We have another appointment with the immunologist on Monday. You need to come.
Hi daddy... Mr. Belly says you smell like smoke.
You tell him he's got a very good nose.
Don't tuck it too tight, she doesn't like it.
Okay, baby. Go to sleep. I'll see you in the morning, bright and early.
I'll be right in.
Better hurry, mister. I've been up for 18 hours, in the mood or no.
Yes, ma'am.

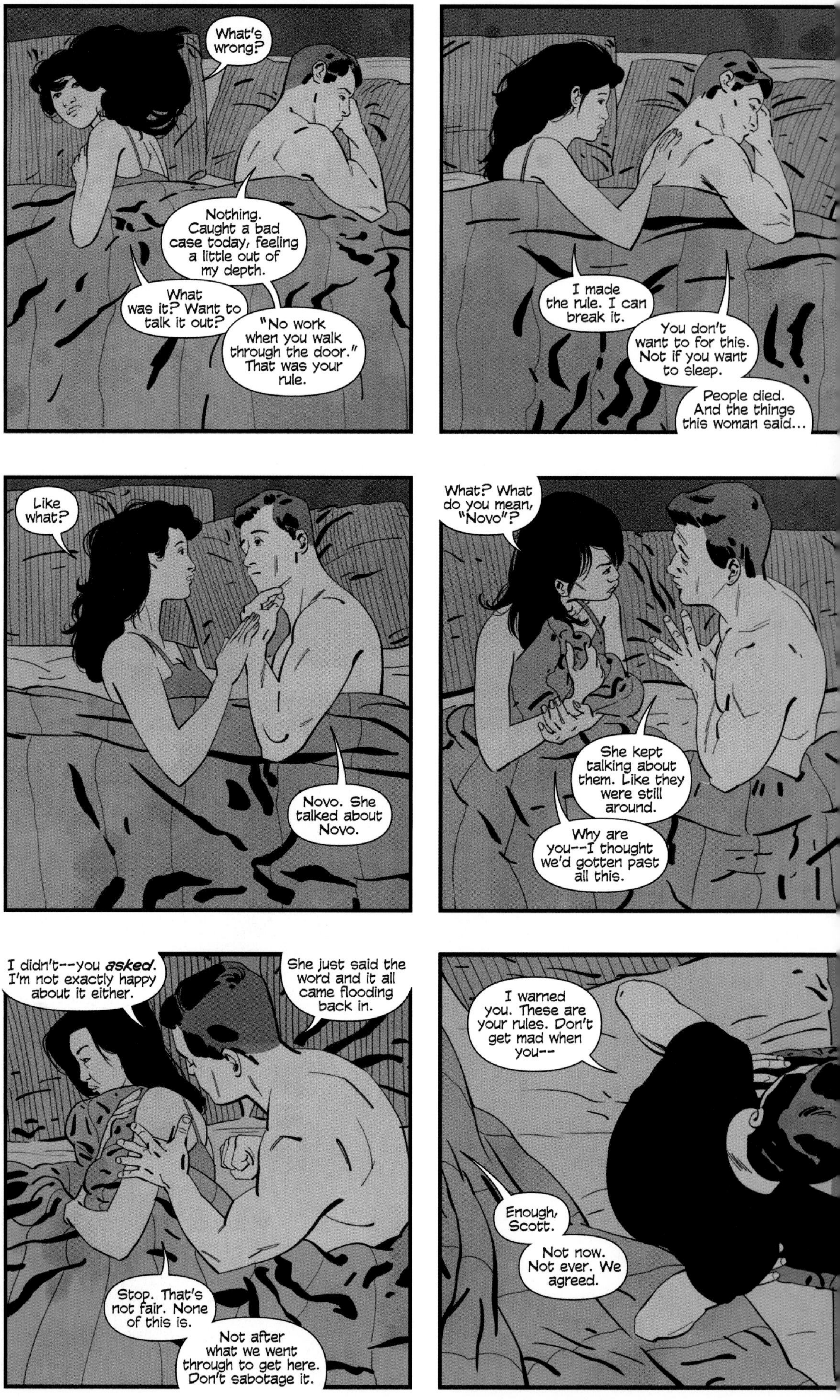
What's wrong?
Nothing. Caught a bad case today, feeling a little out of my depth.
What was it? Want to talk it out?
"No work when you walk through the door." That was your rule.
I made the rule. I can break it.
You don't want to for this. Not if you want to sleep.
People died. And the things this woman said...
Like what?
Novo. She talked about Novo.
What? What do you mean, "Novo"?
She kept talking about them. Like they were still around.
Why are you--I thought we'd gotten past all this.
I didn't--you *asked*. I'm not exactly happy about it either.
She just said the word and it all came flooding back in.
Stop. That's not fair. None of this is.
Not after what we went through to get here. Don't sabotage it.
I warned you. These are your rules. Don't get mad when you--
Enough, Scott.
Not now. Not ever. We agreed.

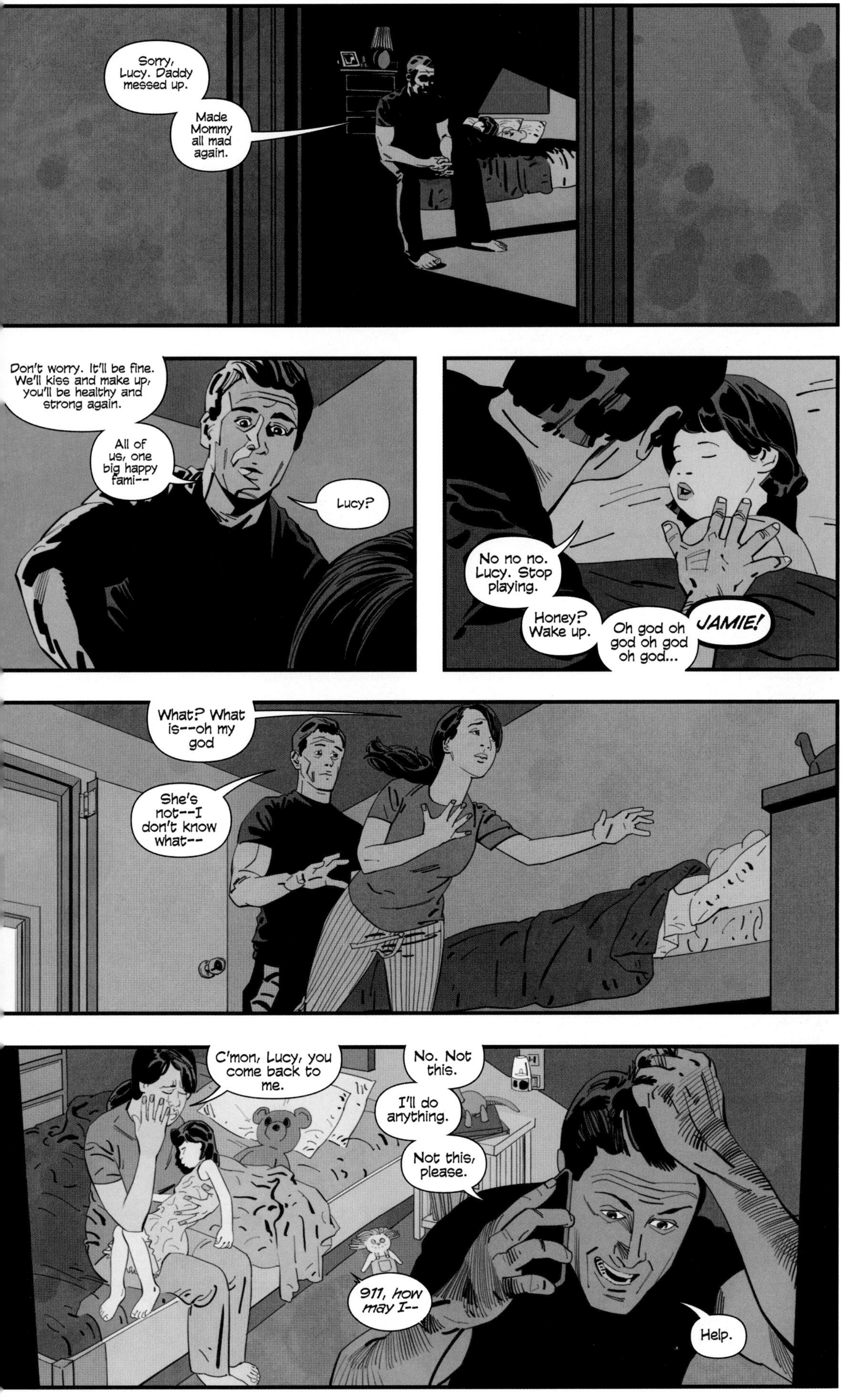
Sorry, Lucy. Daddy messed up.
Made Mommy all mad again.
Don't worry. It'll be fine. We'll kiss and make up, you'll be healthy and strong again.
All of us, one big happy fami--
Lucy?
No no no. Lucy. Stop playing.
Honey? Wake up.
Oh god oh god oh god oh god...
JAMIE!
What? What is--oh my god
She's not--I don't know what--
C'mon, Lucy, you come back to me.
No. Not this.
I'll do anything.
Not this, please.
911, how may I--
Help.

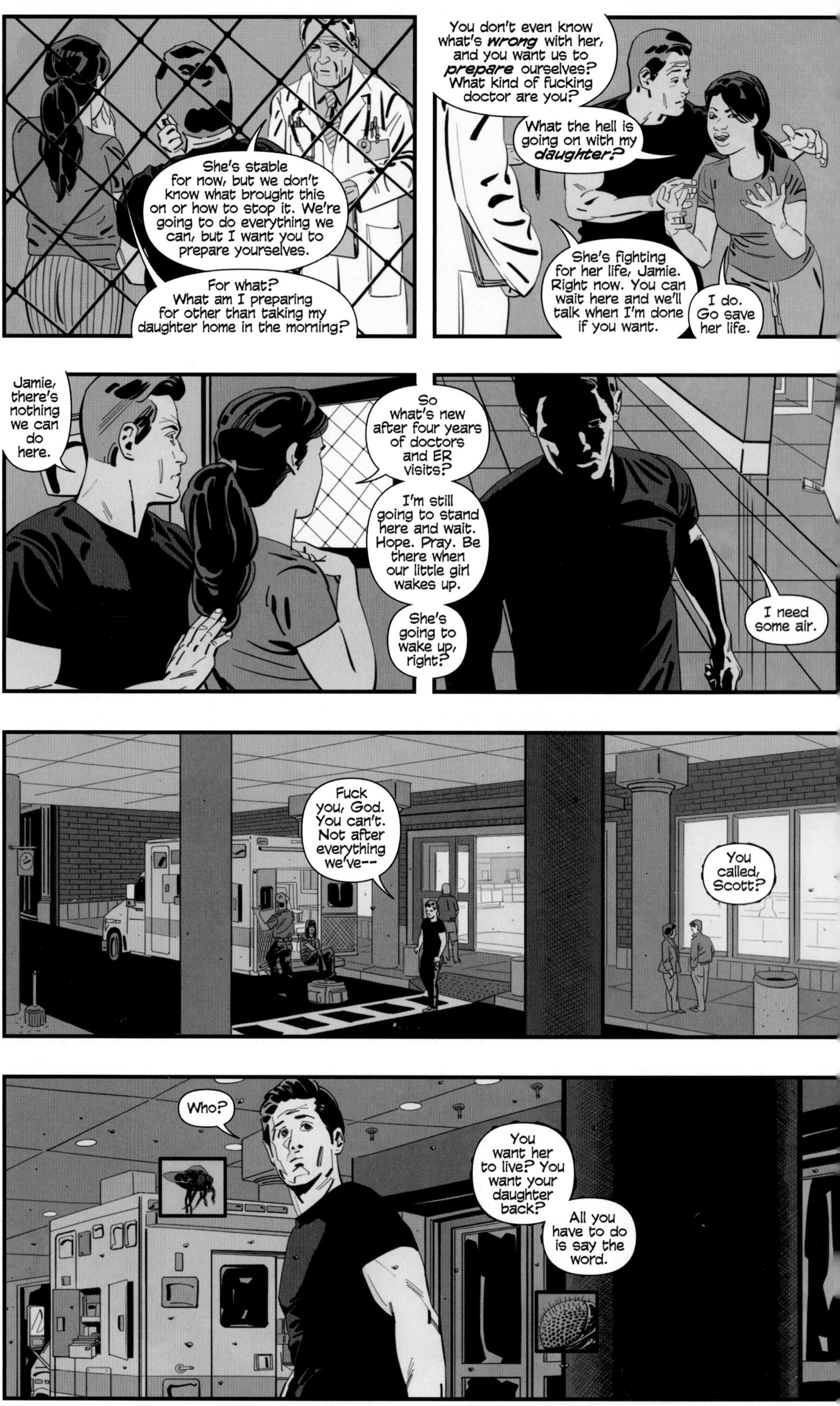
She's stable for now, but we don't know what brought this on or how to stop it. We're going to do everything we can, but I want you to prepare yourselves.
For what? What am I preparing for other than taking my daughter home in the morning?
You don't even know what's *wrong* with her, and you want us to *prepare* ourselves? What kind of fucking doctor are you?
What the hell is going on with my *daughter?*
She's fighting for her life, Jamie. Right now. You can wait here and we'll talk when I'm done if you want.
I do. Go save her life.
Jamie, there's nothing we can do here.
So what's new after four years of doctors and ER visits?
I'm still going to stand here and wait. Hope. Pray. Be there when our little girl wakes up.
She's going to wake up, right?
I need some air.
Fuck you, God. You can't. Not after everything we've--
You called, Scott?
Who?
You want her to live? You want your daughter back?
All you have to do is say the word.

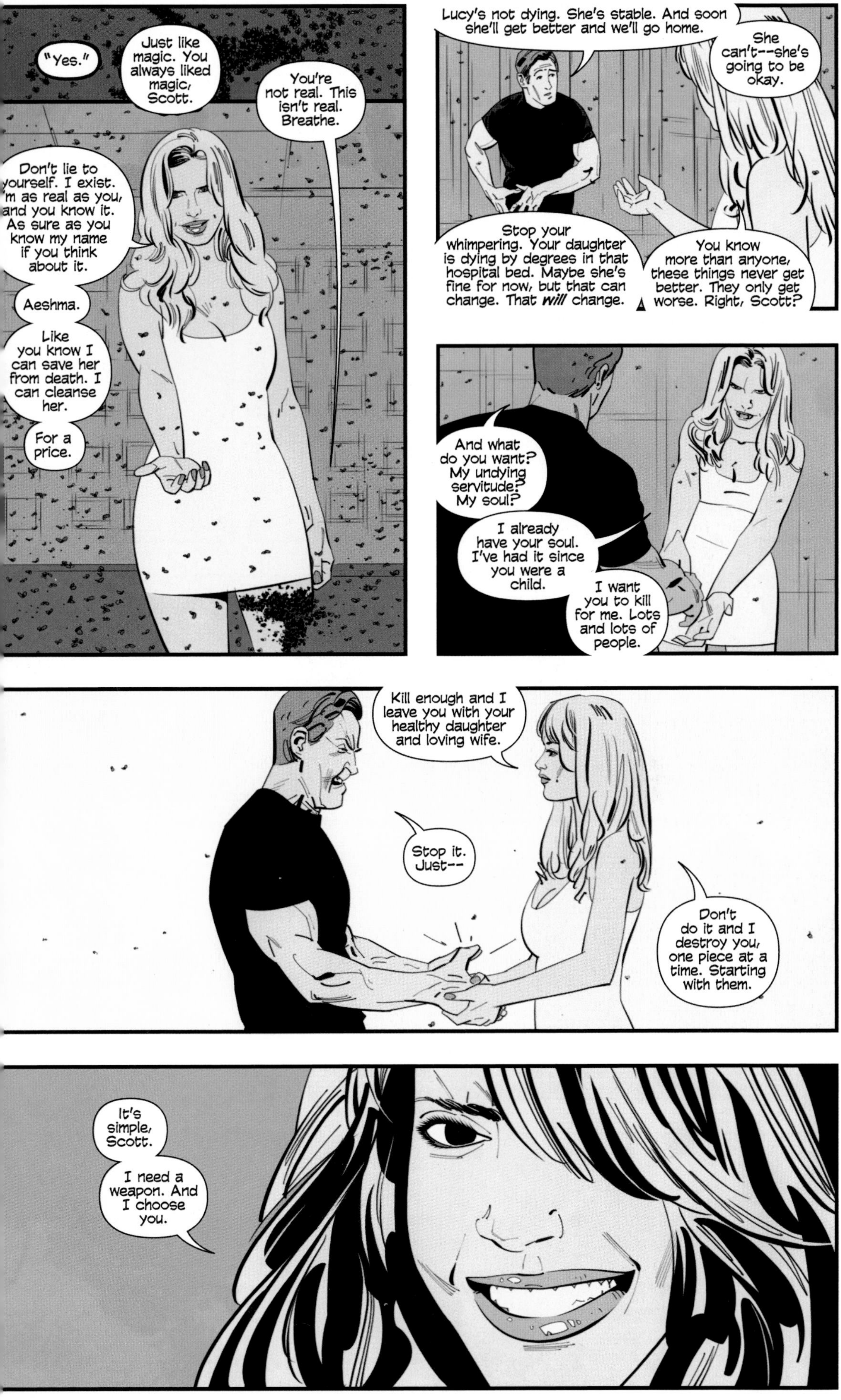
"Yes."
Just like magic. You always liked magic, Scott.
You're not real. This isn't real. Breathe.
Don't lie to yourself. I exist. 'm as real as you, and you know it. As sure as you know my name if you think about it.
Aeshma.
Like you know I can save her from death. I can cleanse her.
For a price.
Lucy's not dying. She's stable. And soon she'll get better and we'll go home.
She can't--she's going to be okay.
Stop your whimpering. Your daughter is dying by degrees in that hospital bed. Maybe she's fine for now, but that can change. That *will* change.
You know more than anyone, these things never get better. They only get worse. Right, Scott?
And what do you want? My undying servitude? My soul?
I already have your soul. I've had it since you were a child.
I want you to kill for me. Lots and lots of people.
Kill enough and I leave you with your healthy daughter and loving wife.
Stop it. Just--
Don't do it and I destroy you, one piece at a time. Starting with them.
It's simple, Scott.
I need a weapon. And I choose you.

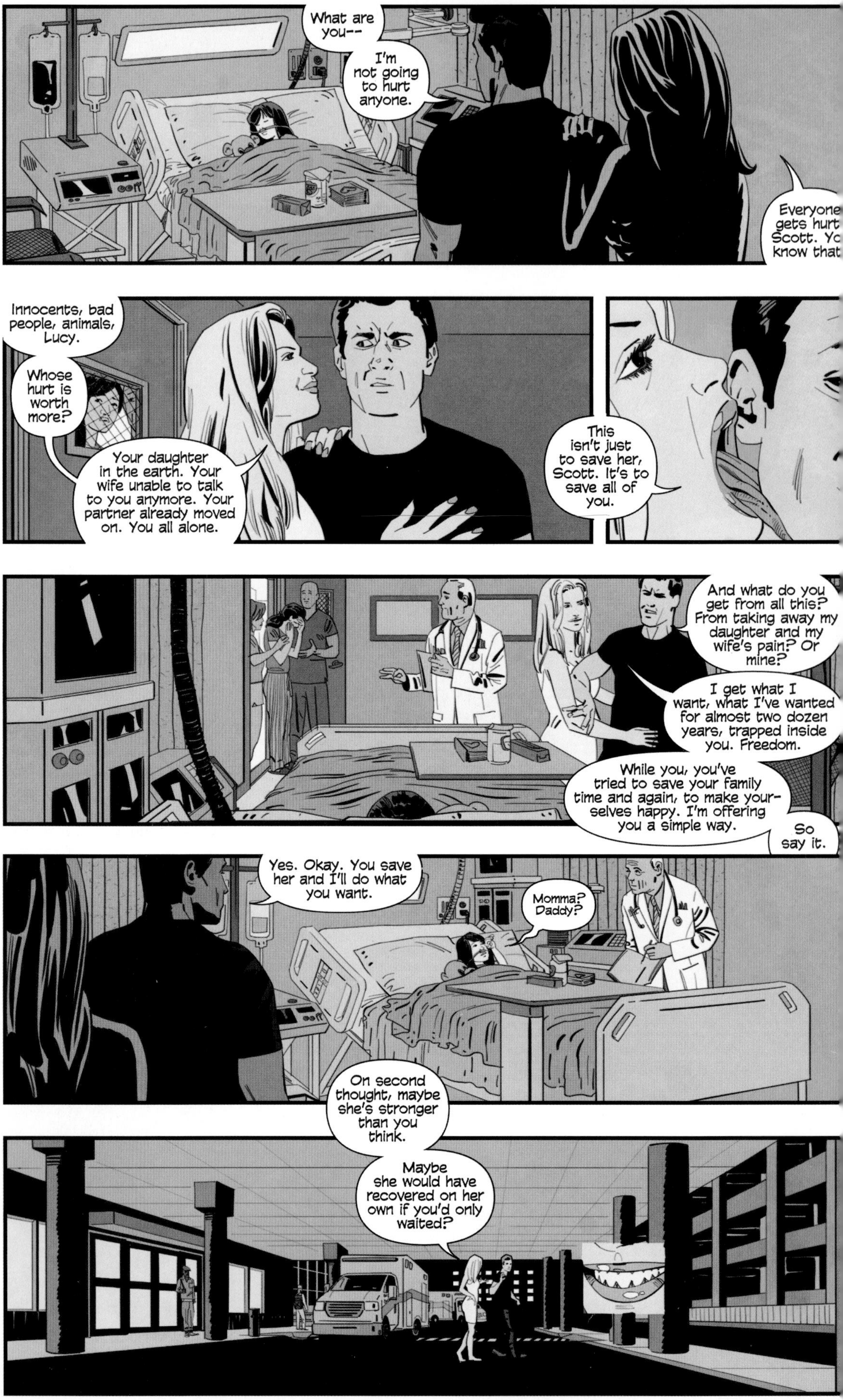
What are you--
I'm not going to hurt anyone.
Everyone gets hurt Scott. Yo know that
Innocents, bad people, animals, Lucy.
Whose hurt is worth more?
Your daughter in the earth. Your wife unable to talk to you anymore. Your partner already moved on. You all alone.
This isn't just to save her, Scott. It's to save all of you.
And what do you get from all this? From taking away my daughter and my wife's pain? Or mine?
I get what I want, what I've wanted for almost two dozen years, trapped inside you. Freedom.
While you, you've tried to save your family time and again, to make your-selves happy. I'm offering you a simple way.
So say it.
Yes. Okay. You save her and I'll do what you want.
Momma? Daddy?
On second thought, maybe she's stronger than you think.
Maybe she would have recovered on her own if you'd only waited?

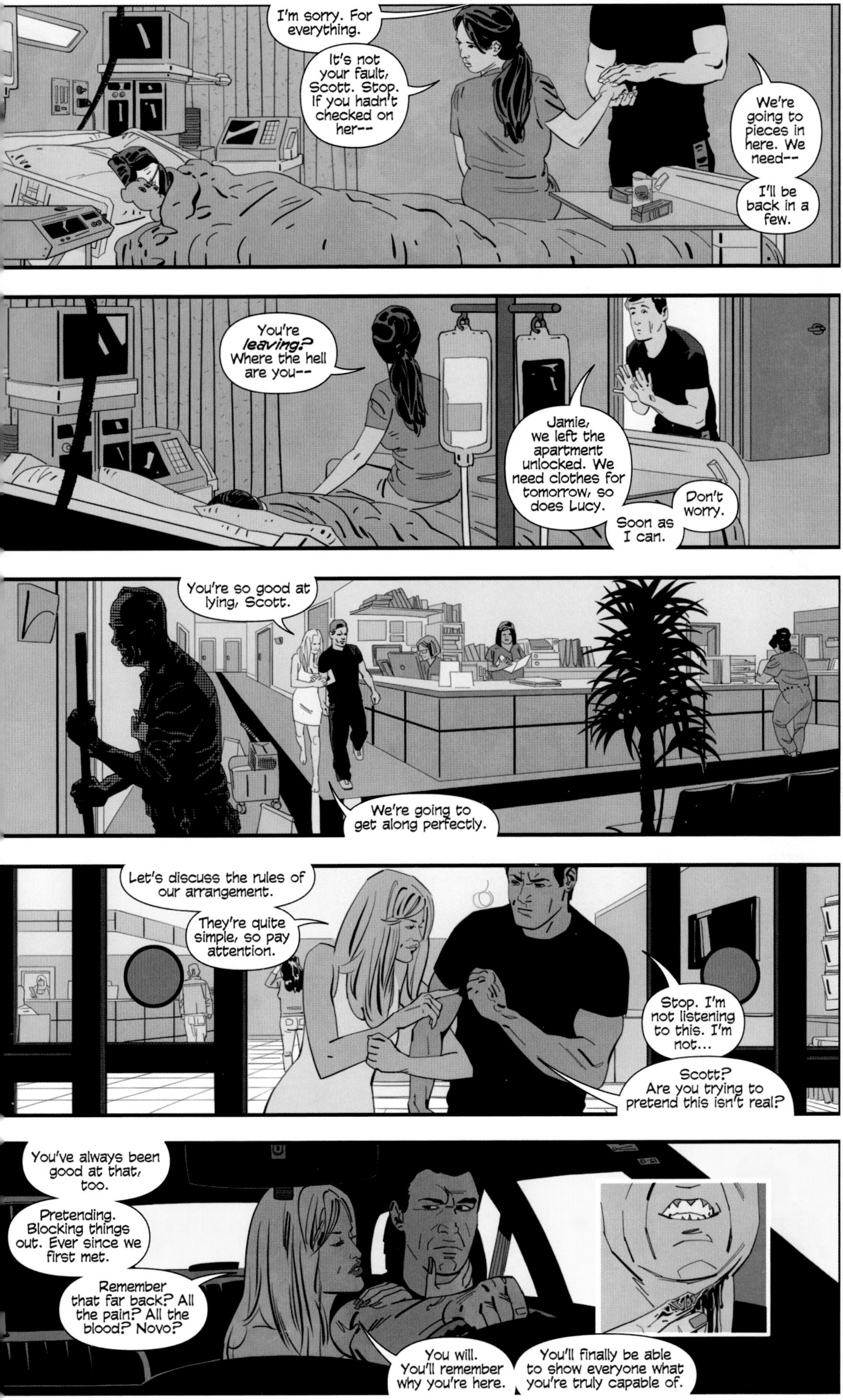
I'm sorry. For everything.
It's not your fault, Scott. Stop. If you hadn't checked on her--
We're going to pieces in here. We need--
I'll be back in a few.
You're *leaving?* Where the hell are you--
Jamie, we left the apartment unlocked. We need clothes for tomorrow, so does Lucy.
Don't worry.
Soon as I can.
You're so good at lying, Scott.
We're going to get along perfectly.
Let's discuss the rules of our arrangement.
They're quite simple, so pay attention.
Stop. I'm not listening to this. I'm not...
Scott? Are you trying to pretend this isn't real?
You've always been good at that, too.
Pretending. Blocking things out. Ever since we first met.
Remember that far back? All the pain? All the blood? Novo?
You will. You'll remember why you're here.
You'll finally be able to show everyone what you're truly capable of.

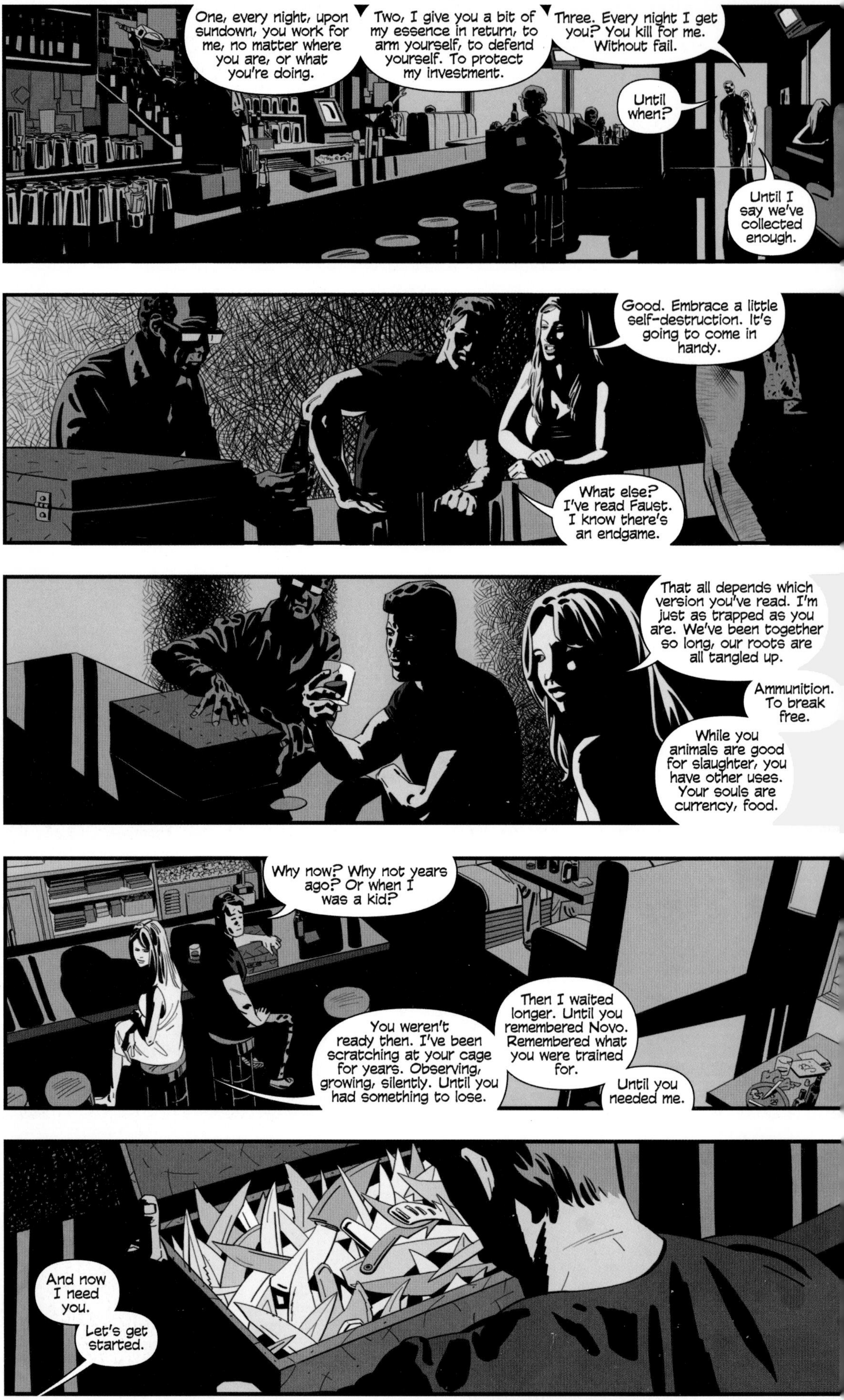
One, every night, upon sundown, you work for me, no matter where you are, or what you're doing.
Two, I give you a bit of my essence in return, to arm yourself, to defend yourself. To protect my investment.
Three. Every night I get you? You kill for me. Without fail.
Until when?
Until I say we've collected enough.
Good. Embrace a little self-destruction. It's going to come in handy.
What else? I've read Faust. I know there's an endgame.
That all depends which version you've read. I'm just as trapped as you are. We've been together so long, our roots are all tangled up.
Ammunition. To break free.
While you animals are good for slaughter, you have other uses. Your souls are currency, food.
Why now? Why not years ago? Or when I was a kid?
You weren't ready then. I've been scratching at your cage for years. Observing, growing, silently. Until you had something to lose.
Then I waited longer. Until you remembered Novo. Remembered what you were trained for.
Until you needed me.
And now I need you.
Let's get started.

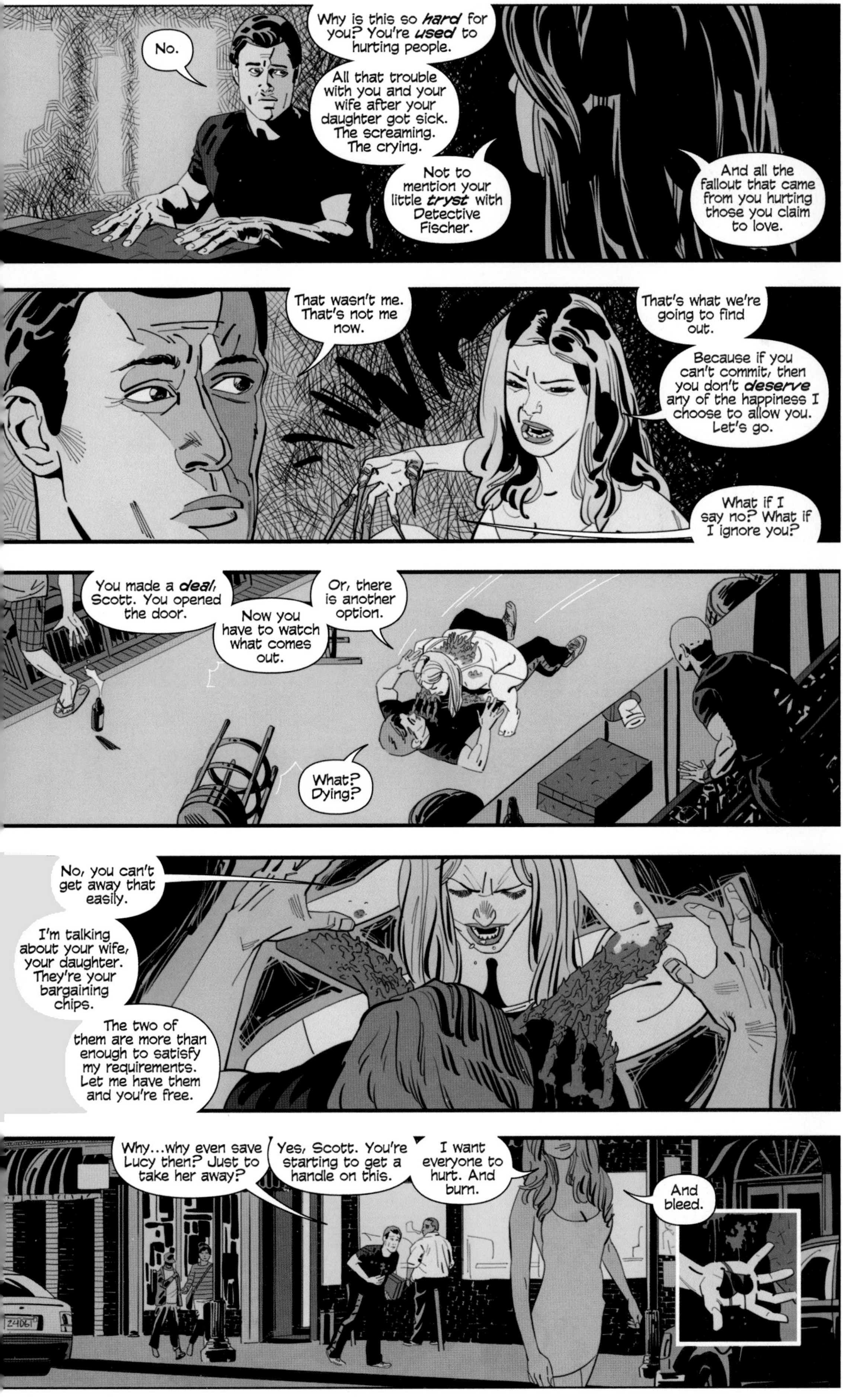
No.
Why is this so *hard* for you? You're *used* to hurting people.
All that trouble with you and your wife after your daughter got sick. The screaming. The crying.
Not to mention your little *tryst* with Detective Fischer.
And all the fallout that came from you hurting those you claim to love.
That wasn't me. That's not me now.
That's what we're going to find out.
Because if you can't commit, then you don't *deserve* any of the happiness I choose to allow you. Let's go.
What if I say no? What if I ignore you?
You made a *deal*, Scott. You opened the door.
Now you have to watch what comes out.
Or, there is another option.
What? Dying?
No, you can't get away that easily.
I'm talking about your wife, your daughter. They're your bargaining chips.
The two of them are more than enough to satisfy my requirements. Let me have them and you're free.
Why...why even save Lucy then? Just to take her away?
Yes, Scott. You're starting to get a handle on this.
I want everyone to hurt. And burn.
And bleed.

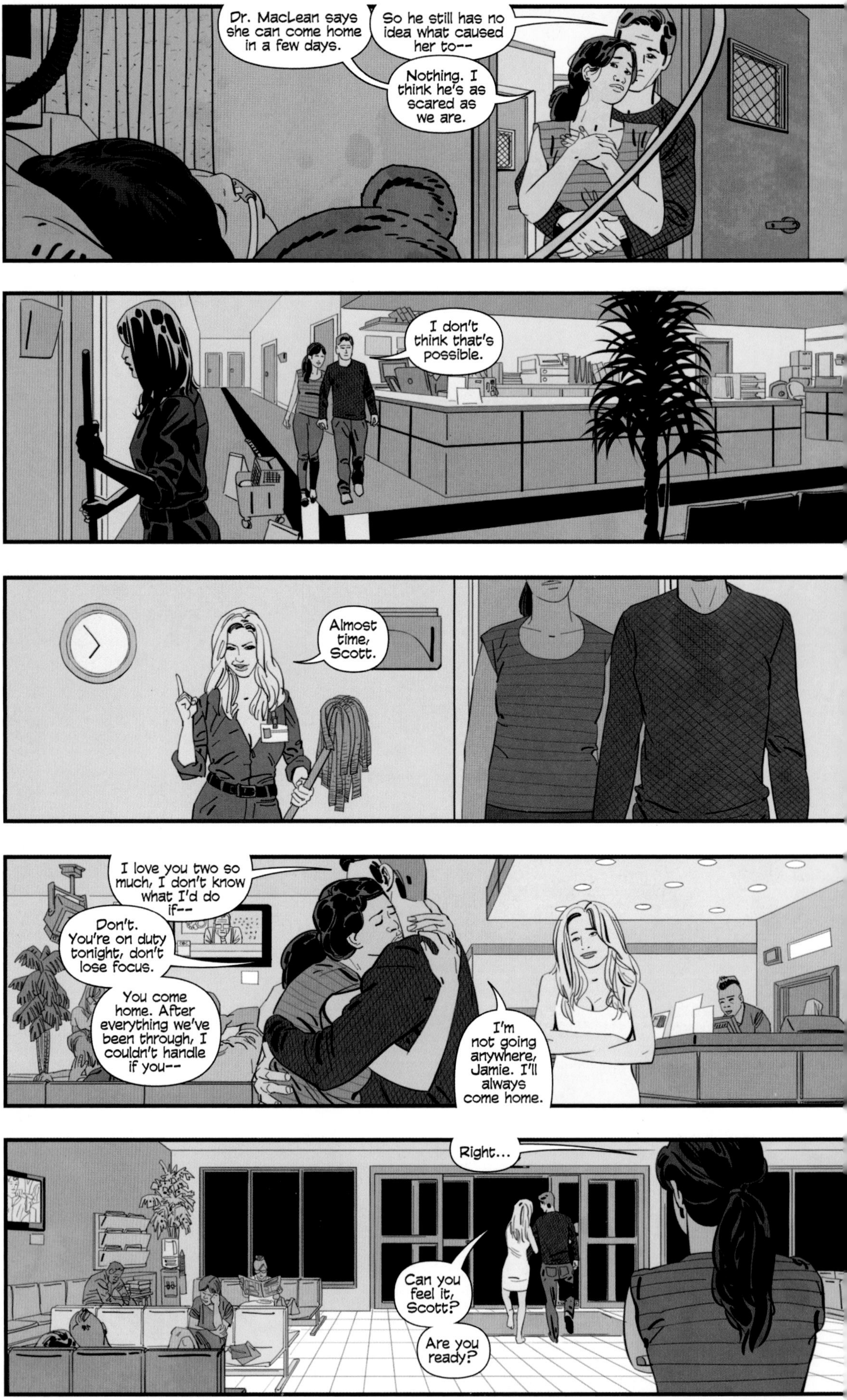
Dr. MacLean says she can come home in a few days.
So he still has no idea what caused her to--
Nothing. I think he's as scared as we are.
I don't think that's possible.
Almost time, Scott.
I love you two so much, I don't know what I'd do if--
Don't. You're on duty tonight, don't lose focus.
You come home. After everything we've been through, I couldn't handle if you--
I'm not going anywhere, Jamie. I'll always come home.
Right...
Can you feel it, Scott?
Are you ready?

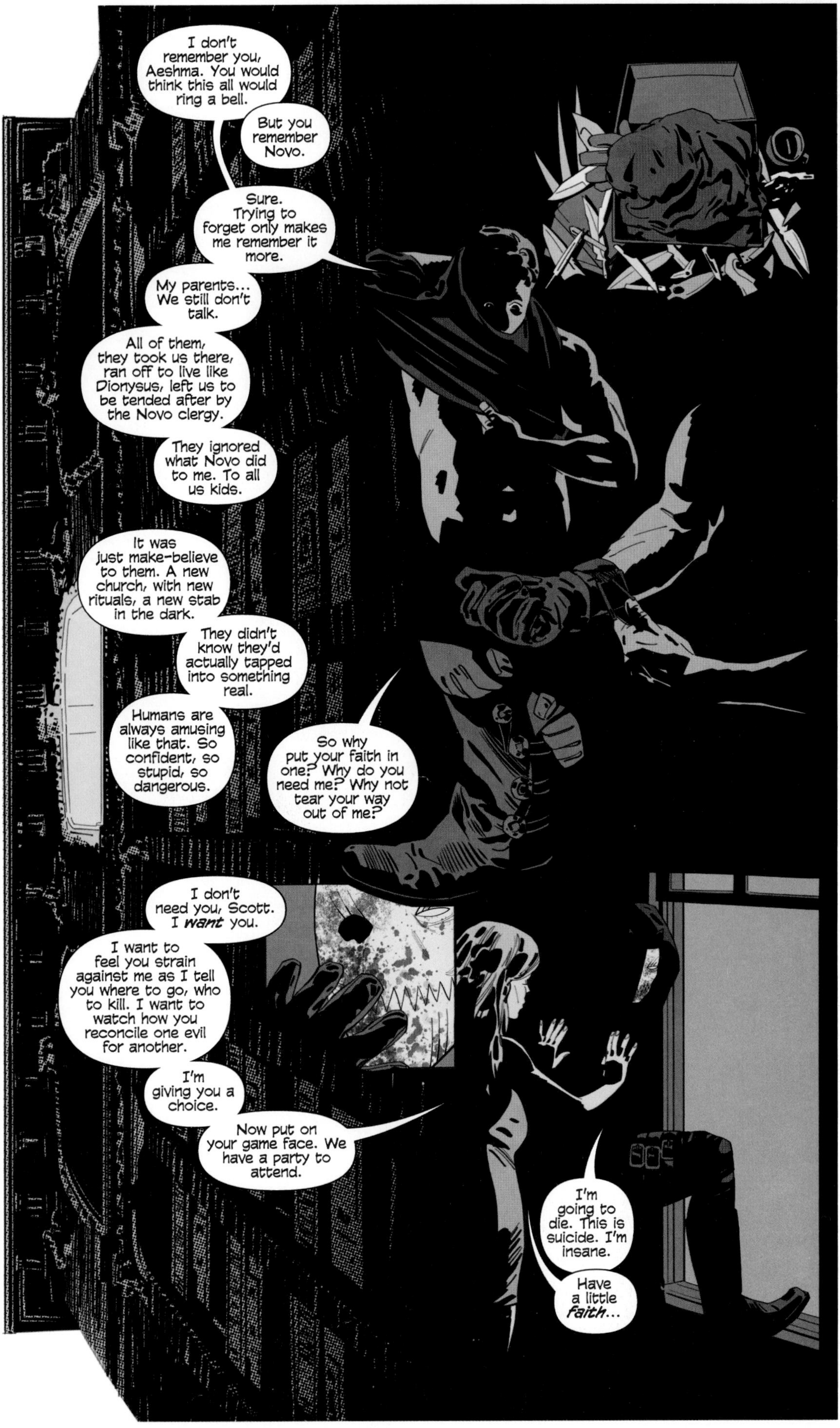
I don't remember you, Aeshma. You would think this all would ring a bell.
But you remember Novo.
Sure. Trying to forget only makes me remember it more.
My parents... We still don't talk.
All of them, they took us there, ran off to live like Dionysus, left us to be tended after by the Novo clergy.
They ignored what Novo did to me. To all us kids.
It was just make-believe to them. A new church, with new rituals, a new stab in the dark.
They didn't know they'd actually tapped into something real.
Humans are always amusing like that. So confident, so stupid, so dangerous.
So why put your faith in one? Why do you need me? Why not tear your way out of me?
I don't need you, Scott. I *want* you.
I want to feel you strain against me as I tell you where to go, who to kill. I want to watch how you reconcile one evil for another.
I'm giving you a choice.
Now put on your game face. We have a party to attend.
I'm going to die. This is suicide. I'm insane.
Have a little *faith*...

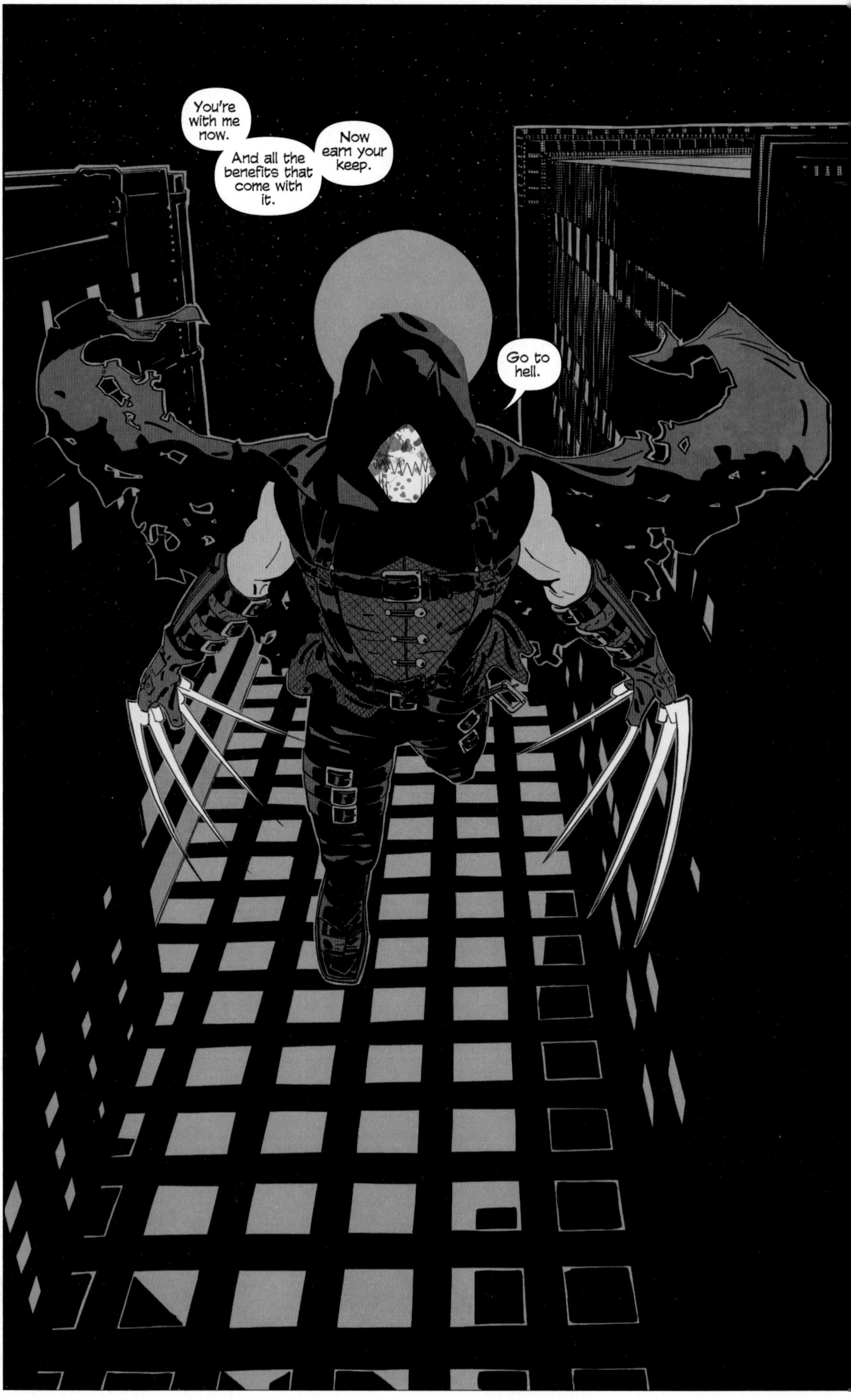
You're with me now.
And all the benefits that come with it.
Now earn your keep.
Go to hell.

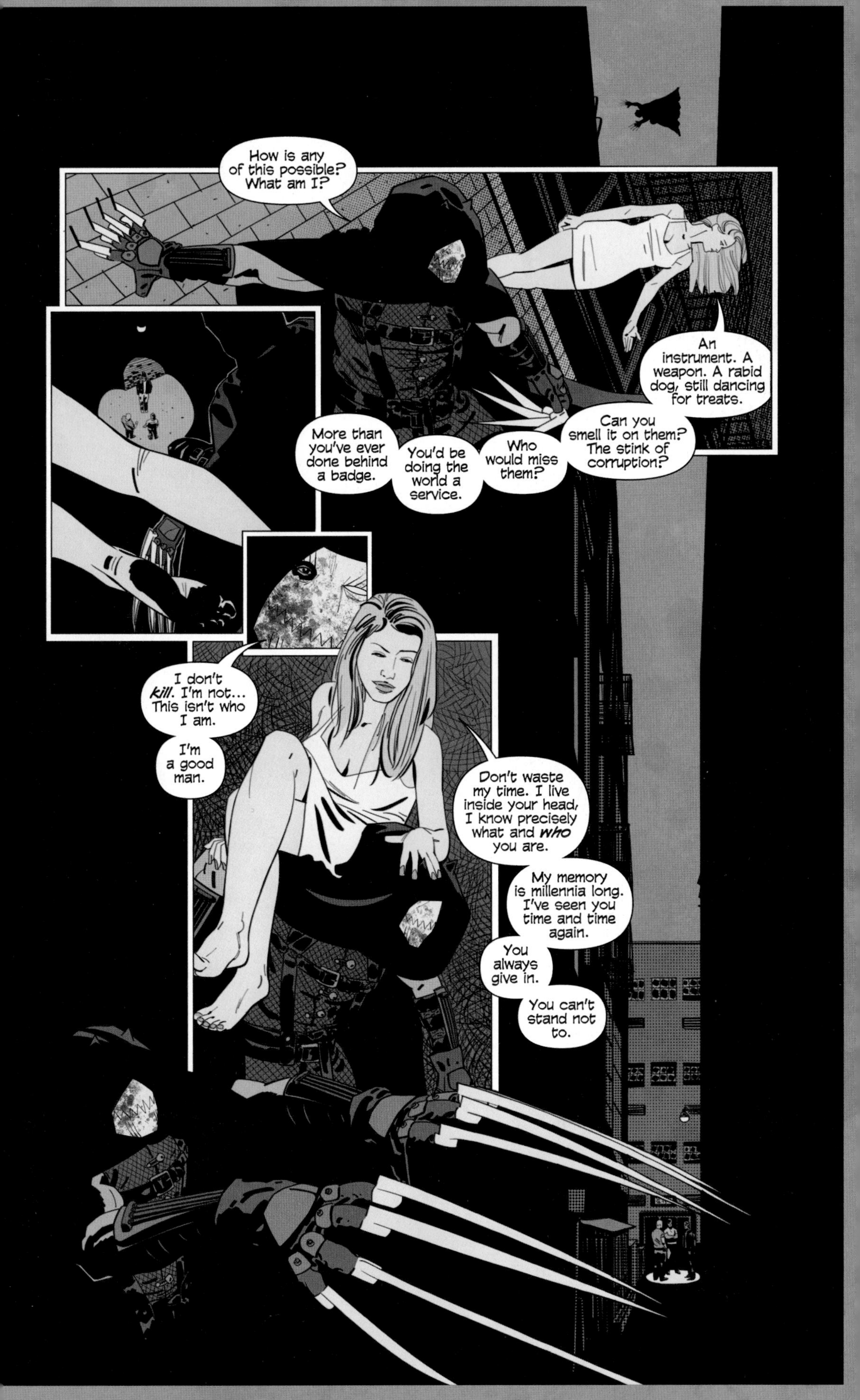
How is any of this possible? What am I?
An instrument. A weapon. A rabid dog, still dancing for treats.
Can you smell it on them? The stink of corruption?
Who would miss them?
You'd be doing the world a service.
More than you've ever done behind a badge.
I don't *kill*. I'm not... This isn't who I am.
I'm a good man.
Don't waste my time. I live inside your head, I know precisely what and *who* you are.
My memory is millennia long. I've seen you time and time again.
You always give in.
You can't stand not to.

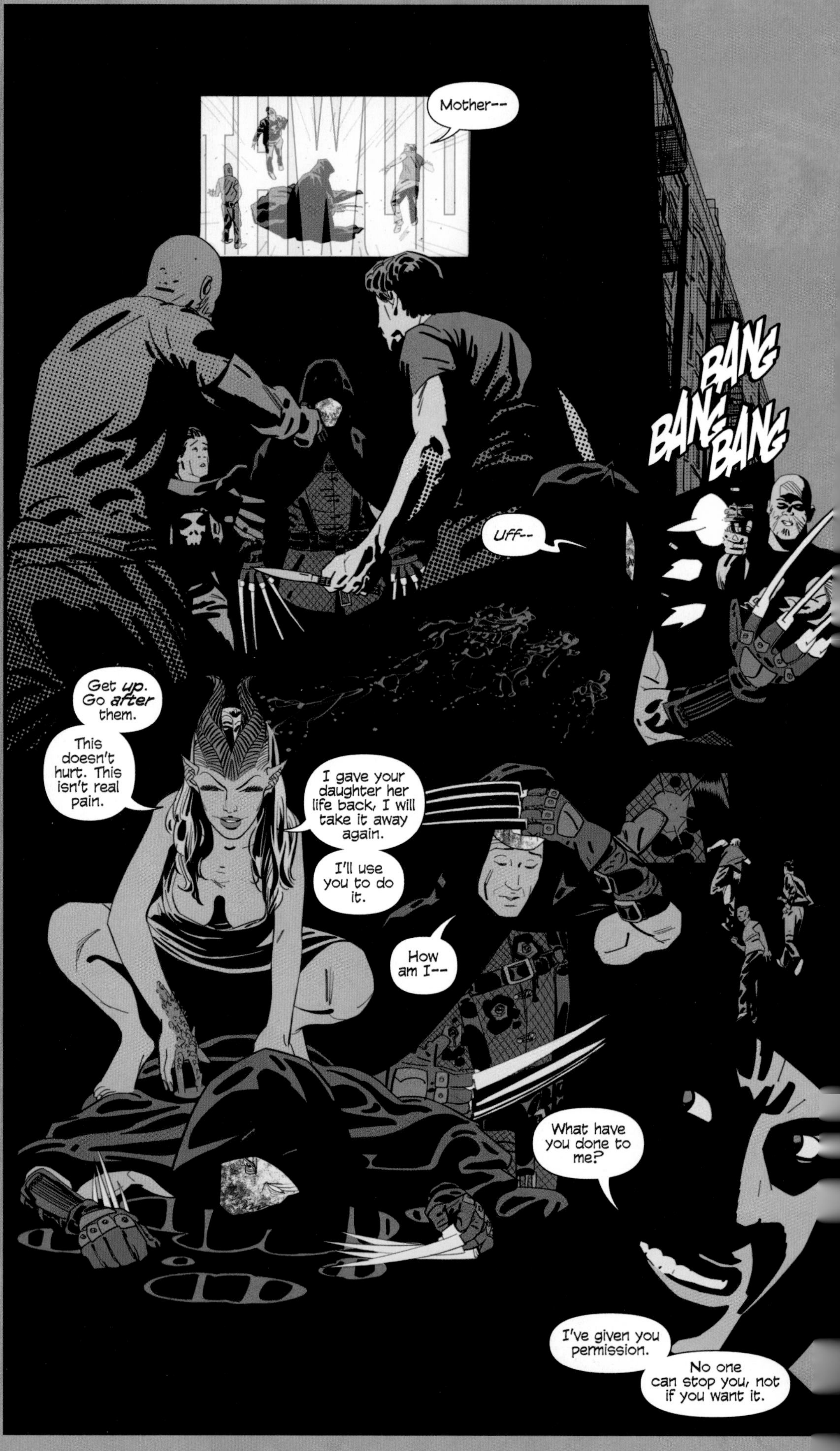
Mother--
BANG BANG BANG BANG
Uff--
Get *up*. Go *after* them.
This doesn't hurt. This isn't real pain.
I gave your daughter her life back, I will take it away again.
I'll use you to do it.
How am I--
What have you done to me?
I've given you permission.
No one can stop you, not if you want it.

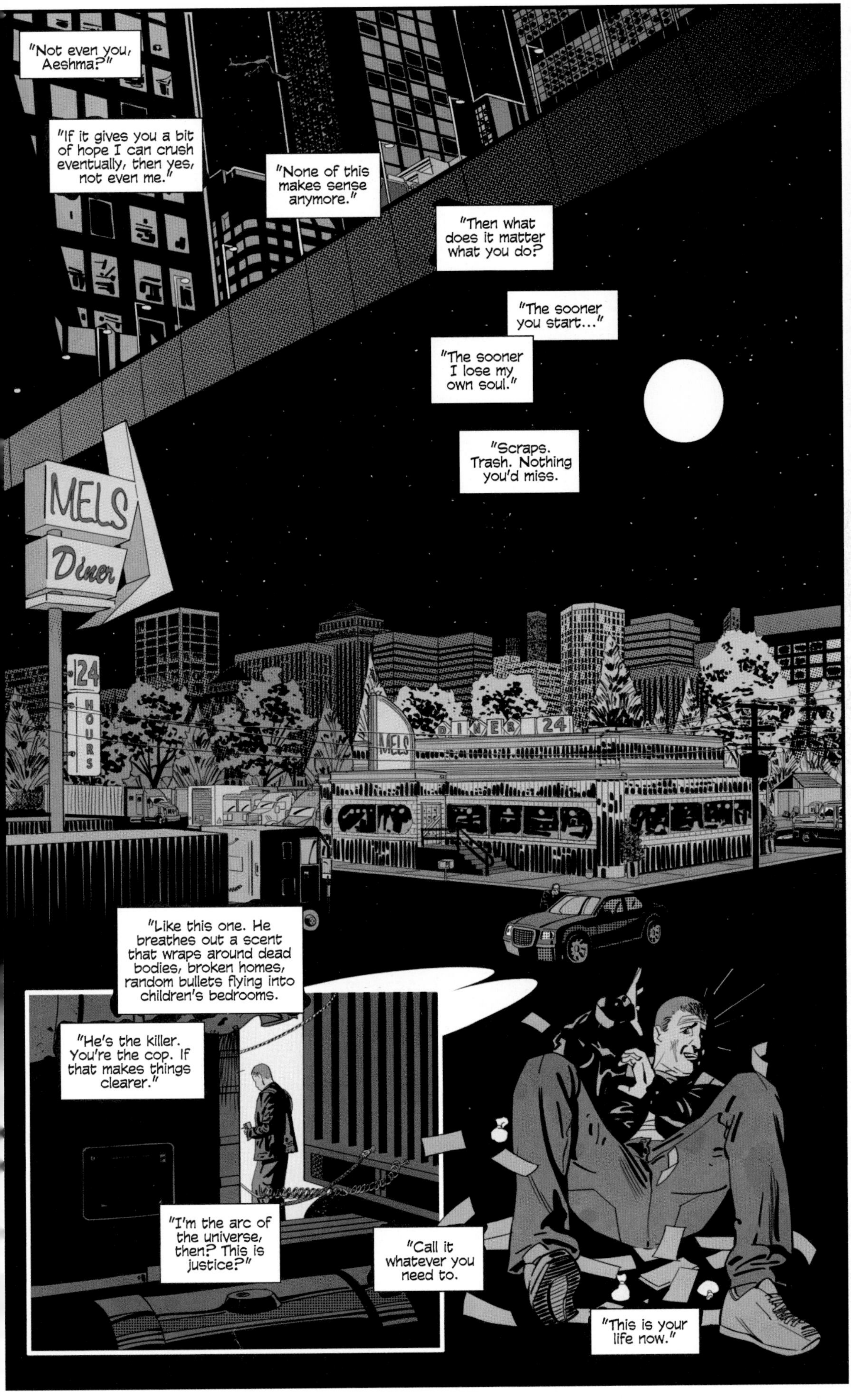

"Not even you, Aeshma?"
"If it gives you a bit of hope I can crush eventually, then yes, not even me."
"None of this makes sense anymore."
"Then what does it matter what you do?
"The sooner you start..."
"The sooner I lose my own soul."
"Scraps. Trash. Nothing you'd miss.
MELS Diner
24 HOURS
MELS
DINER 24
"Like this one. He breathes out a scent that wraps around dead bodies, broken homes, random bullets flying into children's bedrooms.
"He's the killer. You're the cop. If that makes things clearer."
"I'm the arc of the universe, then? This is justice?"
"Call it whatever you need to.
"This is your life now."

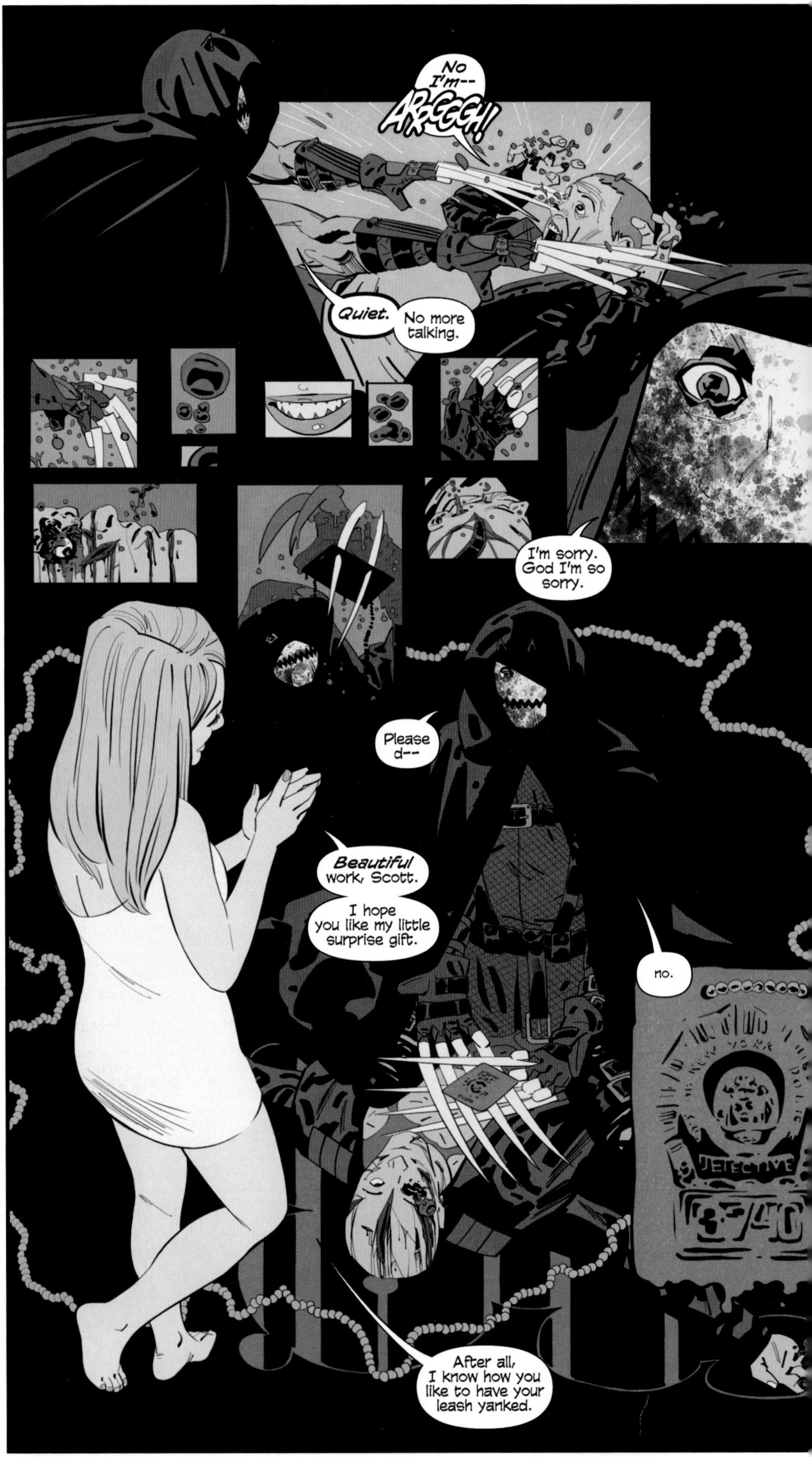
No I'm-- ARRGGH!
Quiet. No more talking.
I'm sorry. God I'm so sorry.
Please d--
Beautiful work, Scott.
I hope you like my little surprise gift.
no.
After all, I know how you like to have your leash yanked.

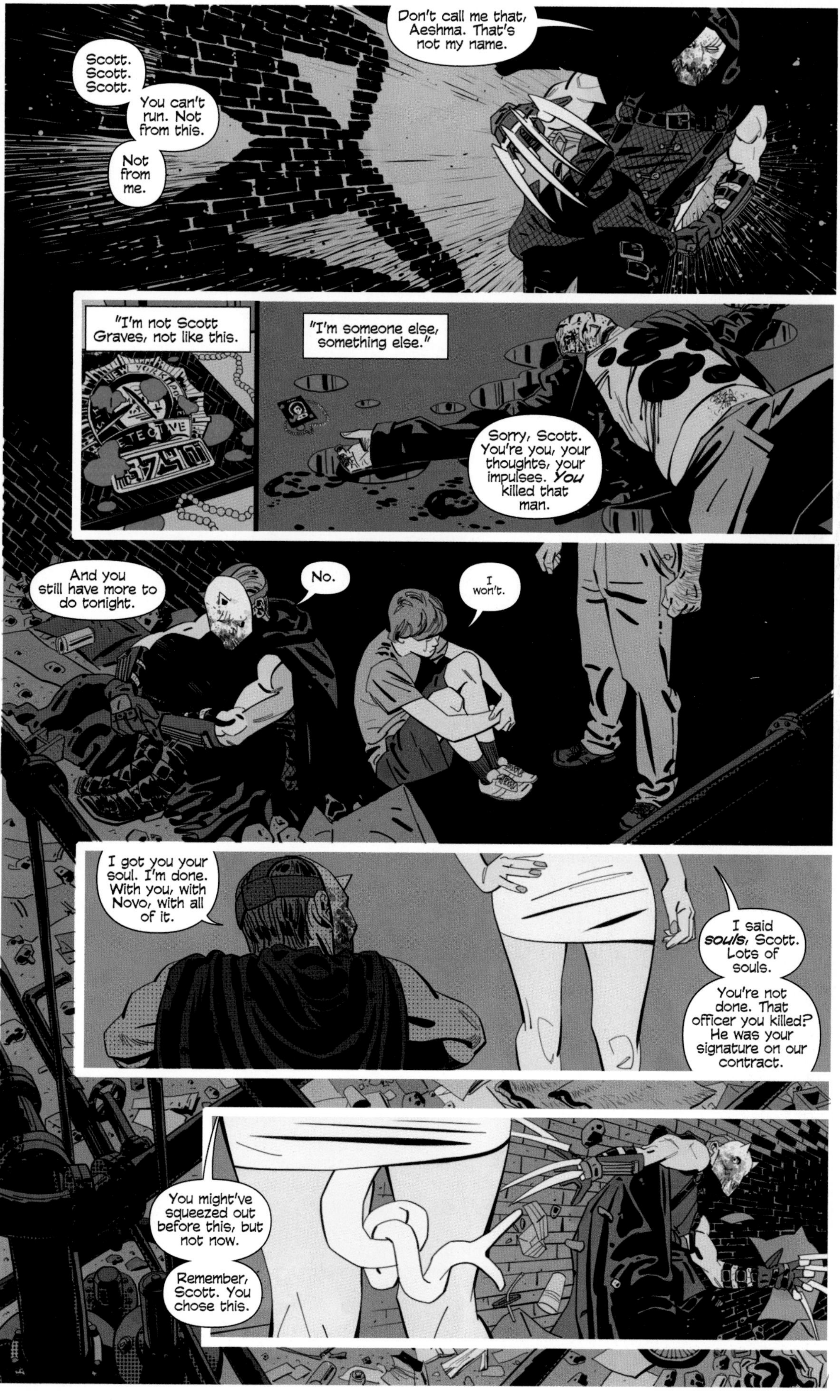
Don't call me that, Aeshma. That's not my name.
Scott. Scott. Scott.
You can't run. Not from this.
Not from me.
"I'm not Scott Graves, not like this.
NEW YORK PO
DETECTIVE
"I'm someone else, something else."
Sorry, Scott. You're you, your thoughts, your impulses. *You* killed that man.
And you still have more to do tonight.
No.
I won't.
I got you your soul. I'm done. With you, with Novo, with all of it.
I said *souls*, Scott. Lots of souls.
You're not done. That officer you killed? He was your signature on our contract.
You might've squeezed out before this, but not now.
Remember, Scott. You chose this.

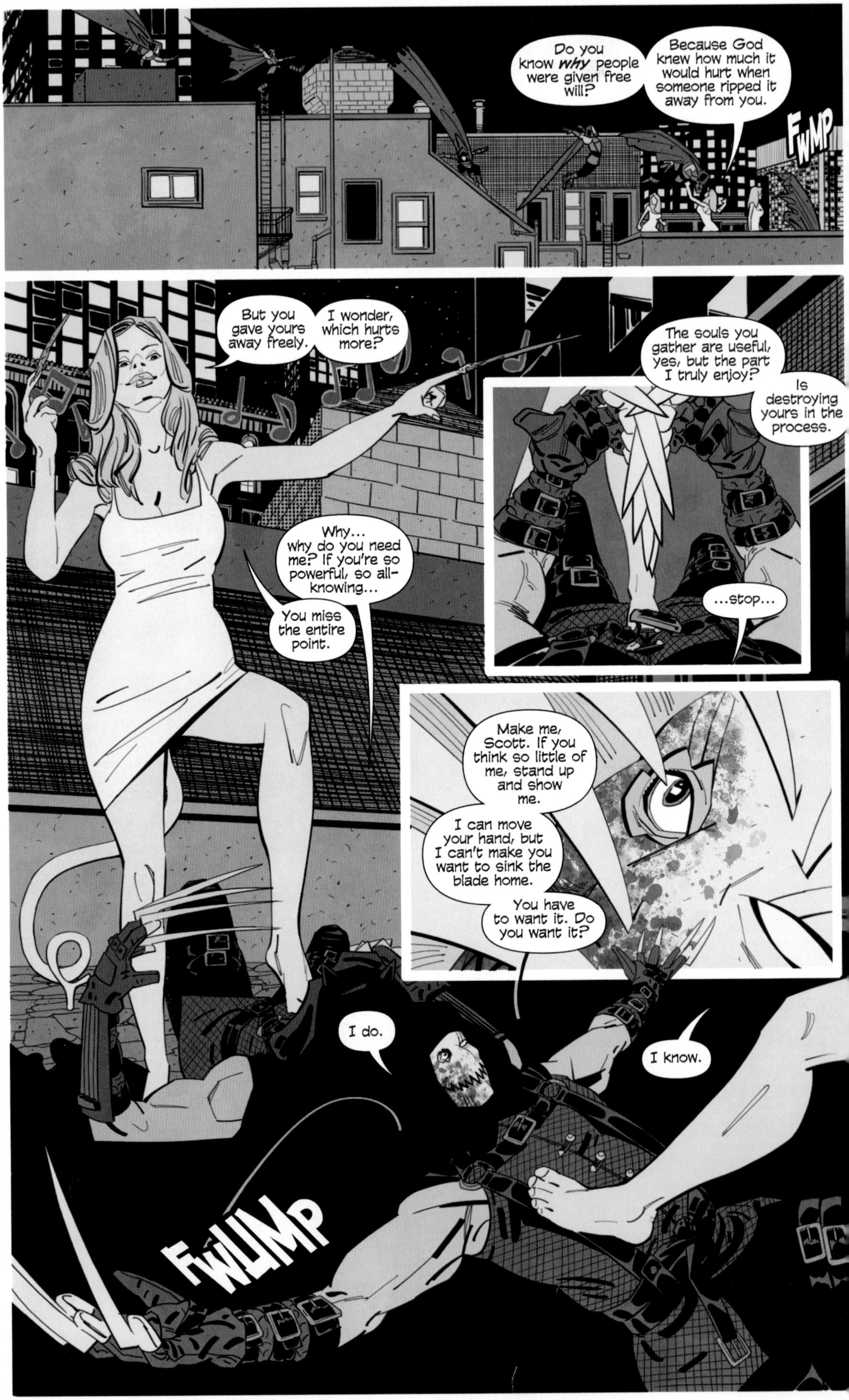
Do you know why people were given free will?
Because God knew how much it would hurt when someone ripped it away from you.
FWMP
But you gave yours away freely.
I wonder, which hurts more?
The souls you gather are useful, yes, but the part I truly enjoy?
Is destroying yours in the process.
Why... why do you need me? If you're so powerful, so all-knowing...
You miss the entire point.
...stop...
Make me, Scott. If you think so little of me, stand up and show me.
I can move your hand, but I can't make you want to sink the blade home.
You have to want it. Do you want it?
I do.
I know.
FWUMP

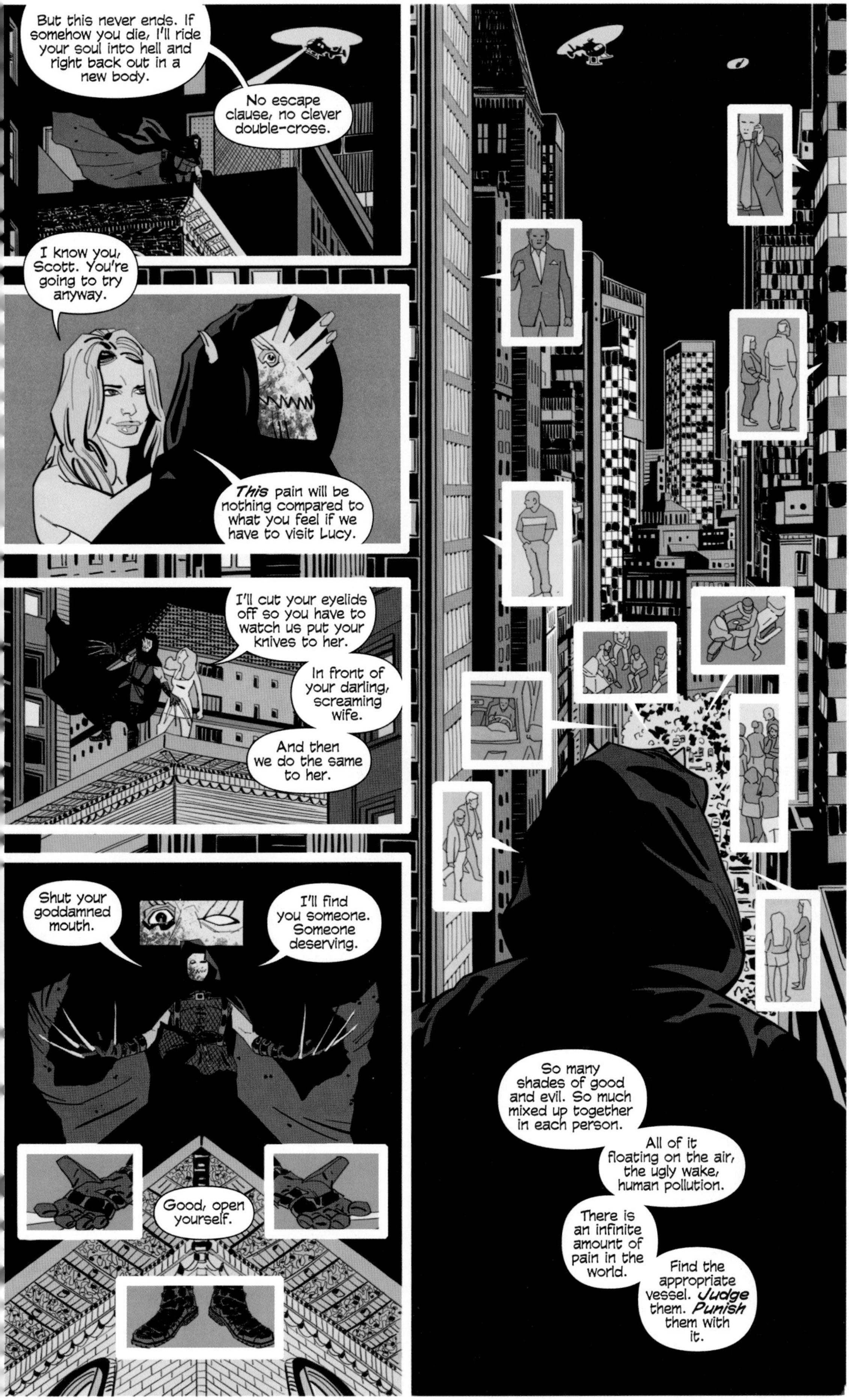
But this never ends. If somehow you die, I'll ride your soul into hell and right back out in a new body.
No escape clause, no clever double-cross.
I know you, Scott. You're going to try anyway.
This pain will be nothing compared to what you feel if we have to visit Lucy.
I'll cut your eyelids off so you have to watch us put your knives to her.
In front of your darling, screaming wife.
And then we do the same to her.
Shut your goddamned mouth.
I'll find you someone. Someone deserving.
Good, open yourself.
So many shades of good and evil. So much mixed up together in each person.
All of it floating on the air, the ugly wake, human pollution.
There is an infinite amount of pain in the world.
Find the appropriate vessel. *Judge* them. *Punish* them with it.

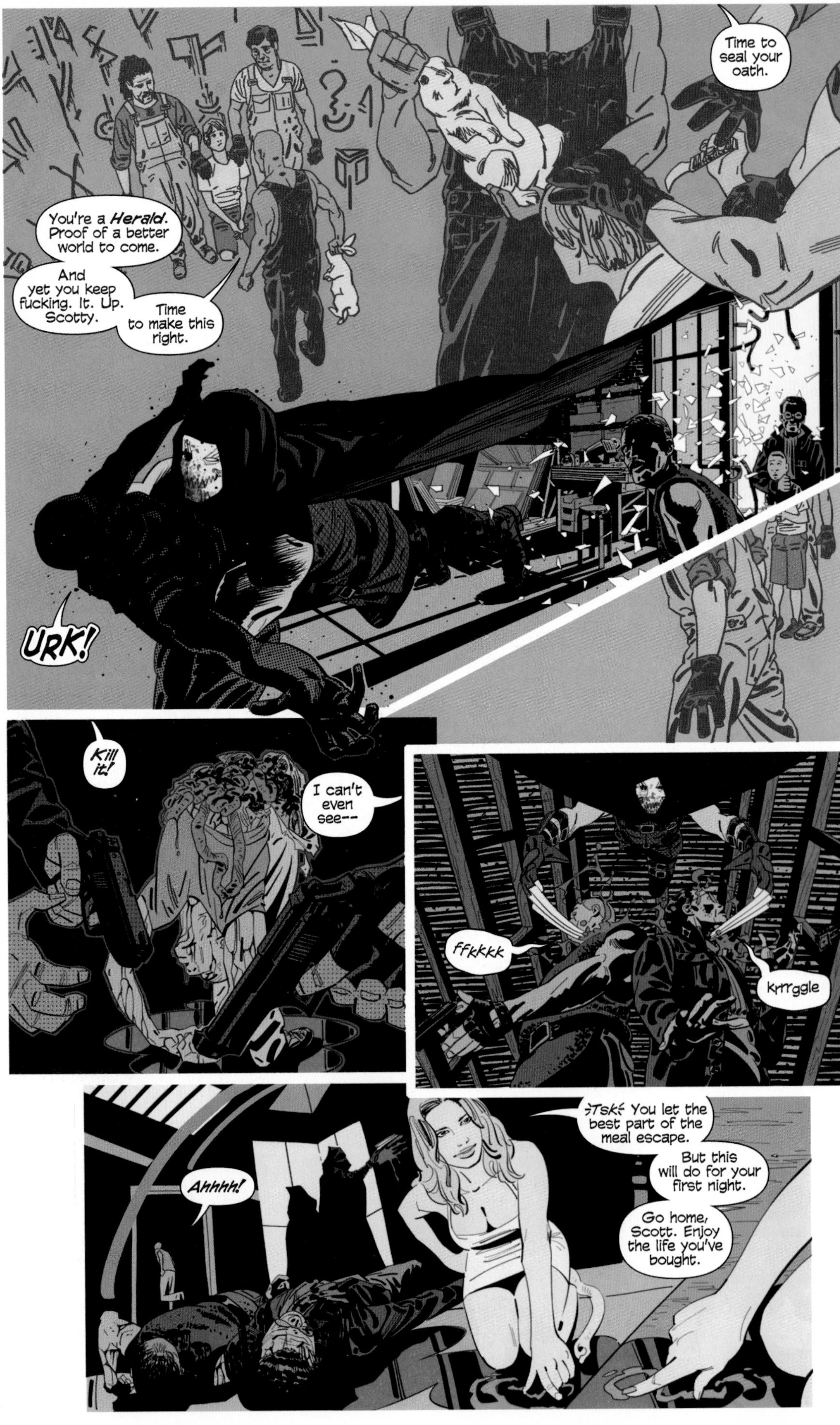
Time to seal your oath.
You're a Herald. Proof of a better world to come.
And yet you keep fucking. It. Up. Scotty.
Time to make this right.
URK!
Kill it!
I can't even see--
ffkkkk
krrrggle
Ahhhh!
-Tsk- You let the best part of the meal escape.
But this will do for your first night.
Go home, Scott. Enjoy the life you've bought.

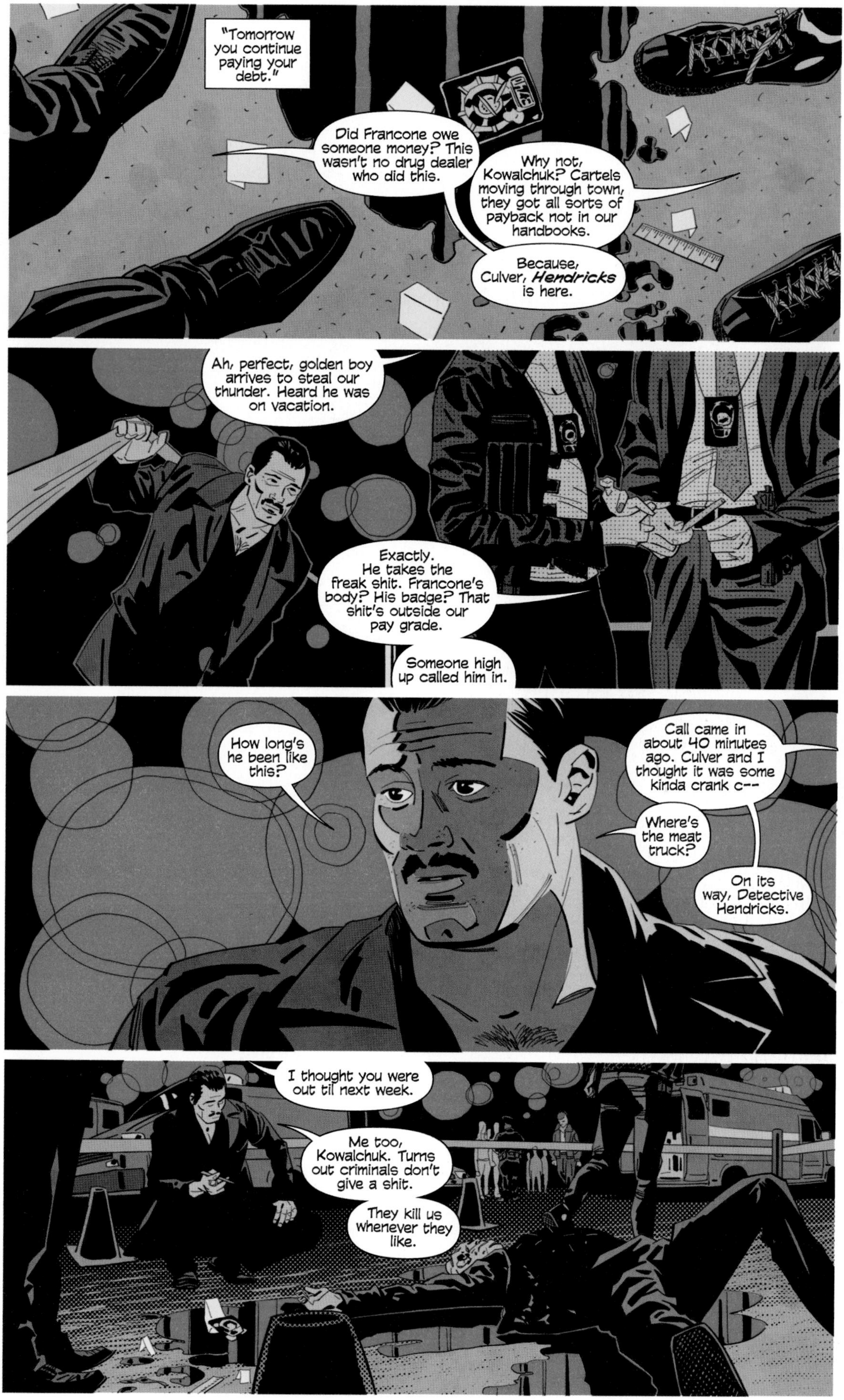
"Tomorrow you continue paying your debt."
Did Francone owe someone money? This wasn't no drug dealer who did this.
Why not, Kowalchuk? Cartels moving through town, they got all sorts of payback not in our handbooks.
Because, Culver, *Hendricks* is here.
Ah, perfect, golden boy arrives to steal our thunder. Heard he was on vacation.
Exactly. He takes the freak shit. Francone's body? His badge? That shit's outside our pay grade.
Someone high up called him in.
How long's he been like this?
Call came in about 40 minutes ago. Culver and I thought it was some kinda crank c--
Where's the meat truck?
On its way, Detective Hendricks.
I thought you were out til next week.
Me too, Kowalchuk. Turns out criminals don't give a shit.
They kill us whenever they like.

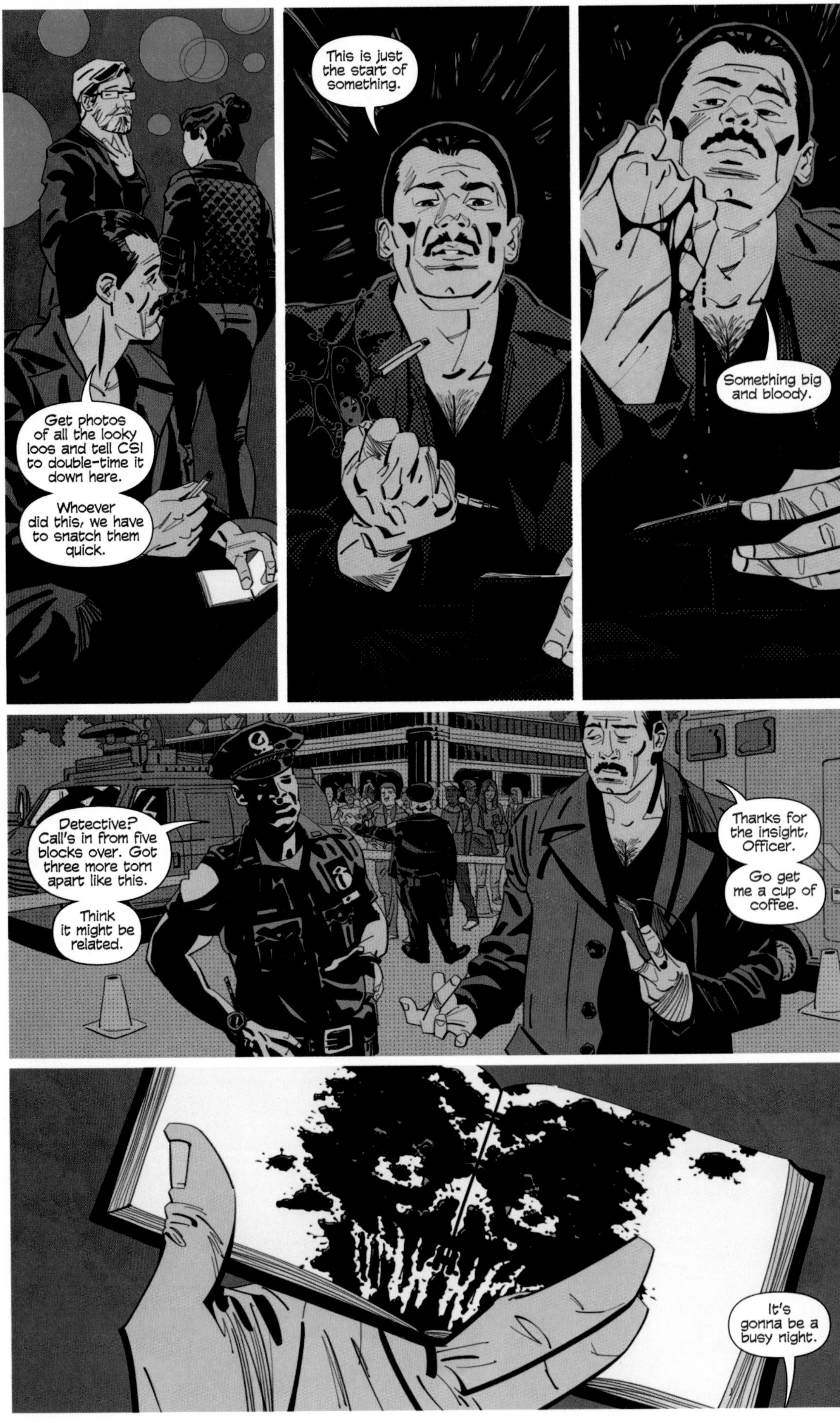
Get photos of all the looky loos and tell CSI to double-time it down here.
Whoever did this, we have to snatch them quick.
This is just the start of something.
Something big and bloody.
Detective? Call's in from five blocks over. Got three more torn apart like this.
Think it might be related.
Thanks for the insight, Officer.
Go get me a cup of coffee.
It's gonna be a busy night.

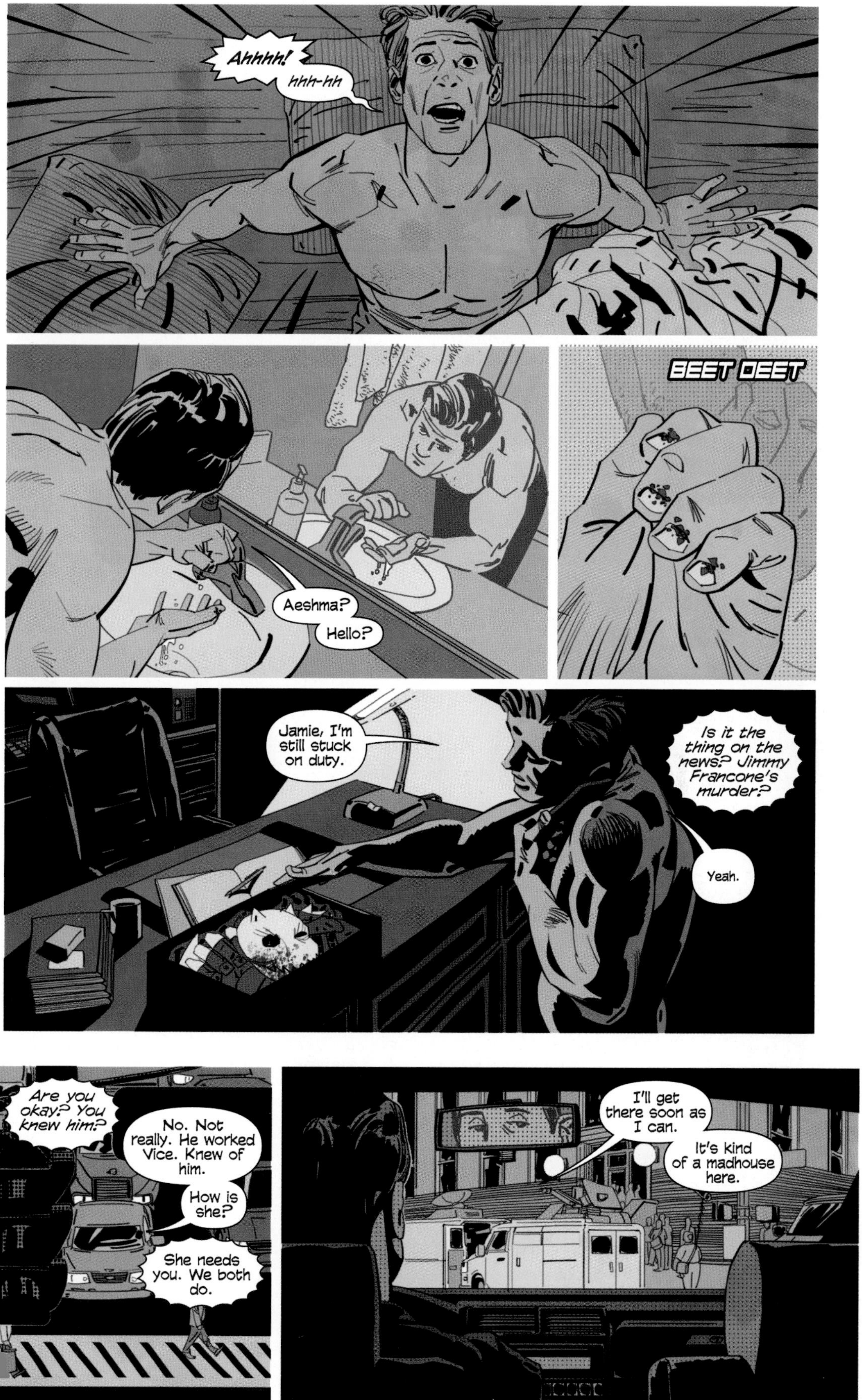
Ahhhh!
hhh-hh
Aeshma?
Hello?
BEET DEET
Jamie, I'm still stuck on duty.
Is it the thing on the news? Jimmy Francone's murder?
Yeah.
Are you okay? You knew him?
No. Not really. He worked Vice. Knew of him.
How is she?
She needs you. We both do.
I'll get there soon as I can.
It's kind of a madhouse here.

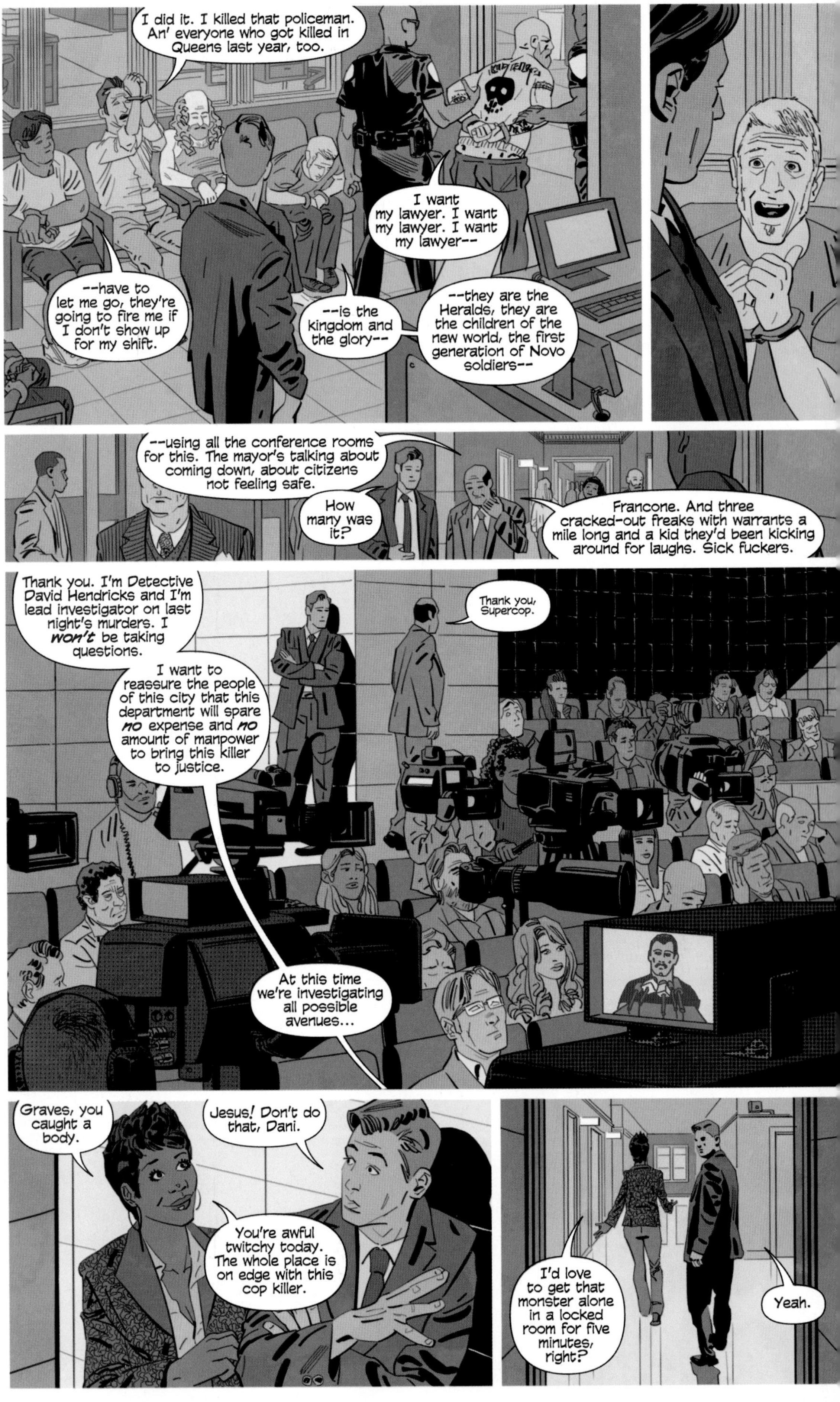
I did it. I killed that policeman. An' everyone who got killed in Queens last year, too.
I want my lawyer. I want my lawyer. I want my lawyer--
--have to let me go, they're going to fire me if I don't show up for my shift.
--is the kingdom and the glory--
--they are the Heralds, they are the children of the new world, the first generation of Novo soldiers--
--using all the conference rooms for this. The mayor's talking about coming down, about citizens not feeling safe.
How many was it?
Francone. And three cracked-out freaks with warrants a mile long and a kid they'd been kicking around for laughs. Sick fuckers.
Thank you. I'm Detective David Hendricks and I'm lead investigator on last night's murders. I *won't* be taking questions.
Thank you, Supercop.
I want to reassure the people of this city that this department will spare *no* expense and *no* amount of manpower to bring this killer to justice.
At this time we're investigating all possible avenues...
Graves, you caught a body.
Jesus! Don't do that, Dani.
You're awful twitchy today. The whole place is on edge with this cop killer.
I'd love to get that monster alone in a locked room for five minutes, right?
Yeah.

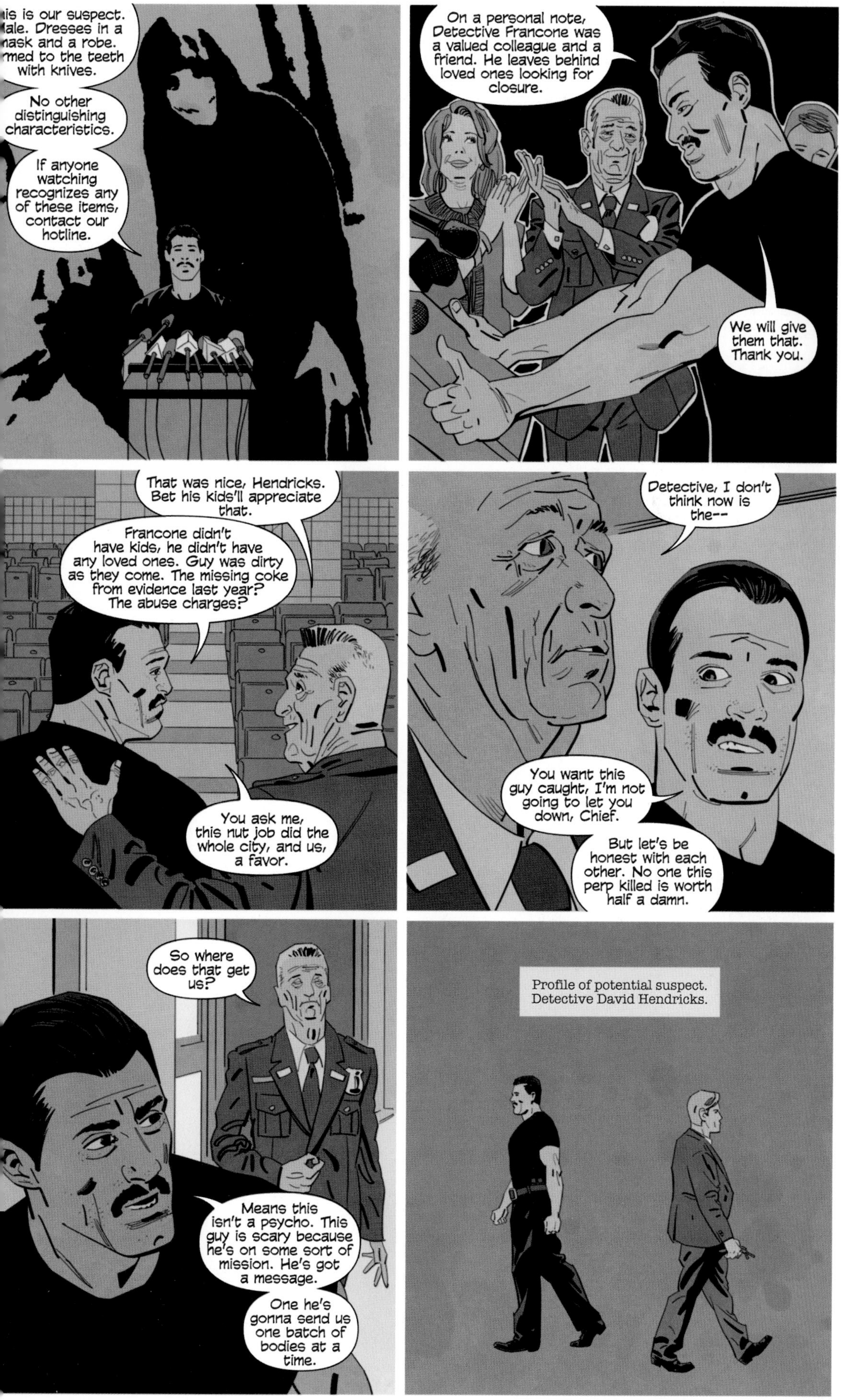

is is our suspect. ale. Dresses in a nask and a robe. rmed to the teeth with knives.
No other distinguishing characteristics.
If anyone watching recognizes any of these items, contact our hotline.
On a personal note, Detective Francone was a valued colleague and a friend. He leaves behind loved ones looking for closure.
We will give them that. Thank you.
That was nice, Hendricks. Bet his kids'll appreciate that.
Francone didn't have kids, he didn't have any loved ones. Guy was dirty as they come. The missing coke from evidence last year? The abuse charges?
You ask me, this nut job did the whole city, and us, a favor.
Detective, I don't think now is the--
You want this guy caught, I'm not going to let you down, Chief.
But let's be honest with each other. No one this perp killed is worth half a damn.
So where does that get us?
Means this isn't a psycho. This guy is scary because he's on some sort of mission. He's got a message.
One he's gonna send us one batch of bodies at a time.
Profile of potential suspect. Detective David Hendricks.

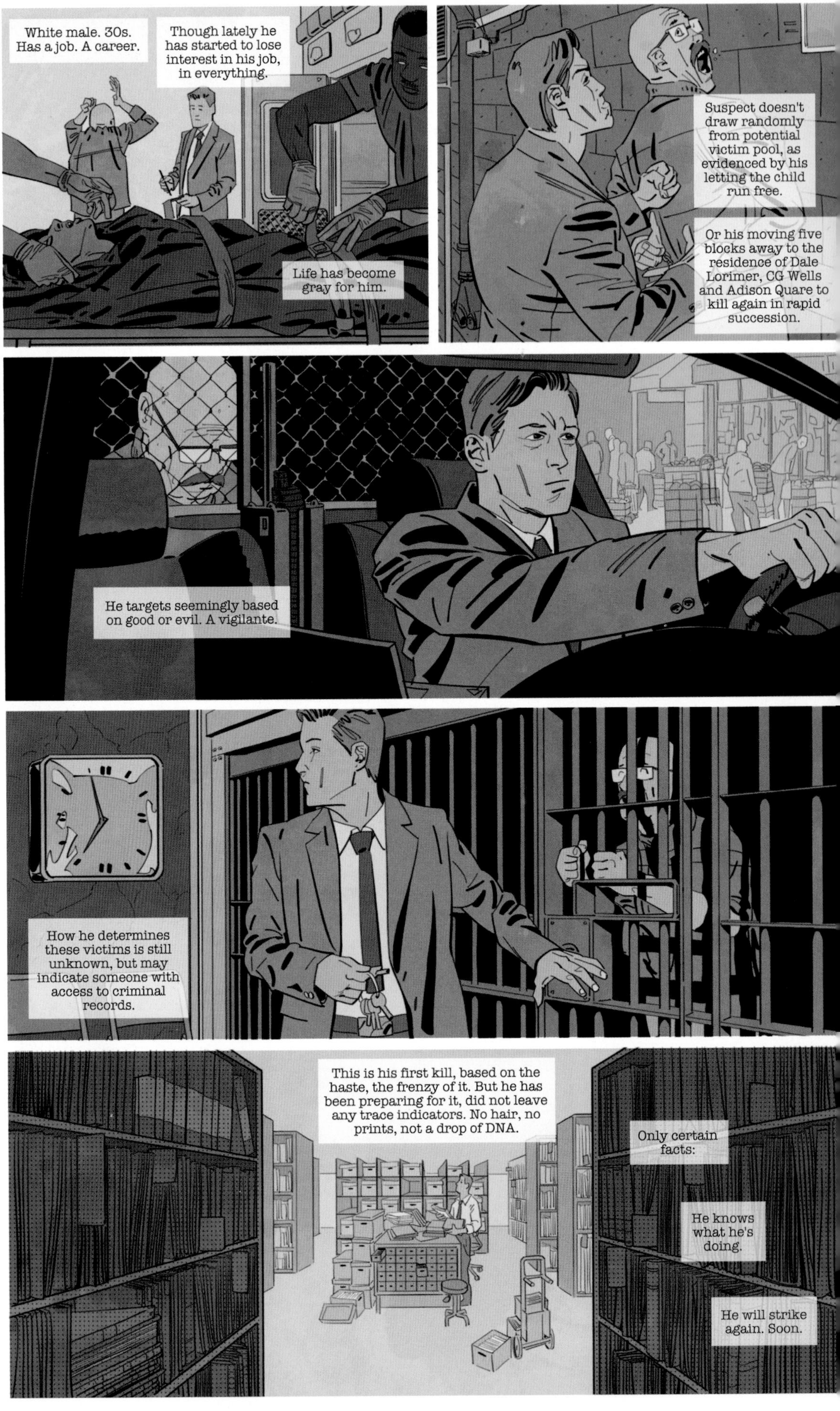
White male. 30s. Has a job. A career.
Though lately he has started to lose interest in his job, in everything.
Life has become gray for him.
Suspect doesn't draw randomly from potential victim pool, as evidenced by his letting the child run free.
Or his moving five blocks away to the residence of Dale Lorimer, CG Wells and Adison Quare to kill again in rapid succession.
He targets seemingly based on good or evil. A vigilante.
How he determines these victims is still unknown, but may indicate someone with access to criminal records.
This is his first kill, based on the haste, the frenzy of it. But he has been preparing for it, did not leave any trace indicators. No hair, no prints, not a drop of DNA.
Only certain facts:
He knows what he's doing.
He will strike again. Soon.

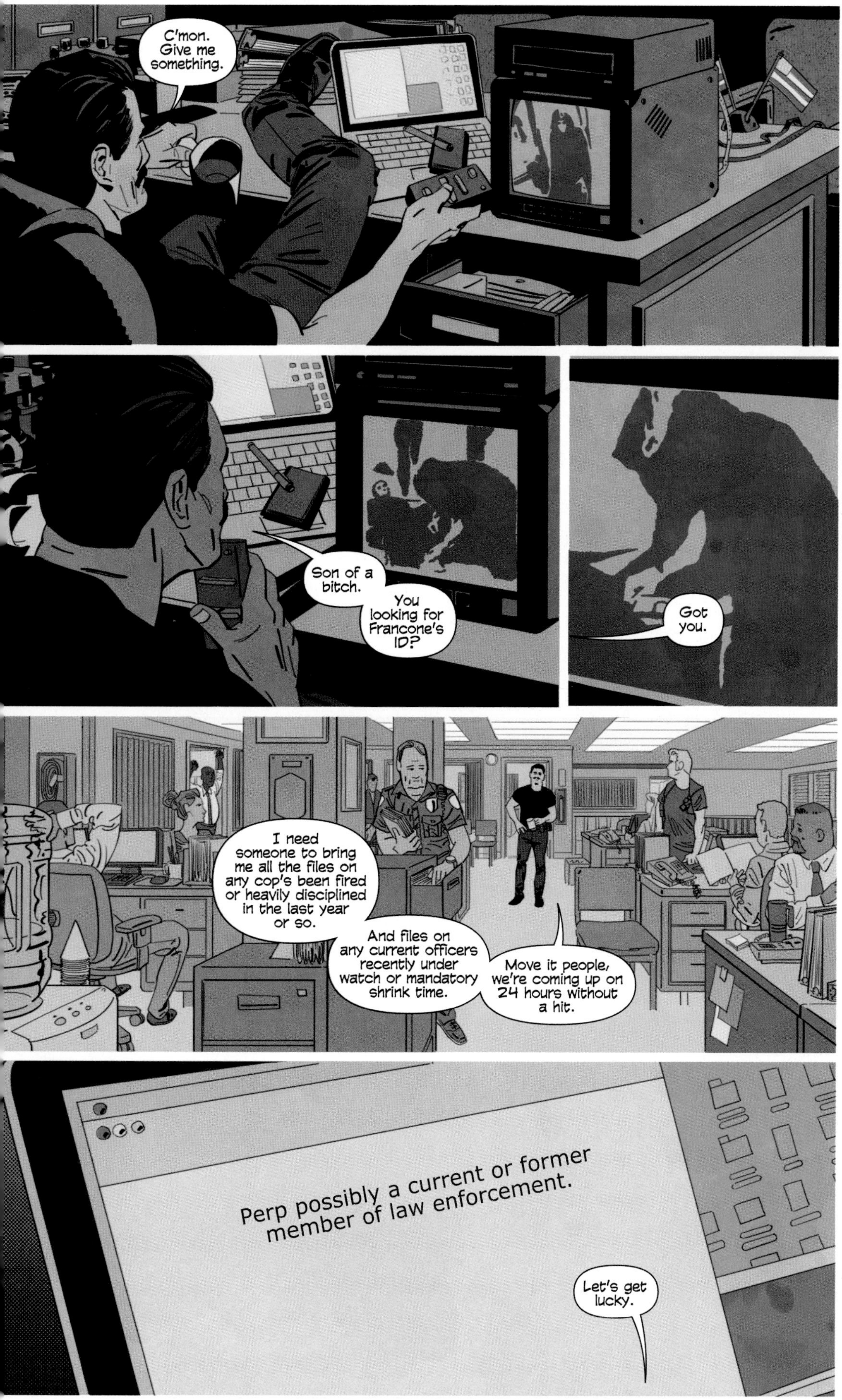
C'mon. Give me something.
Son of a bitch.
You looking for Francone's ID?
Got you.
I need someone to bring me all the files on any cop's been fired or heavily disciplined in the last year or so.
And files on any current officers recently under watch or mandatory shrink time.
Move it people, we're coming up on 24 hours without a hit.
Perp possibly a current or former member of law enforcement.
Let's get lucky.

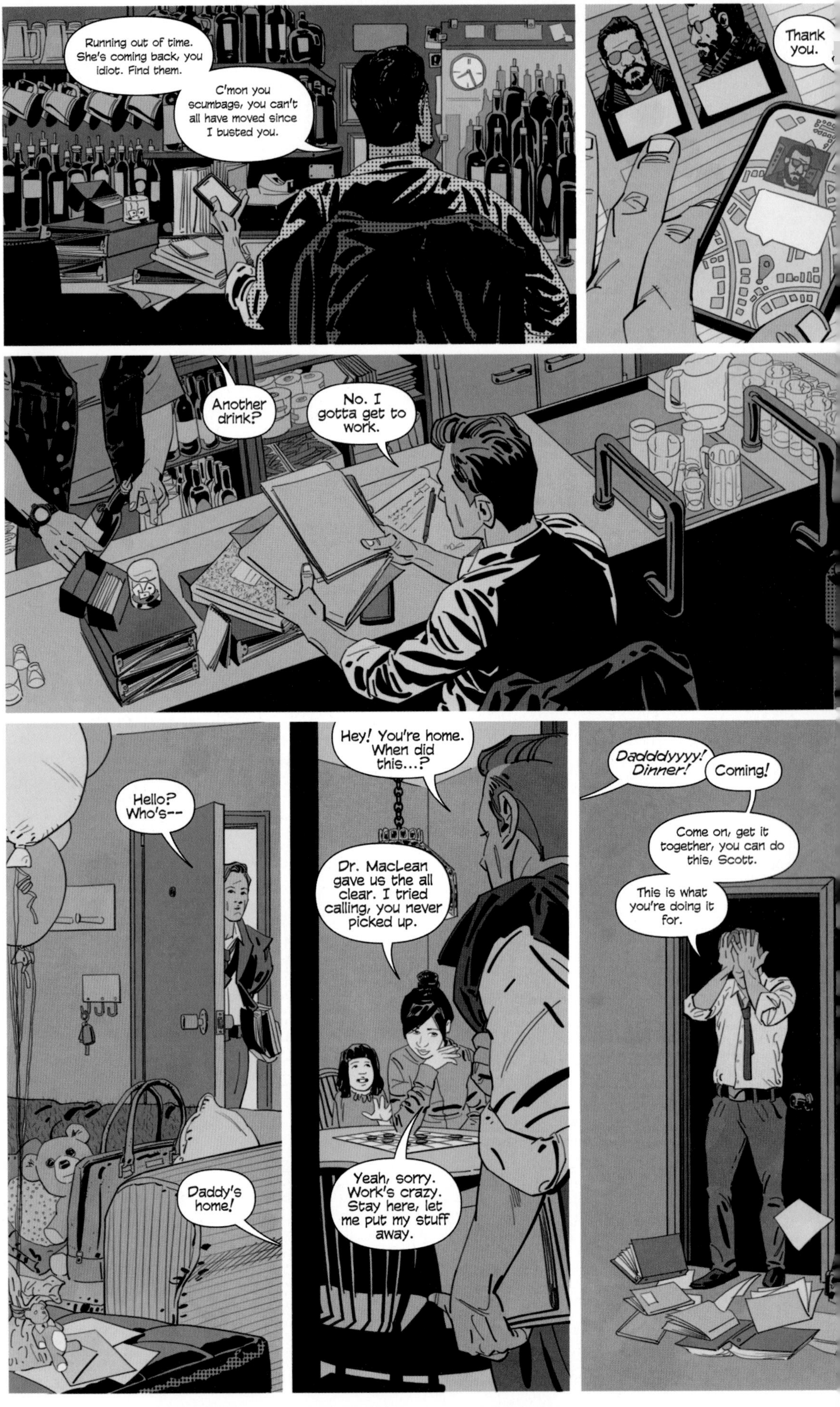

Running out of time. She's coming back, you idiot. Find them.
C'mon you scumbags, you can't all have moved since I busted you.
Thank you.
Another drink?
No. I gotta get to work.
Hello? Who's--
Daddy's home!
Hey! You're home. When did this...?
Dr. MacLean gave us the all clear. I tried calling, you never picked up.
Yeah, sorry. Work's crazy. Stay here, let me put my stuff away.
Daddddyyyy! Dinner!
Coming!
Come on, get it together, you can do this, Scott.
This is what you're doing it for.

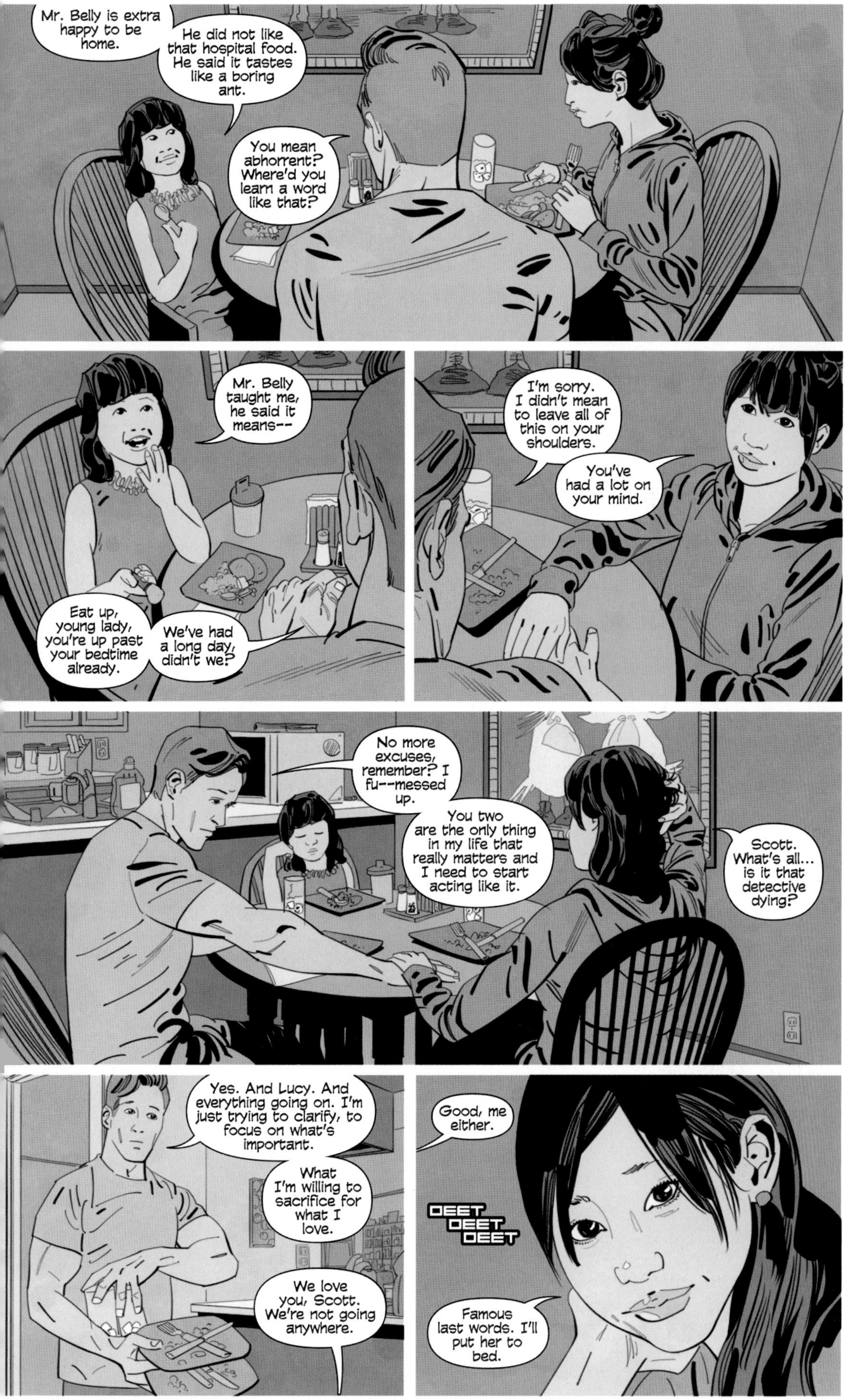

Mr. Belly is extra happy to be home.
He did not like that hospital food. He said it tastes like a boring ant.
You mean abhorrent? Where'd you learn a word like that?
Mr. Belly taught me, he said it means--
Eat up, young lady, you're up past your bedtime already.
We've had a long day, didn't we?
I'm sorry. I didn't mean to leave all of this on your shoulders.
You've had a lot on your mind.
No more excuses, remember? I fu--messed up.
You two are the only thing in my life that really matters and I need to start acting like it.
Scott. What's all... is it that detective dying?
Yes. And Lucy. And everything going on. I'm just trying to clarify, to focus on what's important.
What I'm willing to sacrifice for what I love.
We love you, Scott. We're not going anywhere.
Good, me either.
DEET DEET DEET
Famous last words. I'll put her to bed.

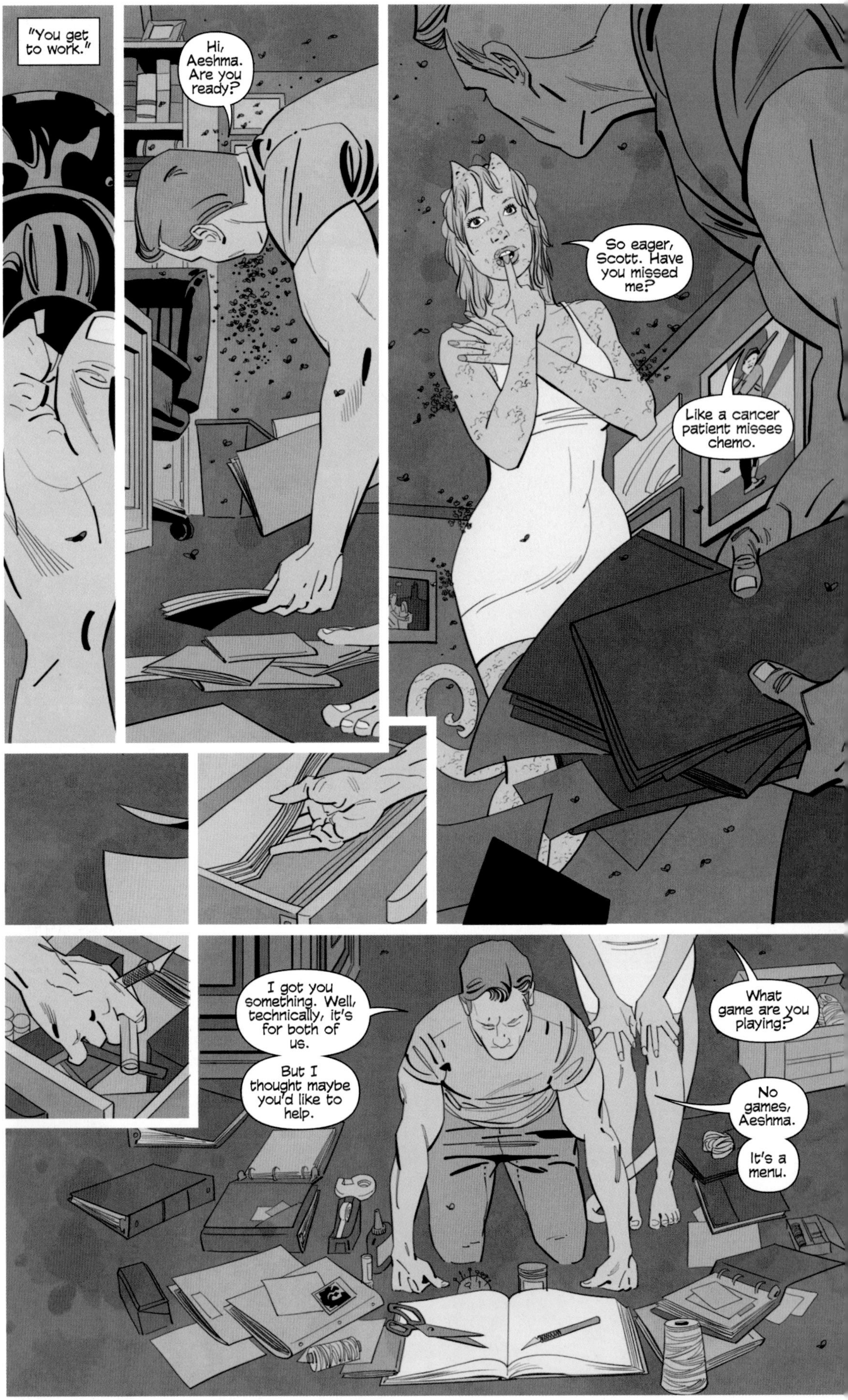
"You get to work."
Hi, Aeshma. Are you ready?
So eager, Scott. Have you missed me?
Like a cancer patient misses chemo.
I got you something. Well, technically, it's for both of us.
But I thought maybe you'd like to help.
What game are you playing?
No games, Aeshma.
It's a menu.

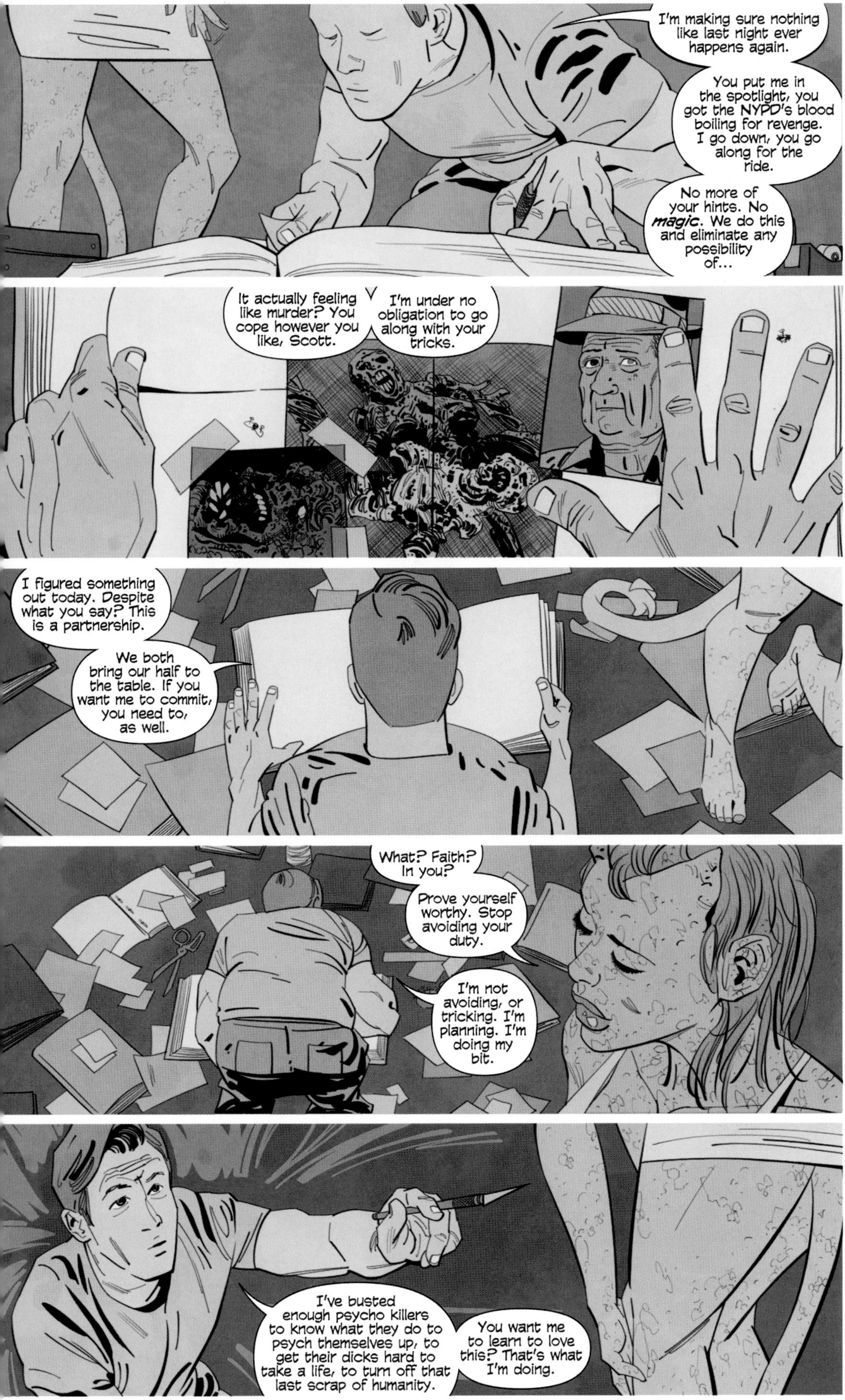

I'm making sure nothing like last night ever happens again.
You put me in the spotlight, you got the NYPD's blood boiling for revenge. I go down, you go along for the ride.
No more of your hints. No *magic*. We do this and eliminate any possibility of...
It actually feeling like murder? You cope however you like, Scott.
I'm under no obligation to go along with your tricks.
I figured something out today. Despite what you say? This is a partnership.
We both bring our half to the table. If you want me to commit, you need to, as well.
What? Faith? In you?
Prove yourself worthy. Stop avoiding your duty.
I'm not avoiding, or tricking. I'm planning. I'm doing my bit.
I've busted enough psycho killers to know what they do to psych themselves up, to get their dicks hard to take a life, to turn off that last scrap of humanity.
You want me to learn to love this? That's what I'm doing.

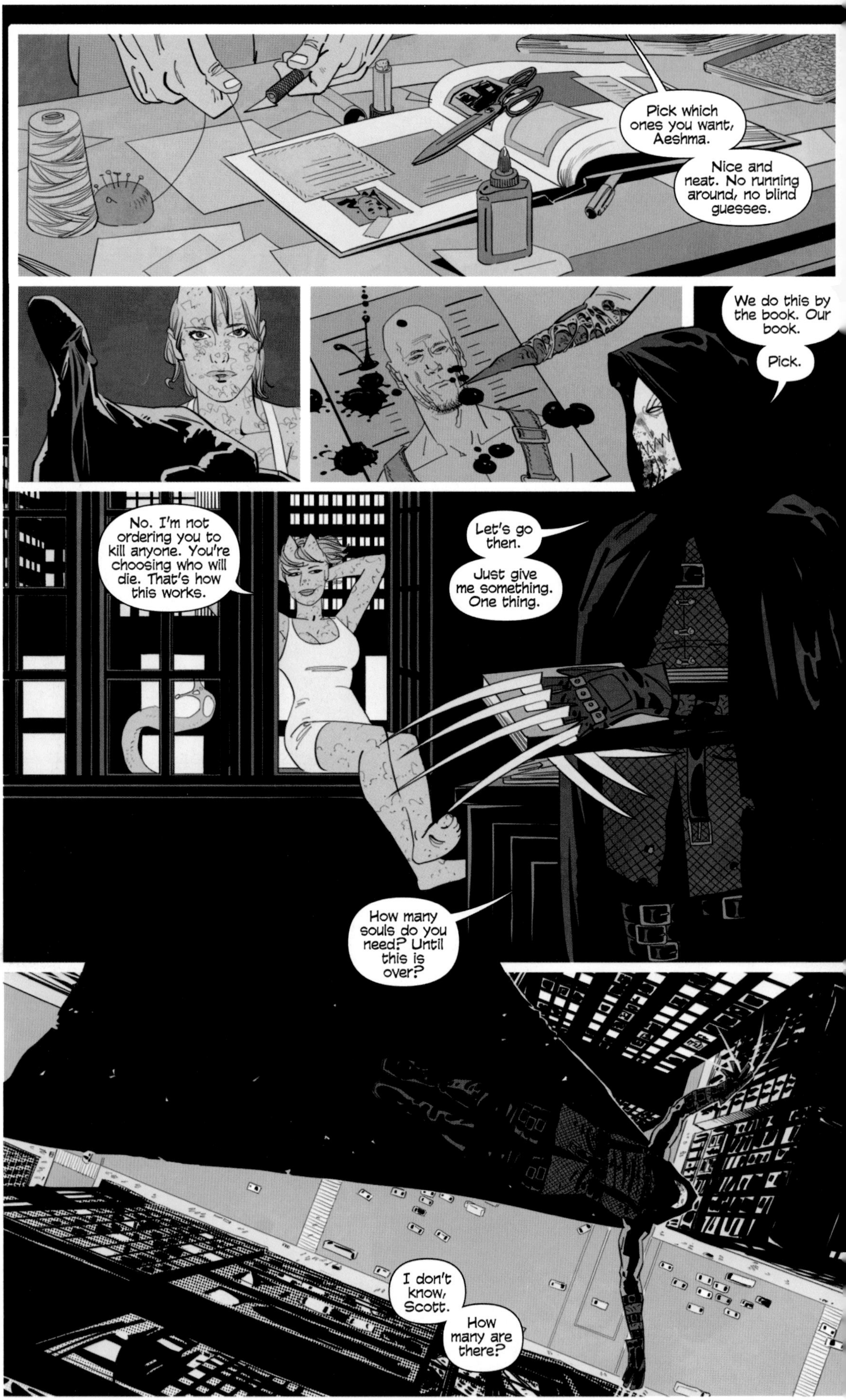
Pick which ones you want, Aeshma.
Nice and neat. No running around, no blind guesses.
We do this by the book. Our book.
Pick.
No. I'm not ordering you to kill anyone. You're choosing who will die. That's how this works.
Let's go then.
Just give me something. One thing.
How many souls do you need? Until this is over?
I don't know, Scott.
How many are there?

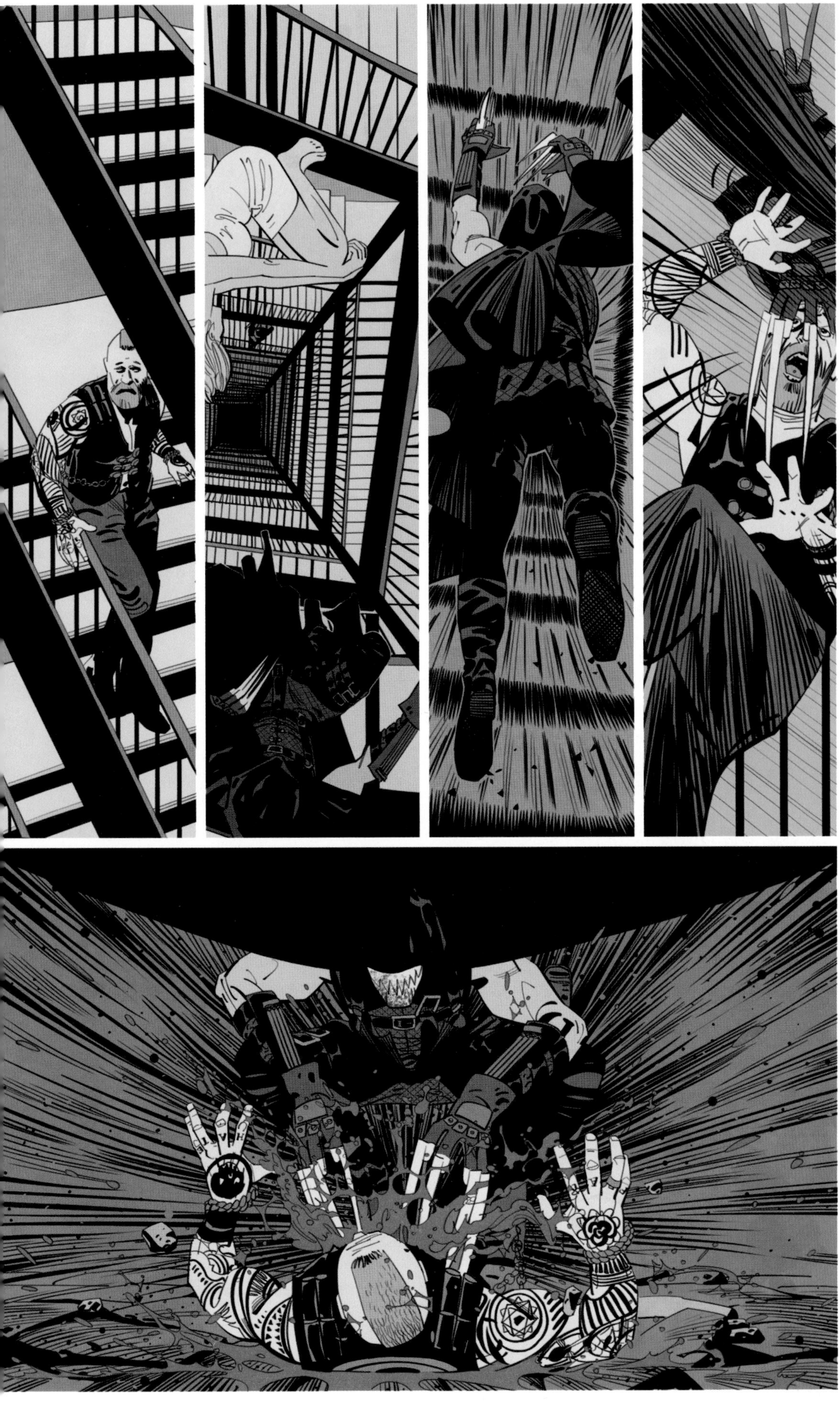

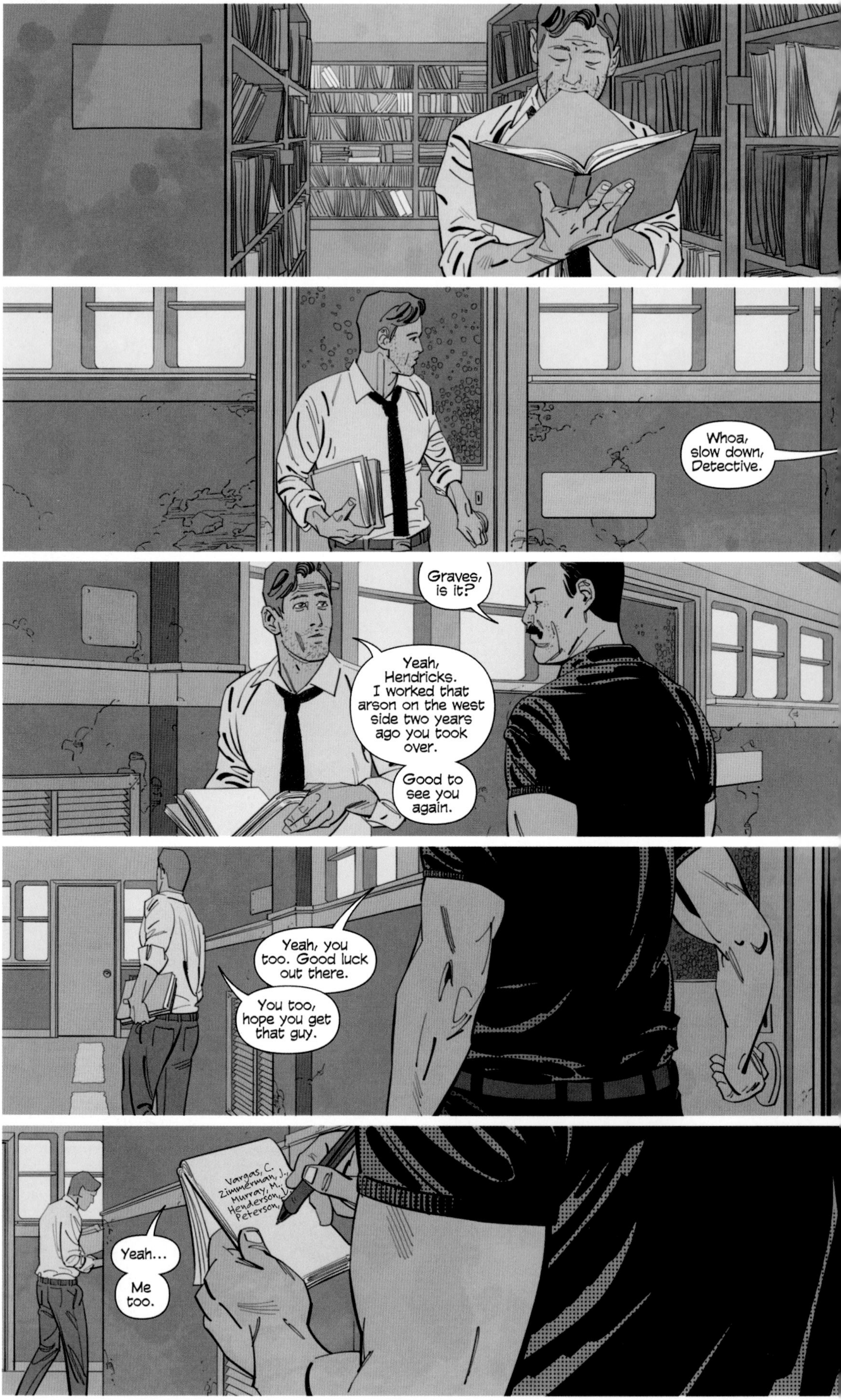
Whoa, slow down, Detective.
Graves, is it?
Yeah, Hendricks. I worked that arson on the west side two years ago you took over.
Good to see you again.
Yeah, you too. Good luck out there.
You too, hope you get that guy.
Vargas, C.
Zimmerman, J.,
Murray, M.,
Henderson,
Peterson,
Yeah...
Me too.

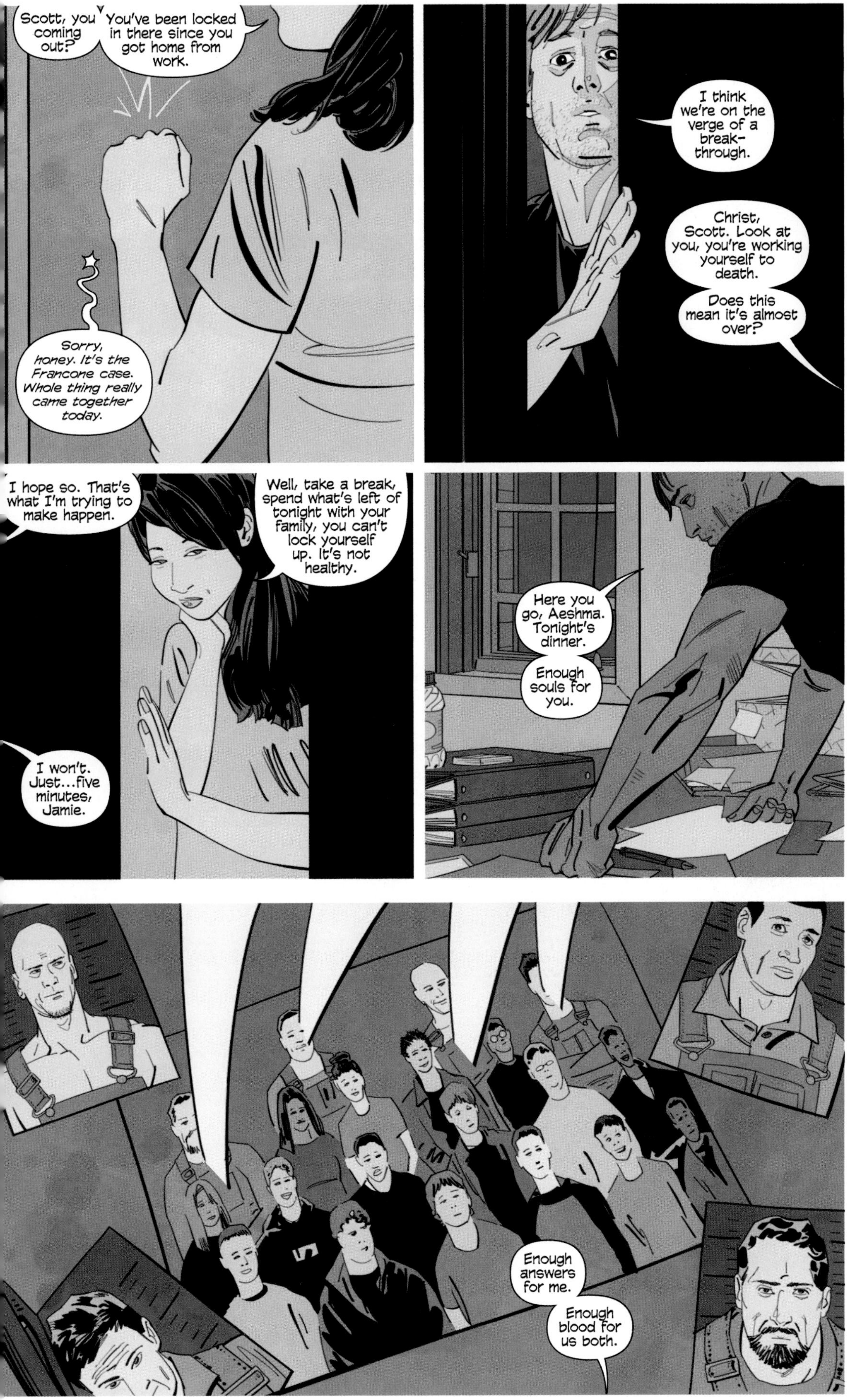
Scott, you coming out?
You've been locked in there since you got home from work.
Sorry, honey. It's the Francone case. Whole thing really came together today.
I think we're on the verge of a break-through.
Christ, Scott. Look at you, you're working yourself to death.
Does this mean it's almost over?
I hope so. That's what I'm trying to make happen.
Well, take a break, spend what's left of tonight with your family, you can't lock yourself up. It's not healthy.
I won't. Just...five minutes, Jamie.
Here you go, Aeshma. Tonight's dinner.
Enough souls for you.
Enough answers for me.
Enough blood for us both.

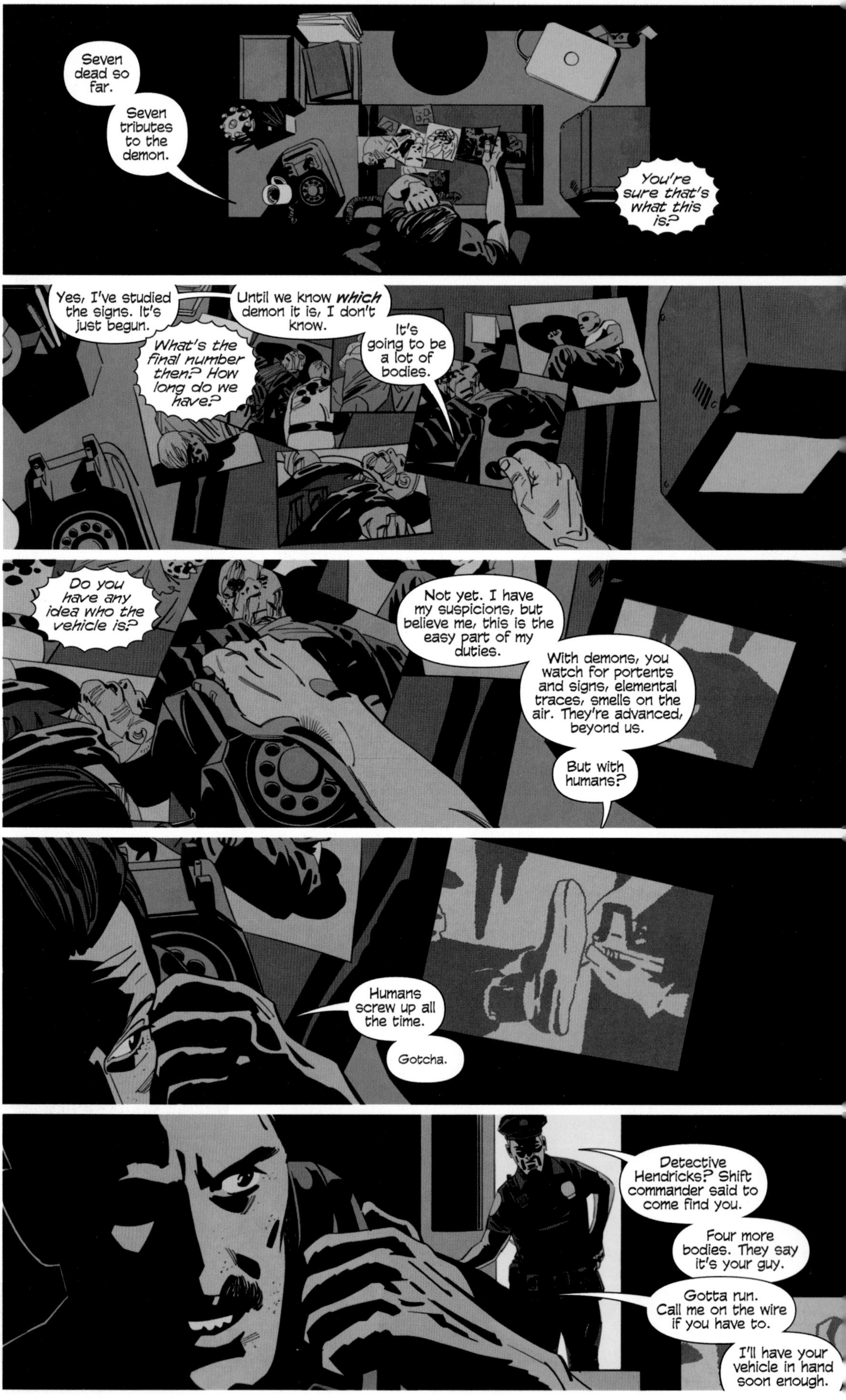

Seven dead so far.
Seven tributes to the demon.
You're sure that's what this is?
Yes, I've studied the signs. It's just begun.
What's the final number then? How long do we have?
Until we know ***which*** demon it is, I don't know.
It's going to be a lot of bodies.
Do you have any idea who the vehicle is?
Not yet. I have my suspicions, but believe me, this is the easy part of my duties.
With demons, you watch for portents and signs, elemental traces, smells on the air. They're advanced, beyond us.
But with humans?
Humans screw up all the time.
Gotcha.
Detective Hendricks? Shift commander said to come find you.
Four more bodies. They say it's your guy.
Gotta run. Call me on the wire if you have to.
I'll have your vehicle in hand soon enough.

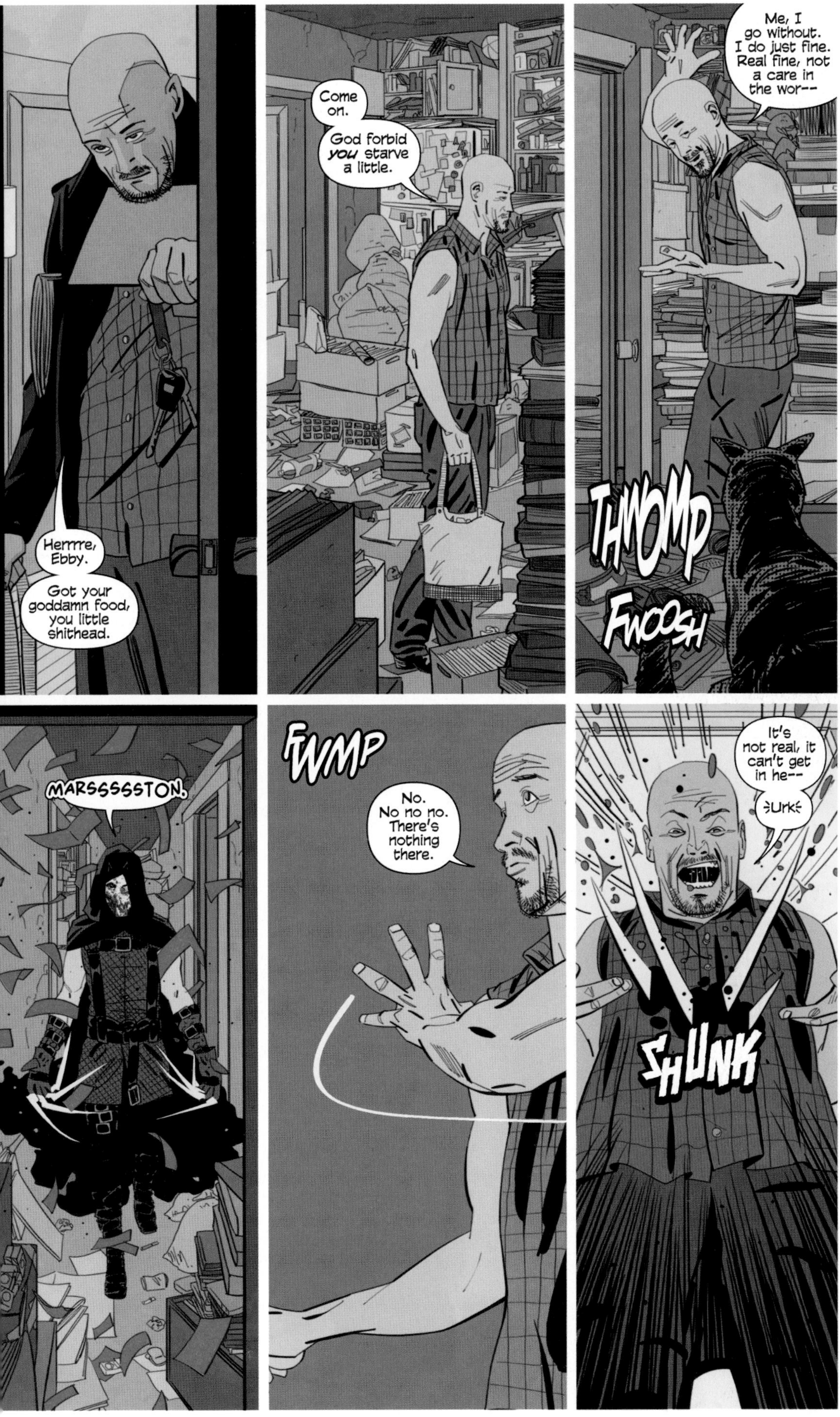
Herrrre, Ebby.
Got your goddamn food, you little shithead.
Come on.
God forbid *you* starve a little.
Me, I go without. I do just fine. Real fine, not a care in the wor--
THWOMP
FWOOSH
MARSSSSSTON.
FWMP
No. No no no. There's nothing there.
It's not real, it can't get in he--
Urk
SHUNK

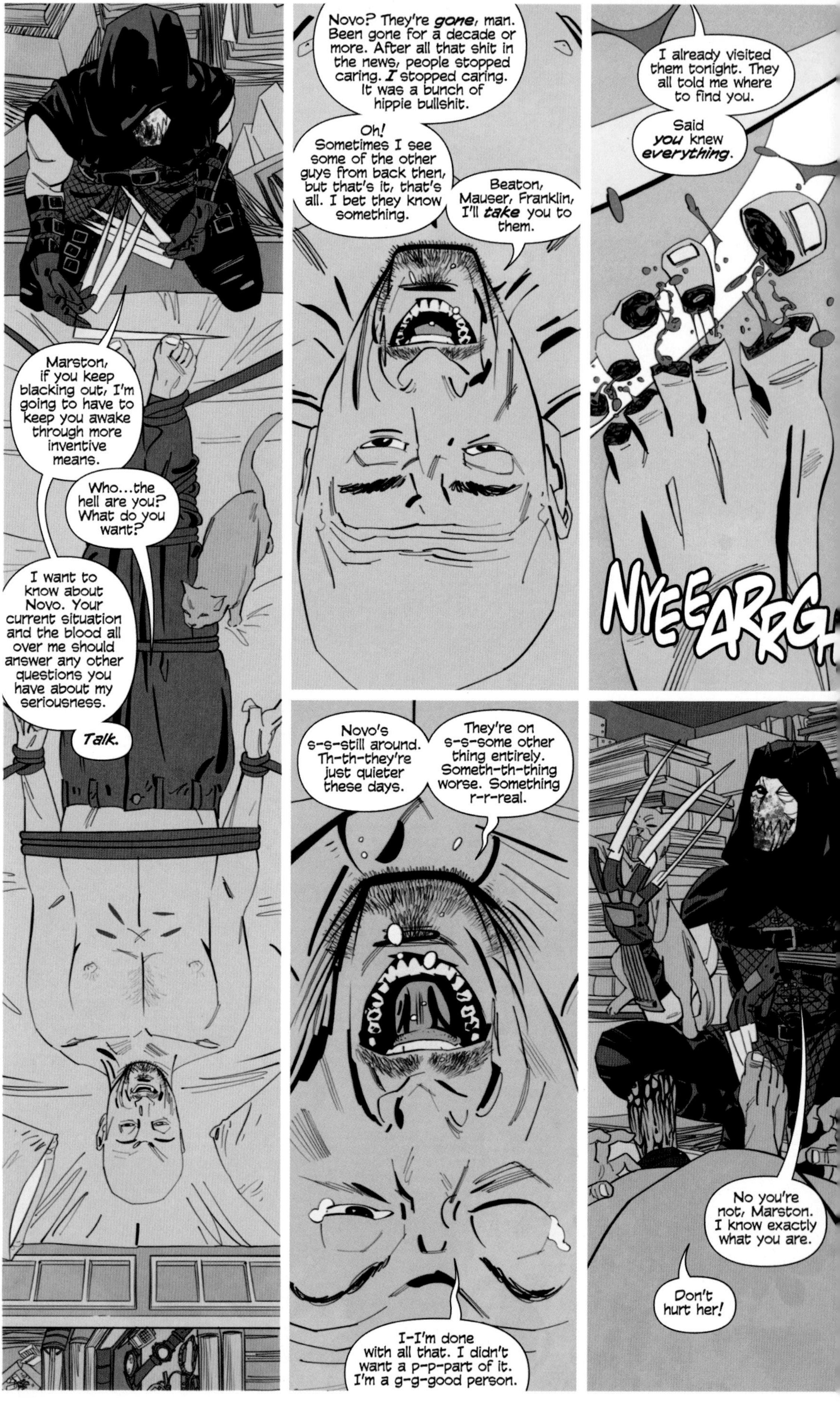

Marston, if you keep blacking out, I'm going to have to keep you awake through more inventive means.
Who...the hell are you? What do you want?
I want to know about Novo. Your current situation and the blood all over me should answer any other questions you have about my seriousness.
Talk.
Novo? They're gone, man. Been gone for a decade or more. After all that shit in the news, people stopped caring. I stopped caring. It was a bunch of hippie bullshit.
Oh! Sometimes I see some of the other guys from back then, but that's it, that's all. I bet they know something.
Beaton, Mauser, Franklin, I'll take you to them.
I already visited them tonight. They all told me where to find you.
Said you knew everything.
NYEEARRGH
Novo's s-s-still around. Th-th-they're just quieter these days.
They're on s-s-some other thing entirely. Someth-th-thing worse. Something r-r-real.
I-I'm done with all that. I didn't want a p-p-part of it. I'm a g-g-good person.
No you're not, Marston. I know exactly what you are.
Don't hurt her!

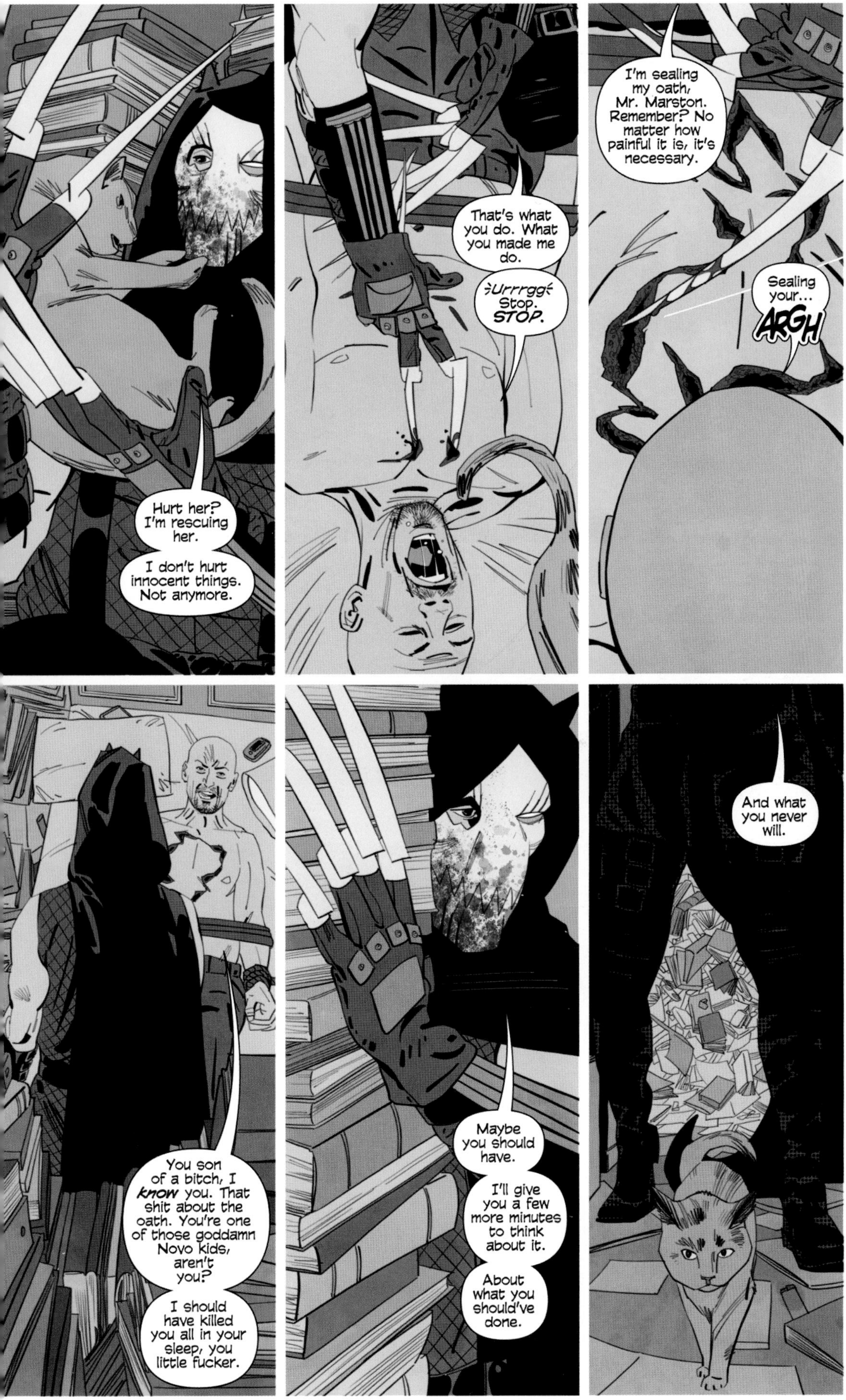
Hurt her? I'm rescuing her.
I don't hurt innocent things. Not anymore.
That's what you do. What you made me do.
Urrrgg Stop. STOP.
I'm sealing my oath, Mr. Marston. Remember? No matter how painful it is, it's necessary.
Sealing your... ARGH
You son of a bitch, I KNOW you. That shit about the oath. You're one of those goddamn Novo kids, aren't you?
I should have killed you all in your sleep, you little fucker.
Maybe you should have.
I'll give you a few more minutes to think about it.
About what you should've done.
And what you never will.

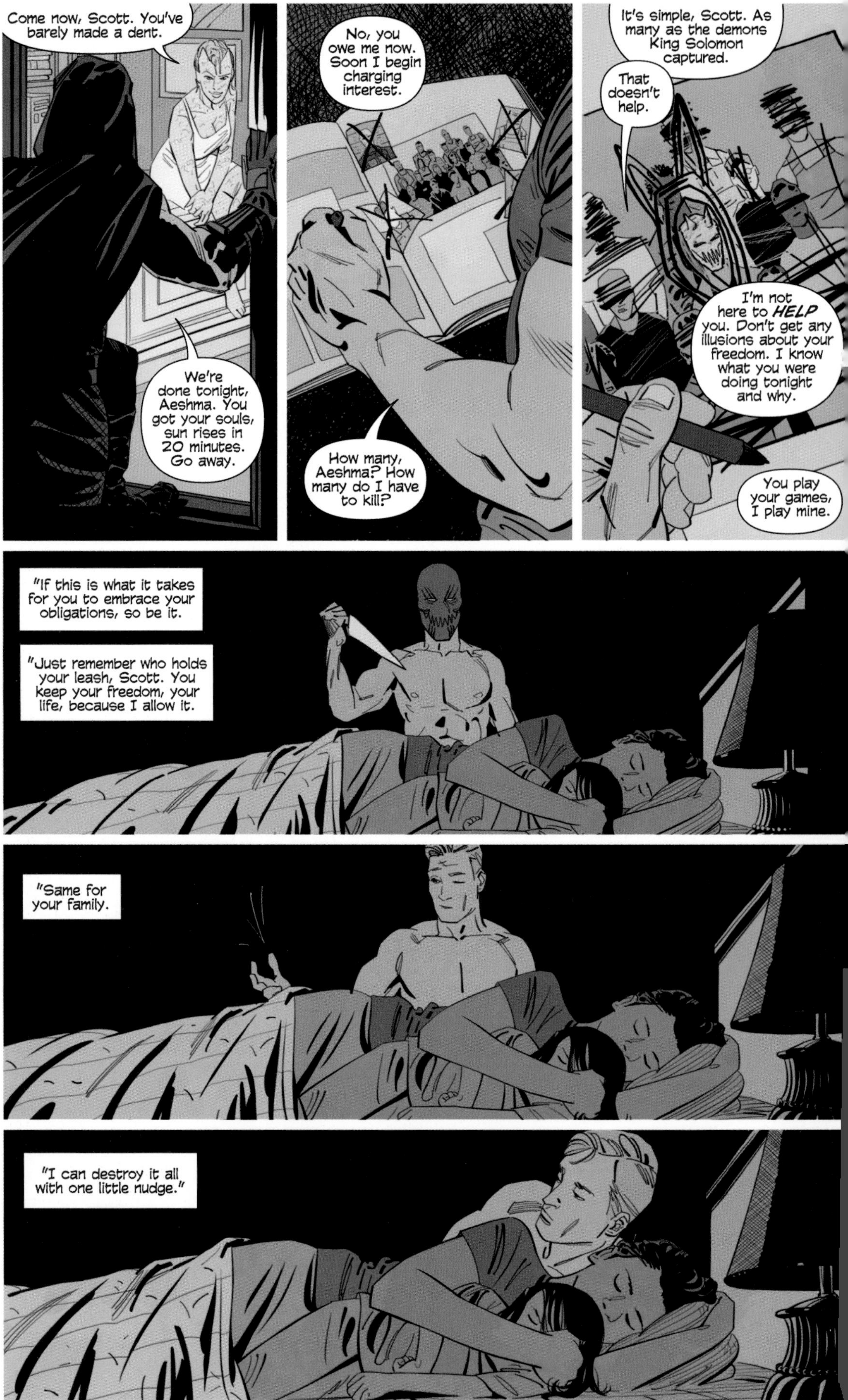

Come now, Scott. You've barely made a dent.
We're done tonight, Aeshma. You got your souls, sun rises in 20 minutes. Go away.
No, you owe me now. Soon I begin charging interest.
How many, Aeshma? How many do I have to kill?
It's simple, Scott. As many as the demons King Solomon captured.
That doesn't help.
I'm not here to HELP you. Don't get any illusions about your freedom. I know what you were doing tonight and why.
You play your games, I play mine.
"If this is what it takes for you to embrace your obligations, so be it.
"Just remember who holds your leash, Scott. You keep your freedom, your life, because I allow it.
"Same for your family.
"I can destroy it all with one little nudge."

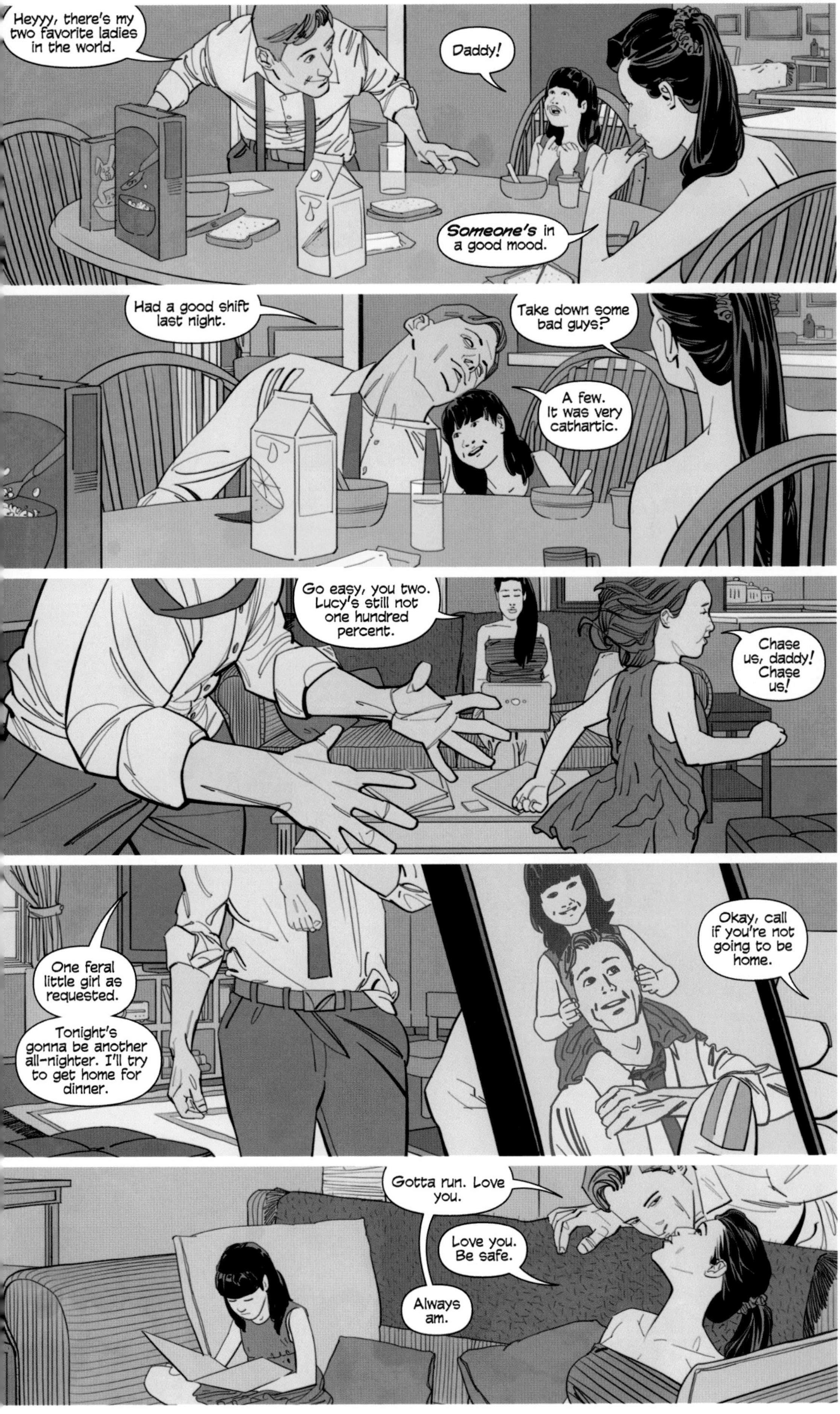

Heyyy, there's my two favorite ladies in the world.
Daddy!
Someone's in a good mood.
Had a good shift last night.
Take down some bad guys?
A few. It was very cathartic.
Go easy, you two. Lucy's still not one hundred percent.
Chase us, daddy! Chase us!
One feral little girl as requested.
Tonight's gonna be another all-nighter. I'll try to get home for dinner.
Okay, call if you're not going to be home.
Gotta run. Love you.
Love you. Be safe.
Always am.

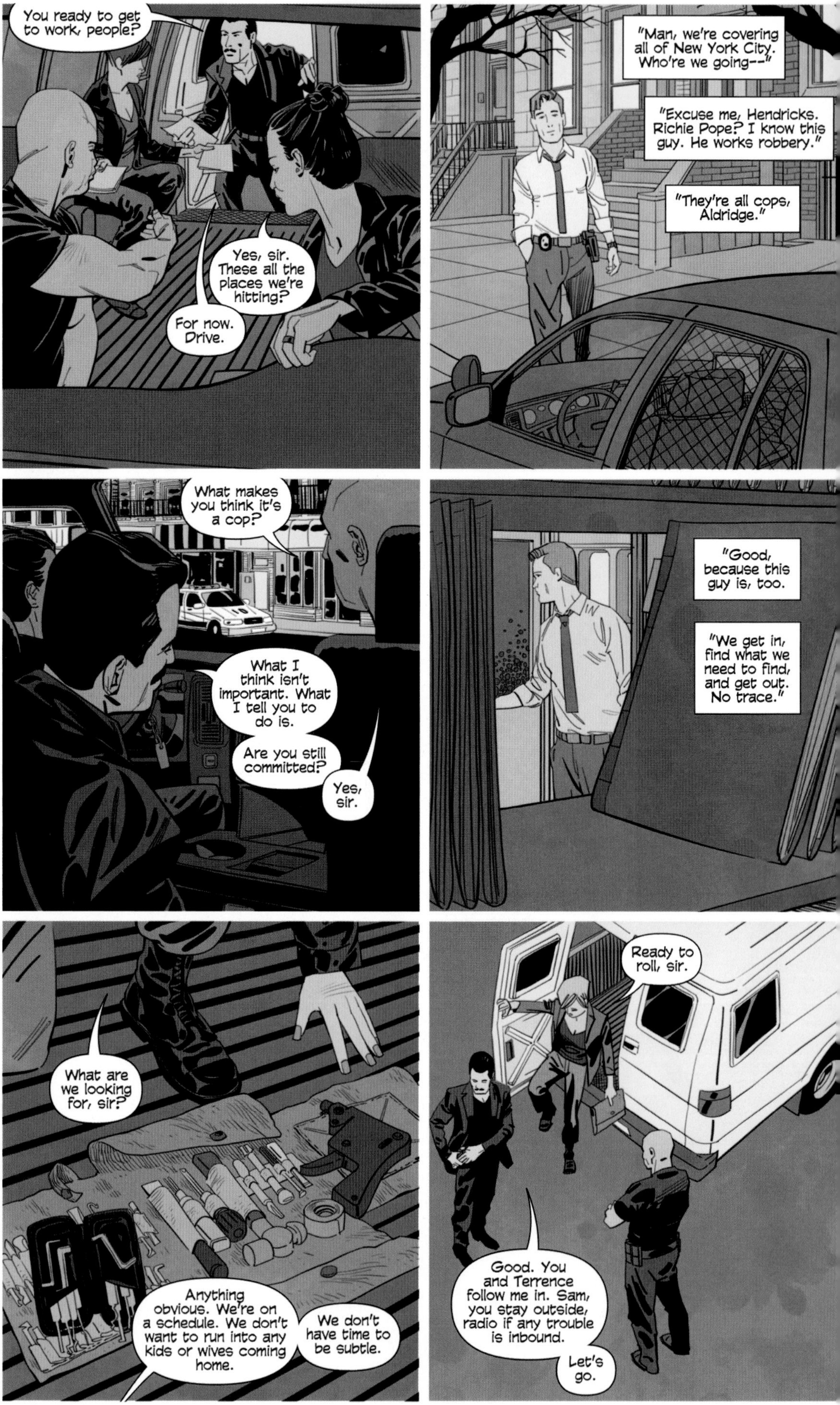
You ready to get to work, people?
Yes, sir. These all the places we're hitting?
For now. Drive.
"Man, we're covering all of New York City. Who're we going--"
"Excuse me, Hendricks. Richie Pope? I know this guy. He works robbery."
"They're all cops, Aldridge."
What makes you think it's a cop?
What I think isn't important. What I tell you to do is.
Are you still committed?
Yes, sir.
"Good, because this guy is, too.
"We get in, find what we need to find, and get out. No trace."
What are we looking for, sir?
Anything obvious. We're on a schedule. We don't want to run into any kids or wives coming home.
We don't have time to be subtle.
Ready to roll, sir.
Good. You and Terrence follow me in. Sam, you stay outside, radio if any trouble is inbound.
Let's go.

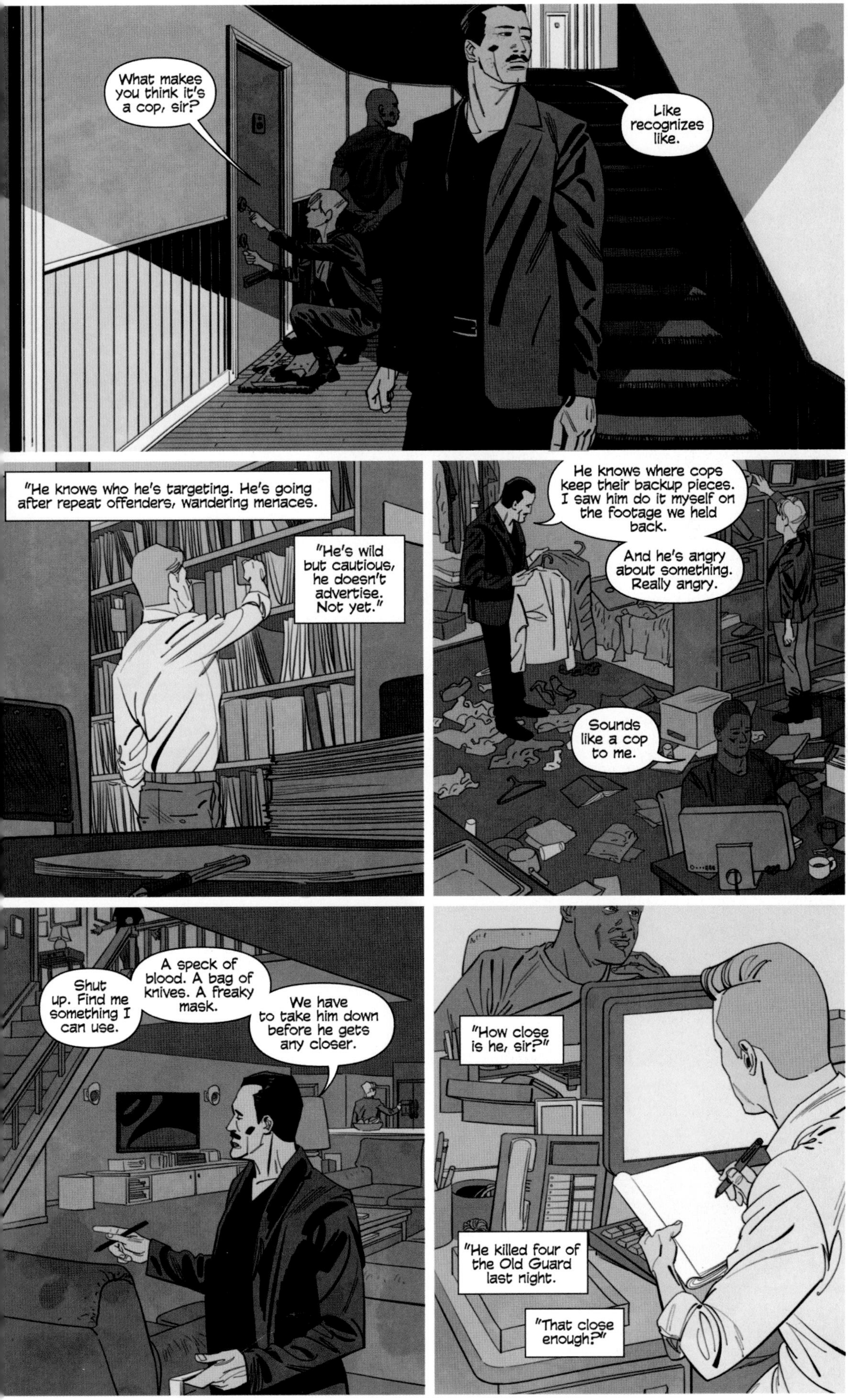
What makes you think it's a cop, sir?
Like recognizes like.
"He knows who he's targeting. He's going after repeat offenders, wandering menaces.
"He's wild but cautious, he doesn't advertise. Not yet."
He knows where cops keep their backup pieces. I saw him do it myself on the footage we held back.
And he's angry about something. Really angry.
Sounds like a cop to me.
Shut up. Find me something I can use.
A speck of blood. A bag of knives. A freaky mask.
We have to take him down before he gets any closer.
"How close is he, sir?"
"He killed four of the Old Guard last night.
"That close enough?"

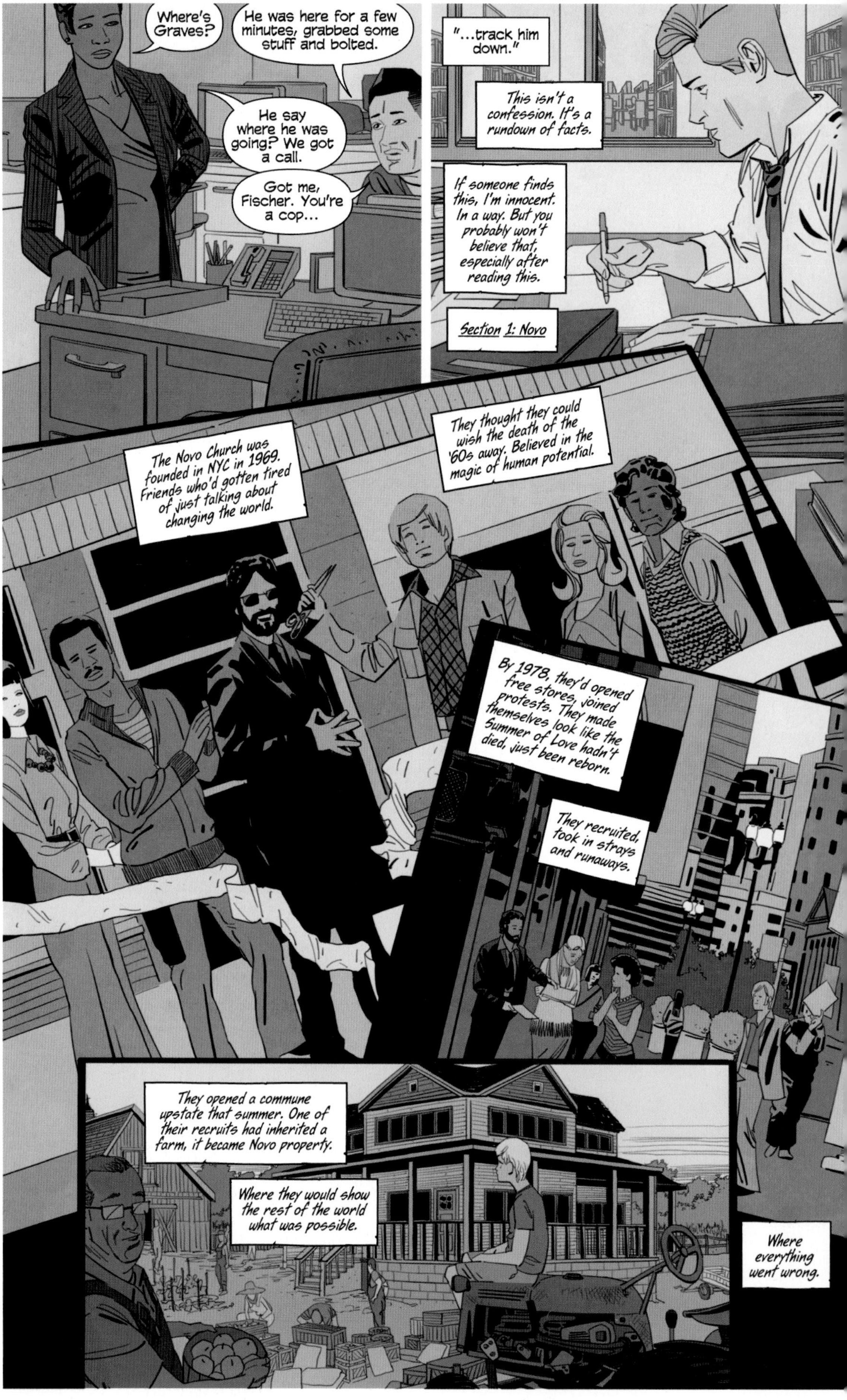
Where's Graves?
He was here for a few minutes, grabbed some stuff and bolted.
He say where he was going? We got a call.
Got me, Fischer. You're a cop...
"...track him down."
This isn't a confession. It's a rundown of facts.
If someone finds this, I'm innocent. In a way. But you probably won't believe that, especially after reading this.
Section 1: Novo
The Novo Church was founded in NYC in 1969. Friends who'd gotten tired of just talking about changing the world.
They thought they could wish the death of the '60s away. Believed in the magic of human potential.
By 1978, they'd opened free stores, joined protests. They made themselves look like the Summer of Love hadn't died, just been reborn.
They recruited, took in strays and runaways.
They opened a commune upstate that summer. One of their recruits had inherited a farm, it became Novo property.
Where they would show the rest of the world what was possible.
Where everything went wrong.

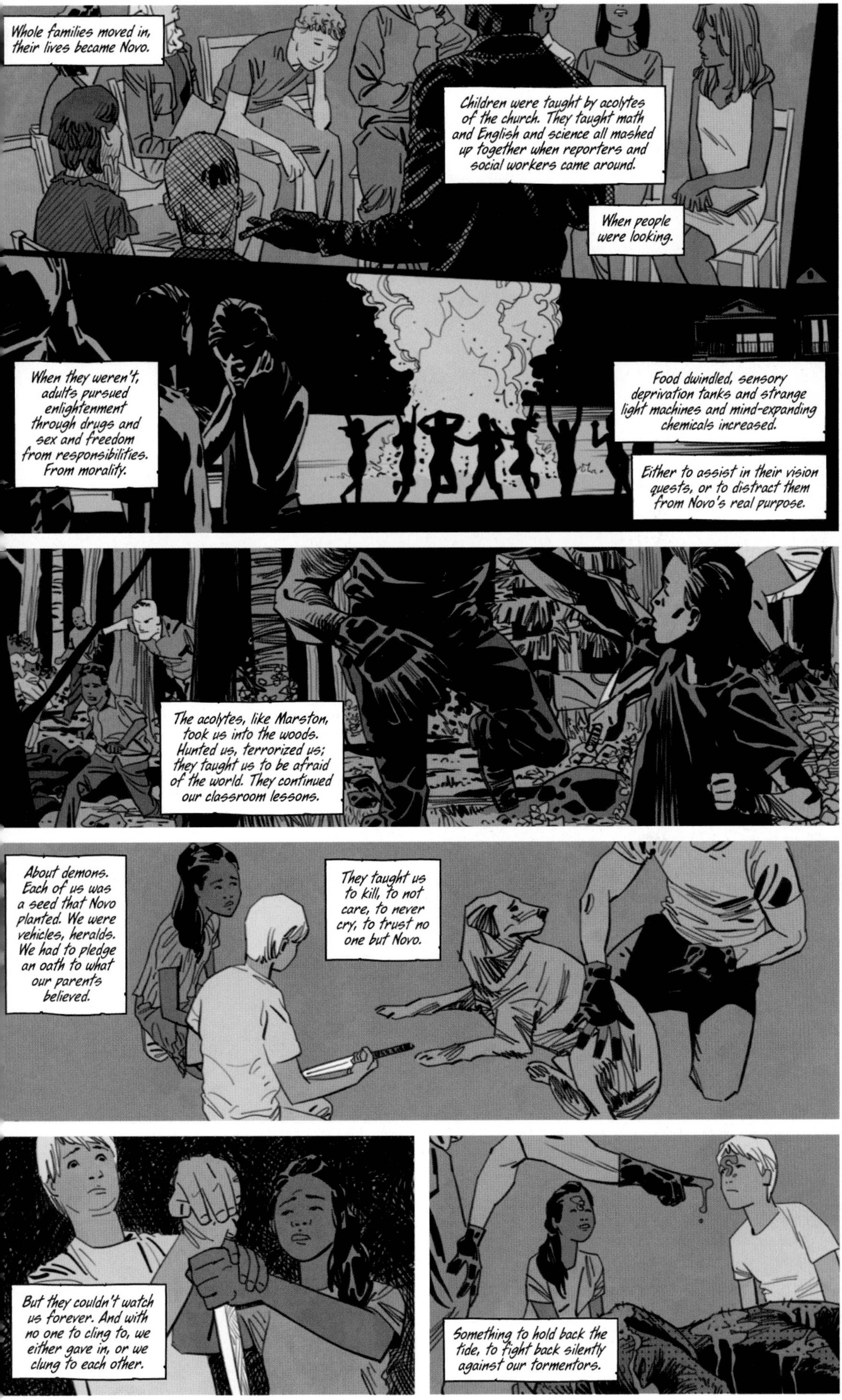

Whole families moved in, their lives became Novo.
Children were taught by acolytes of the church. They taught math and English and science all mashed up together when reporters and social workers came around.
When people were looking.
When they weren't, adults pursued enlightenment through drugs and sex and freedom from responsibilities. From morality.
Food dwindled, sensory deprivation tanks and strange light machines and mind-expanding chemicals increased.
Either to assist in their vision quests, or to distract them from Novo's real purpose.
The acolytes, like Marston, took us into the woods. Hunted us, terrorized us; they taught us to be afraid of the world. They continued our classroom lessons.
About demons. Each of us was a seed that Novo planted. We were vehicles, heralds. We had to pledge an oath to what our parents believed.
They taught us to kill, to not care, to never cry, to trust no one but Novo.
But they couldn't watch us forever. And with no one to cling to, we either gave in, or we clung to each other.
Something to hold back the tide, to fight back silently against our tormentors.

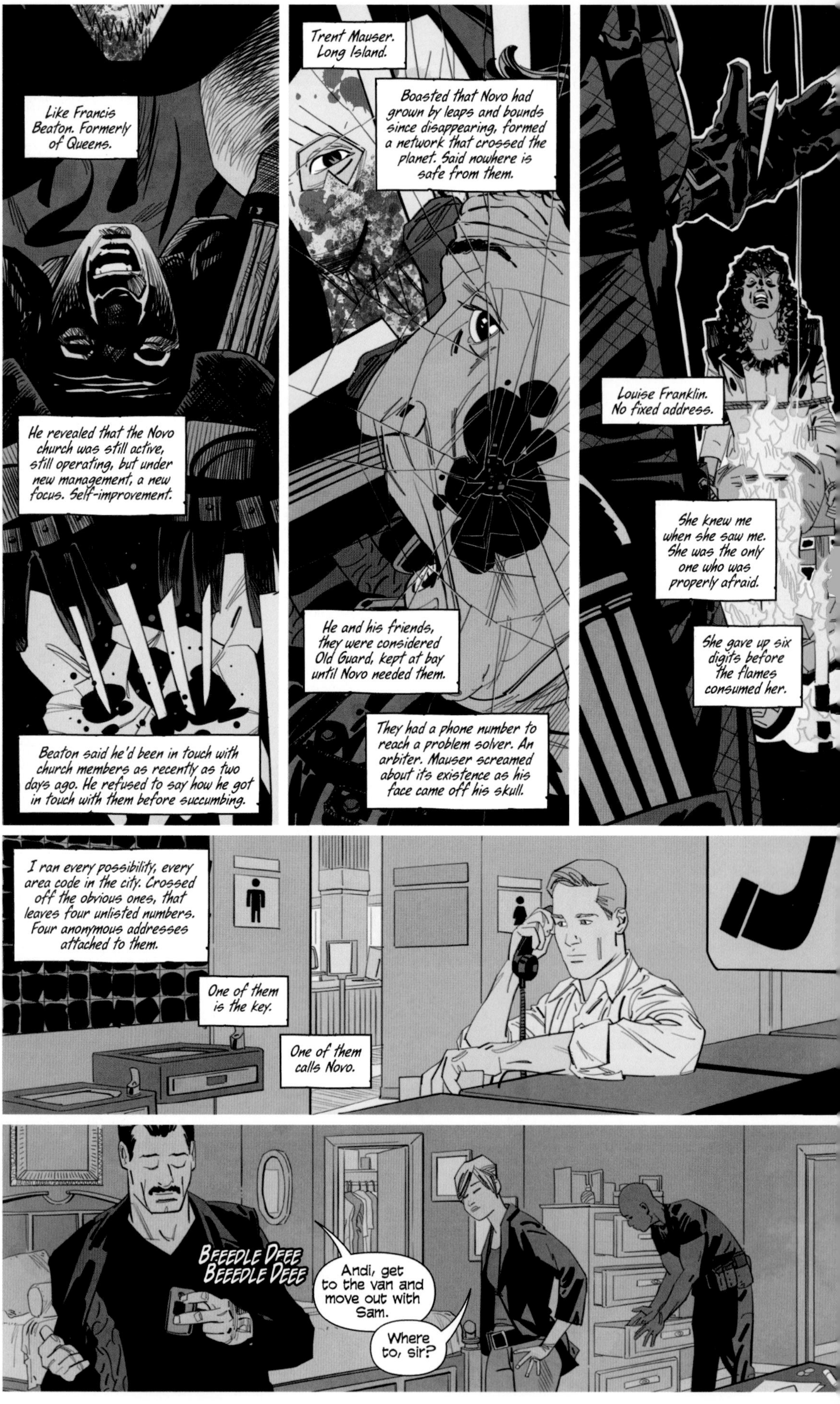
Like Francis Beaton. Formerly of Queens.
He revealed that the Novo church was still active, still operating, but under new management, a new focus. Self-improvement.
Beaton said he'd been in touch with church members as recently as two days ago. He refused to say how he got in touch with them before succumbing.
Trent Mauser. Long Island.
Boasted that Novo had grown by leaps and bounds since disappearing, formed a network that crossed the planet. Said nowhere is safe from them.
He and his friends, they were considered Old Guard, kept at bay until Novo needed them.
They had a phone number to reach a problem solver. An arbiter. Mauser screamed about its existence as his face came off his skull.
Louise Franklin. No fixed address.
She knew me when she saw me. She was the only one who was properly afraid.
She gave up six digits before the flames consumed her.
I ran every possibility, every area code in the city. Crossed off the obvious ones, that leaves four unlisted numbers. Four anonymous addresses attached to them.
One of them is the key.
One of them calls Novo.
BEEEDLE DEEE BEEEDLE DEEE
Andi, get to the van and move out with Sam.
Where to, sir?

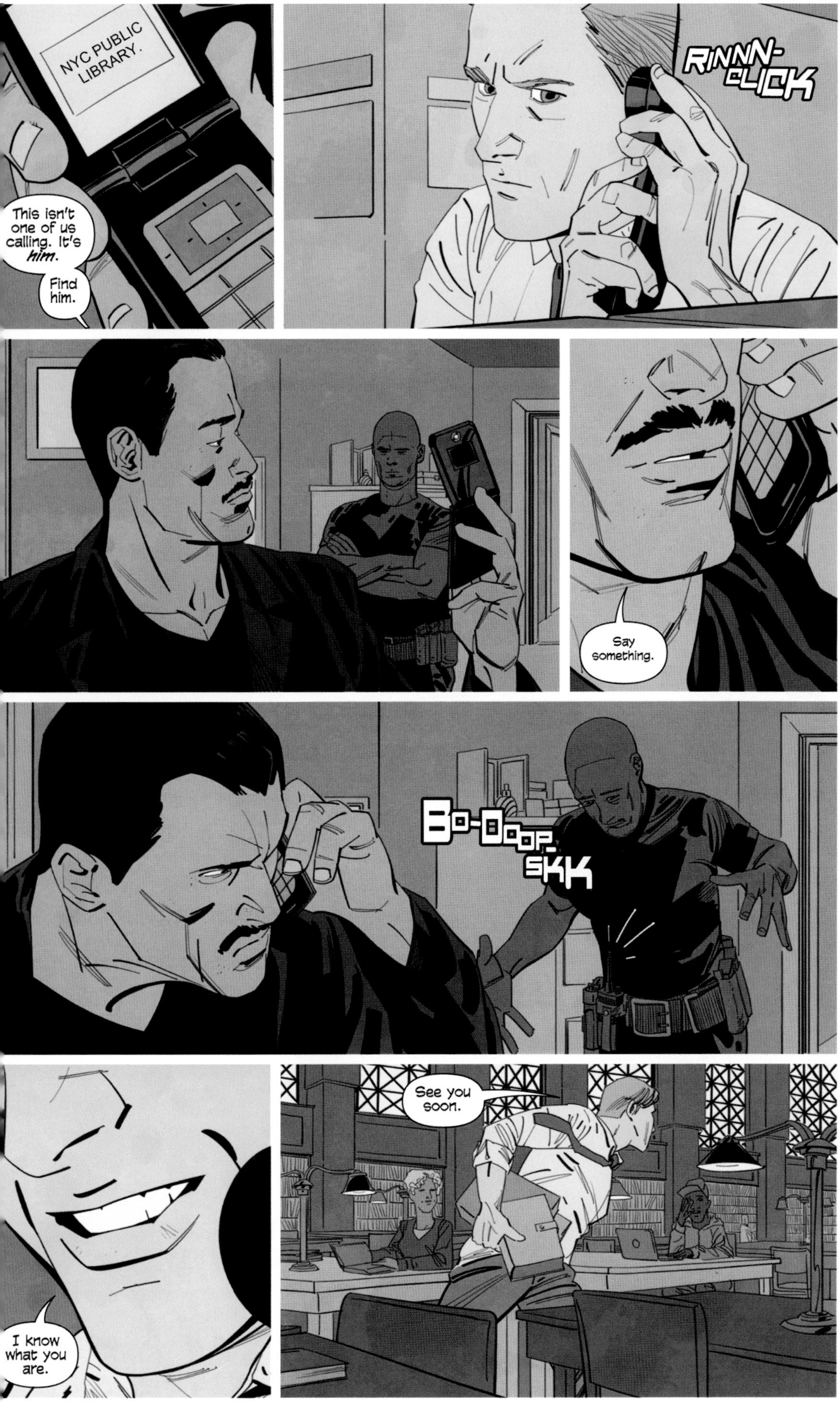
NYC PUBLIC LIBRARY.
RINNN-CLICK
This isn't one of us calling. It's *him*.
Find him.
Say something.
BO-BOOP. SKK
I know what you are.
See you soon.

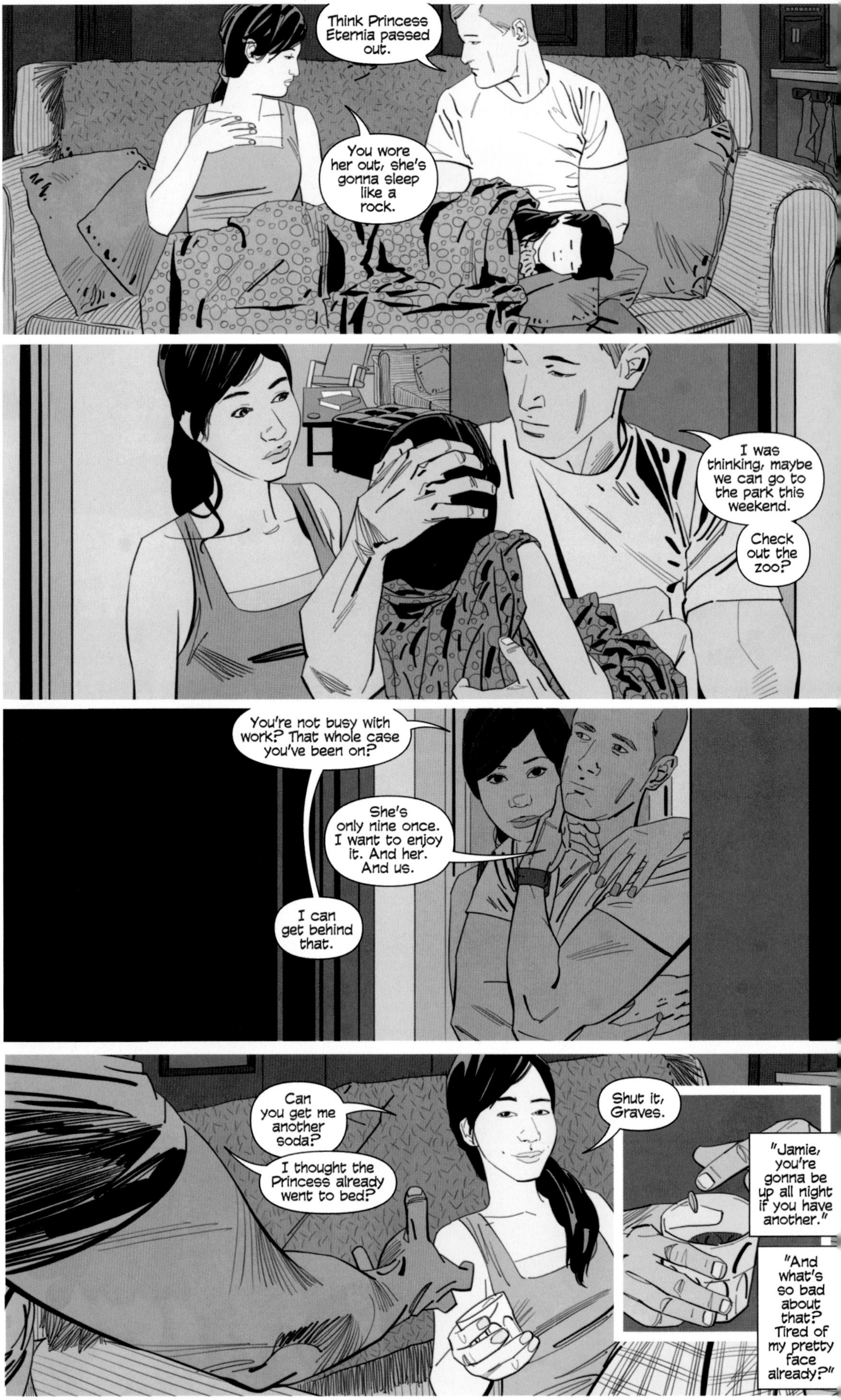
Think Princess Eternia passed out.
You wore her out, she's gonna sleep like a rock.
I was thinking, maybe we can go to the park this weekend.
Check out the zoo?
You're not busy with work? That whole case you've been on?
She's only nine once. I want to enjoy it. And her. And us.
I can get behind that.
Can you get me another soda?
I thought the Princess already went to bed?
Shut it, Graves.
"Jamie, you're gonna be up all night if you have another."
"And what's so bad about that? Tired of my pretty face already?"

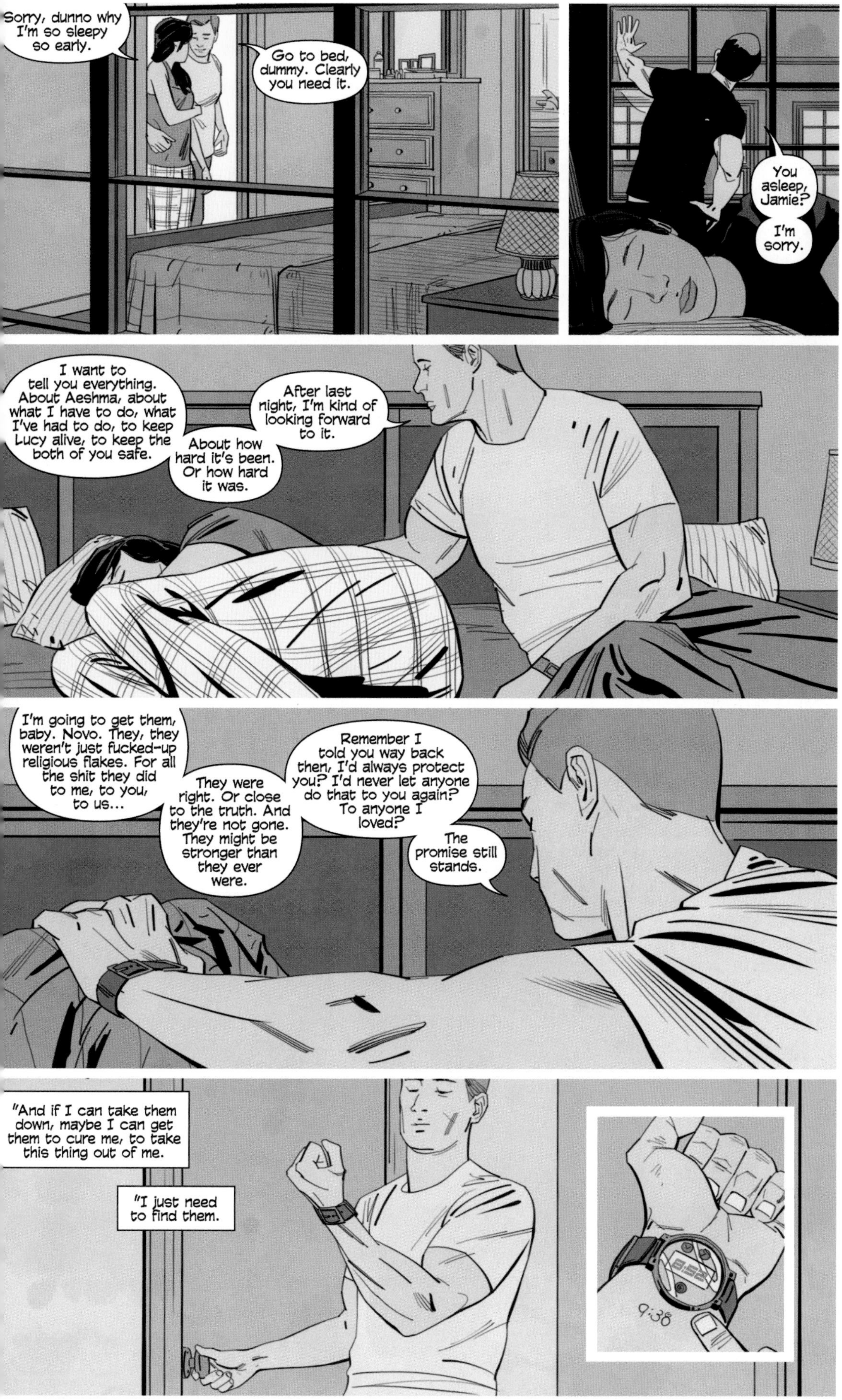

Sorry, dunno why I'm so sleepy so early.
Go to bed, dummy. Clearly you need it.
You asleep, Jamie?
I'm sorry.
I want to tell you everything. About Aeshma, about what I have to do, what I've had to do, to keep Lucy alive, to keep the both of you safe.
About how hard it's been. Or how hard it was.
After last night, I'm kind of looking forward to it.
I'm going to get them, baby. Novo. They, they weren't just fucked-up religious flakes. For all the shit they did to me, to you, to us...
They were right. Or close to the truth. And they're not gone. They might be stronger than they ever were.
Remember I told you way back then, I'd always protect you? I'd never let anyone do that to you again? To anyone I loved?
The promise still stands.
"And if I can take them down, maybe I can get them to cure me, to take this thing out of me.
"I just need to find them.
9:38

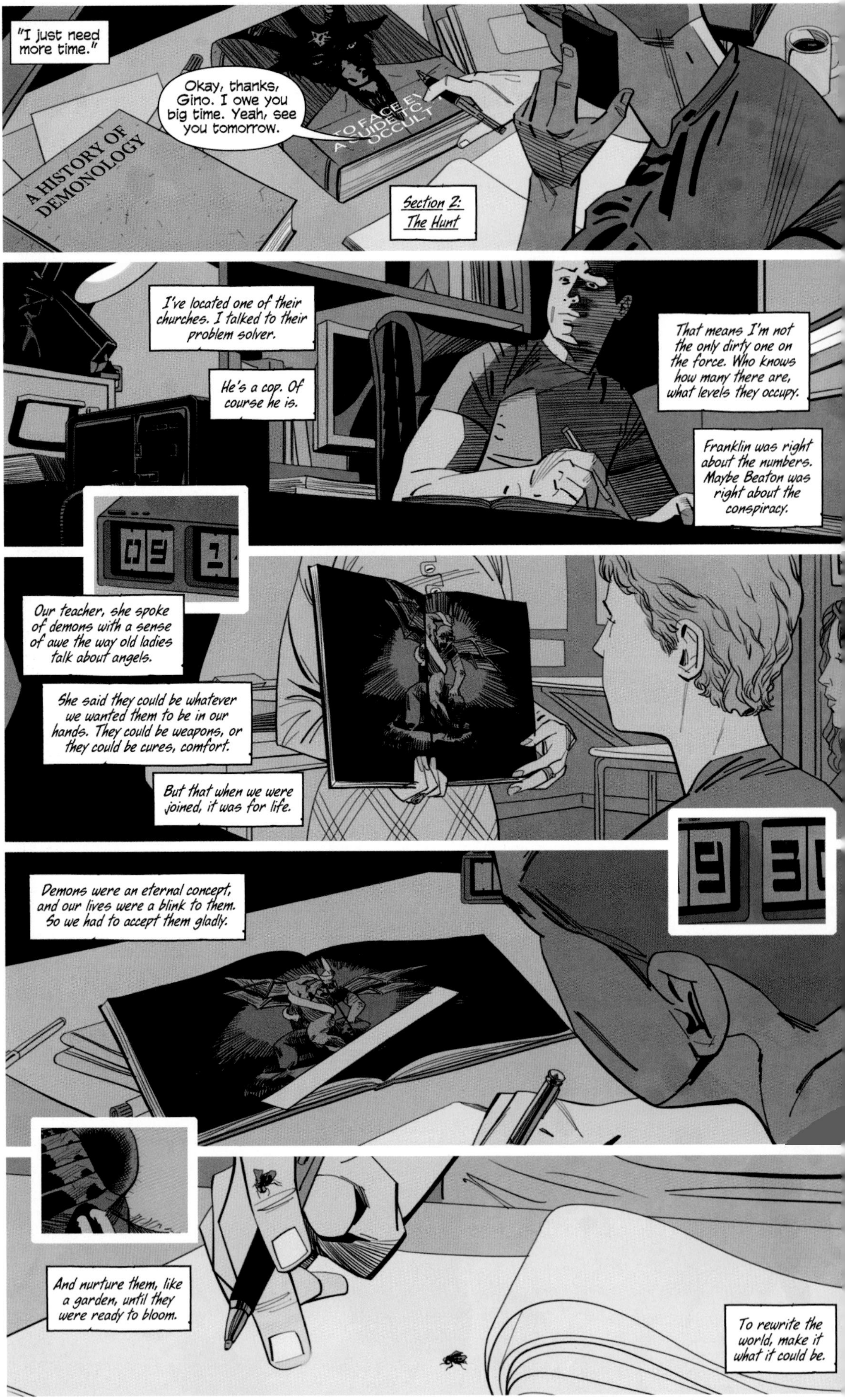
"I just need more time."
Okay, thanks, Gino. I owe you big time. Yeah, see you tomorrow.
A HISTORY OF DEMONOLOGY
Section 2: The Hunt
I've located one of their churches. I talked to their problem solver.
He's a cop. Of course he is.
That means I'm not the only dirty one on the force. Who knows how many there are, what levels they occupy.
Franklin was right about the numbers. Maybe Beaton was right about the conspiracy.
Our teacher, she spoke of demons with a sense of awe the way old ladies talk about angels.
She said they could be whatever we wanted them to be in our hands. They could be weapons, or they could be cures, comfort.
But that when we were joined, it was for life.
Demons were an eternal concept, and our lives were a blink to them. So we had to accept them gladly.
And nurture them, like a garden, until they were ready to bloom.
To rewrite the world, make it what it could be.

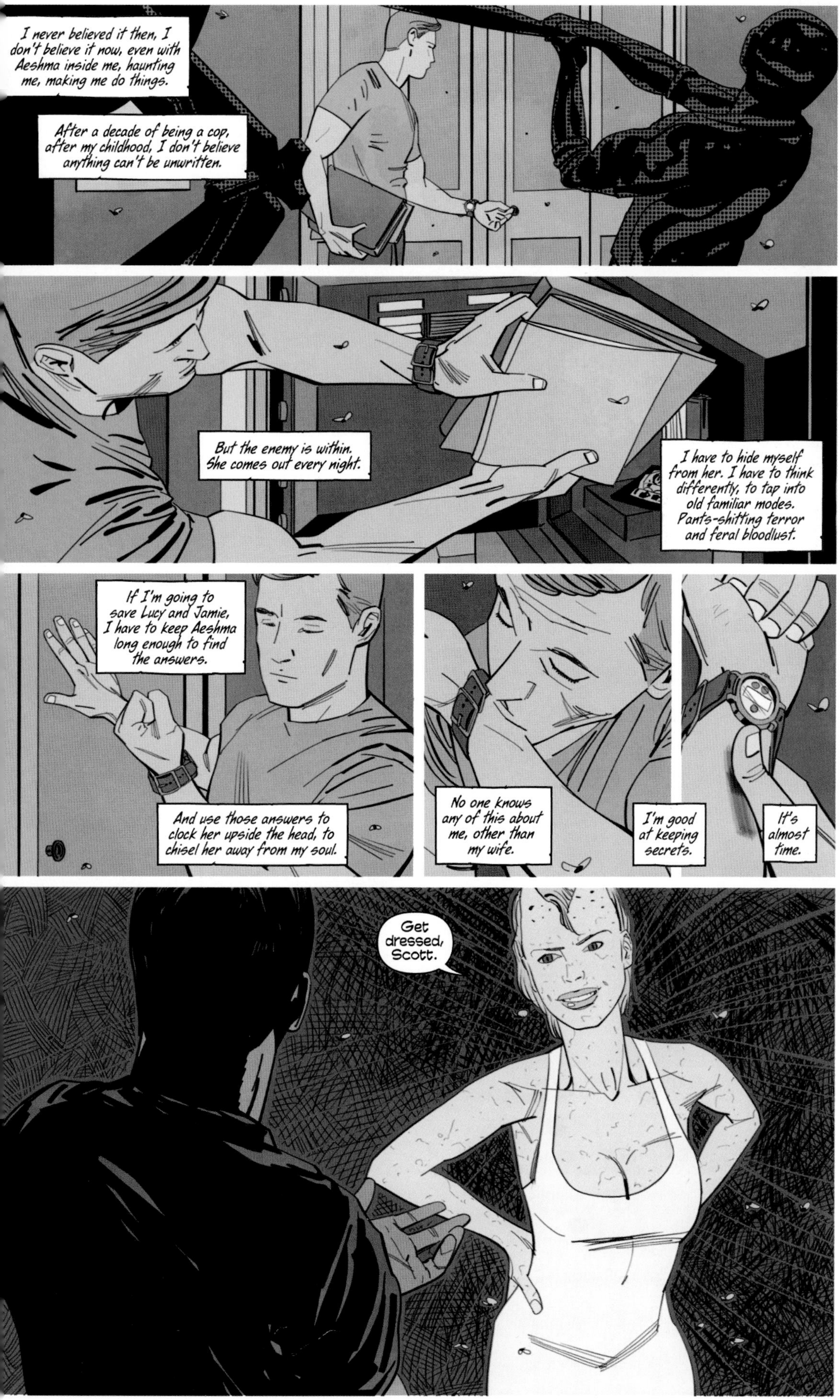
I never believed it then, I don't believe it now, even with Aeshma inside me, haunting me, making me do things.
After a decade of being a cop, after my childhood, I don't believe anything can't be unwritten.
But the enemy is within. She comes out every night.
I have to hide myself from her. I have to think differently, to tap into old familiar modes. Pants-shitting terror and feral bloodlust.
If I'm going to save Lucy and Jamie, I have to keep Aeshma long enough to find the answers.
And use those answers to clock her upside the head, to chisel her away from my soul.
No one knows any of this about me, other than my wife.
I'm good at keeping secrets.
It's almost time.
Get dressed, Scott.

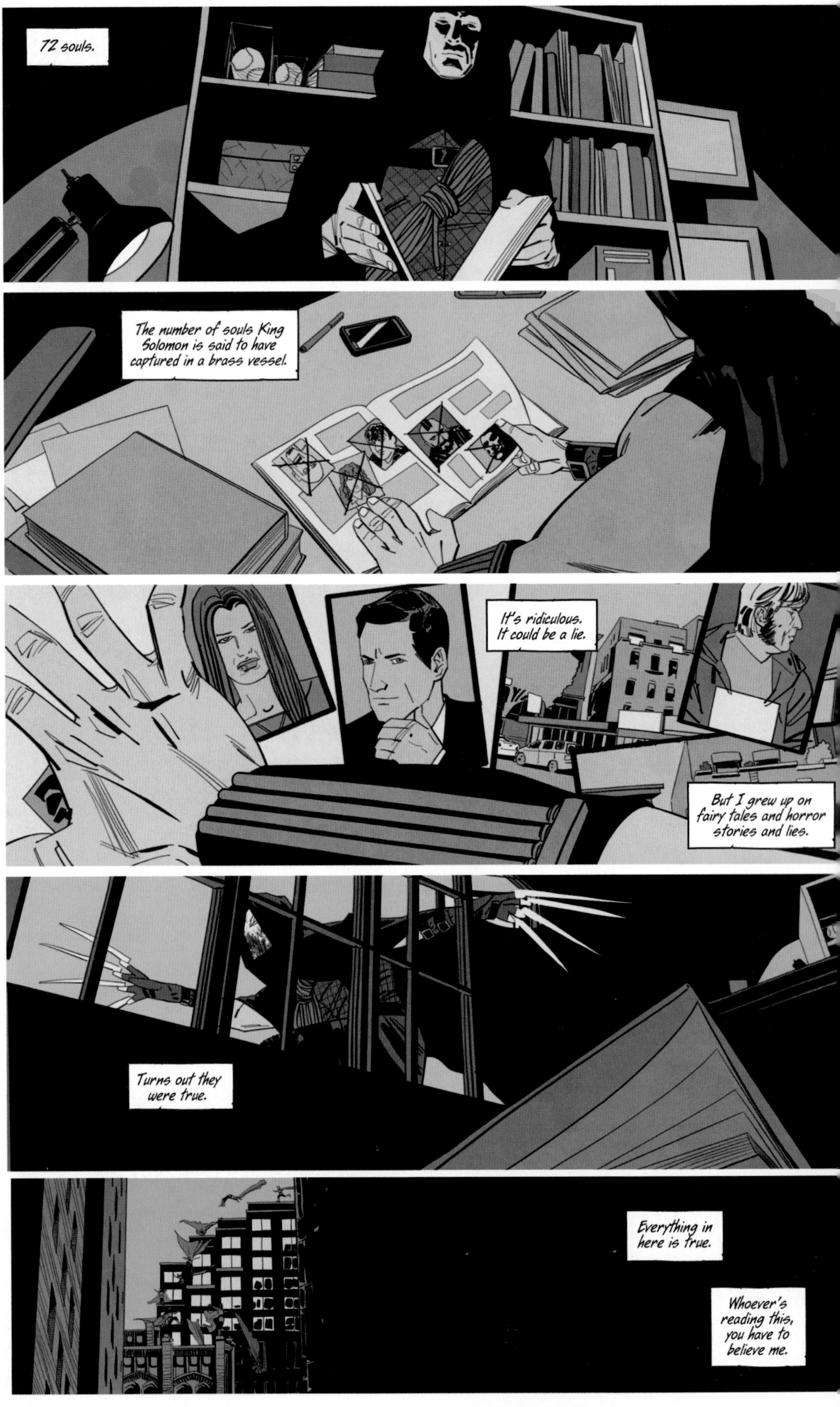
72 souls.
The number of souls King Solomon is said to have captured in a brass vessel.
It's ridiculous. It could be a lie.
But I grew up on fairy tales and horror stories and lies.
Turns out they were true.
Everything in here is true.
Whoever's reading this, you have to believe me.

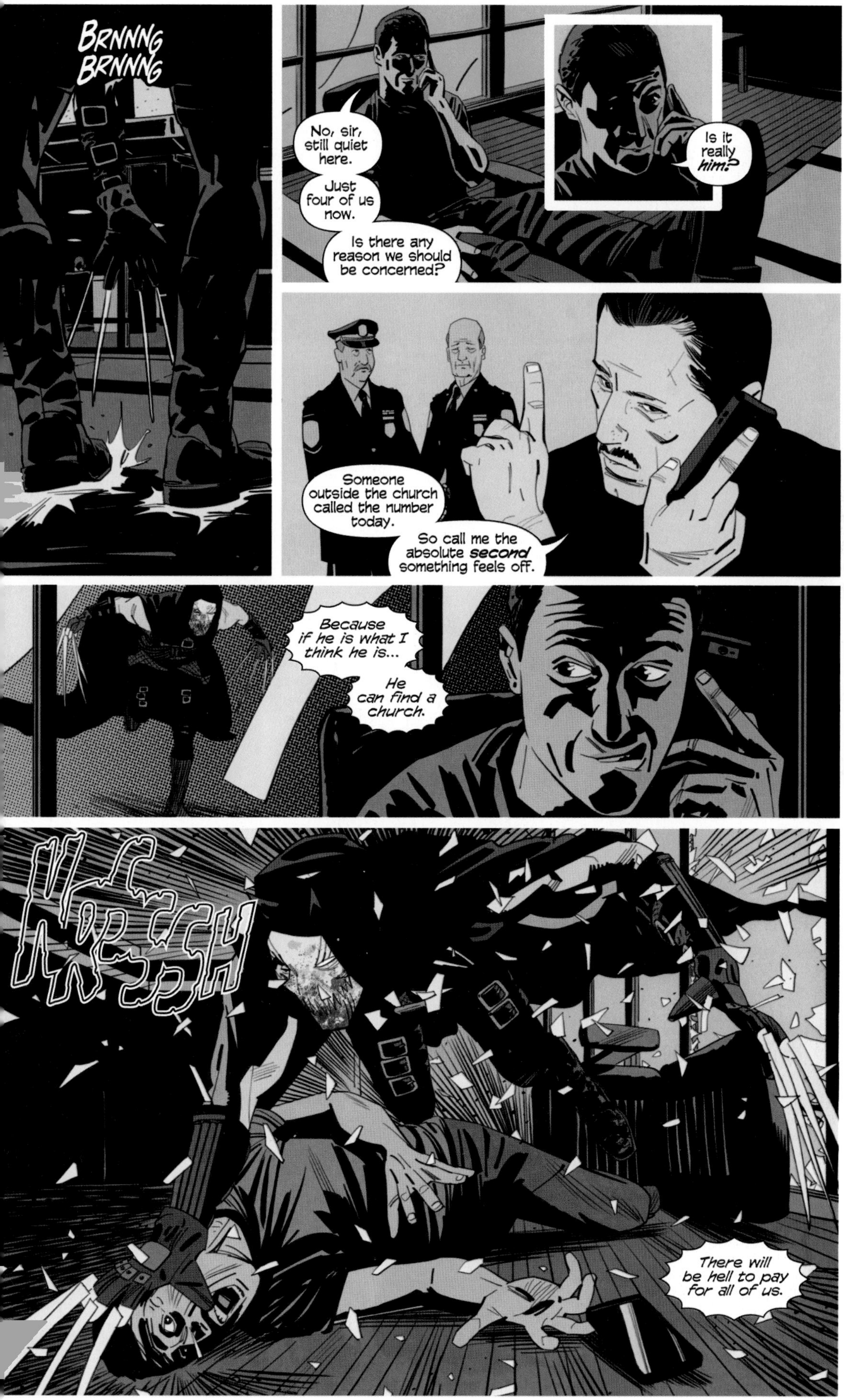

BRNNNG BRNNNG
No, sir, still quiet here.
Just four of us now.
Is there any reason we should be concerned?
Is it really *him?*
Someone outside the church called the number today.
So call me the absolute ***second*** something feels off.
Because if he is what I think he is...
He can find a church.
KRSSSH
There will be hell to pay for all of us.

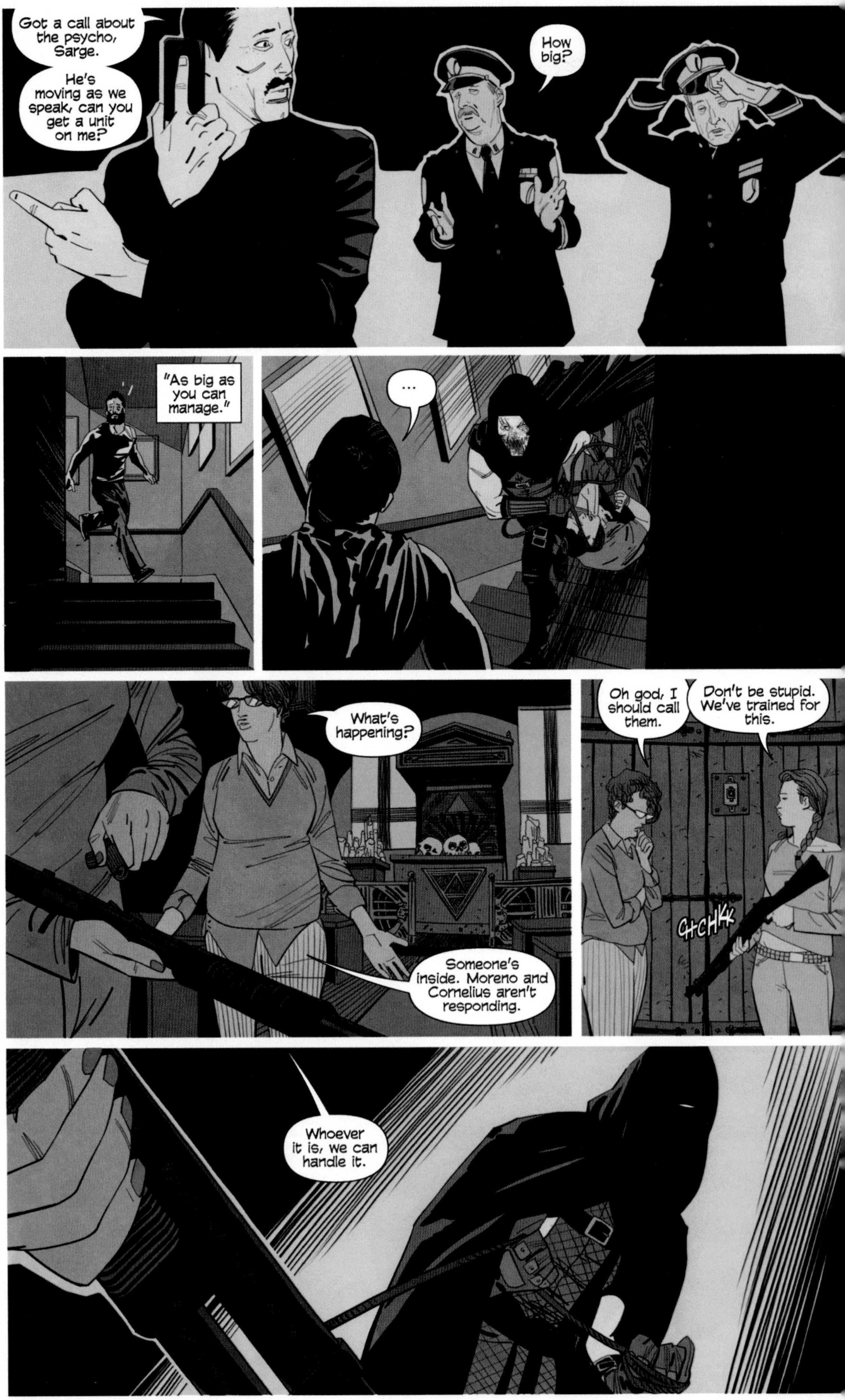
Got a call about the psycho, Sarge.
He's moving as we speak, can you get a unit on me?
How big?
"As big as you can manage."
...
What's happening?
Someone's inside. Moreno and Cornelius aren't responding.
Oh god, I should call them.
Don't be stupid. We've trained for this.
CHCHKK
Whoever it is, we can handle it.

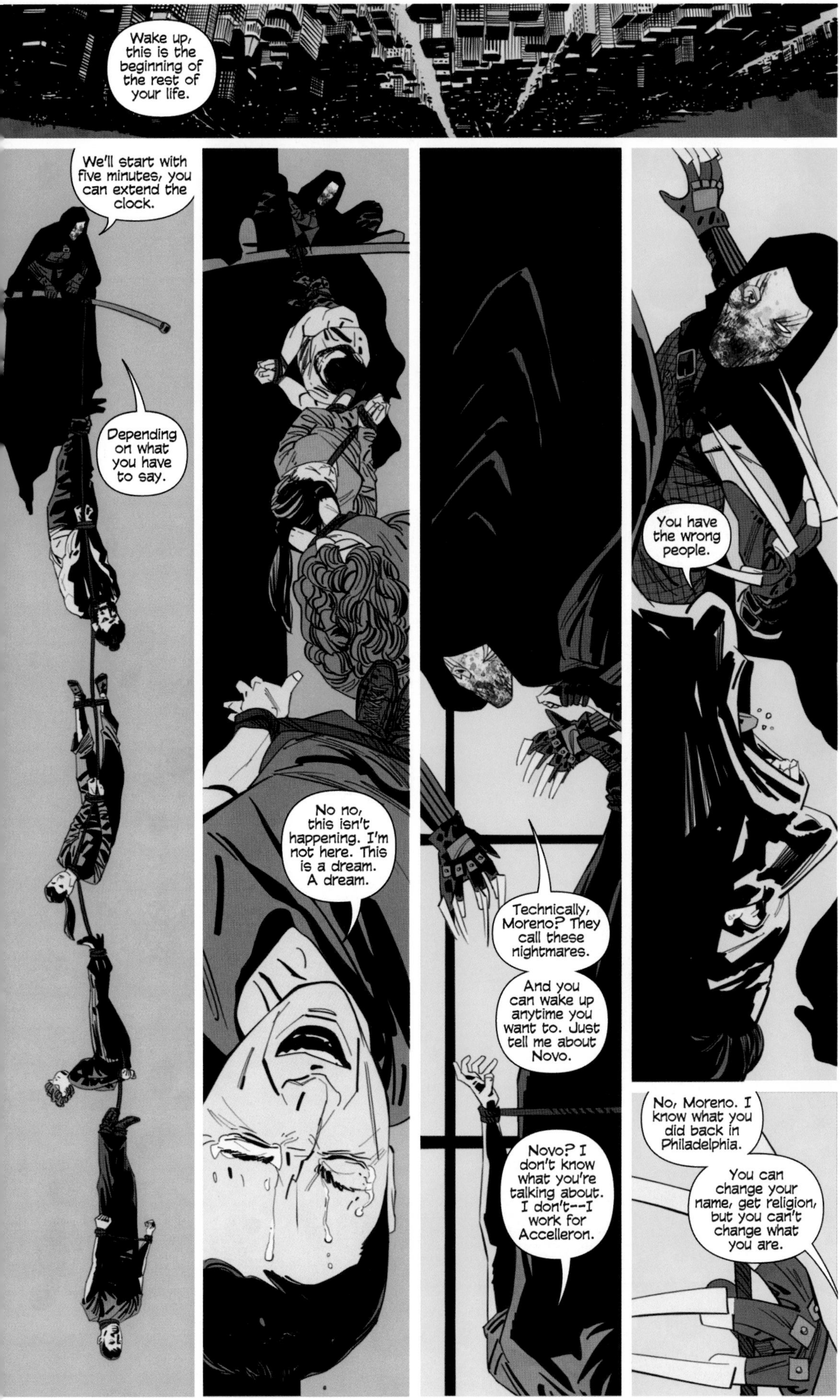
Wake up, this is the beginning of the rest of your life.
We'll start with five minutes, you can extend the clock.
Depending on what you have to say.
No no, this isn't happening. I'm not here. This is a dream. A dream.
Technically, Moreno? They call these nightmares.
And you can wake up anytime you want to. Just tell me about Novo.
Novo? I don't know what you're talking about. I don't--I work for Accelleron.
You have the wrong people.
No, Moreno. I know what you did back in Philadelphia.
You can change your name, get religion, but you can't change what you are.

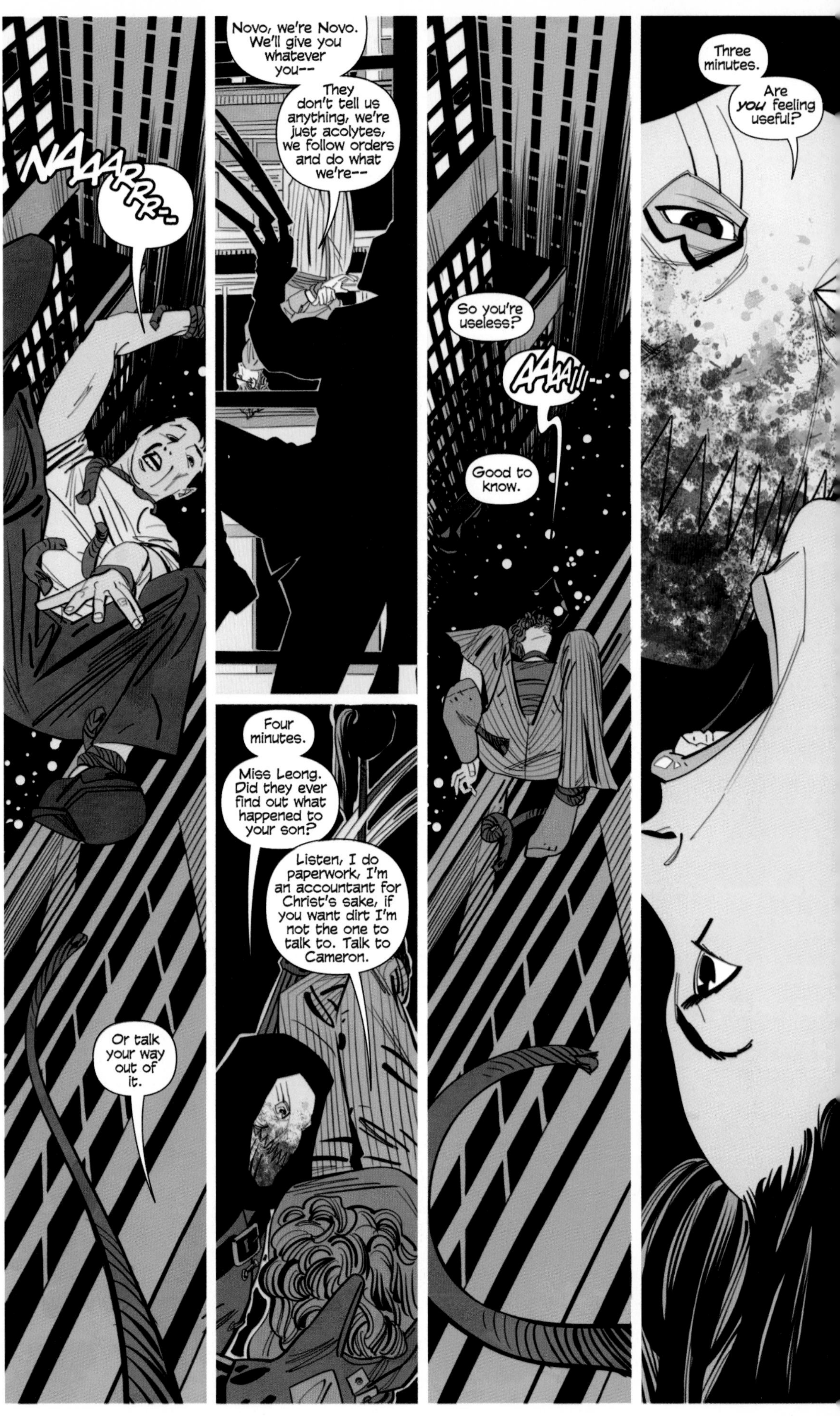
NAAARRR--
Or talk your way out of it.
Novo, we're Novo. We'll give you whatever you--
They don't tell us anything, we're just acolytes, we follow orders and do what we're--
Four minutes.
Miss Leong. Did they ever find out what happened to your son?
Listen, I do paperwork, I'm an accountant for Christ's sake, if you want dirt I'm not the one to talk to. Talk to Cameron.
So you're useless?
AAAA!!--
Good to know.
Three minutes.
Are *you* feeling useful?

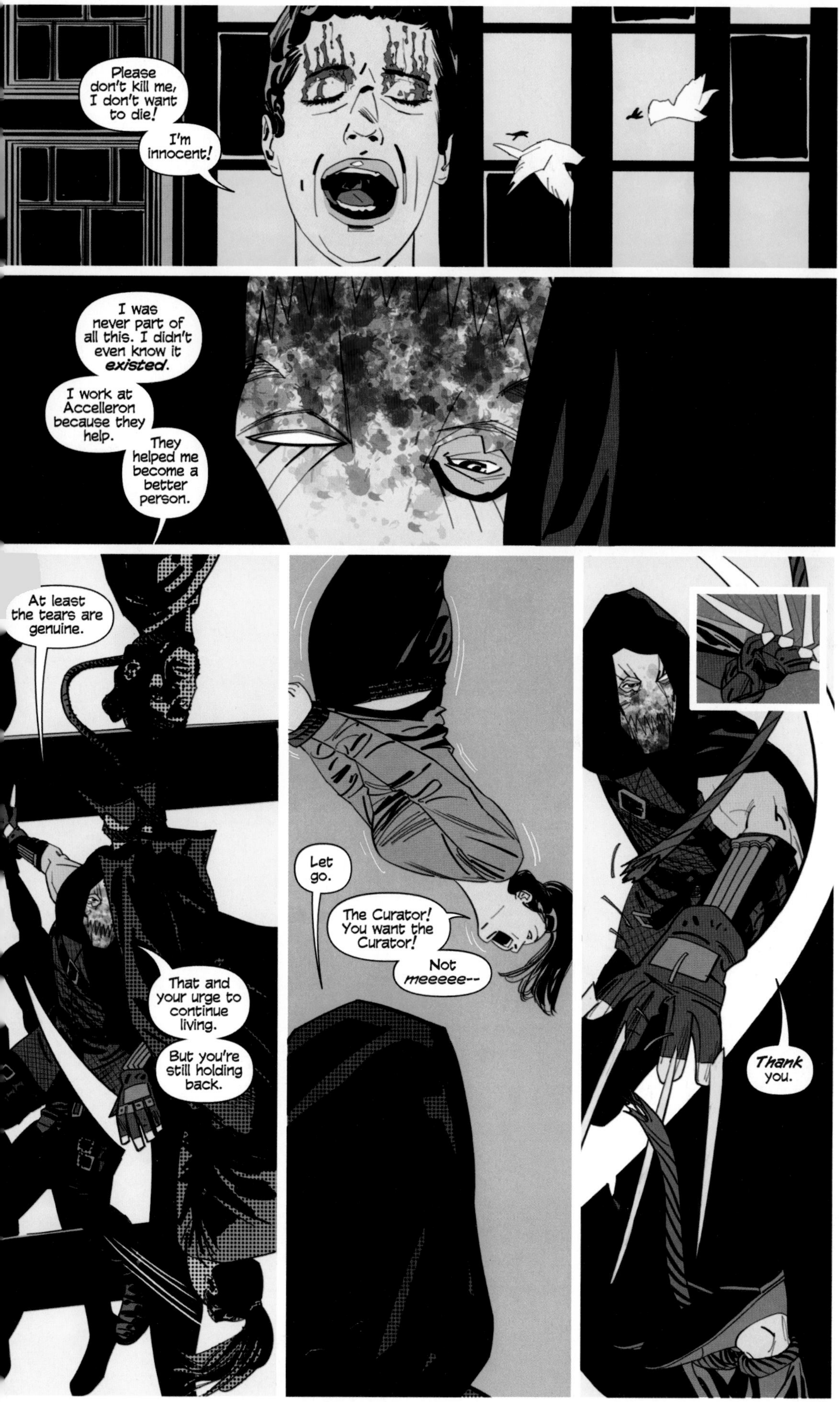
Please don't kill me, I don't want to die!
I'm innocent!
I was never part of all this. I didn't even know it *existed*.
I work at Accelleron because they help.
They helped me become a better person.
At least the tears are genuine.
That and your urge to continue living.
But you're still holding back.
Let go.
The Curator! You want the Curator!
Not *meeeee--*
Thank you.

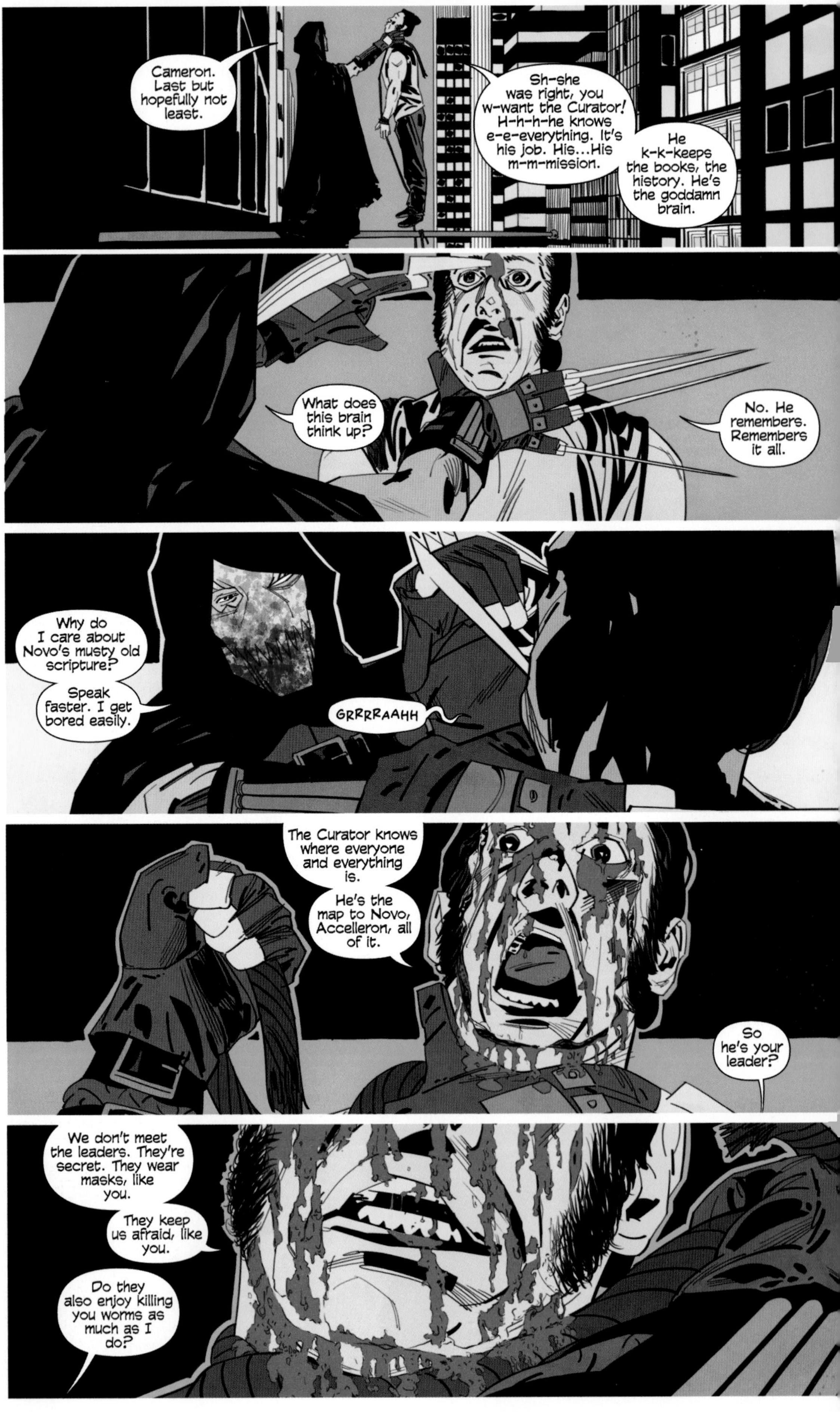
Cameron. Last but hopefully not least.
Sh-she was right, you w-want the Curator! H-h-h-he knows e-e-everything. It's his job. His...His m-m-mission.
He k-k-keeps the books, the history. He's the goddamn brain.
What does this brain think up?
No. He remembers. Remembers it all.
Why do I care about Novo's musty old scripture?
Speak faster. I get bored easily.
GRRRRAAHH
The Curator knows where everyone and everything is.
He's the map to Novo, Accelleron, all of it.
So he's your leader?
We don't meet the leaders. They're secret. They wear masks, like you.
They keep us afraid, like you.
Do they also enjoy killing you worms as much as I do?

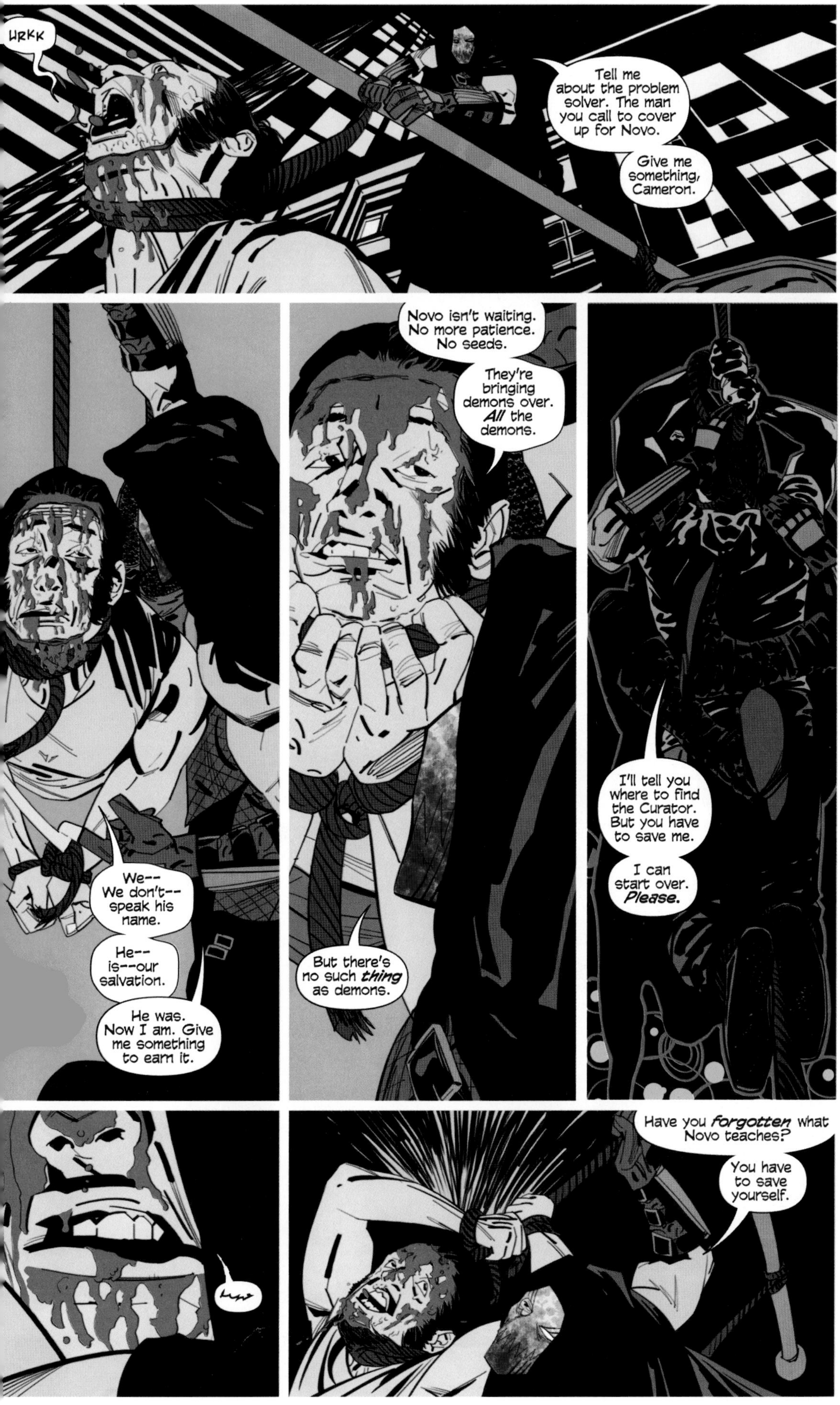
URKK
Tell me about the problem solver. The man you call to cover up for Novo.
Give me something, Cameron.
We-- We don't-- speak his name.
He-- is--our salvation.
He was. Now I am. Give me something to earn it.
Novo isn't waiting. No more patience. No seeds.
They're bringing demons over. *All* the demons.
But there's no such *thing* as demons.
I'll tell you where to find the Curator. But you have to save me.
I can start over. *Please.*
Have you *forgotten* what Novo teaches?
You have to save yourself.

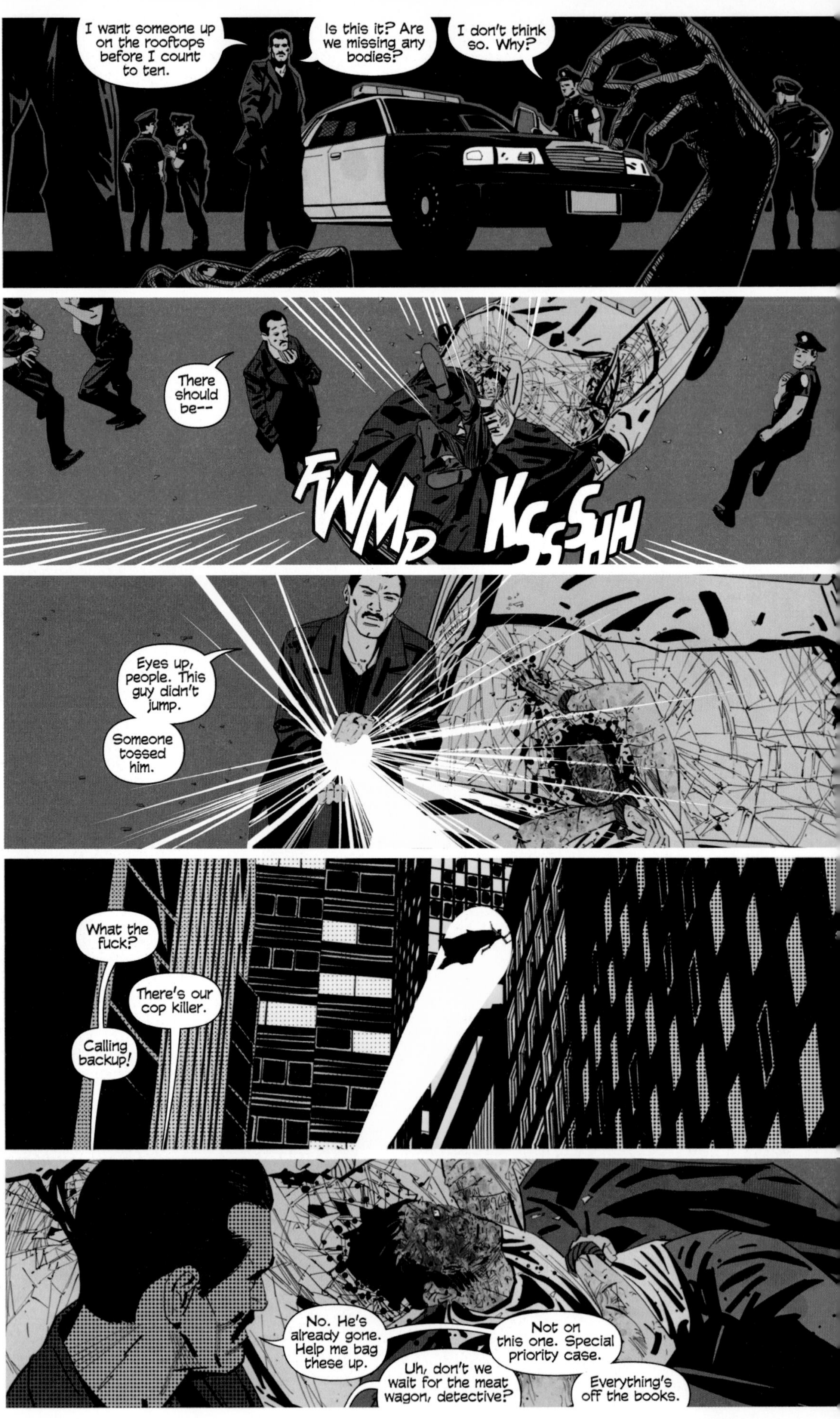
I want someone up on the rooftops before I count to ten.
Is this it? Are we missing any bodies?
I don't think so. Why?
There should be--
FWMP
KSSSHH
Eyes up, people. This guy didn't jump.
Someone tossed him.
What the fuck?
There's our cop killer.
Calling backup!
No. He's already gone. Help me bag these up.
Uh, don't we wait for the meat wagon, detective?
Not on this one. Special priority case.
Everything's off the books.

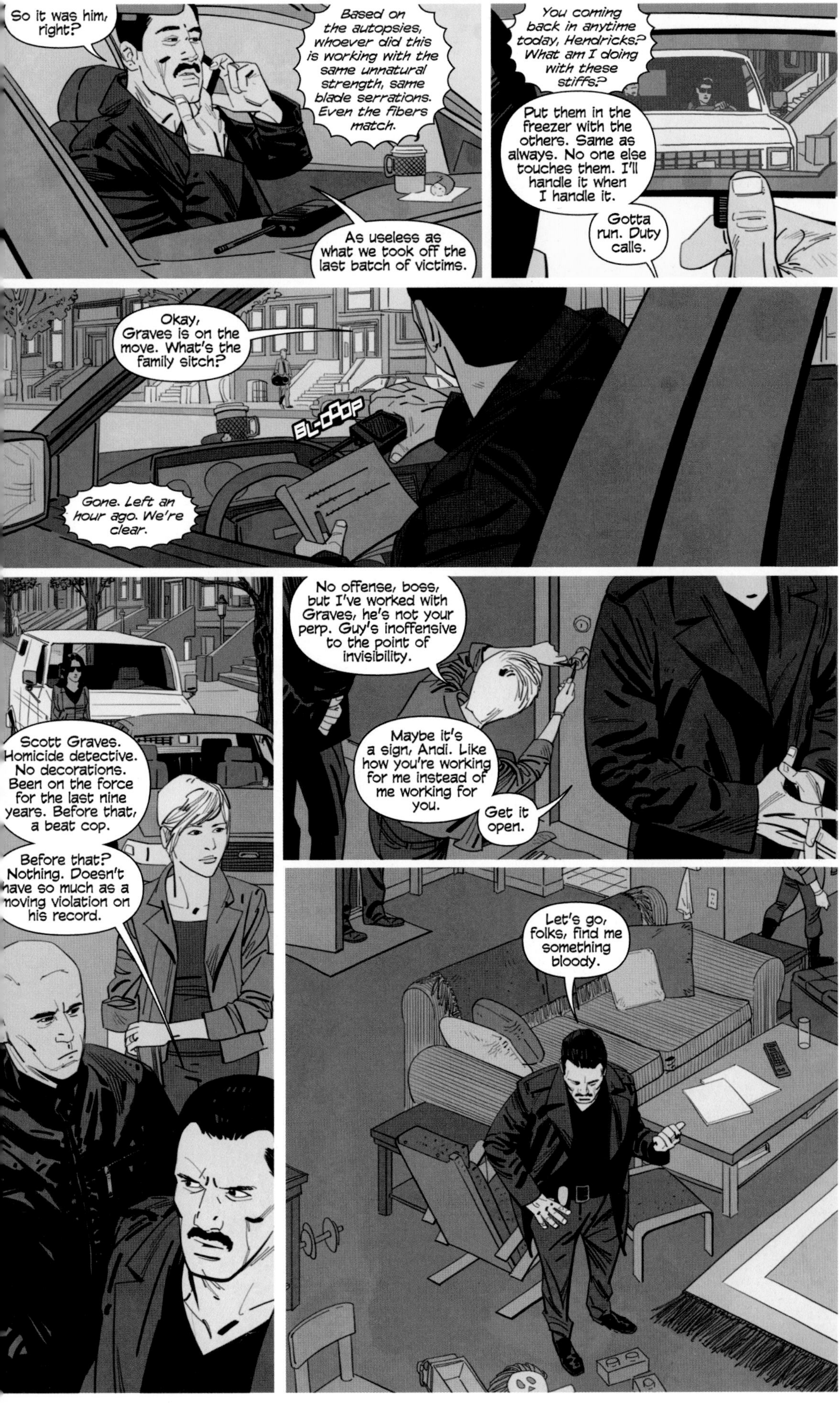
So it was him, right?
Based on the autopsies, whoever did this is working with the same unnatural strength, same blade serrations. Even the fibers match.
As useless as what we took off the last batch of victims.
You coming back in anytime today, Hendricks? What am I doing with these stiffs?
Put them in the freezer with the others. Same as always. No one else touches them. I'll handle it when I handle it.
Gotta run. Duty calls.
Okay, Graves is on the move. What's the family sitch?
BL-OOP
Gone. Left an hour ago. We're clear.
Scott Graves. Homicide detective. No decorations. Been on the force for the last nine years. Before that, a beat cop.
Before that? Nothing. Doesn't have so much as a moving violation on his record.
No offense, boss, but I've worked with Graves, he's not your perp. Guy's inoffensive to the point of invisibility.
Maybe it's a sign, Andi. Like how you're working for me instead of me working for you.
Get it open.
Let's go, folks, find me something bloody.

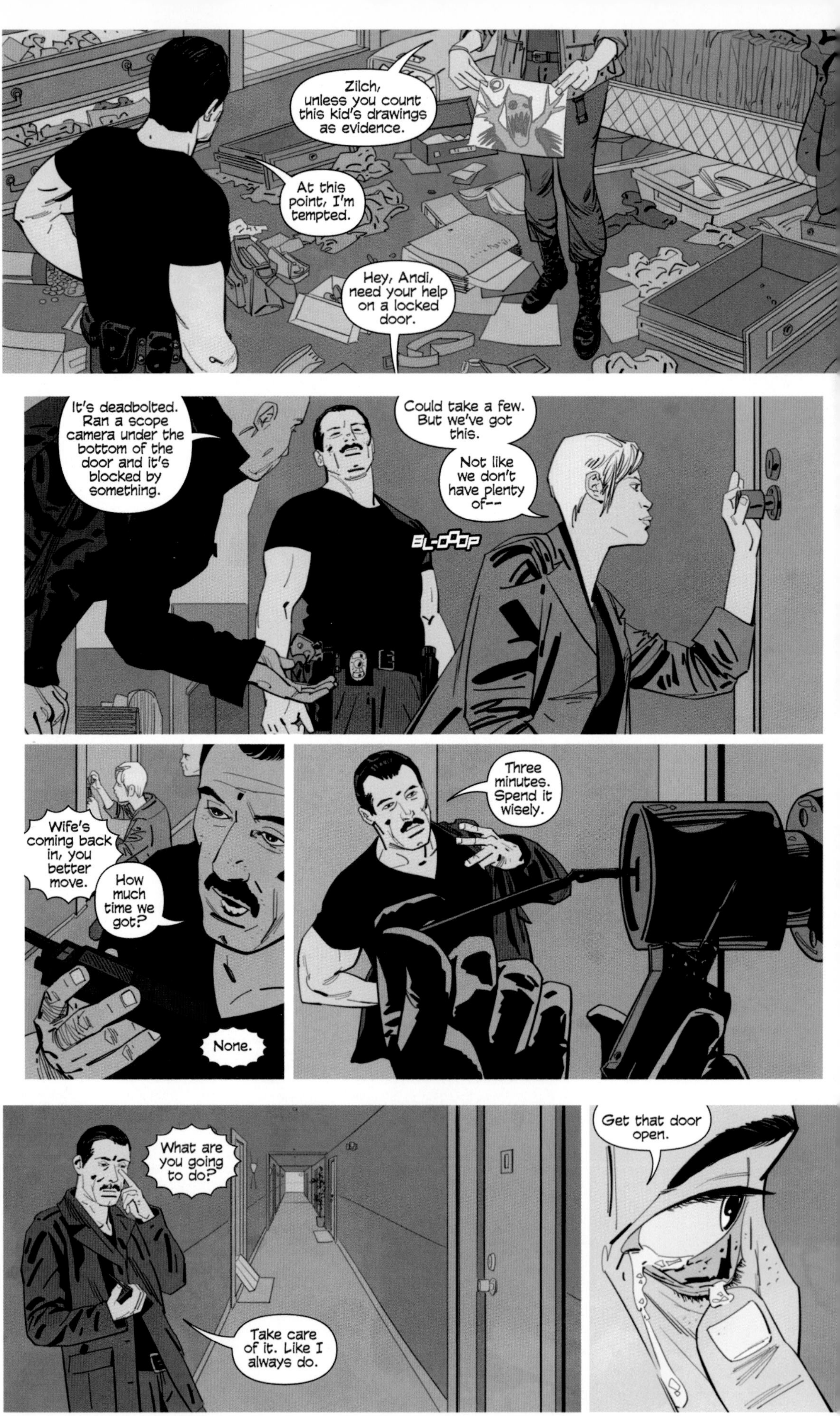
Zilch, unless you count this kid's drawings as evidence.
At this point, I'm tempted.
Hey, Andi, need your help on a locked door.
It's deadbolted. Ran a scope camera under the bottom of the door and it's blocked by something.
Could take a few. But we've got this.
Not like we don't have plenty of--
BL-DOOP
Wife's coming back in, you better move.
How much time we got?
None.
Three minutes. Spend it wisely.
What are you going to do?
Take care of it. Like I always do.
Get that door open.

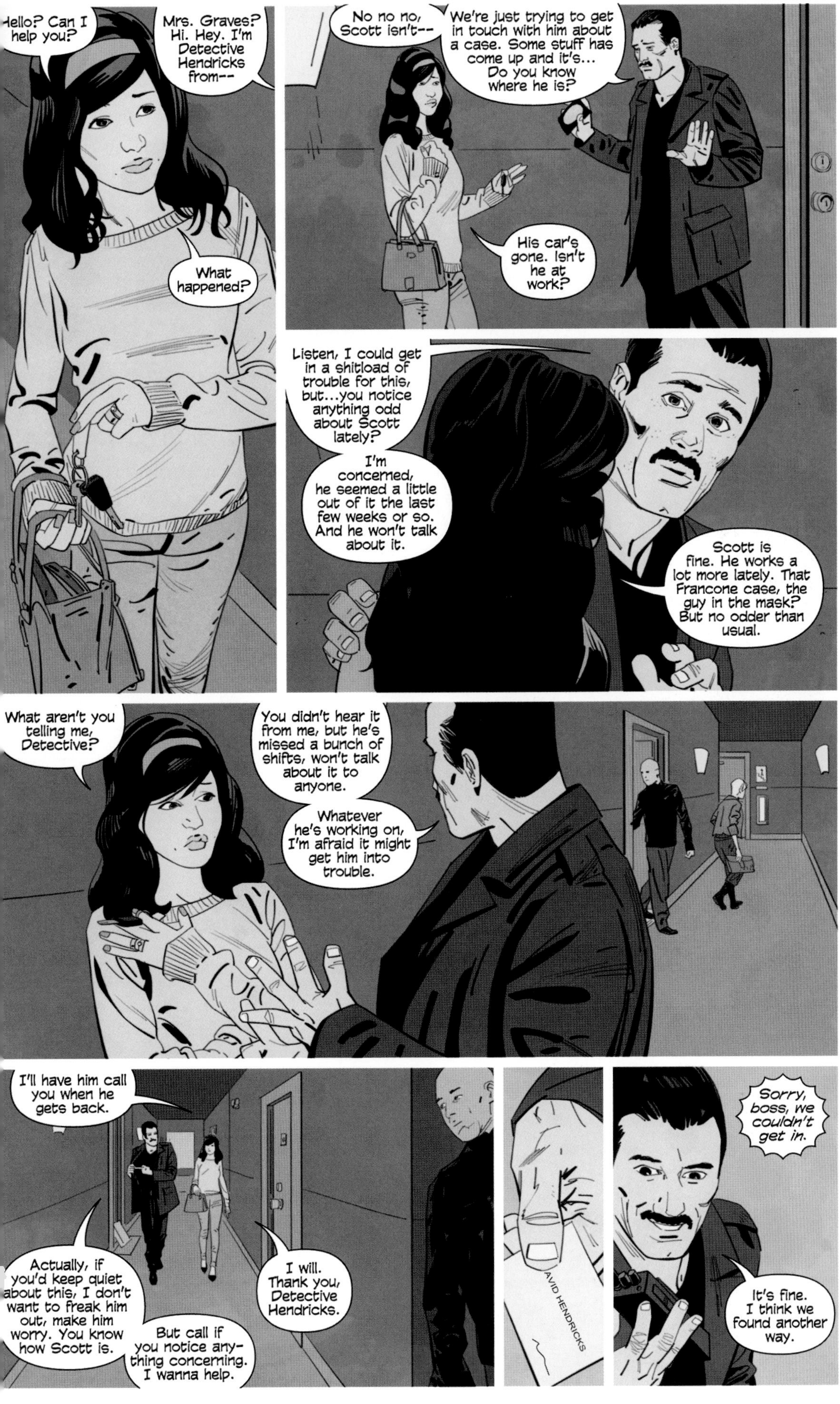
Hello? Can I help you?
Mrs. Graves? Hi. Hey. I'm Detective Hendricks from--
What happened?
No no no, Scott isn't--
We're just trying to get in touch with him about a case. Some stuff has come up and it's... Do you know where he is?
His car's gone. Isn't he at work?
Listen, I could get in a shitload of trouble for this, but...you notice anything odd about Scott lately?
I'm concerned, he seemed a little out of it the last few weeks or so. And he won't talk about it.
Scott is fine. He works a lot more lately. That Francone case, the guy in the mask? But no odder than usual.
What aren't you telling me, Detective?
You didn't hear it from me, but he's missed a bunch of shifts, won't talk about it to anyone.
Whatever he's working on, I'm afraid it might get him into trouble.
I'll have him call you when he gets back.
Actually, if you'd keep quiet about this, I don't want to freak him out, make him worry. You know how Scott is.
But call if you notice anything concerning. I wanna help.
I will. Thank you, Detective Hendricks.
AVID HENDRICKS
Sorry, boss, we couldn't get in.
It's fine. I think we found another way.

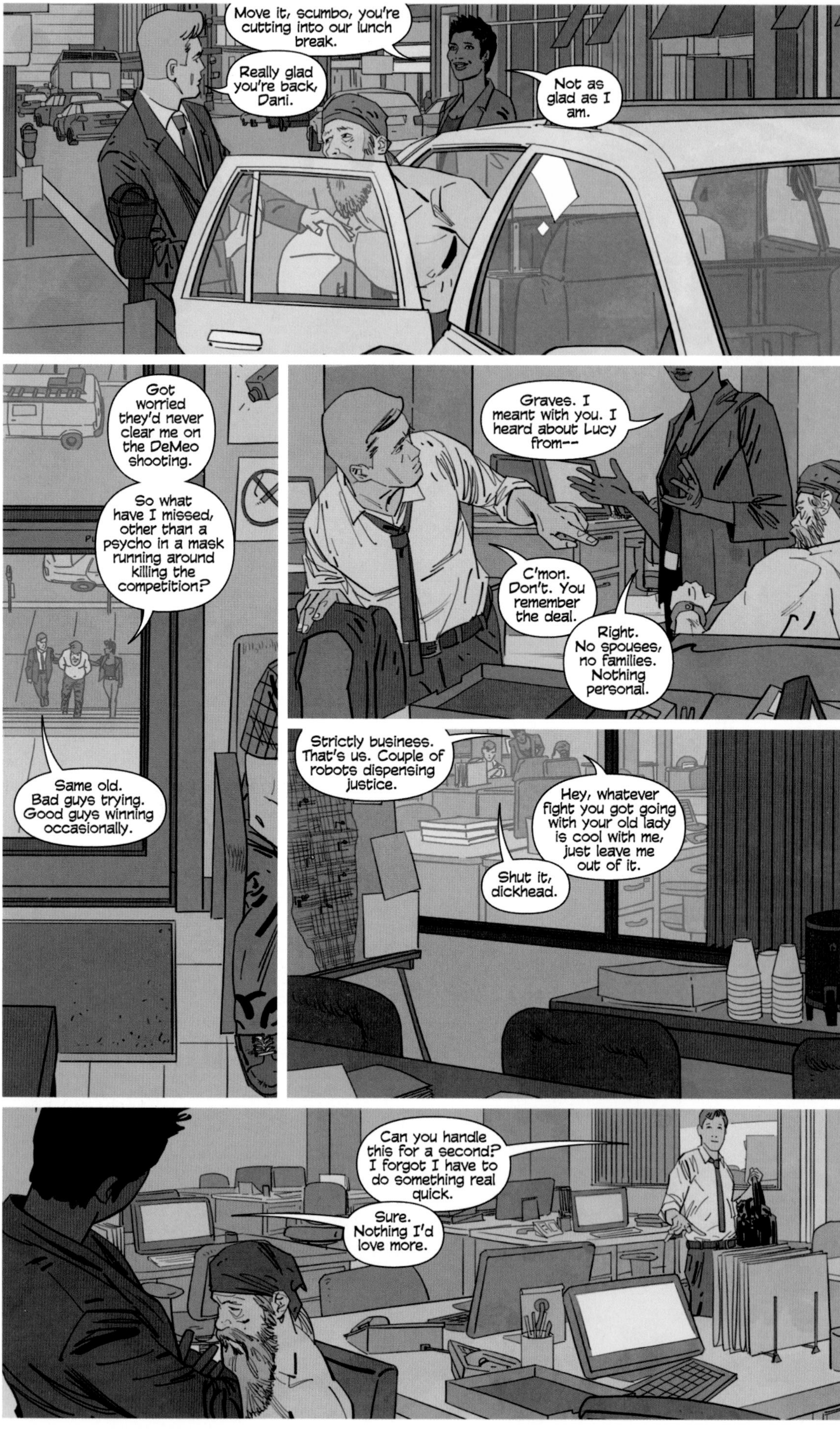
Move it, scumbo, you're cutting into our lunch break.
Really glad you're back, Dani.
Not as glad as I am.
Got worried they'd never clear me on the DeMeo shooting.
So what have I missed, other than a psycho in a mask running around killing the competition?
Same old. Bad guys trying. Good guys winning occasionally.
Graves. I meant with you. I heard about Lucy from--
C'mon. Don't. You remember the deal.
Right. No spouses, no families. Nothing personal.
Strictly business. That's us. Couple of robots dispensing justice.
Hey, whatever fight you got going with your old lady is cool with me, just leave me out of it.
Shut it, dickhead.
Can you handle this for a second? I forgot I have to do something real quick.
Sure. Nothing I'd love more.

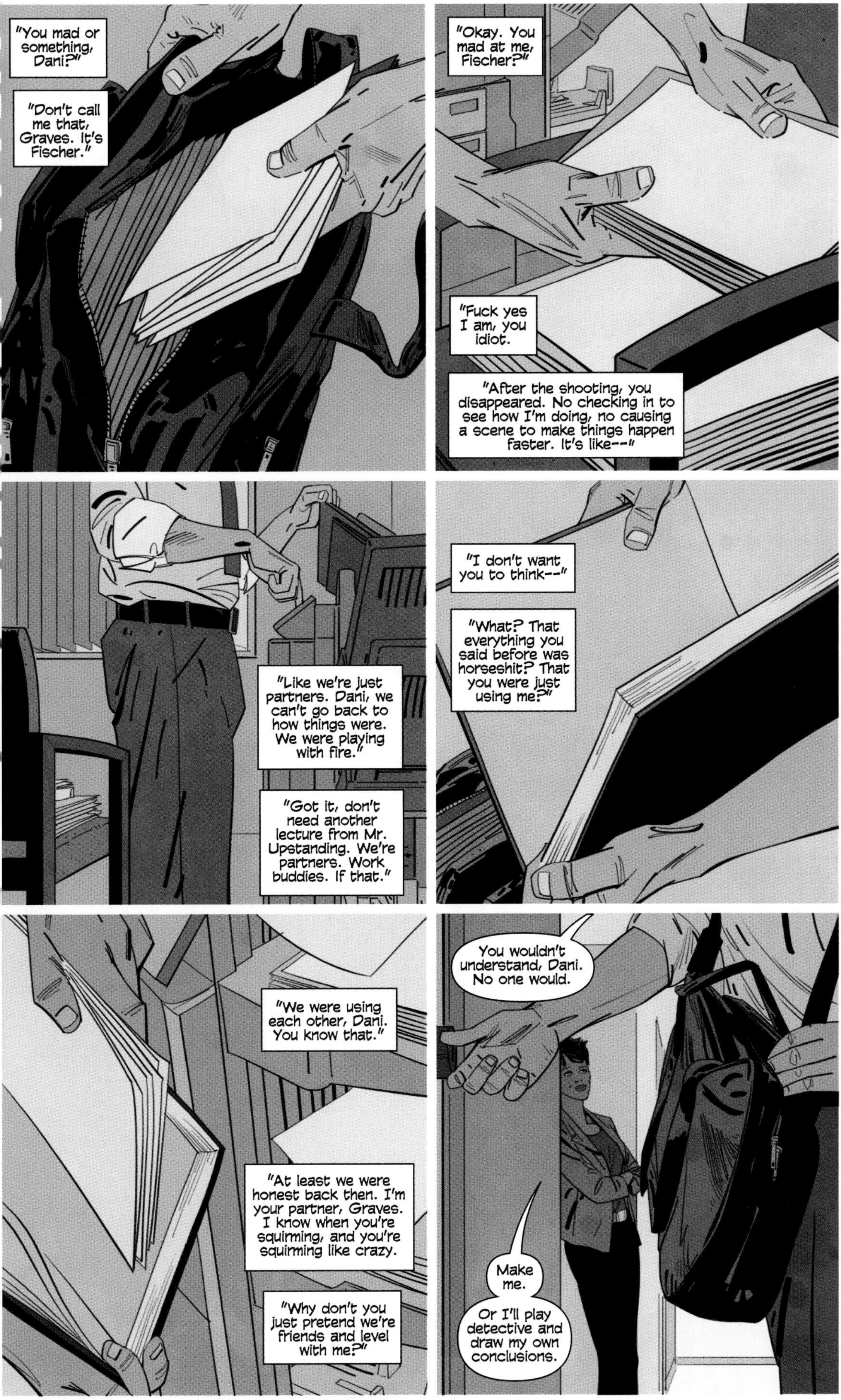
"You mad or something, Dani?"
"Don't call me that, Graves. It's Fischer."
"Okay. You mad at me, Fischer?"
"Fuck yes I am, you idiot.
"After the shooting, you disappeared. No checking in to see how I'm doing, no causing a scene to make things happen faster. It's like--"
"Like we're just partners. Dani, we can't go back to how things were. We were playing with fire."
"Got it, don't need another lecture from Mr. Upstanding. We're partners. Work buddies. If that."
"I don't want you to think--"
"What? That everything you said before was horseshit? That you were just using me?"
"We were using each other, Dani. You know that."
"At least we were honest back then. I'm your partner, Graves. I know when you're squirming, and you're squirming like crazy.
"Why don't you just pretend we're friends and level with me?"
You wouldn't understand, Dani. No one would.
Make me.
Or I'll play detective and draw my own conclusions.

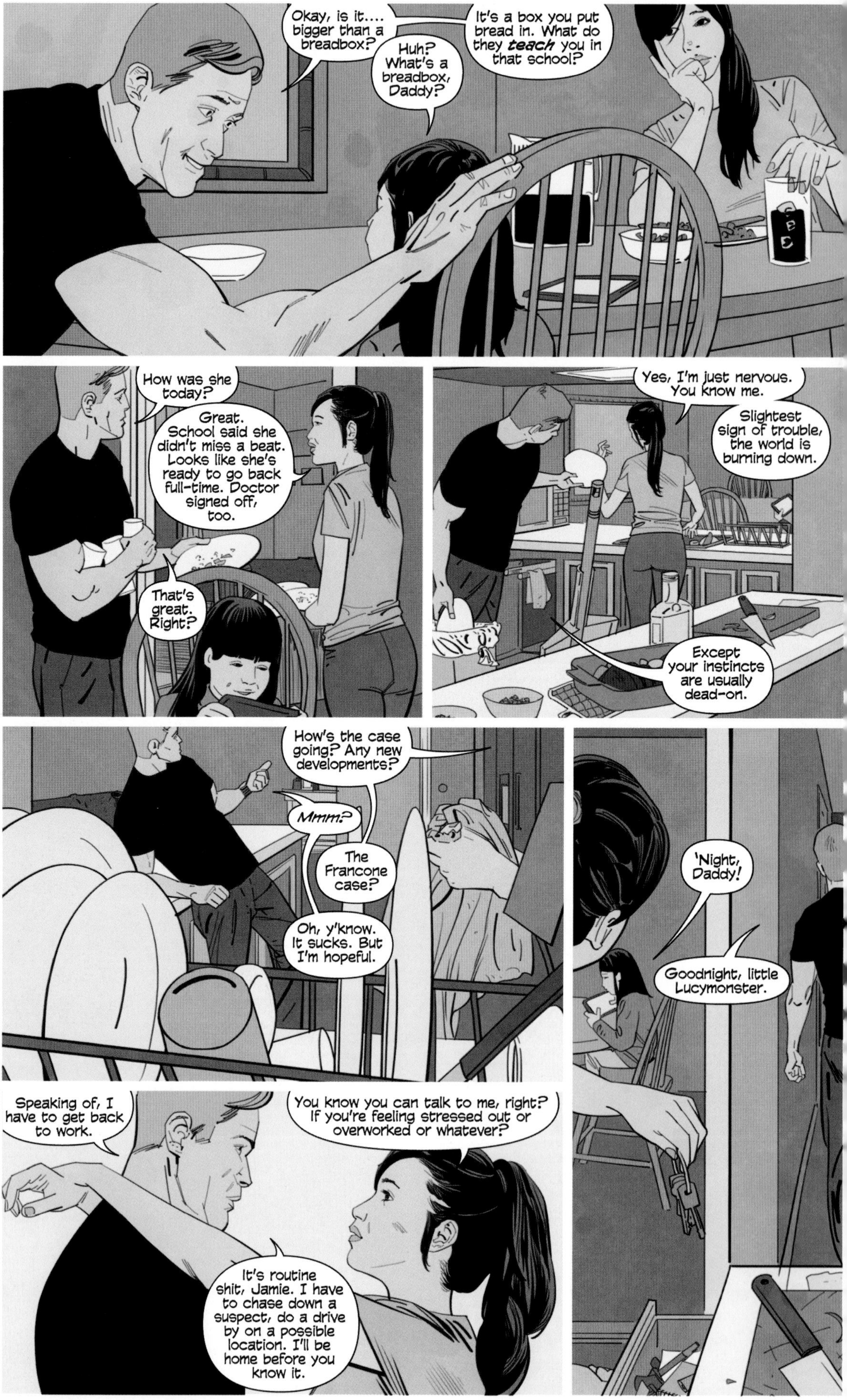
Okay, is it.... bigger than a breadbox?
Huh? What's a breadbox, Daddy?
It's a box you put bread in. What do they *teach* you in that school?
How was she today?
Great. School said she didn't miss a beat. Looks like she's ready to go back full-time. Doctor signed off, too.
That's great. Right?
Yes, I'm just nervous. You know me.
Slightest sign of trouble, the world is burning down.
Except your instincts are usually dead-on.
How's the case going? Any new developments?
Mmm?
The Francone case?
Oh, y'know. It sucks. But I'm hopeful.
Speaking of, I have to get back to work.
You know you can talk to me, right? If you're feeling stressed out or overworked or whatever?
It's routine shit, Jamie. I have to chase down a suspect, do a drive by on a possible location. I'll be home before you know it.
'Night, Daddy!
Goodnight, little Lucymonster.

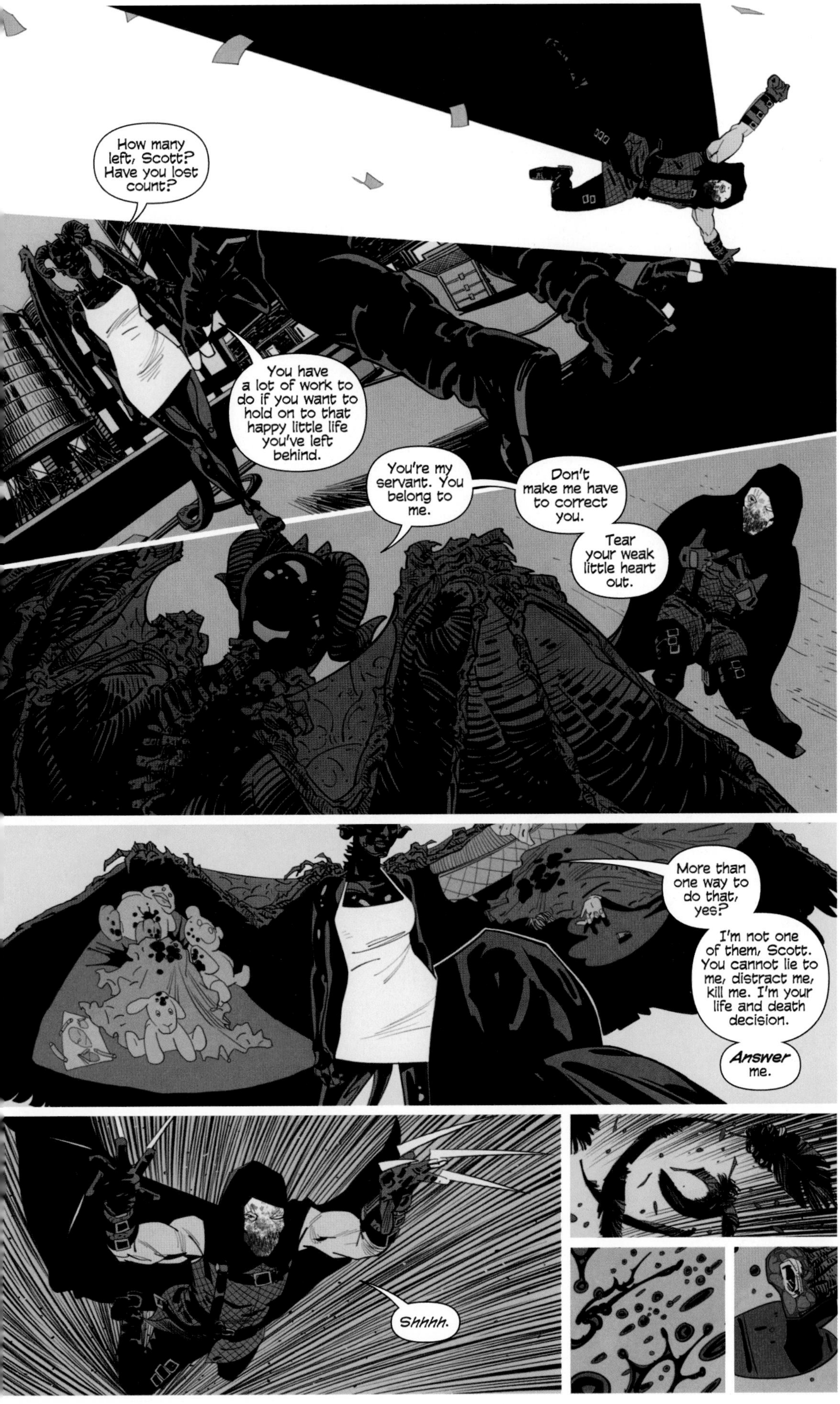
How many left, Scott? Have you lost count?
You have a lot of work to do if you want to hold on to that happy little life you've left behind.
You're my servant. You belong to me.
Don't make me have to correct you.
Tear your weak little heart out.
More than one way to do that, yes?
I'm not one of them, Scott. You cannot lie to me, distract me, kill me. I'm your life and death decision.
Answer me.
Shhhh.

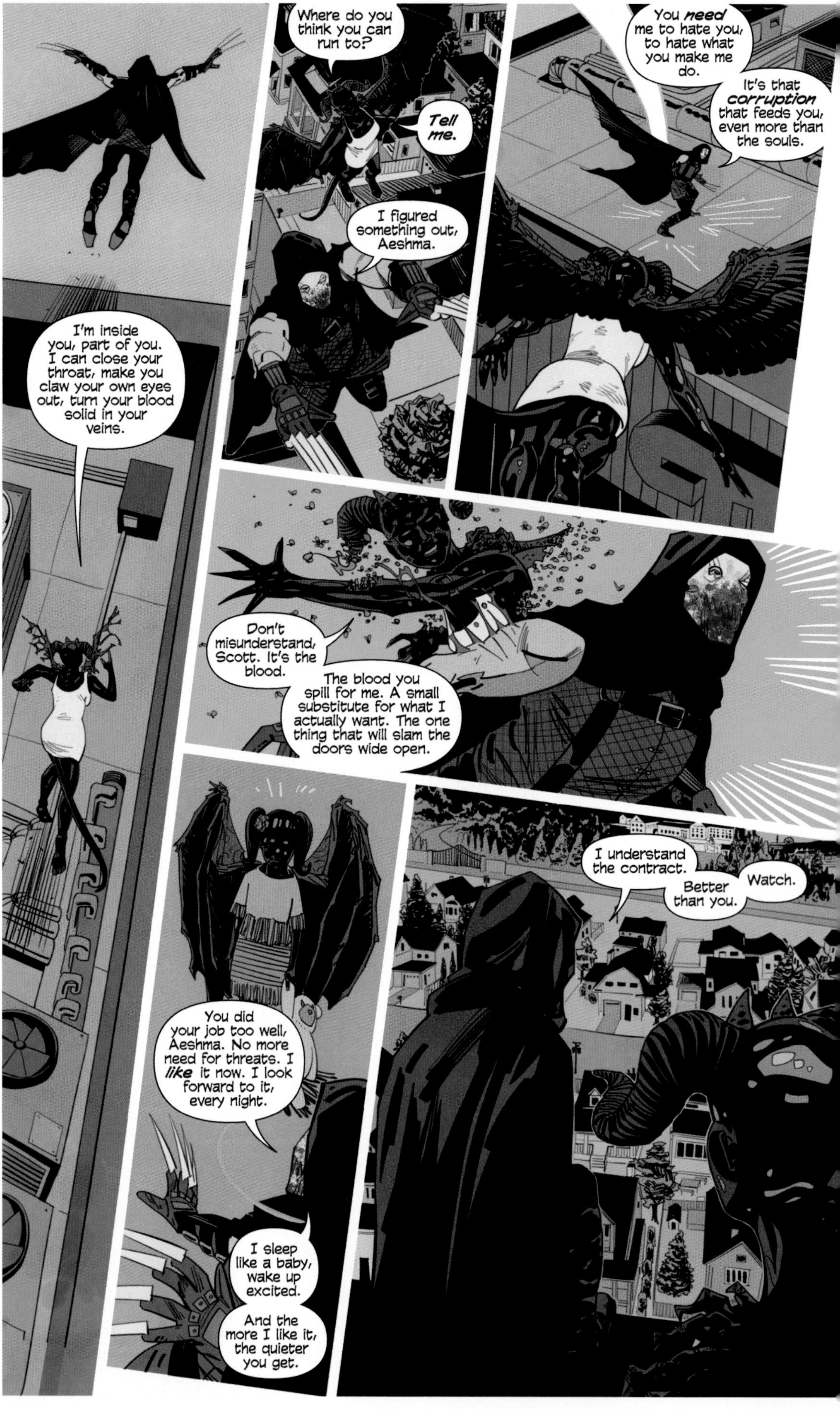
I'm inside you, part of you. I can close your throat, make you claw your own eyes out, turn your blood solid in your veins.
Where do you think you can run to?
Tell me.
I figured something out, Aeshma.
You need me to hate you, to hate what you make me do.
It's that corruption that feeds you, even more than the souls.
Don't misunderstand, Scott. It's the blood.
The blood you spill for me. A small substitute for what I actually want. The one thing that will slam the doors wide open.
You did your job too well, Aeshma. No more need for threats. I like it now. I look forward to it, every night.
I sleep like a baby, wake up excited.
And the more I like it, the quieter you get.
I understand the contract.
Better than you.
Watch.

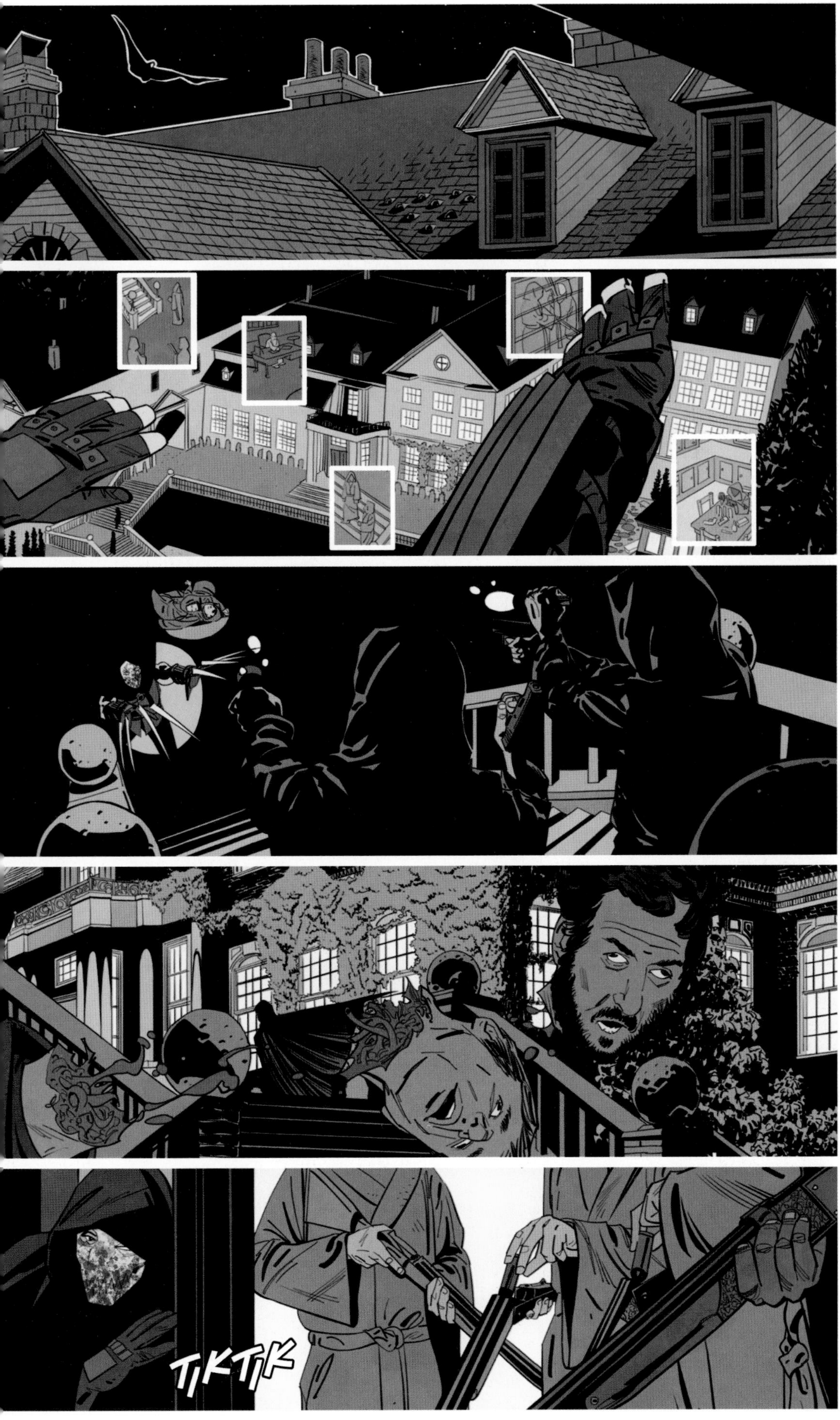
TIKTIK

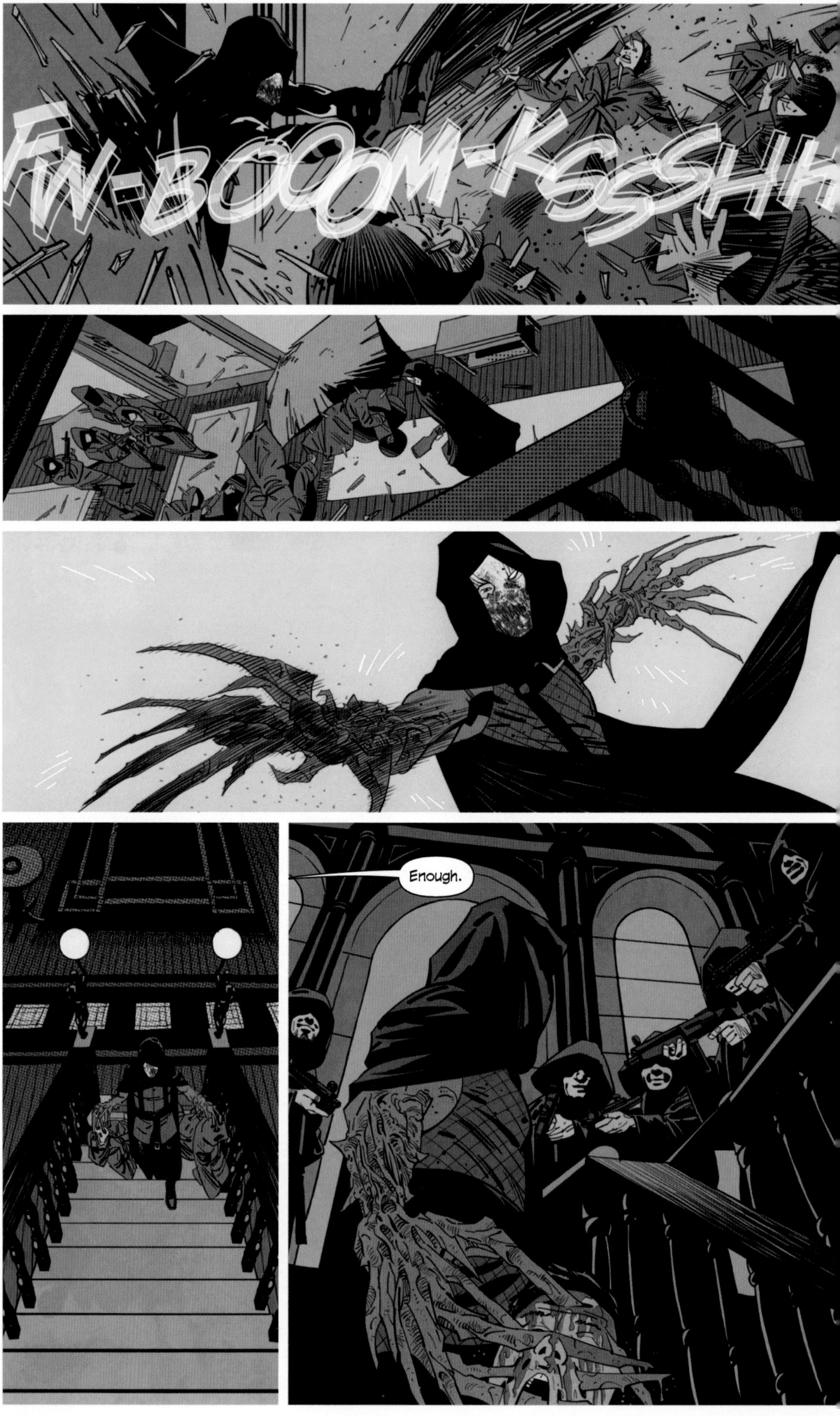
FW-BOOOOM-KSSSHH
Enough.

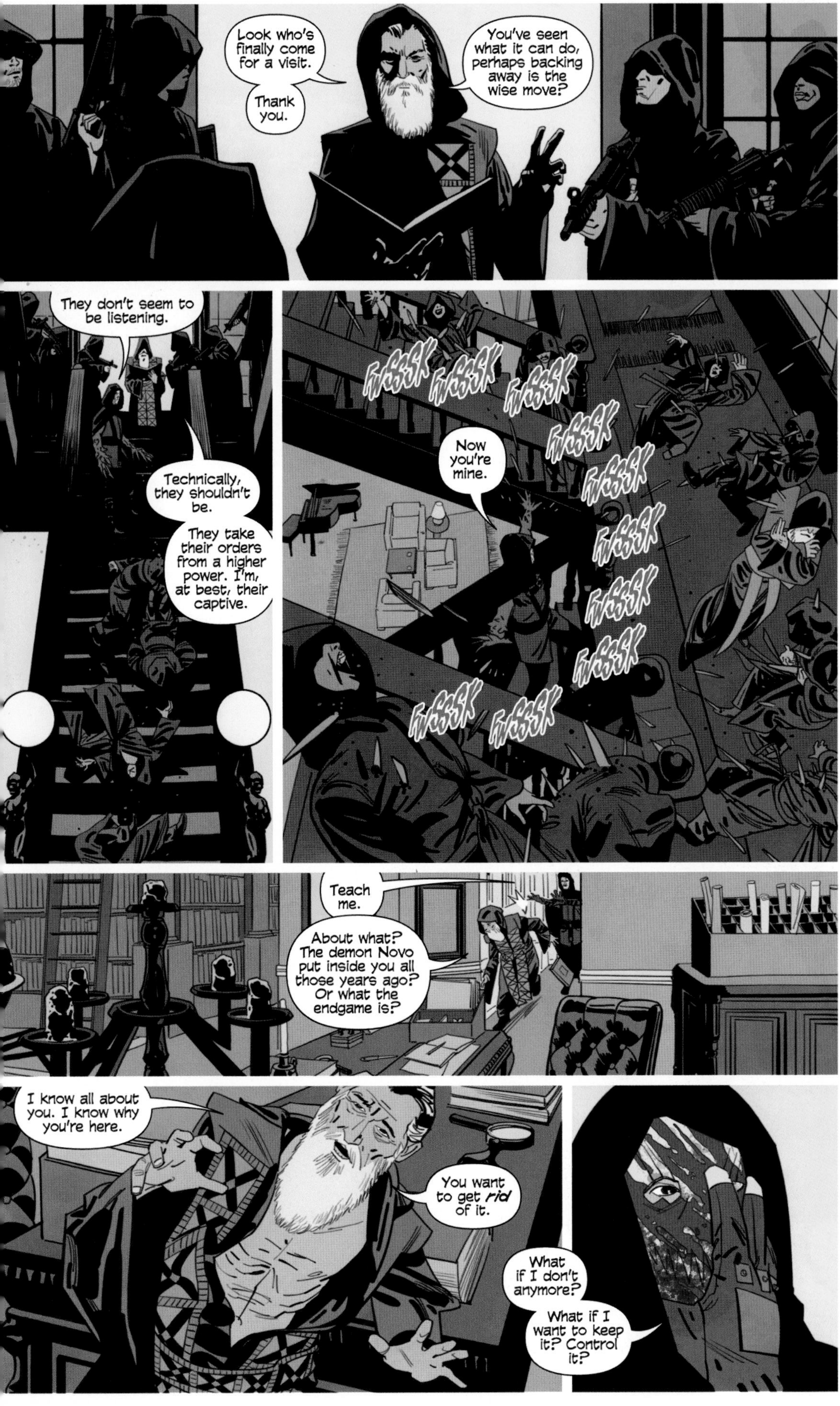
Look who's finally come for a visit.
Thank you.
You've seen what it can do, perhaps backing away is the wise move?
They don't seem to be listening.
Technically, they shouldn't be.
They take their orders from a higher power. I'm, at best, their captive.
FWSSSK
FWSSSK
FWSSSK
FWSSSK
FWSSSK
FWSSSK
FWSSSK
FWSSSK
Now you're mine.
FWSSSK
FWSSSK
Teach me.
About what? The demon Novo put inside you all those years ago? Or what the endgame is?
I know all about you. I know why you're here.
You want to get *rid* of it.
What if I don't anymore?
What if I want to keep it? Control it?

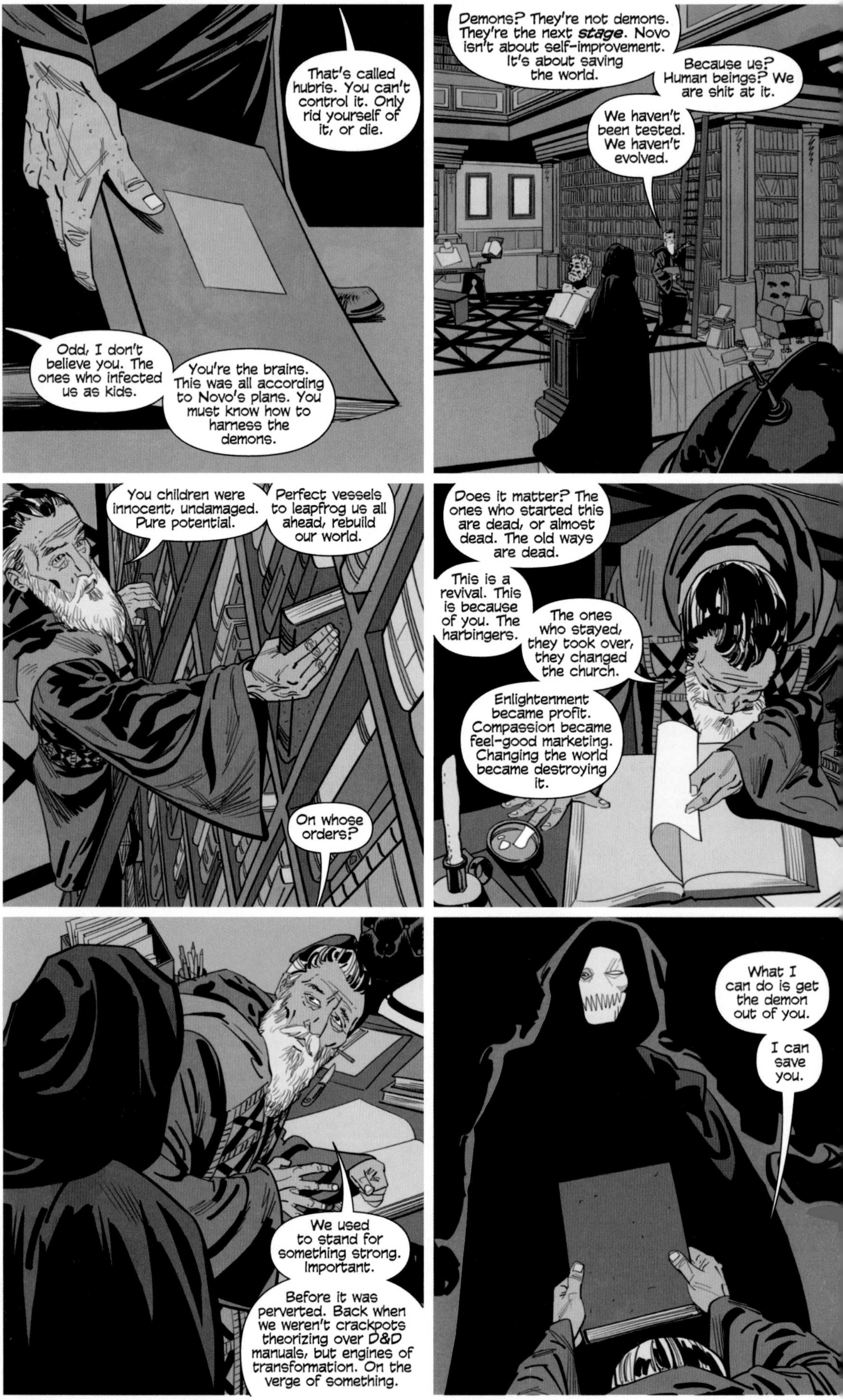
That's called hubris. You can't control it. Only rid yourself of it, or die.
Odd, I don't believe you. The ones who infected us as kids.
You're the brains. This was all according to Novo's plans. You must know how to harness the demons.
Demons? They're not demons. They're the next *stage*. Novo isn't about self-improvement. It's about saving the world.
Because us? Human beings? We are shit at it.
We haven't been tested. We haven't evolved.
You children were innocent, undamaged. Pure potential.
Perfect vessels to leapfrog us all ahead, rebuild our world.
On whose orders?
Does it matter? The ones who started this are dead, or almost dead. The old ways are dead.
This is a revival. This is because of you. The harbingers.
The ones who stayed, they took over, they changed the church.
Enlightenment became profit. Compassion became feel-good marketing. Changing the world became destroying it.
We used to stand for something strong. Important.
Before it was perverted. Back when we weren't crackpots theorizing over D&D manuals, but engines of transformation. On the verge of something.
What I can do is get the demon out of you.
I can save you.

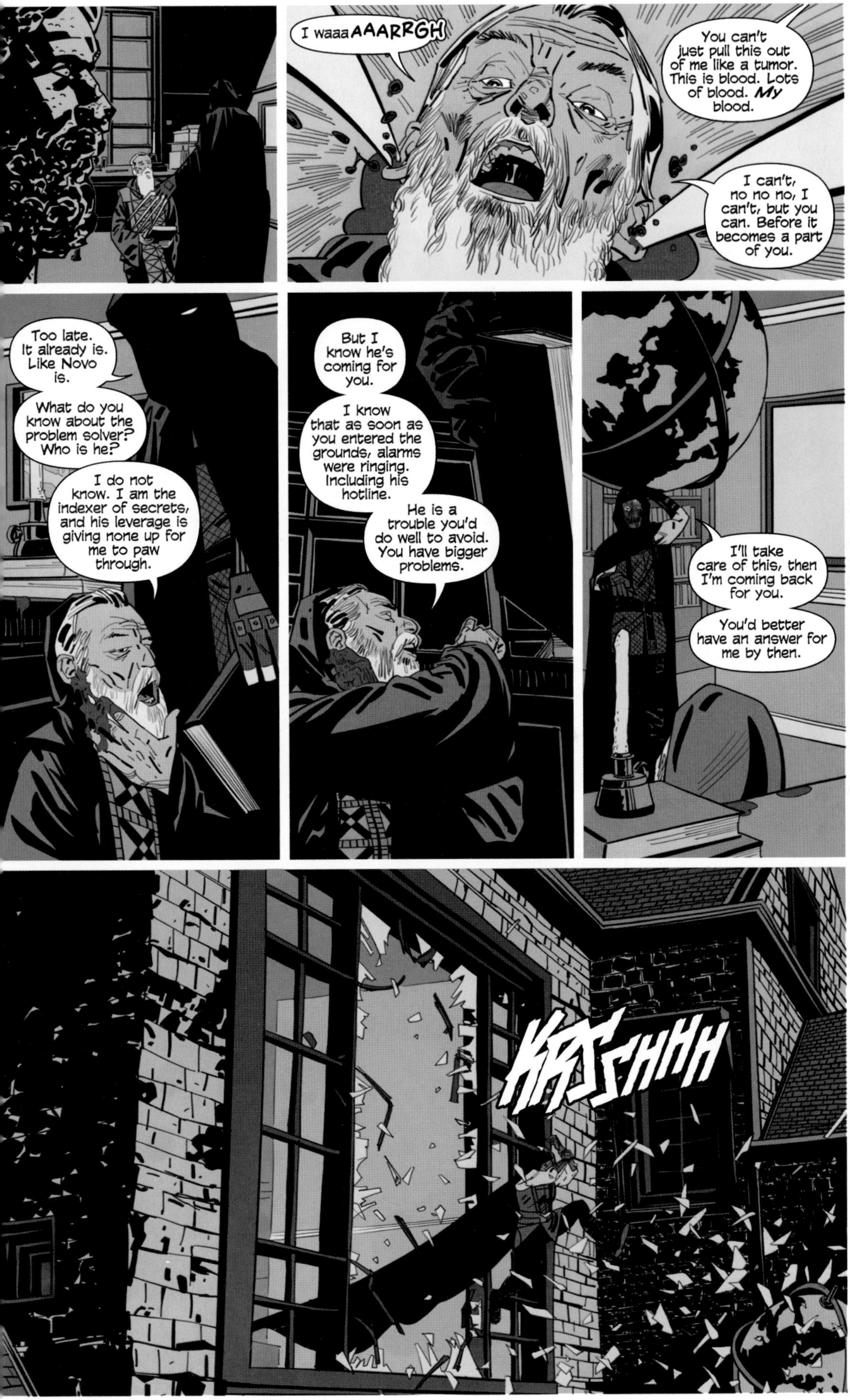
I waaa AAARRGH
You can't just pull this out of me like a tumor. This is blood. Lots of blood. *My* blood.
I can't, no no no, I can't, but you can. Before it becomes a part of you.
Too late. It already is. Like Novo is.
What do you know about the problem solver? Who is he?
I do not know. I am the indexer of secrets, and his leverage is giving none up for me to paw through.
But I know he's coming for you.
I know that as soon as you entered the grounds, alarms were ringing. Including his hotline.
He is a trouble you'd do well to avoid. You have bigger problems.
I'll take care of this, then I'm coming back for you.
You'd better have an answer for me by then.
KRSSHHH

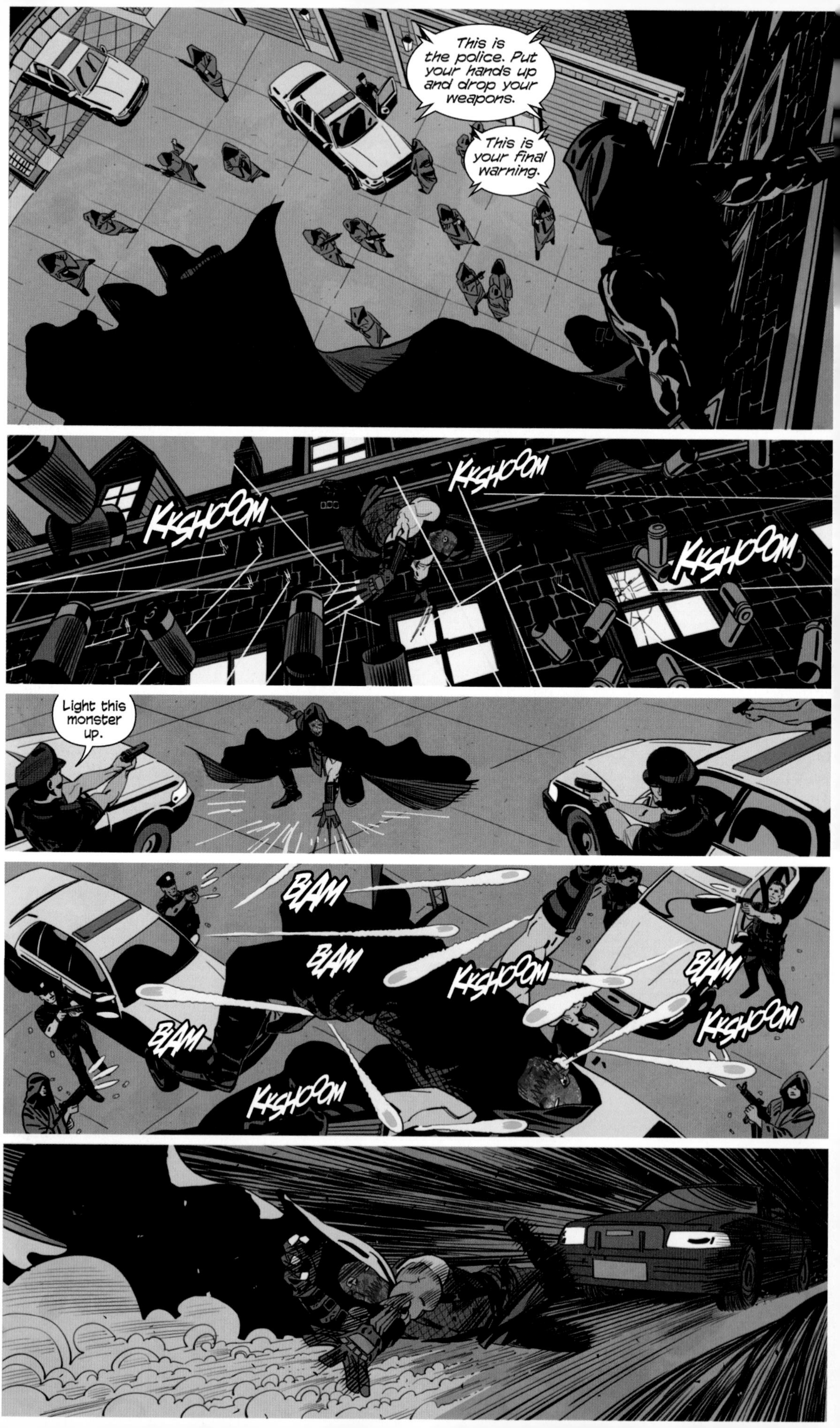

This is the police. Put your hands up and drop your weapons.
This is your final warning.
KKSHOOOM
KKSHOOOM
KKSHOOOM
Light this monster up.
BLAM
BLAM
KKSHOOOM
BLAM
KKSHOOOM
BLAM
KKSHOOOM

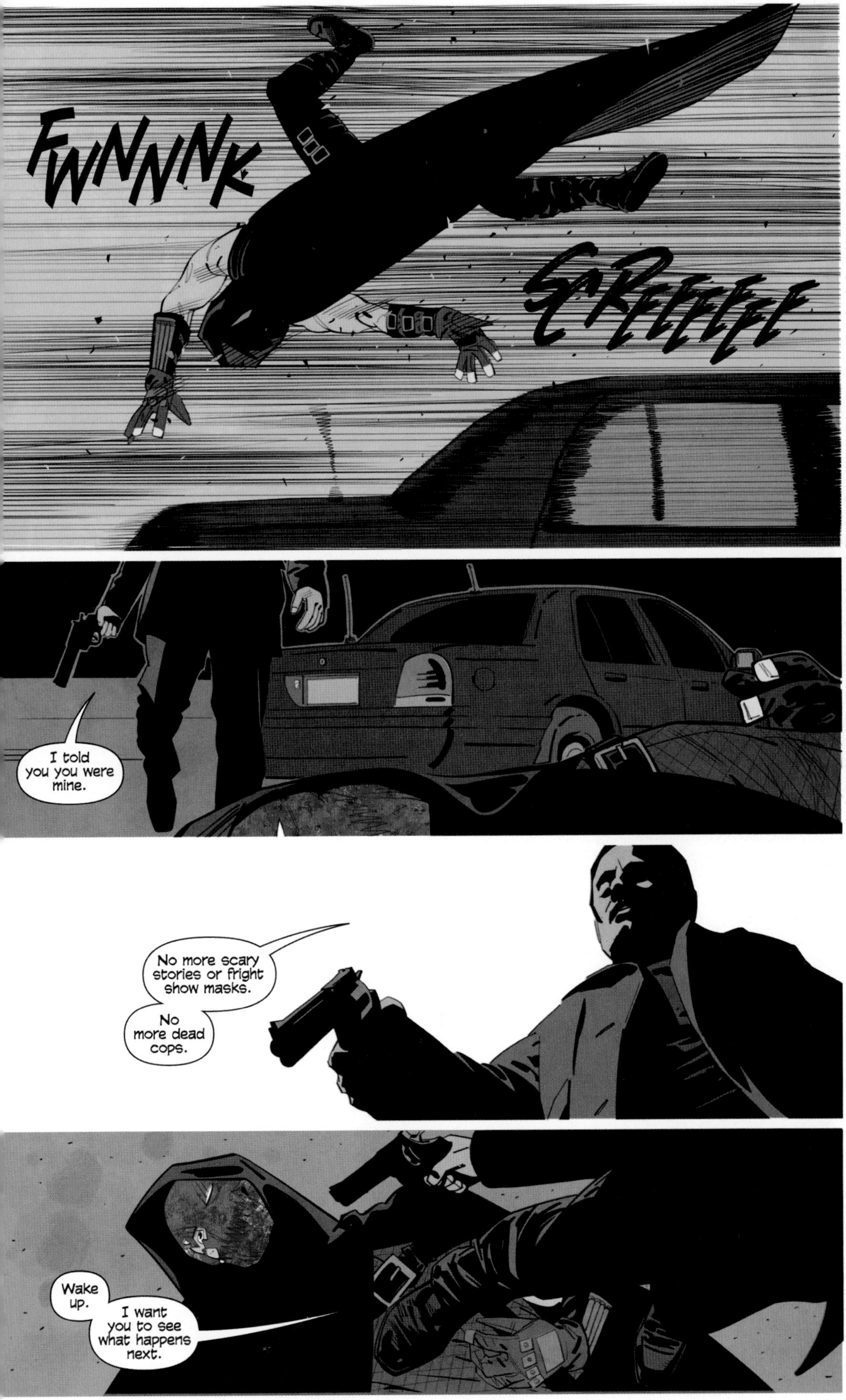
FWNNNK
SCREEEEE
I told you you were mine.
No more scary stories or fright show masks.
No more dead cops.
Wake up.
I want you to see what happens next.

What do you mean? He left here hours ago to do some legwork on a case.
Sorry, ma'am. Roster has him off duty until noon tomorrow. Unless it's something urgent, you might want to try back then.
Sure.
I'll talk to him later.
Nothing urgent.
It's just our life.

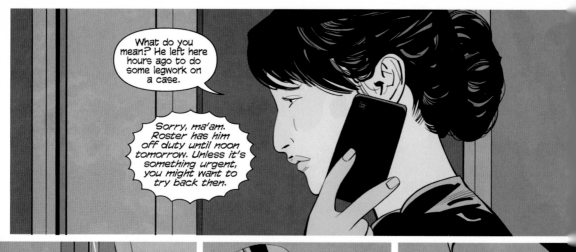

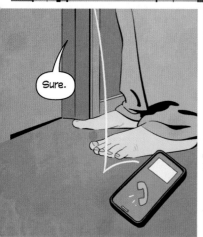

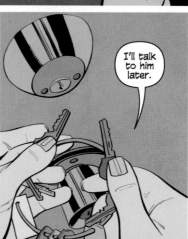

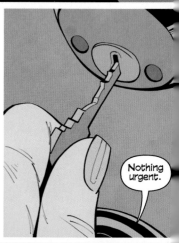

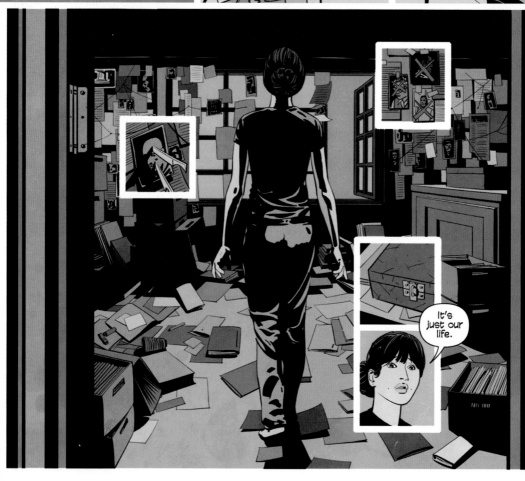

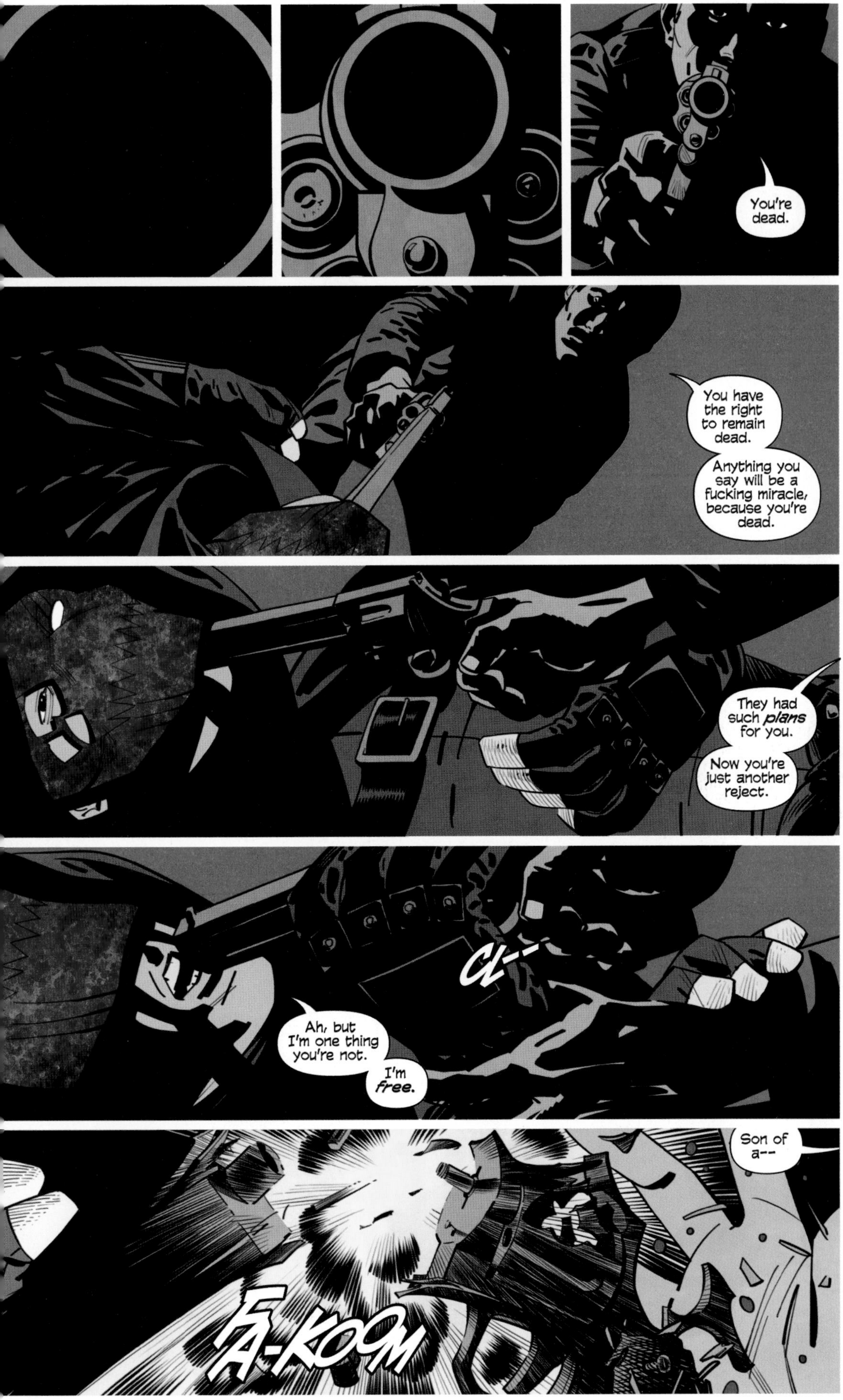
You're dead.
You have the right to remain dead.
Anything you say will be a fucking miracle, because you're dead.
They had such *plans* for you.
Now you're just another reject.
CL--
Ah, but I'm one thing you're not.
I'm *free*.
Son of a--
BA-KOOM

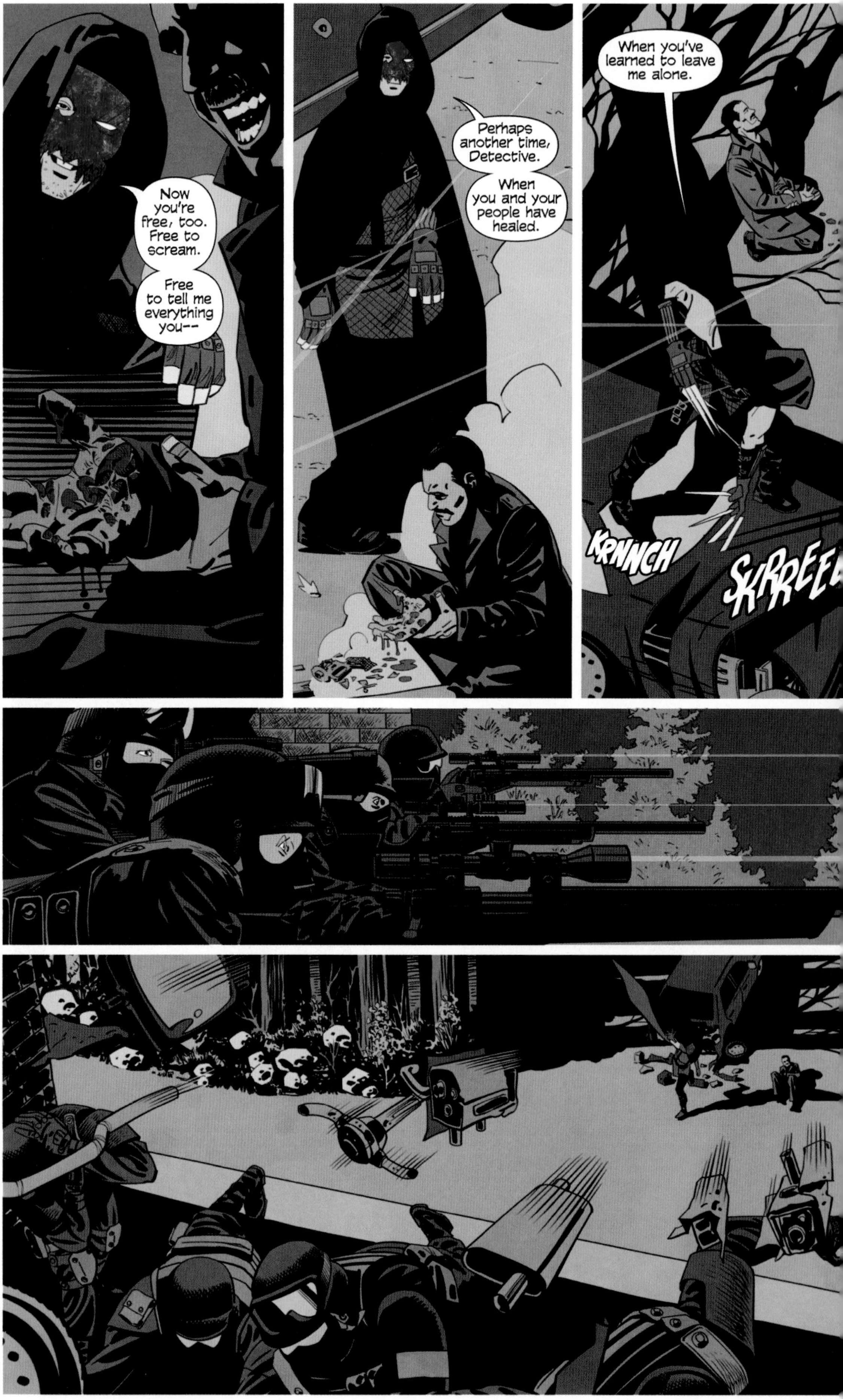
Now you're free, too. Free to scream.
Free to tell me everything you--
Perhaps another time, Detective.
When you and your people have healed.
When you've learned to leave me alone.
KRNNCH
SKRREEE

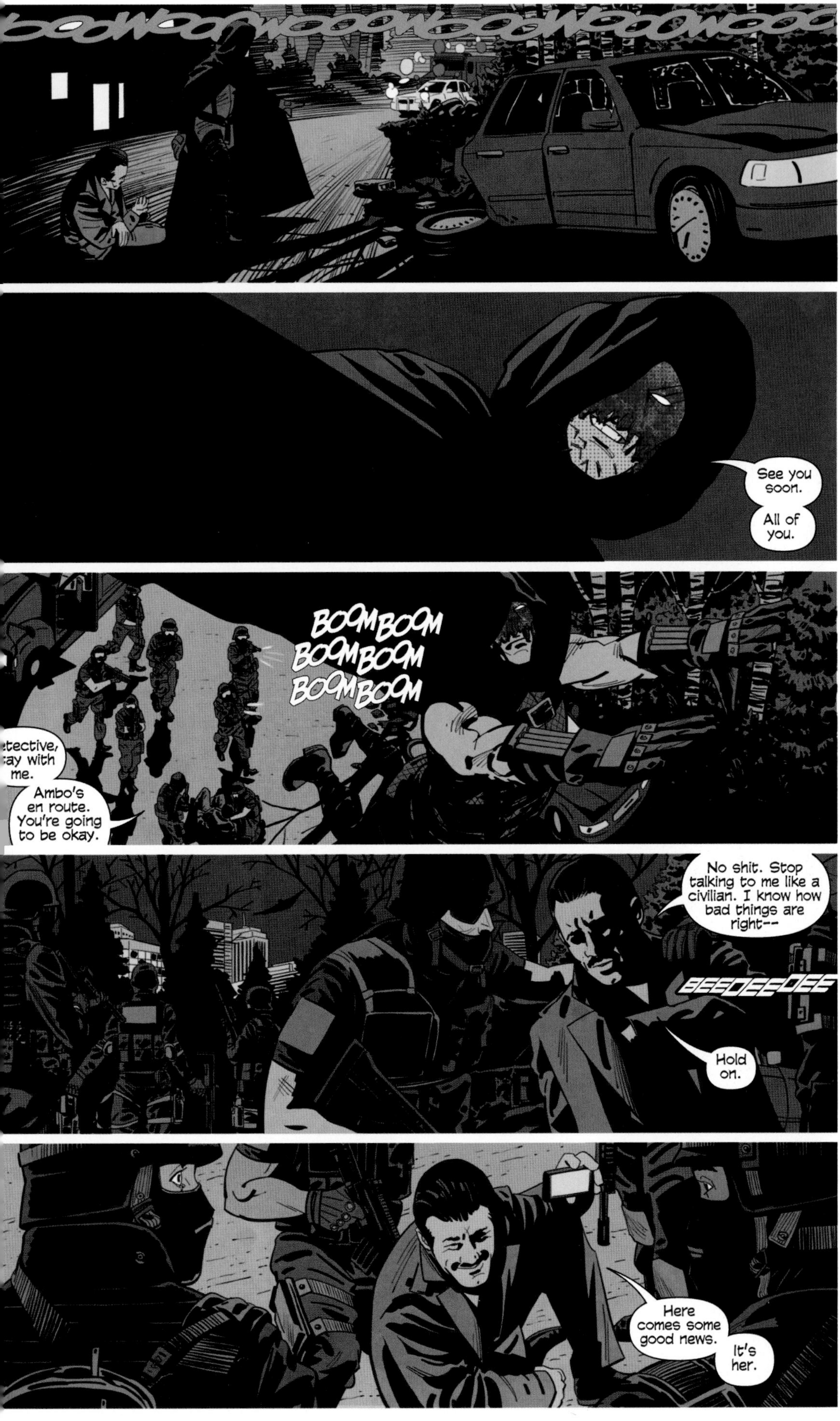
See you soon.
All of you.
BOOMBOOM BOOMBOOM BOOMBOOM
etective, tay with me.
Ambo's en route. You're going to be okay.
No shit. Stop talking to me like a civilian. I know how bad things are right--
BEEDEEDEE
Hold on.
Here comes some good news.
It's her.

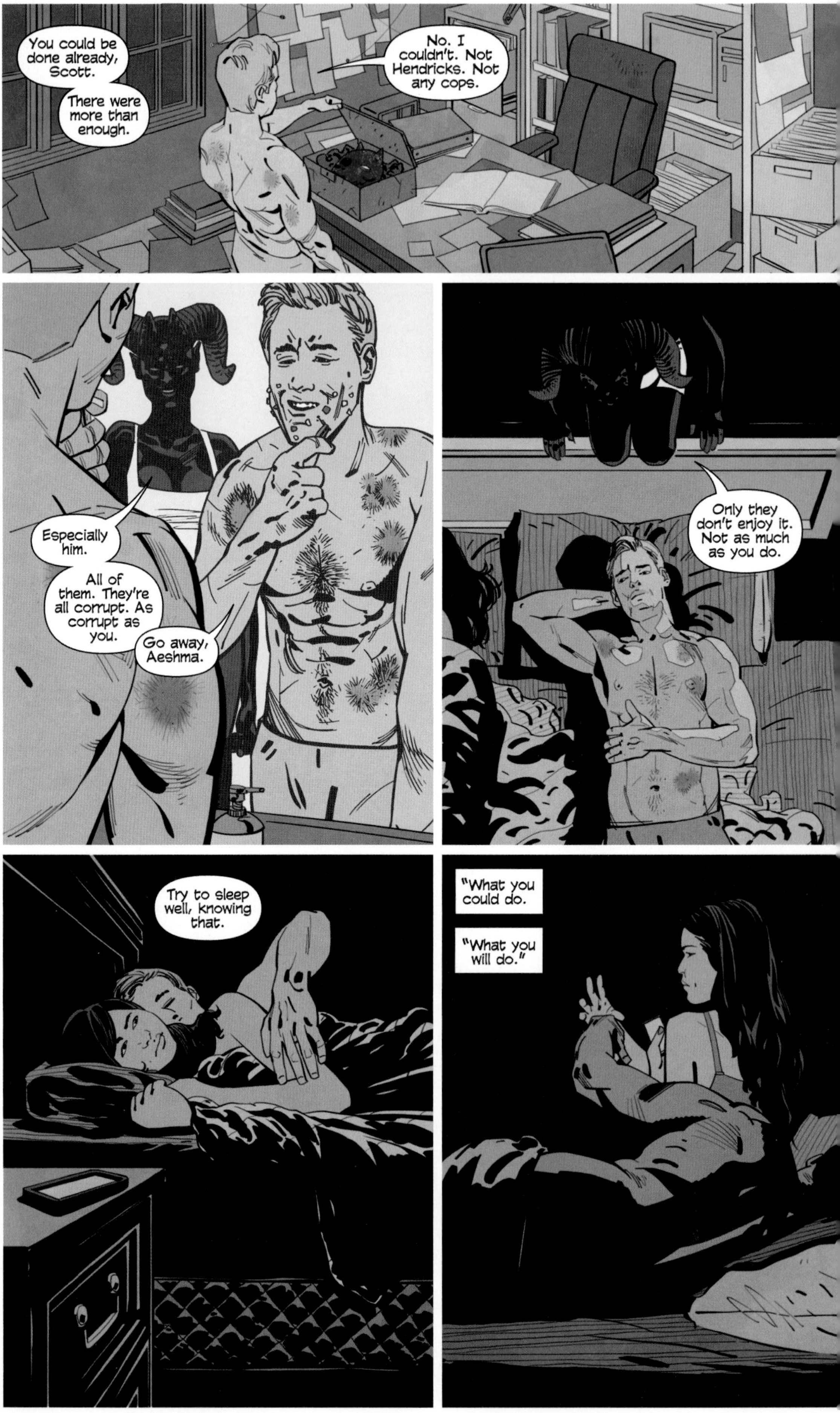
You could be done already, Scott.
There were more than enough.
No. I couldn't. Not Hendricks. Not any cops.
Especially him.
All of them. They're all corrupt. As corrupt as you.
Go away, Aeshma.
Only they don't enjoy it. Not as much as you do.
Try to sleep well, knowing that.
"What you could do.
"What you will do."

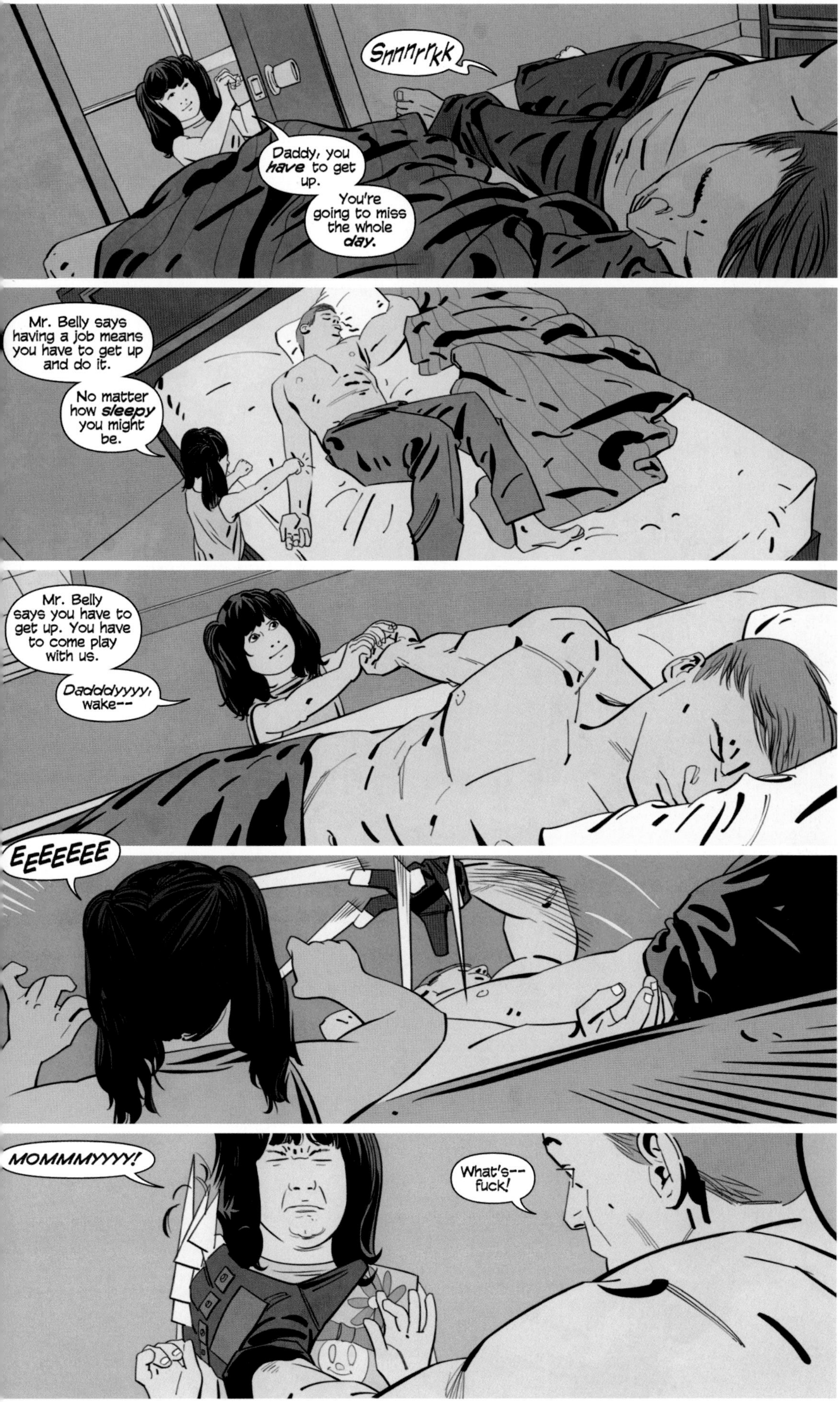
Snnnrrkk
Daddy, you *have* to get up.
You're going to miss the whole *day.*
Mr. Belly says having a job means you have to get up and do it.
No matter how *sleepy* you might be.
Mr. Belly says you have to get up. You have to come play with us.
Daddddyyyy, wake--
EEEEEEE
MOMMMYYYY!
What's-- fuck!

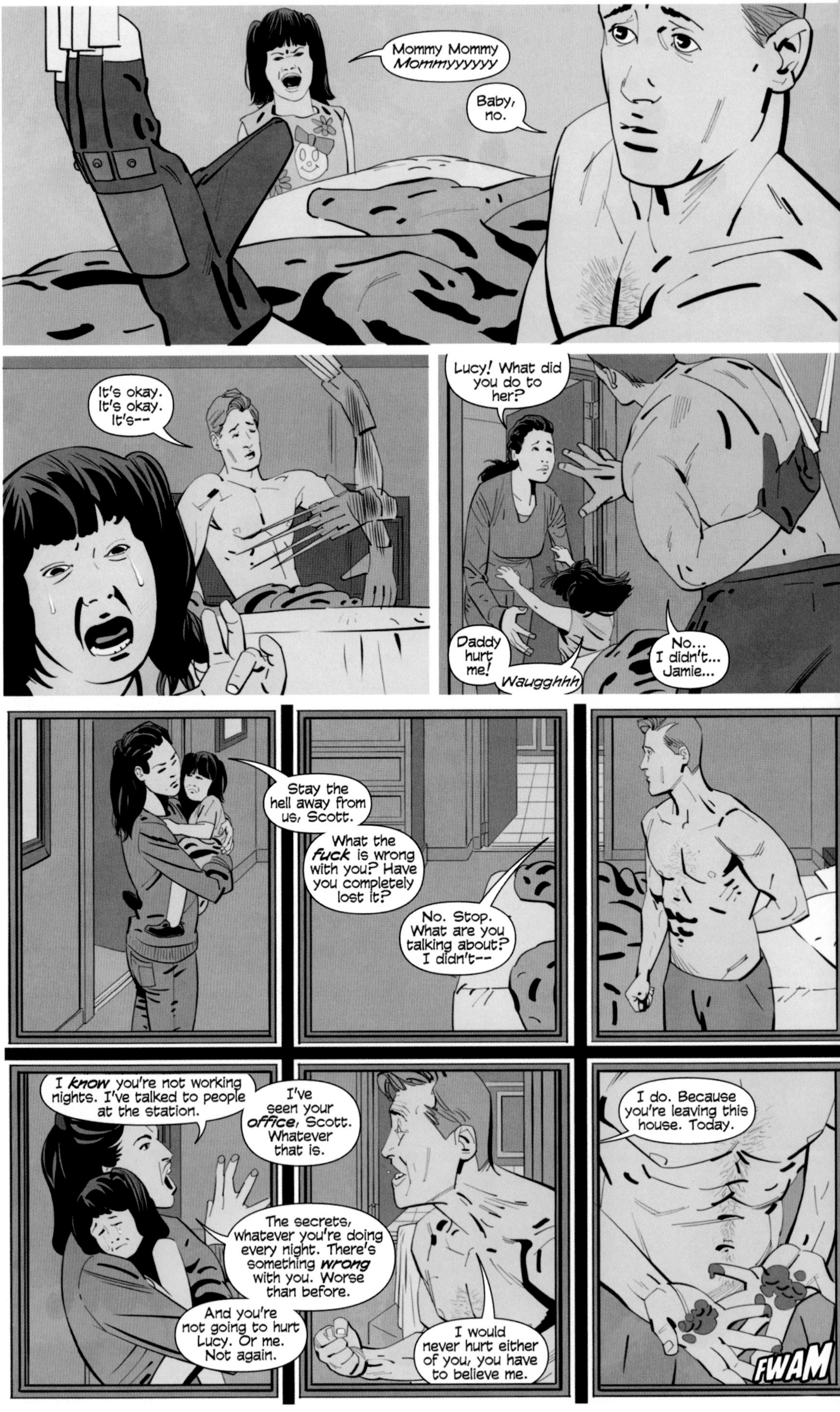
Mommy Mommy *Mommyyyyyy*
Baby, no.
It's okay. It's okay. It's--
Lucy! What did you do to her?
Daddy hurt me!
Waugghhh
No... I didn't... Jamie...
Stay the hell away from us, Scott.
What the ***fuck*** is wrong with you? Have you completely lost it?
No. Stop. What are you talking about? I didn't--
I ***know*** you're not working nights. I've talked to people at the station.
I've seen your ***office***, Scott. Whatever that is.
The secrets, whatever you're doing every night. There's something ***wrong*** with you. Worse than before.
And you're not going to hurt Lucy. Or me. Not again.
I would never hurt either of you, you have to believe me.
I do. Because you're leaving this house. Today.
FWAM

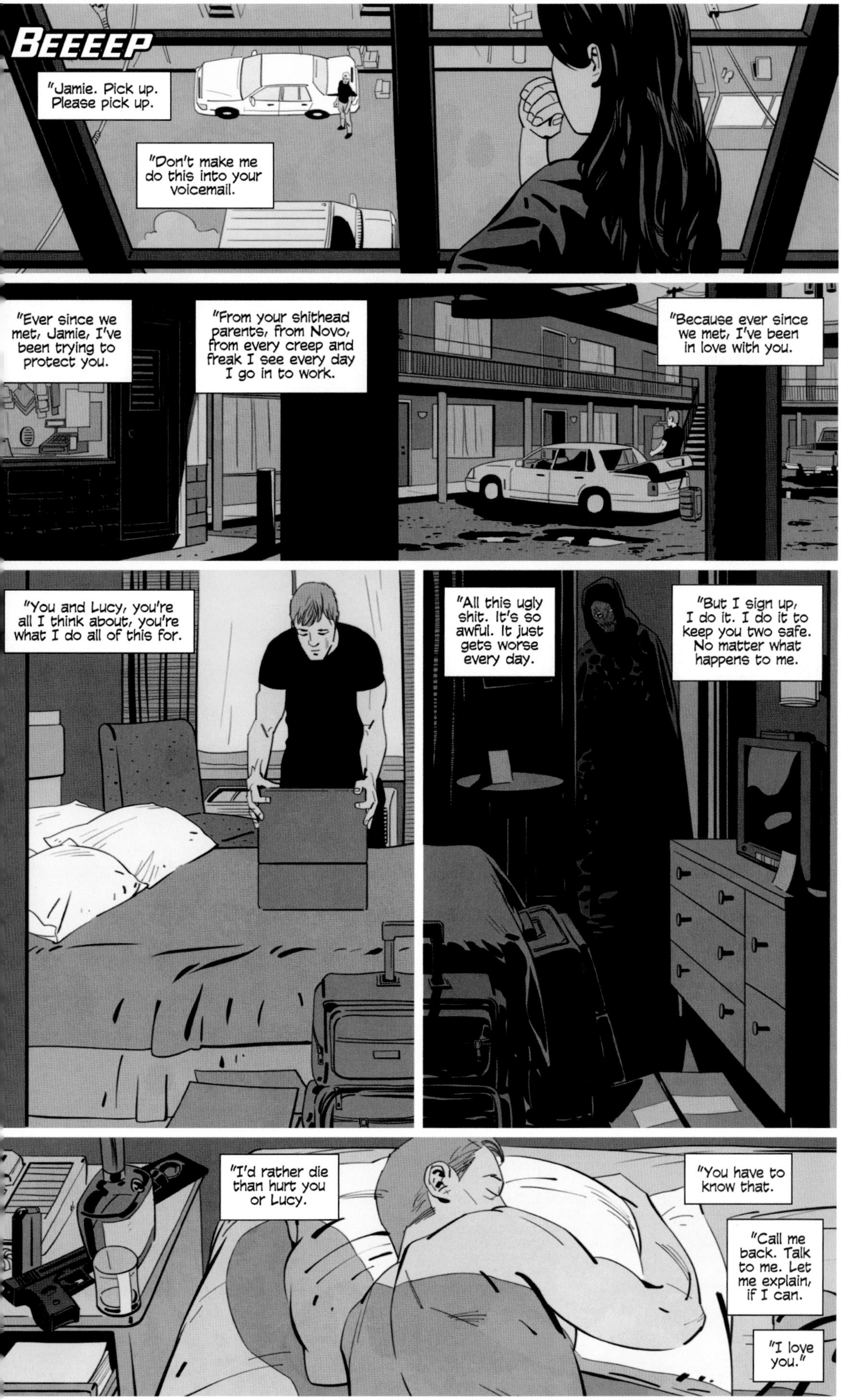
BEEEEP
"Jamie. Pick up. Please pick up.
"Don't make me do this into your voicemail.
"Ever since we met, Jamie, I've been trying to protect you.
"From your shithead parents, from Novo, from every creep and freak I see every day I go in to work.
"Because ever since we met, I've been in love with you.
"You and Lucy, you're all I think about, you're what I do all of this for.
"All this ugly shit. It's so awful. It just gets worse every day.
"But I sign up, I do it. I do it to keep you two safe. No matter what happens to me.
"I'd rather die than hurt you or Lucy.
"You have to know that.
"Call me back. Talk to me. Let me explain, if I can.
"I love you."

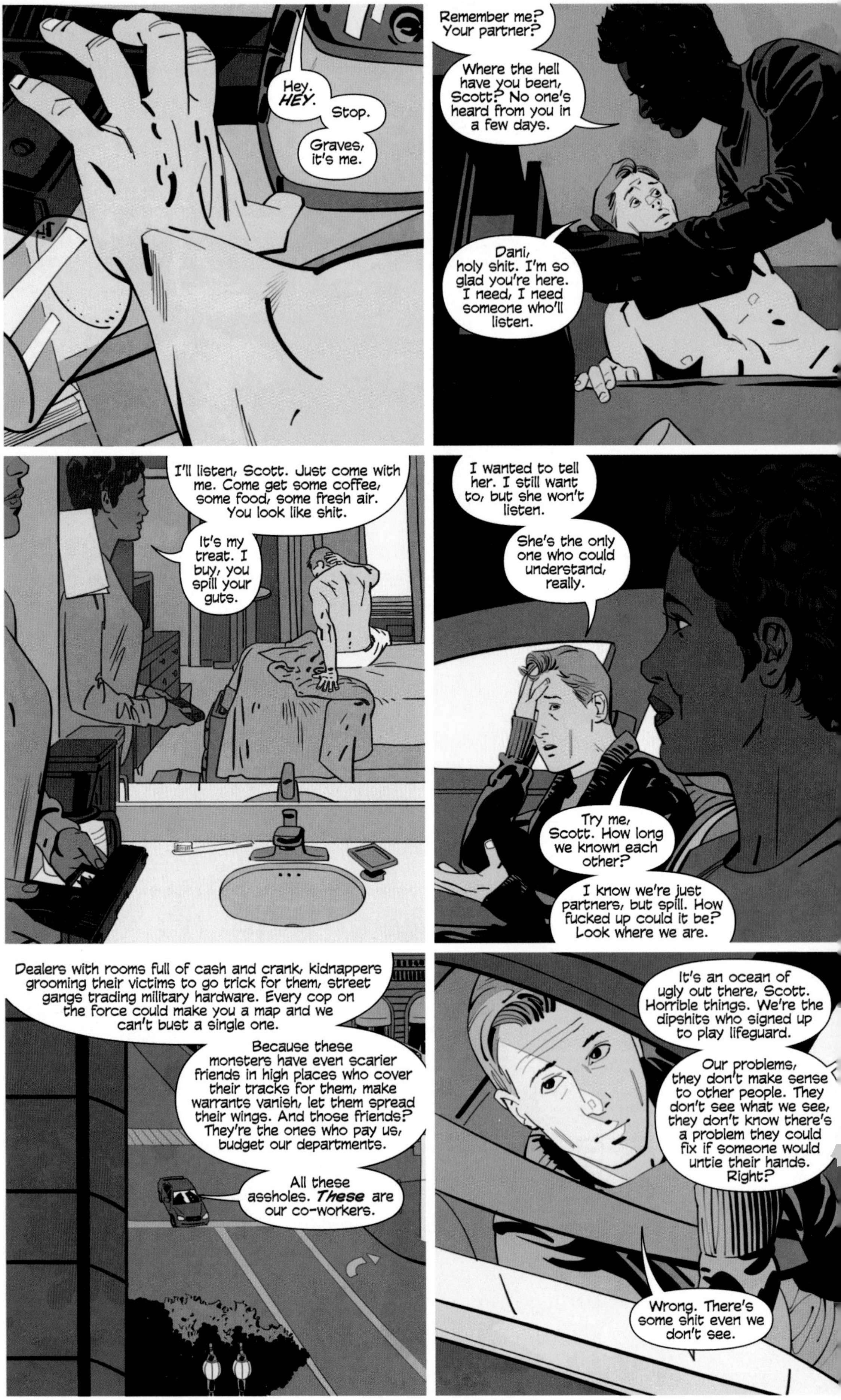
Hey. HEY.
Stop.
Graves, it's me.
Remember me? Your partner?
Where the hell have you been, Scott? No one's heard from you in a few days.
Dani, holy shit. I'm so glad you're here. I need, I need someone who'll listen.
I'll listen, Scott. Just come with me. Come get some coffee, some food, some fresh air. You look like shit.
It's my treat. I buy, you spill your guts.
I wanted to tell her. I still want to, but she won't listen.
She's the only one who could understand, really.
Try me, Scott. How long we known each other?
I know we're just partners, but spill. How fucked up could it be? Look where we are.
Dealers with rooms full of cash and crank, kidnappers grooming their victims to go trick for them, street gangs trading military hardware. Every cop on the force could make you a map and we can't bust a single one.
Because these monsters have even scarier friends in high places who cover their tracks for them, make warrants vanish, let them spread their wings. And those friends? They're the ones who pay us, budget our departments.
All these assholes. These are our co-workers.
It's an ocean of ugly out there, Scott. Horrible things. We're the dipshits who signed up to play lifeguard.
Our problems, they don't make sense to other people. They don't see what we see, they don't know there's a problem they could fix if someone would untie their hands. Right?
Wrong. There's some shit even we don't see.

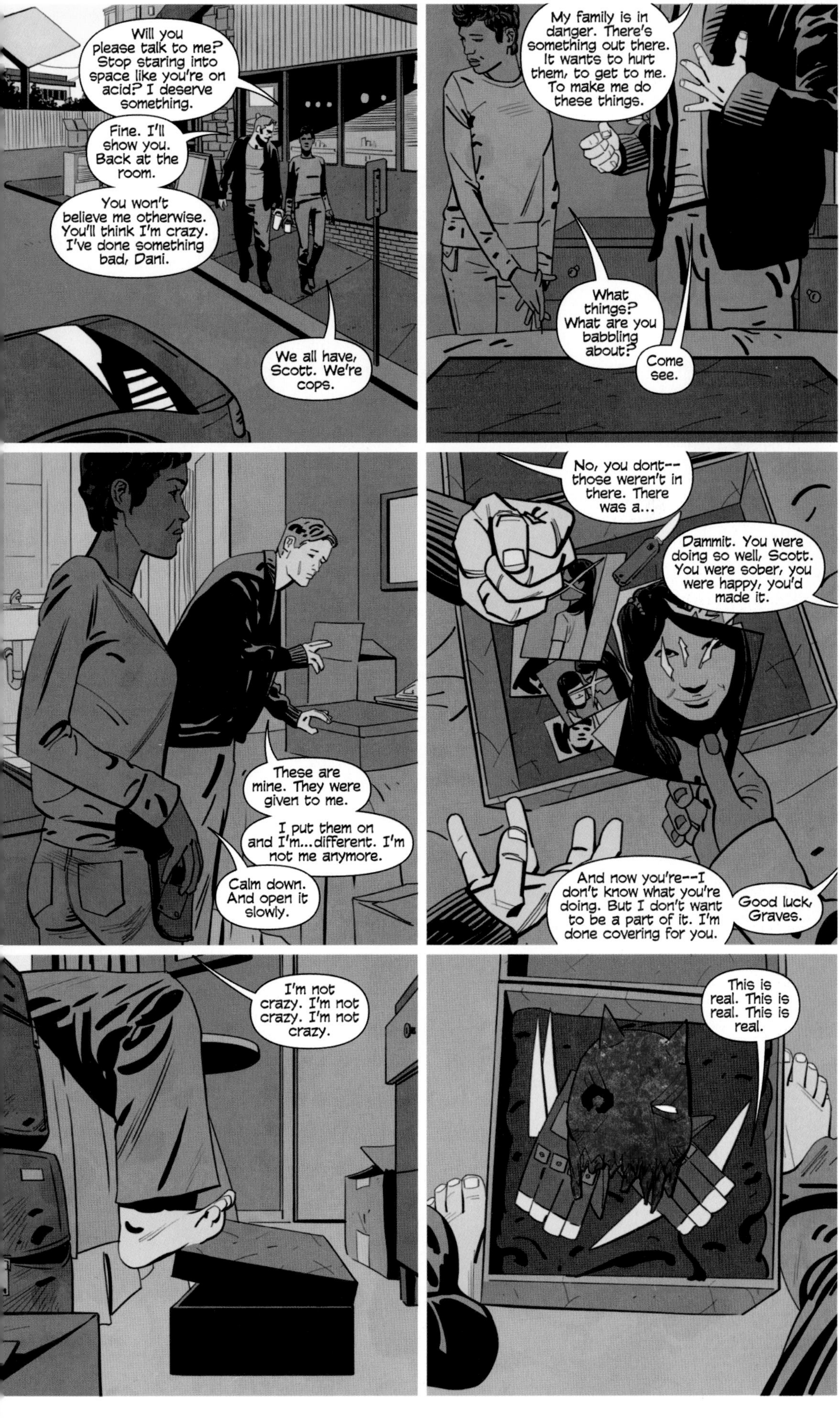
Will you please talk to me? Stop staring into space like you're on acid? I deserve something.
Fine. I'll show you. Back at the room.
You won't believe me otherwise. You'll think I'm crazy. I've done something bad, Dani.
We all have, Scott. We're cops.
My family is in danger. There's something out there. It wants to hurt them, to get to me. To make me do these things.
What things? What are you babbling about?
Come see.
These are mine. They were given to me.
I put them on and I'm...different. I'm not me anymore.
Calm down. And open it slowly.
No, you dont-- those weren't in there. There was a...
Dammit. You were doing so well, Scott. You were sober, you were happy, you'd made it.
And now you're--I don't know what you're doing. But I don't want to be a part of it. I'm done covering for you.
Good luck, Graves.
I'm not crazy. I'm not crazy. I'm not crazy.
This is real. This is real. This is real.

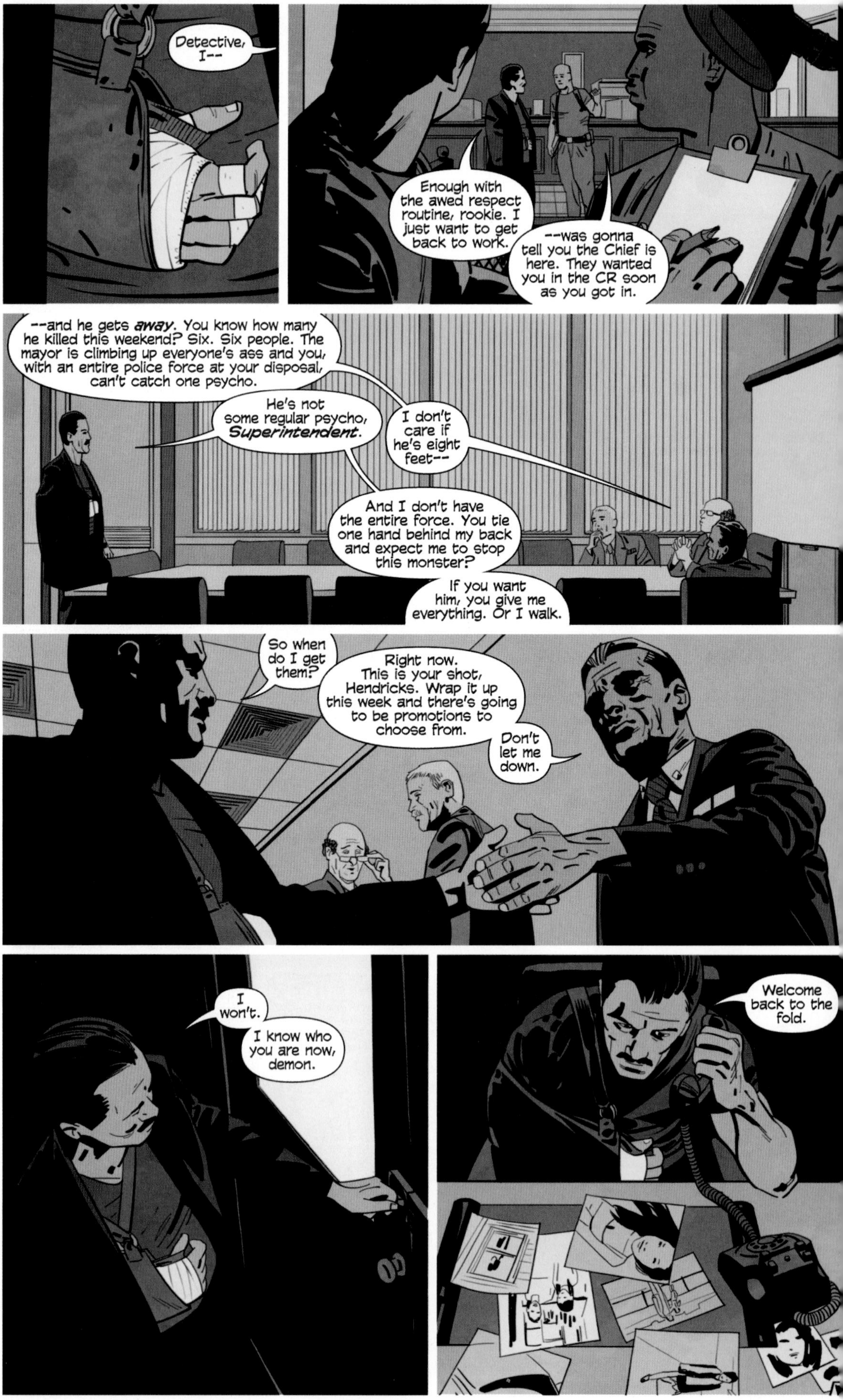
Detective, I--
Enough with the awed respect routine, rookie. I just want to get back to work.
--was gonna tell you the Chief is here. They wanted you in the CR soon as you got in.
--and he gets *away*. You know how many he killed this weekend? Six. Six people. The mayor is climbing up everyone's ass and you, with an entire police force at your disposal, can't catch one psycho.
He's not some regular psycho, *Superintendent*.
I don't care if he's eight feet--
And I don't have the entire force. You tie one hand behind my back and expect me to stop this monster?
If you want him, you give me everything. Or I walk.
So when do I get them?
Right now. This is your shot, Hendricks. Wrap it up this week and there's going to be promotions to choose from.
Don't let me down.
I won't.
I know who you are now, demon.
Welcome back to the fold.

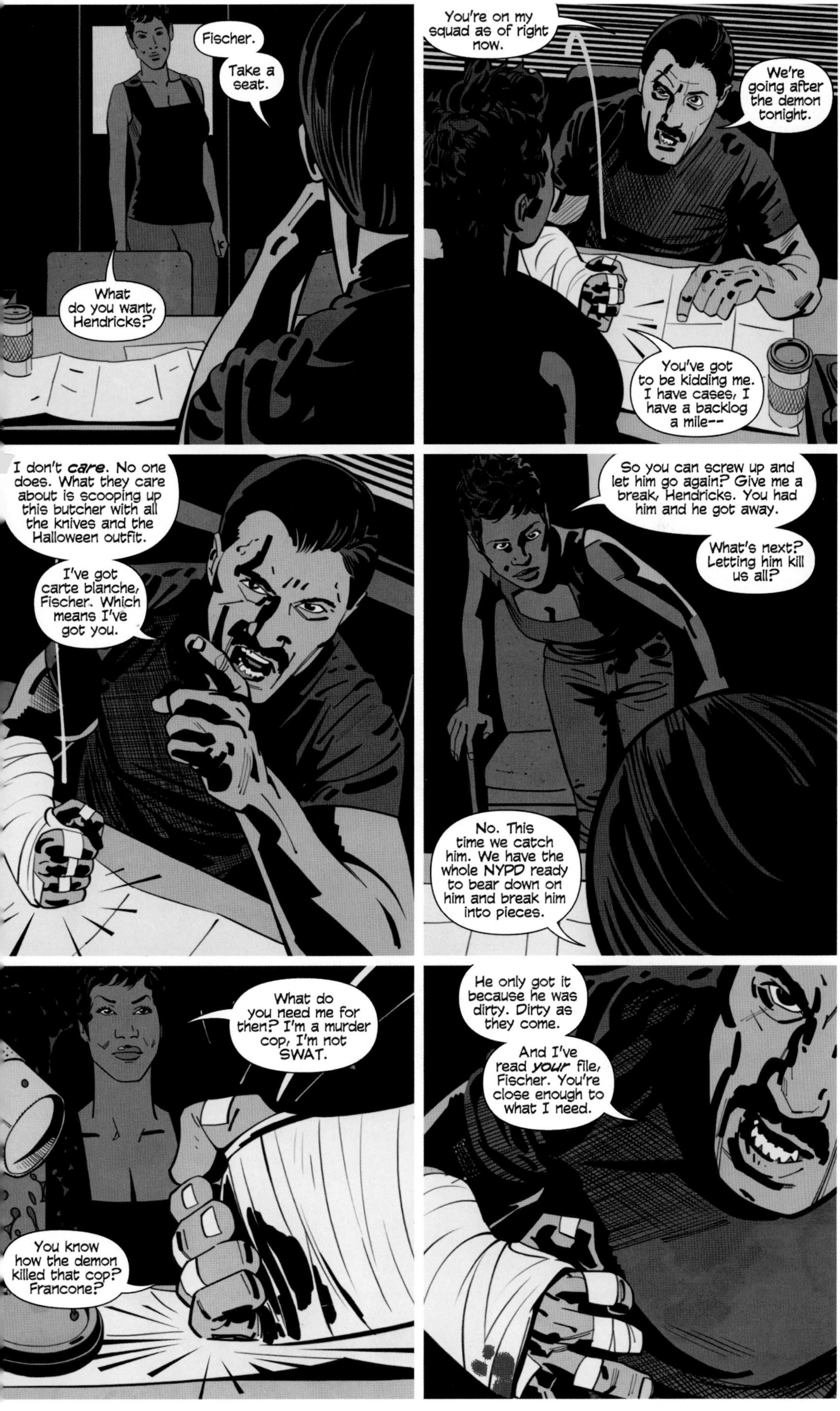
Fischer.
Take a seat.
What do you want, Hendricks?
You're on my squad as of right now.
We're going after the demon tonight.
You've got to be kidding me. I have cases, I have a backlog a mile--
I don't *care*. No one does. What they care about is scooping up this butcher with all the knives and the Halloween outfit.
I've got carte blanche, Fischer. Which means I've got you.
So you can screw up and let him go again? Give me a break, Hendricks. You had him and he got away.
What's next? Letting him kill us all?
No. This time we catch him. We have the whole NYPD ready to bear down on him and break him into pieces.
What do you need me for then? I'm a murder cop, I'm not SWAT.
You know how the demon killed that cop? Francone?
He only got it because he was dirty. Dirty as they come.
And I've read *your* file, Fischer. You're close enough to what I need.

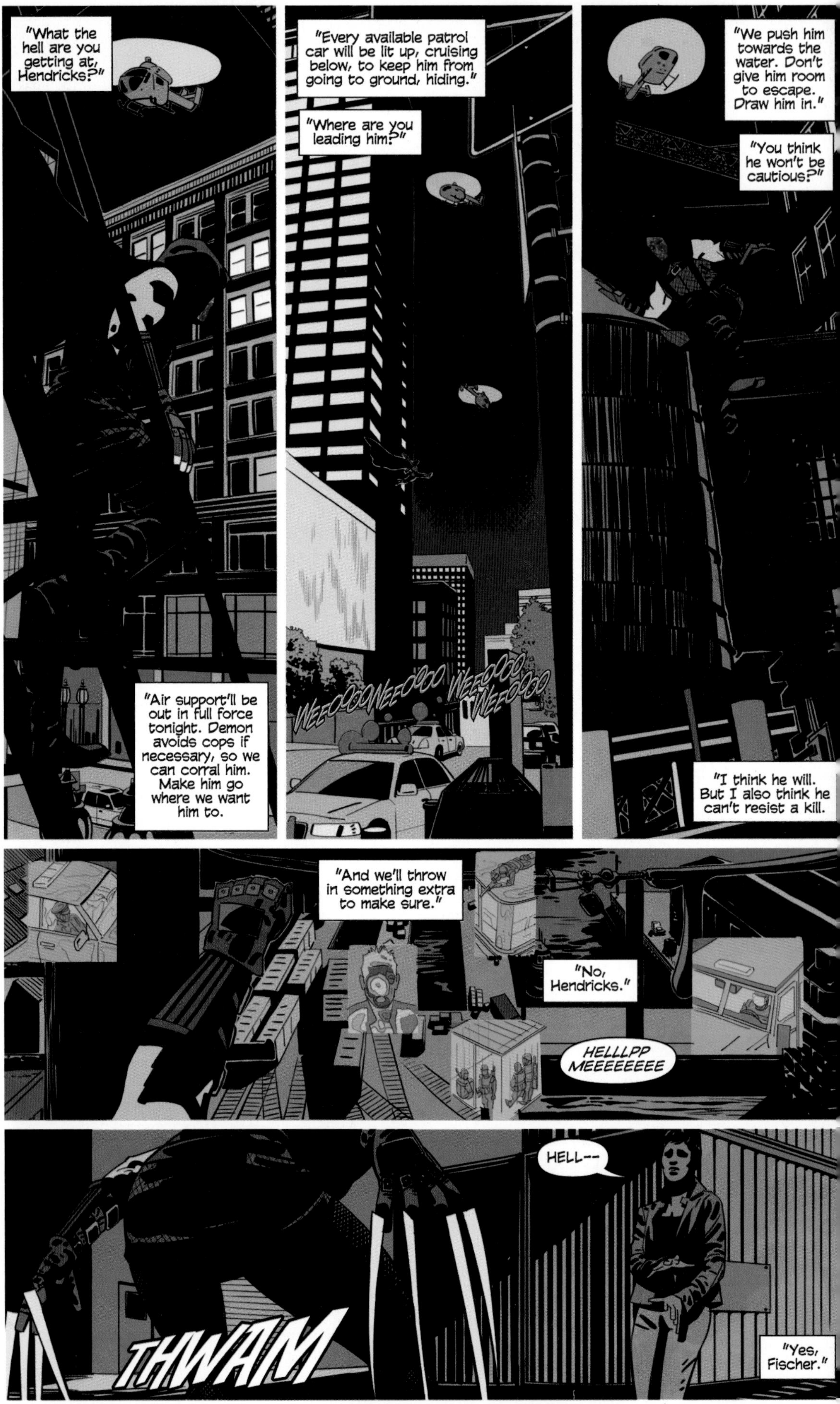
"What the hell are you getting at, Hendricks?"
"Air support'll be out in full force tonight. Demon avoids cops if necessary, so we can corral him. Make him go where we want him to.
"Every available patrol car will be lit up, cruising below, to keep him from going to ground, hiding."
"Where are you leading him?"
WEEOOOOWEEOOOO WEEOOOO WEEOOOO
"We push him towards the water. Don't give him room to escape. Draw him in."
"You think he won't be cautious?"
"I think he will. But I also think he can't resist a kill.
"And we'll throw in something extra to make sure."
"No, Hendricks."
HELLLPP MEEEEEEEE
HELL--
THWAM
"Yes, Fischer."

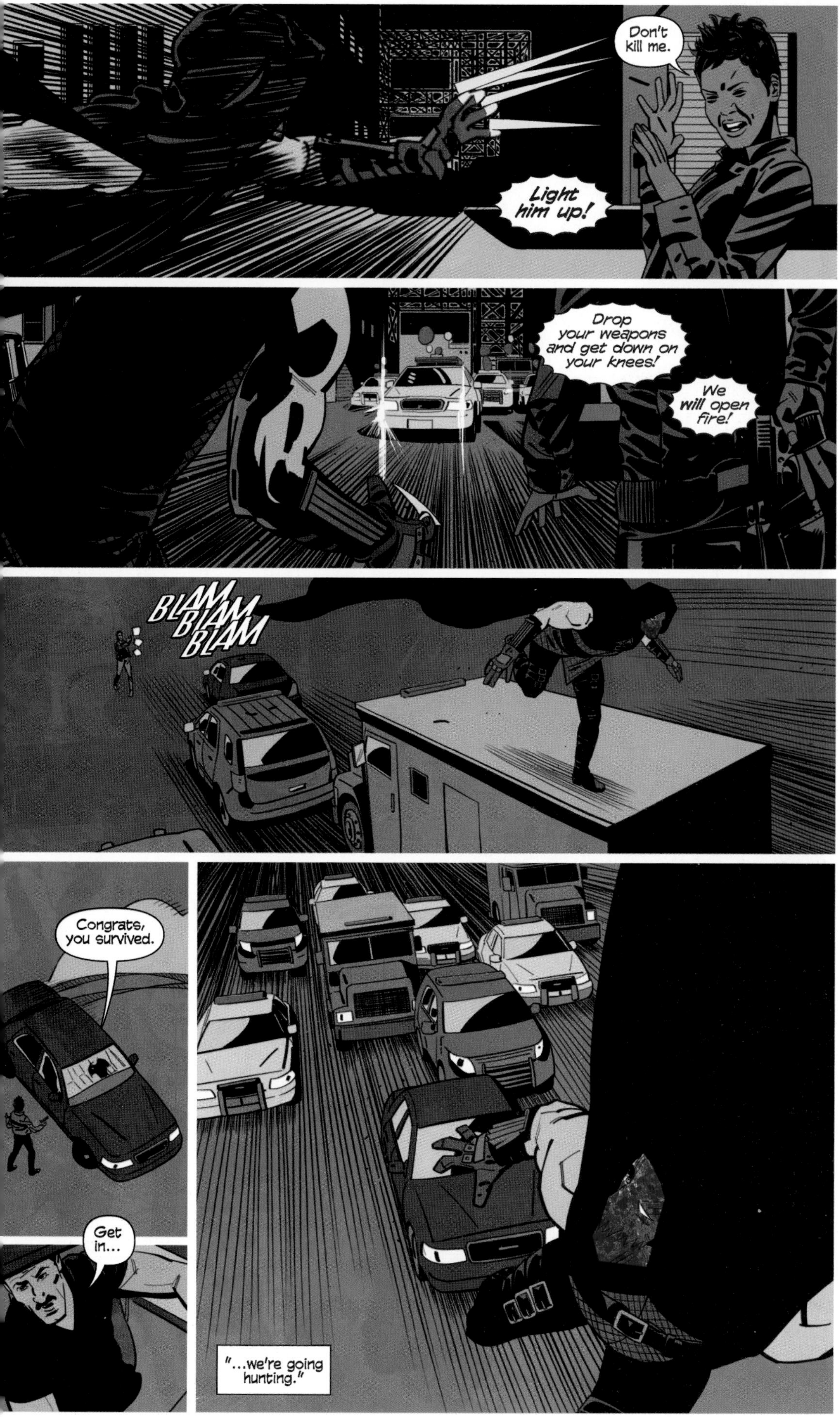
Don't kill me.
Light him up!
Drop your weapons and get down on your knees!
We will open fire!
BLAM BLAM BLAM
Congrats, you survived.
Get in...
"...we're going hunting."

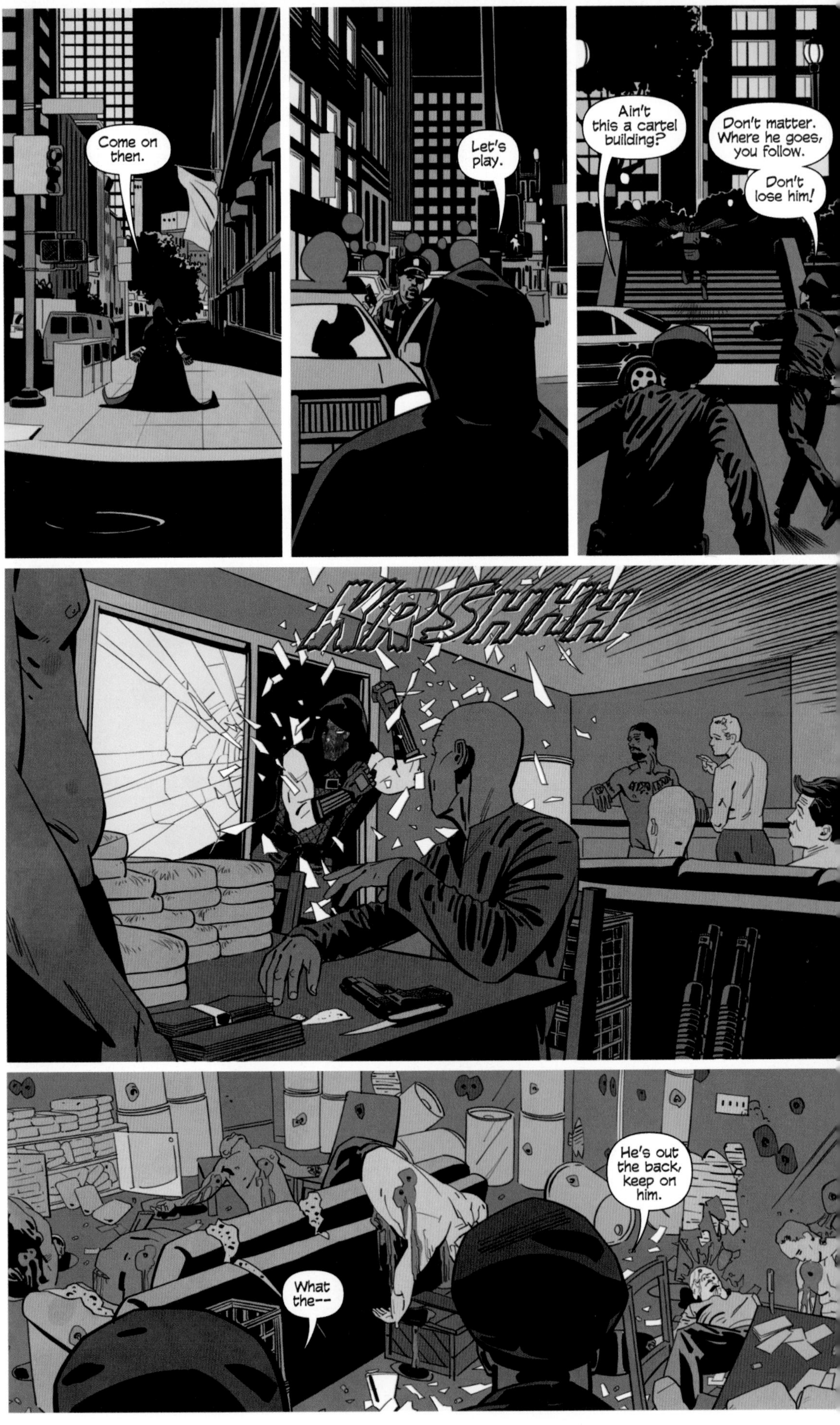
Come on then.
Let's play.
Ain't this a cartel building?
Don't matter. Where he goes, you follow.
Don't lose him!
KRSHHH
He's out the back, keep on him.
What the--

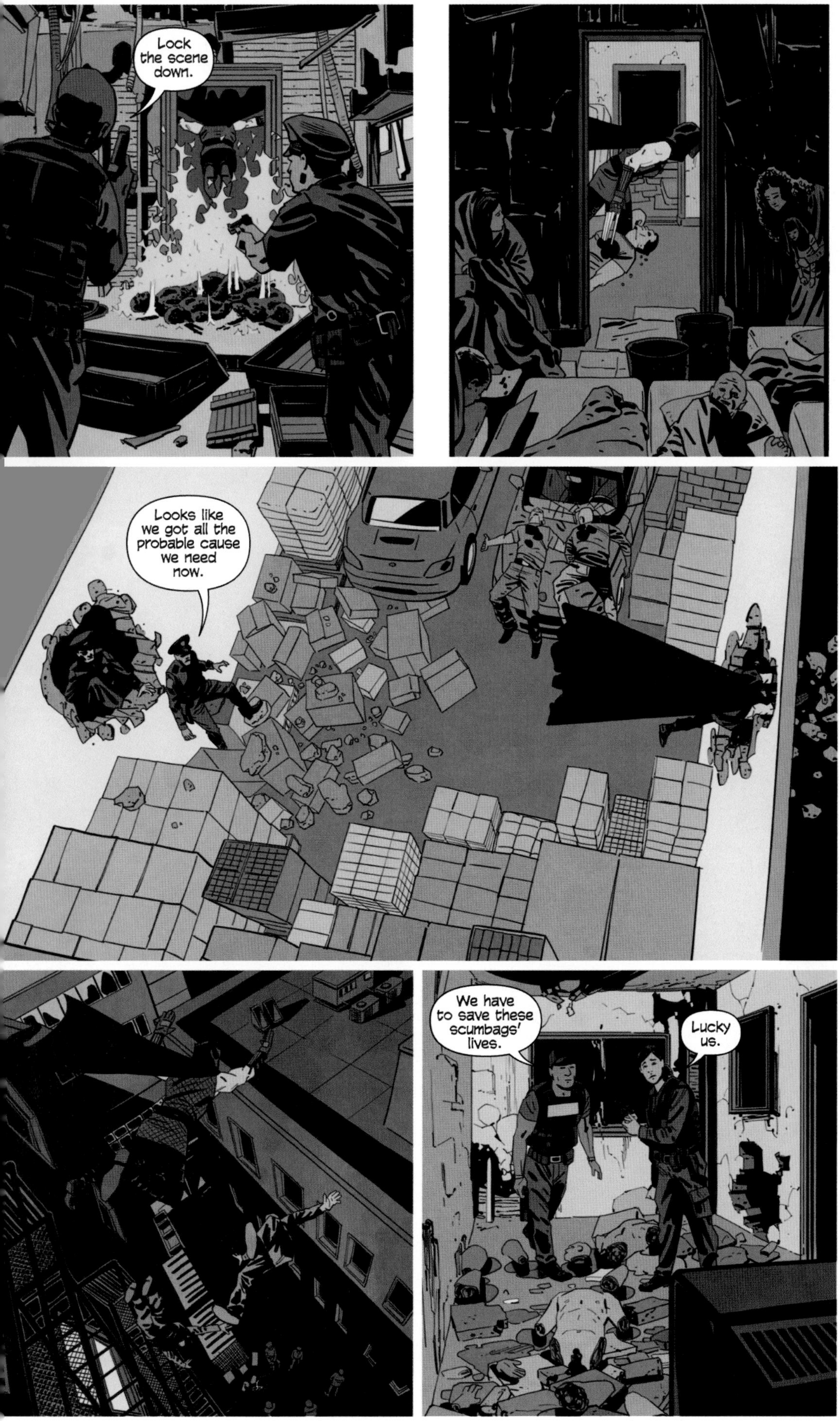

Lock the scene down.
Looks like we got all the probable cause we need now.
We have to save these scumbags' lives.
Lucky us.

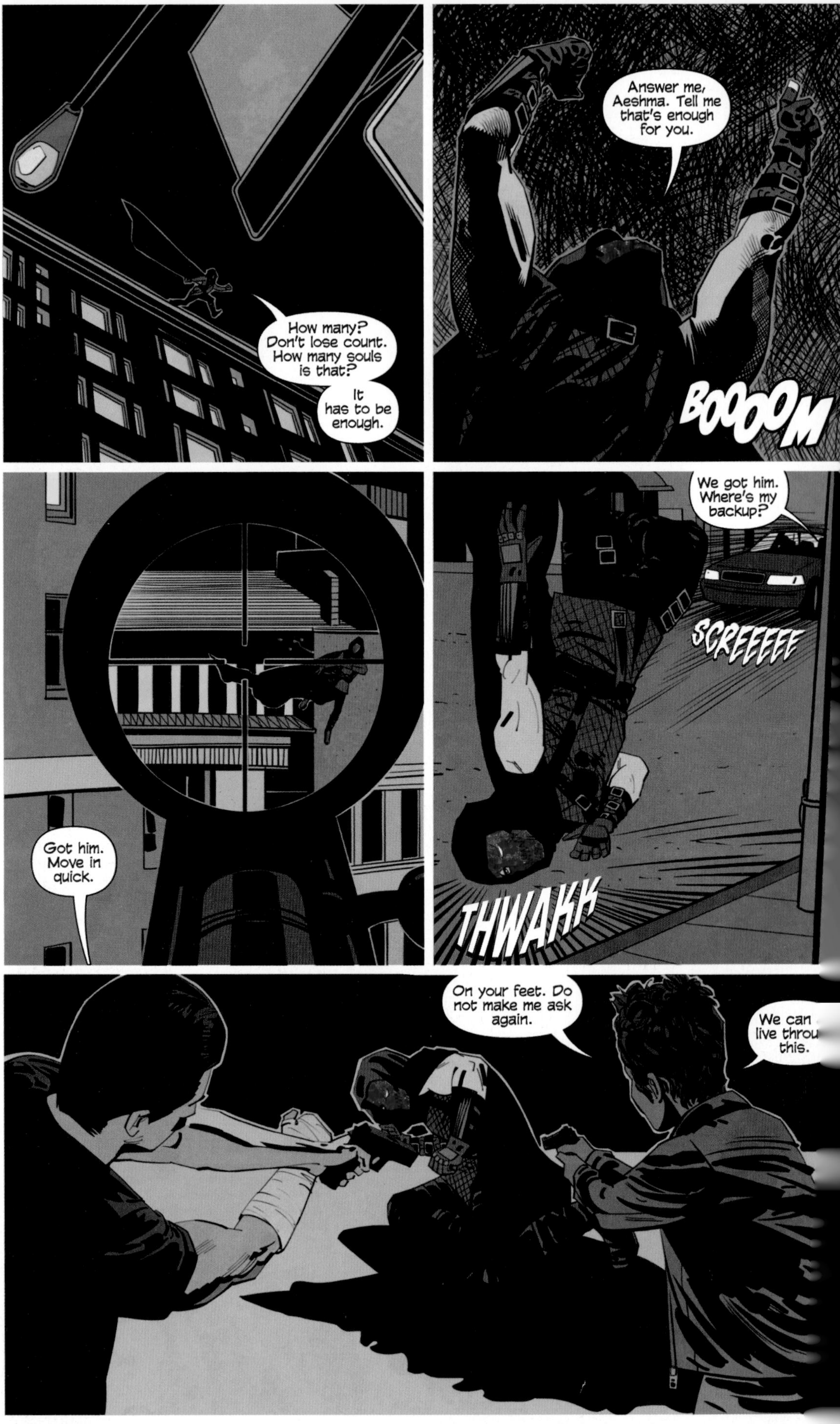
How many? Don't lose count. How many souls is that?
It has to be enough.
Answer me, Aeshma. Tell me that's enough for you.
BOOOOM
Got him. Move in quick.
We got him. Where's my backup?
SCREEEEE
THWAKK
On your feet. Do not make me ask again.

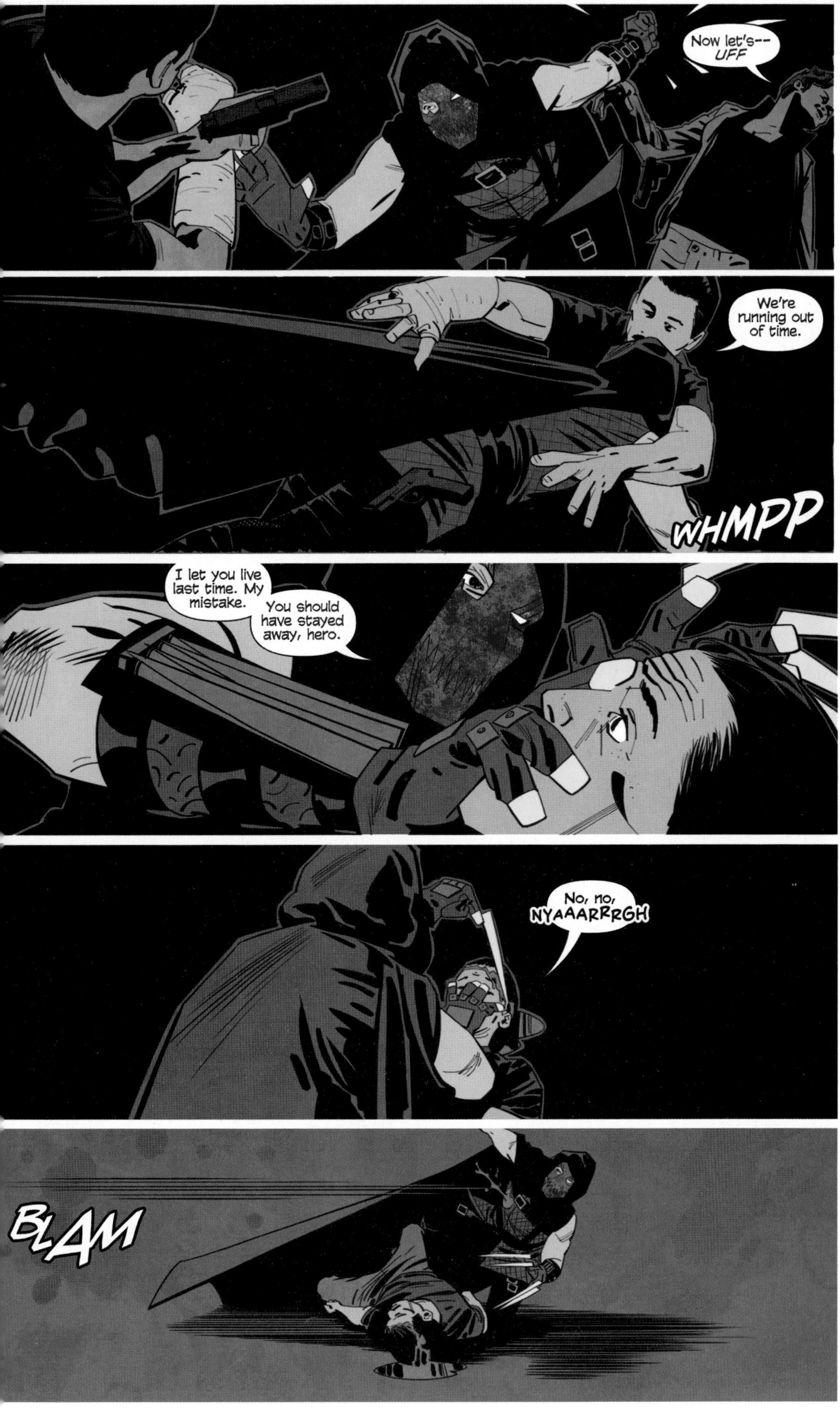

Now let's-- UFF
We're running out of time.
WHMPP
I let you live last time. My mistake.
You should have stayed away, hero.
No, no, NYAAARRRGH
BLAM

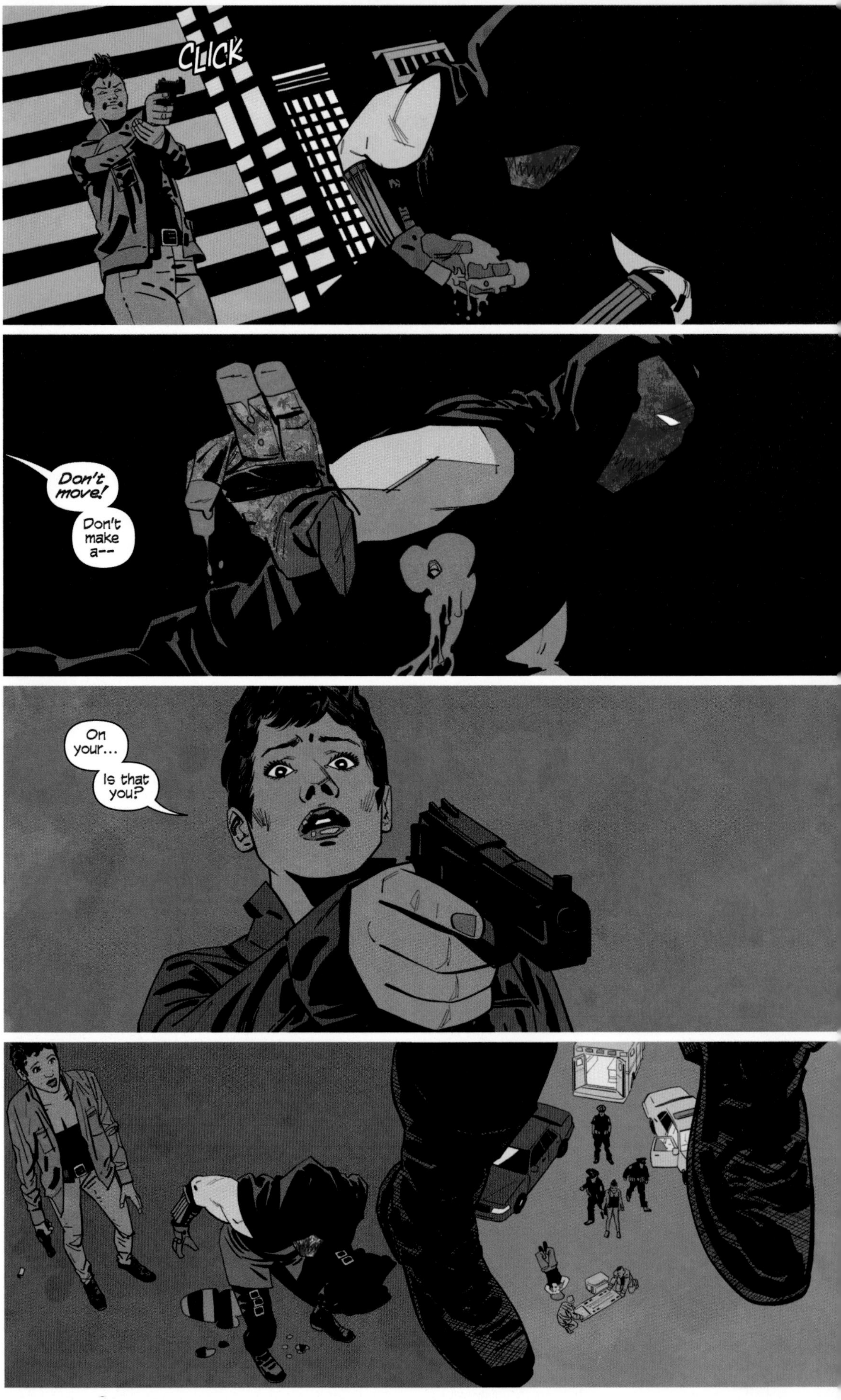
CLICK
Don't move!
Don't make a--
On your...
Is that you?

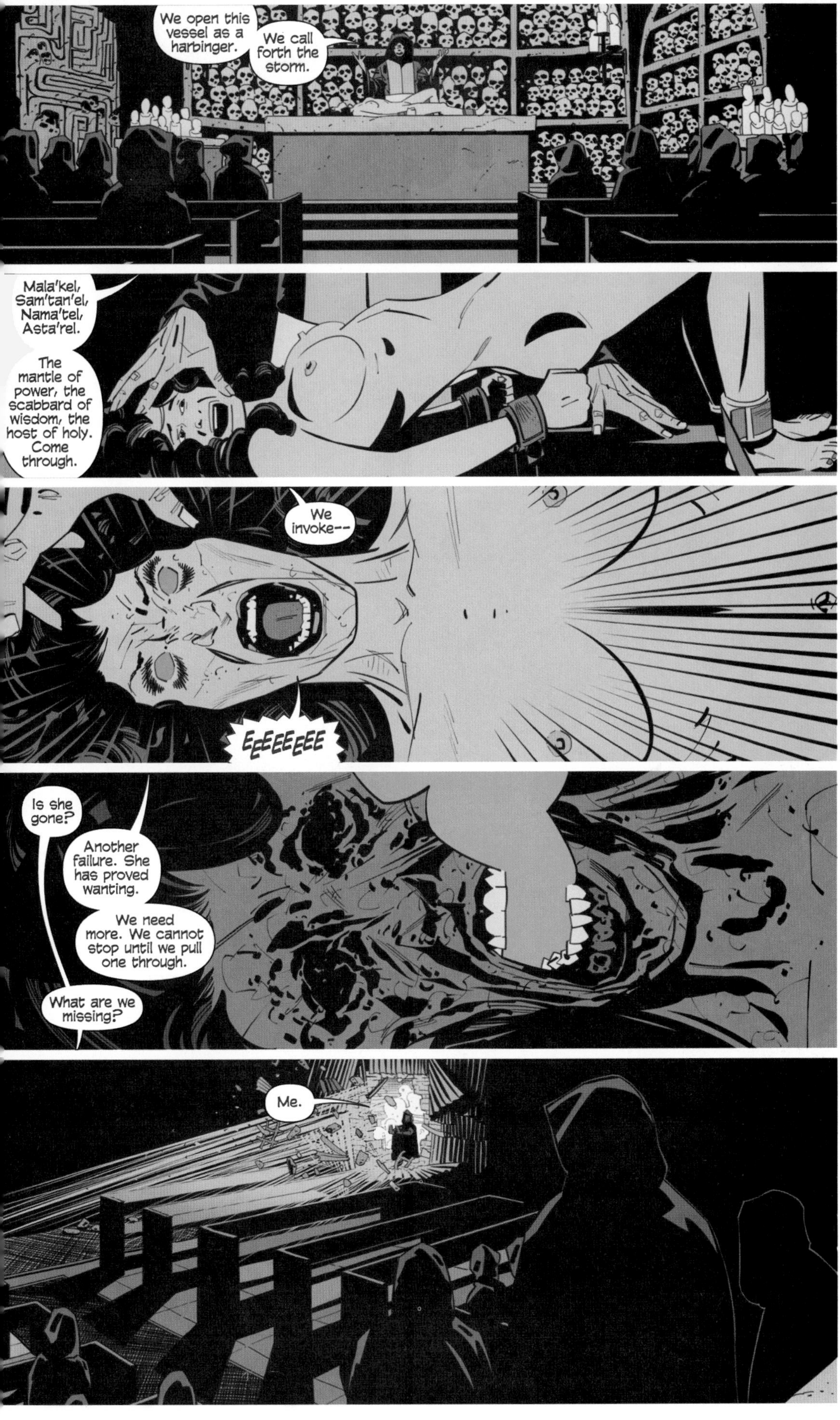
We open this vessel as a harbinger.
We call forth the storm.
Mala'kel, Sam'tan'el, Nama'tel, Asta'rel.
The mantle of power, the scabbard of wisdom, the host of holy. Come through.
We invoke--
EEEEEEEE
Is she gone?
Another failure. She has proved wanting.
We need more. We cannot stop until we pull one through.
What are we missing?
Me.

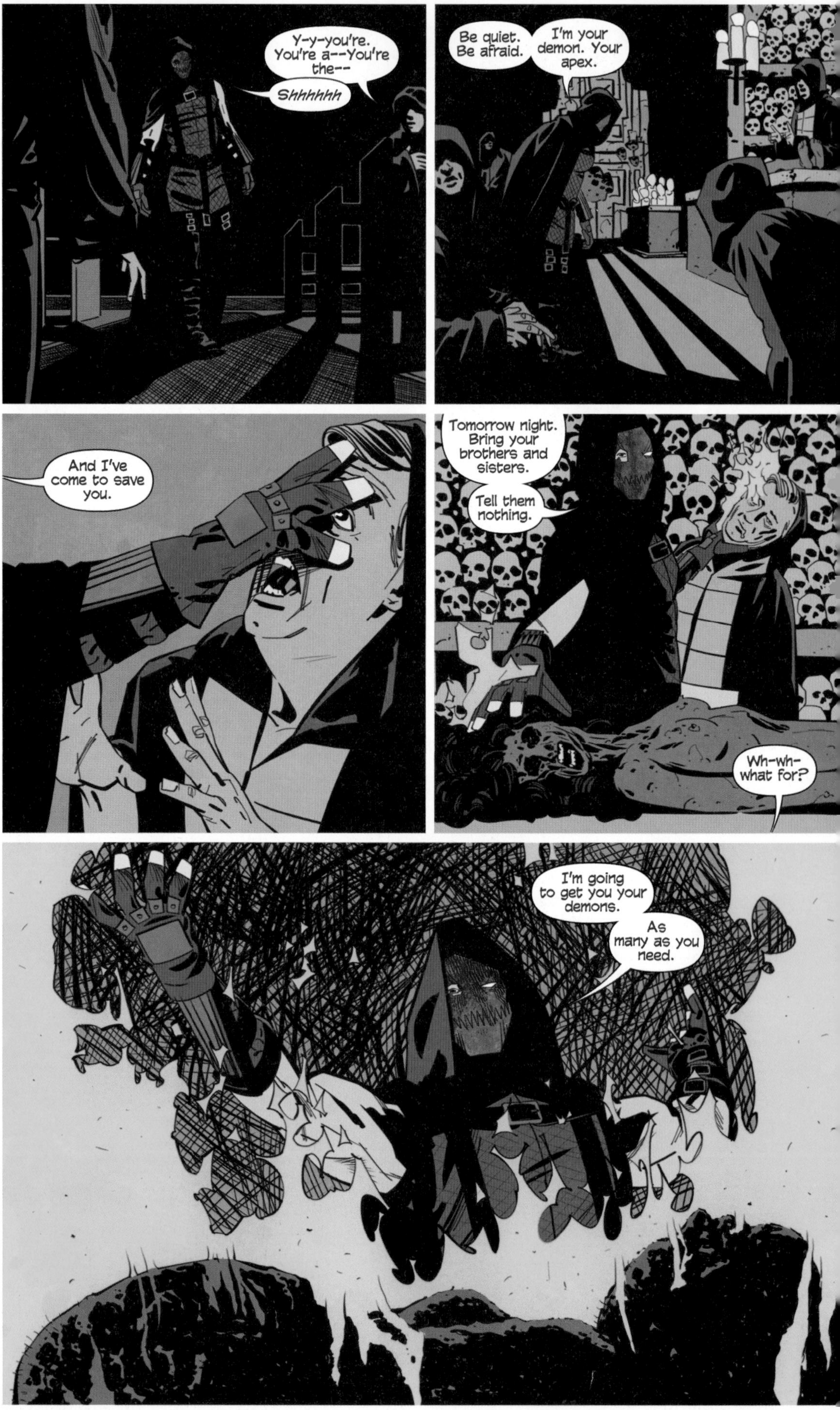
Y-y-you're. You're a--You're the--
Shhhhhh
Be quiet. Be afraid.
I'm your demon. Your apex.
And I've come to save you.
Tomorrow night. Bring your brothers and sisters.
Tell them nothing.
Wh-wh-what for?
I'm going to get you your demons.
As many as you need.

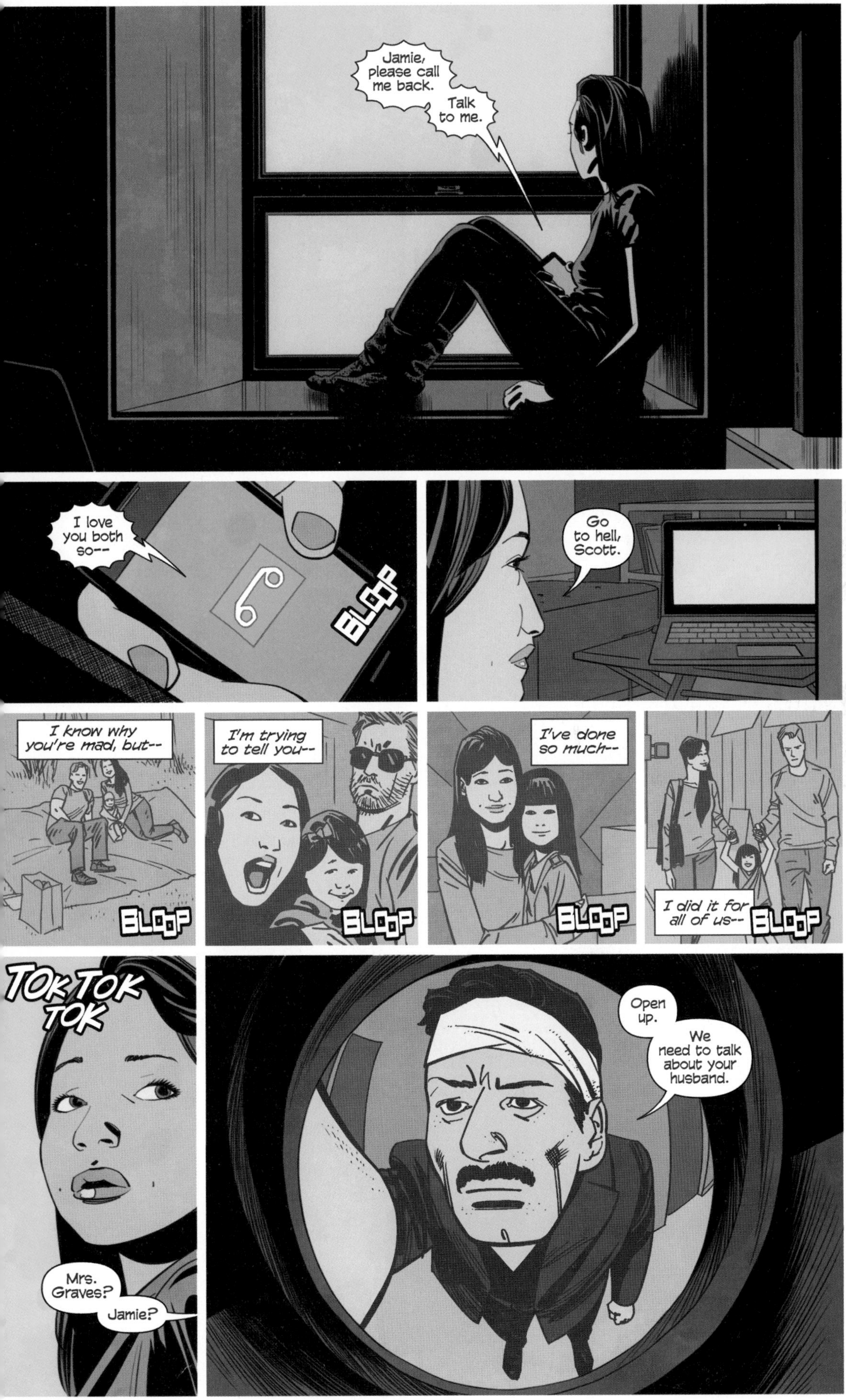
Jamie, please call me back.
Talk to me.
I love you both so--
BLOOP
Go to hell, Scott.
I know why you're mad, but--
BLOOP
I'm trying to tell you--
BLOOP
I've done so much--
BLOOP
I did it for all of us--
BLOOP
TOK TOK TOK
Mrs. Graves?
Jamie?
Open up.
We need to talk about your husband.

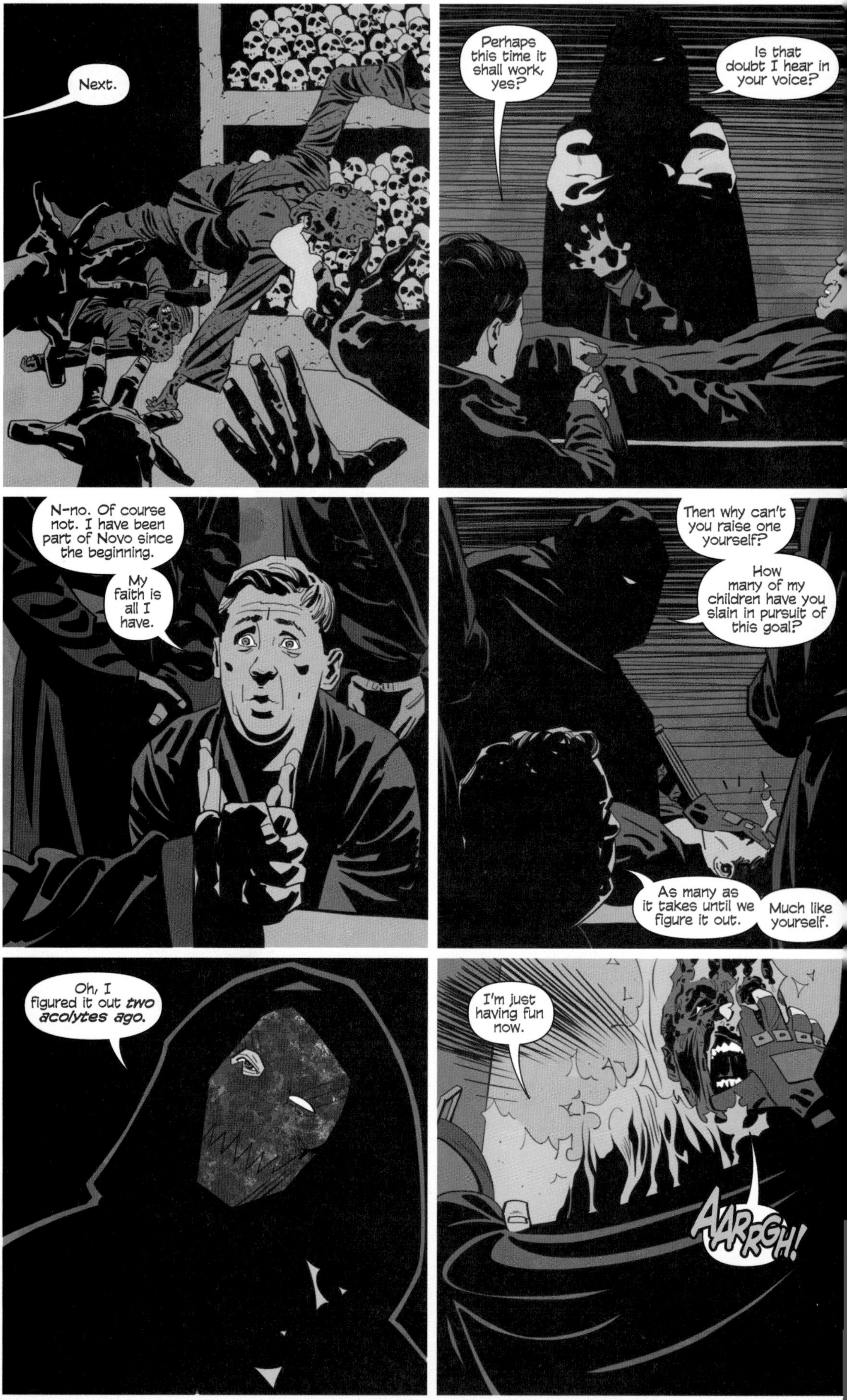
Next.
Perhaps this time it shall work, yes?
Is that doubt I hear in your voice?
N-no. Of course not. I have been part of Novo since the beginning.
My faith is all I have.
Then why can't you raise one yourself?
How many of my children have you slain in pursuit of this goal?
As many as it takes until we figure it out.
Much like yourself.
Oh, I figured it out *two acolytes ago.*
I'm just having fun now.
AARRGH!

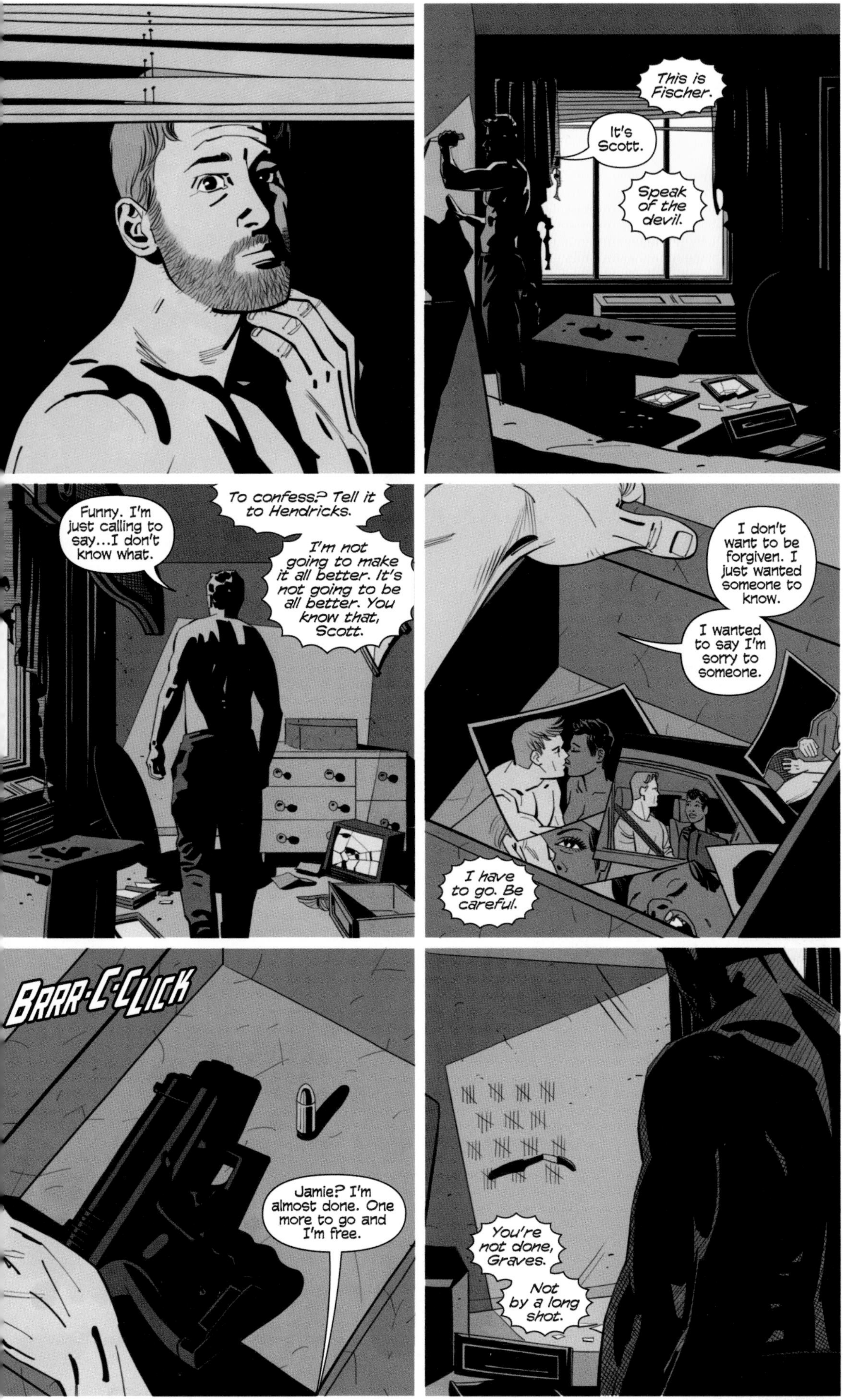

This is Fischer.
It's Scott.
Speak of the devil.
Funny. I'm just calling to say...I don't know what.
To confess? Tell it to Hendricks.
I'm not going to make it all better. It's not going to be all better. You know that, Scott.
I don't want to be forgiven. I just wanted someone to know.
I wanted to say I'm sorry to someone.
I have to go. Be careful.
BRRR-C-CLICK
Jamie? I'm almost done. One more to go and I'm free.
You're not done, Graves.
Not by a long shot.

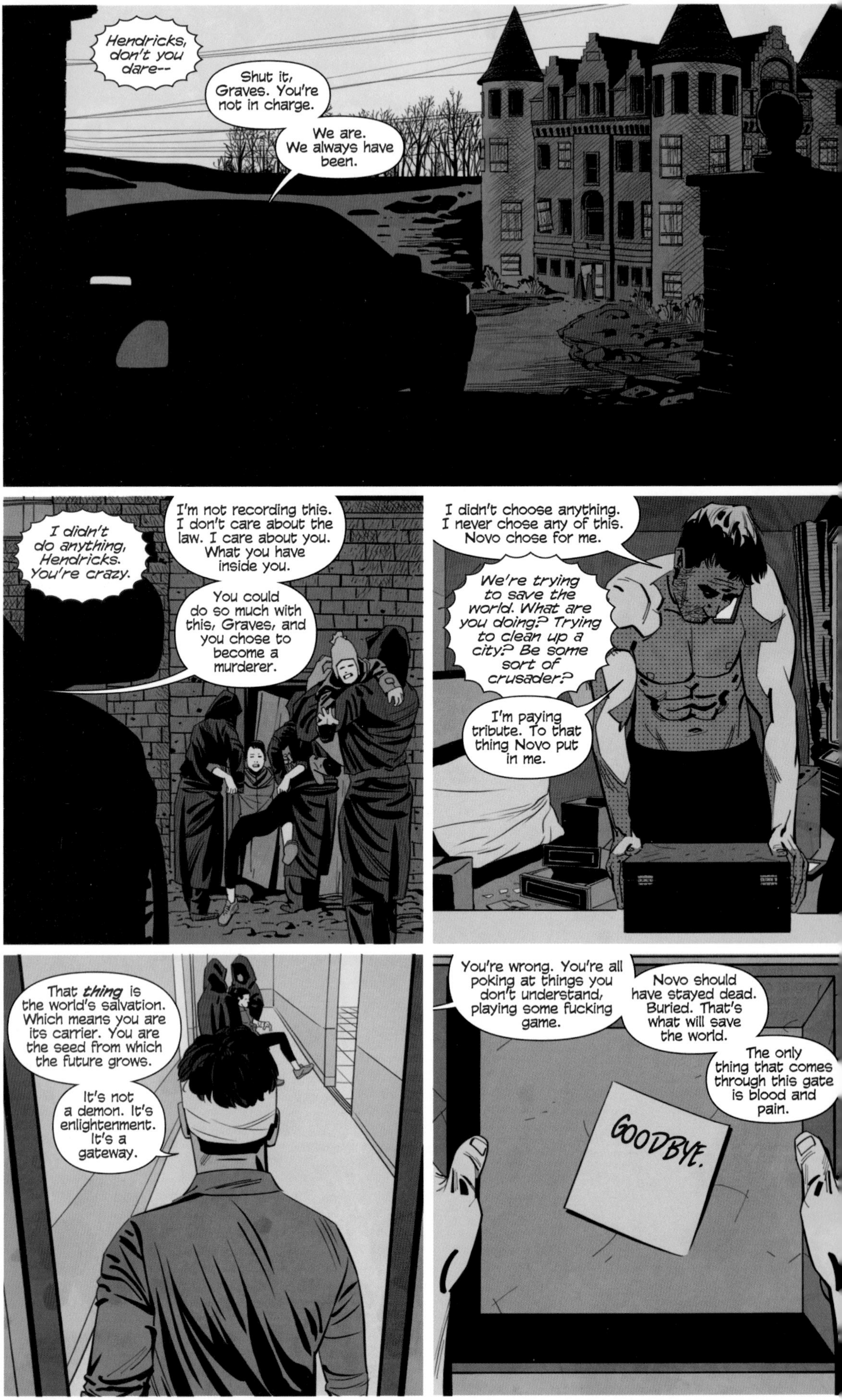
Hendricks, don't you dare--
Shut it, Graves. You're not in charge.
We are. We always have been.
I didn't do anything, Hendricks. You're crazy.
I'm not recording this. I don't care about the law. I care about you. What you have inside you.
You could do so much with this, Graves, and you chose to become a murderer.
I didn't choose anything. I never chose any of this. Novo chose for me.
We're trying to save the world. What are you doing? Trying to clean up a city? Be some sort of crusader?
I'm paying tribute. To that thing Novo put in me.
That *thing* is the world's salvation. Which means you are its carrier. You are the seed from which the future grows.
It's not a demon. It's enlightenment. It's a gateway.
You're wrong. You're all poking at things you don't understand, playing some fucking game.
Novo should have stayed dead. Buried. That's what will save the world.
The only thing that comes through this gate is blood and pain.
GOODBYE.

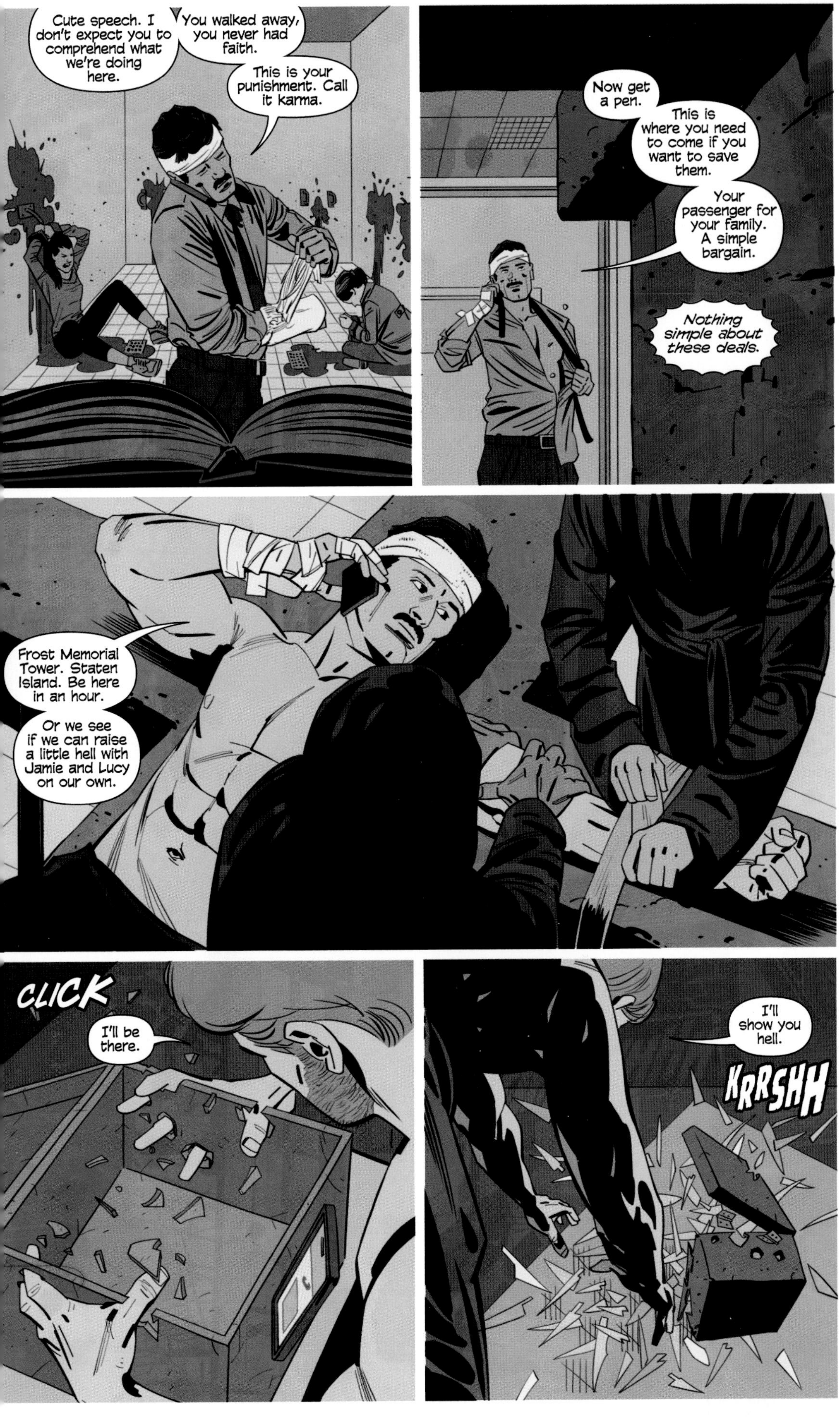
Cute speech. I don't expect you to comprehend what we're doing here.
You walked away, you never had faith.
This is your punishment. Call it karma.
Now get a pen.
This is where you need to come if you want to save them.
Your passenger for your family. A simple bargain.
Nothing simple about these deals.
Frost Memorial Tower. Staten Island. Be here in an hour.
Or we see if we can raise a little hell with Jamie and Lucy on our own.
CLICK
I'll be there.
I'll show you hell.
KRRSHH

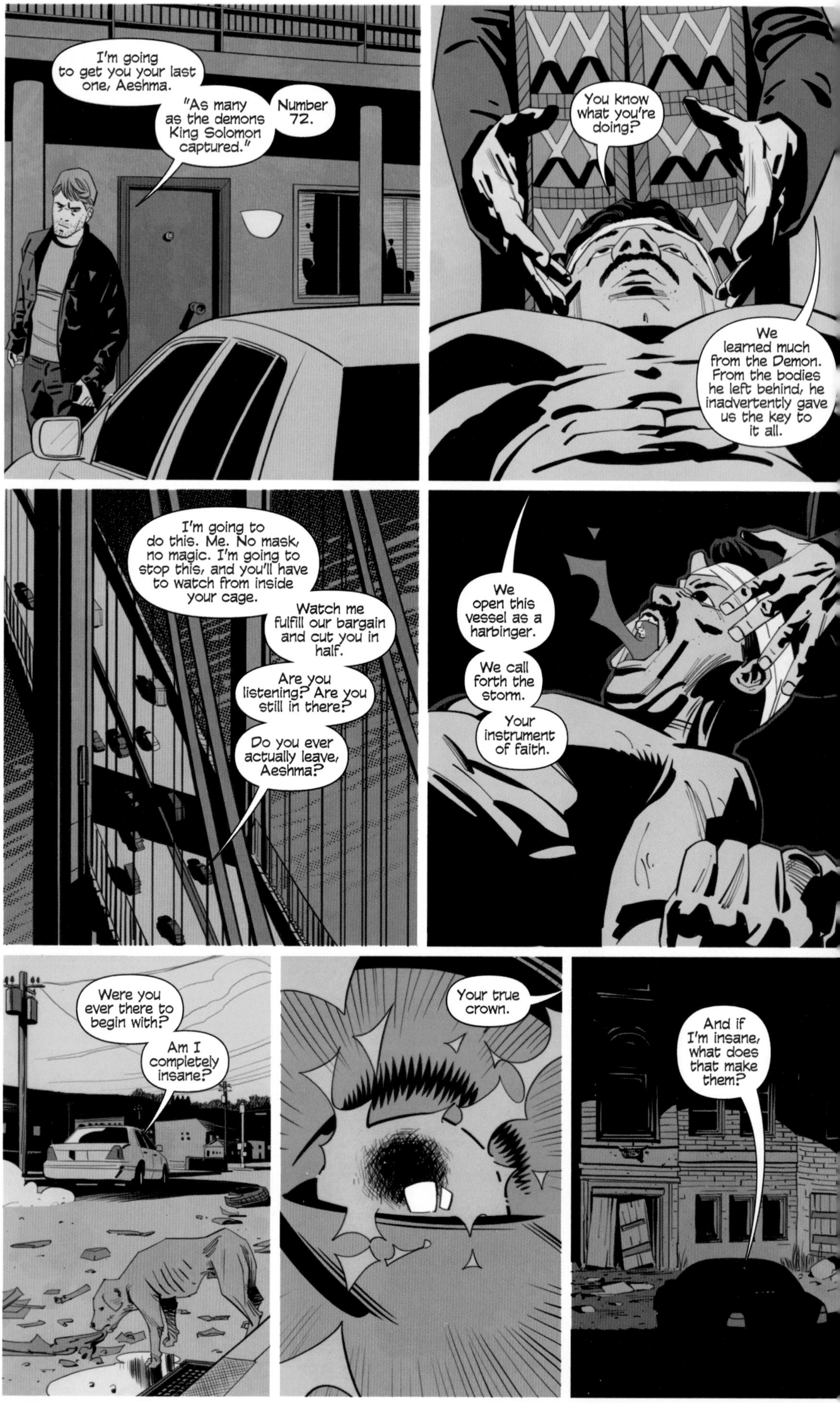
I'm going to get you your last one, Aeshma.
"As many as the demons King Solomon captured."
Number 72.
You know what you're doing?
We learned much from the Demon. From the bodies he left behind, he inadvertently gave us the key to it all.
I'm going to do this. Me. No mask, no magic. I'm going to stop this, and you'll have to watch from inside your cage.
Watch me fulfill our bargain and cut you in half.
Are you listening? Are you still in there?
Do you ever actually leave, Aeshma?
We open this vessel as a harbinger.
We call forth the storm.
Your instrument of faith.
Were you ever there to begin with?
Am I completely insane?
Your true crown.
And if I'm insane, what does that make them?

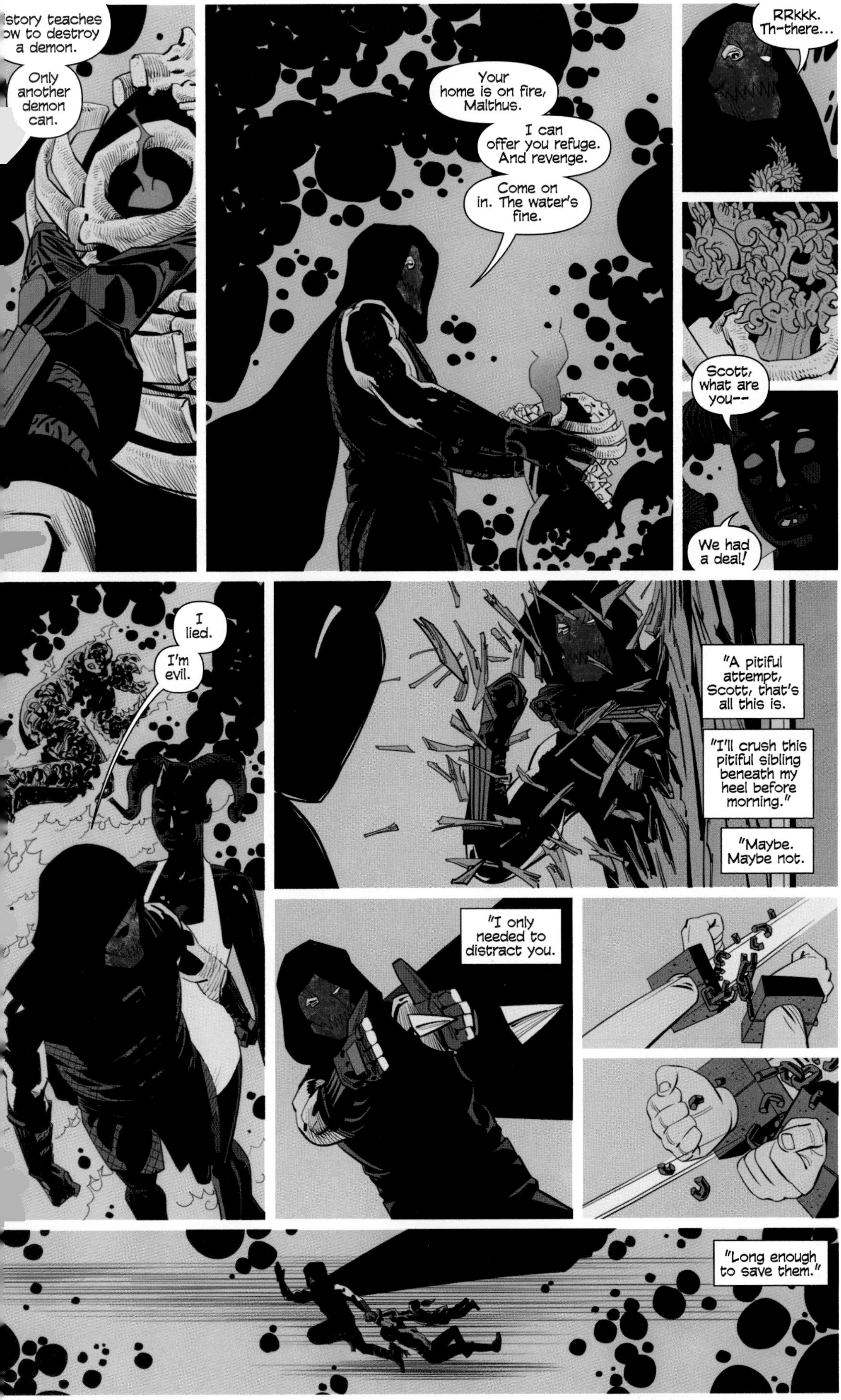

istory teaches
ow to destroy
a demon.
Only another demon can.
Your home is on fire, Malthus.
I can offer you refuge. And revenge.
Come on in. The water's fine.
RRkkk. Th-there...
Scott, what are you--
We had a deal!
I lied.
I'm evil.
"A pitiful attempt, Scott, that's all this is.
"I'll crush this pitiful sibling beneath my heel before morning."
"Maybe. Maybe not.
"I only needed to distract you.
"Long enough to save them."

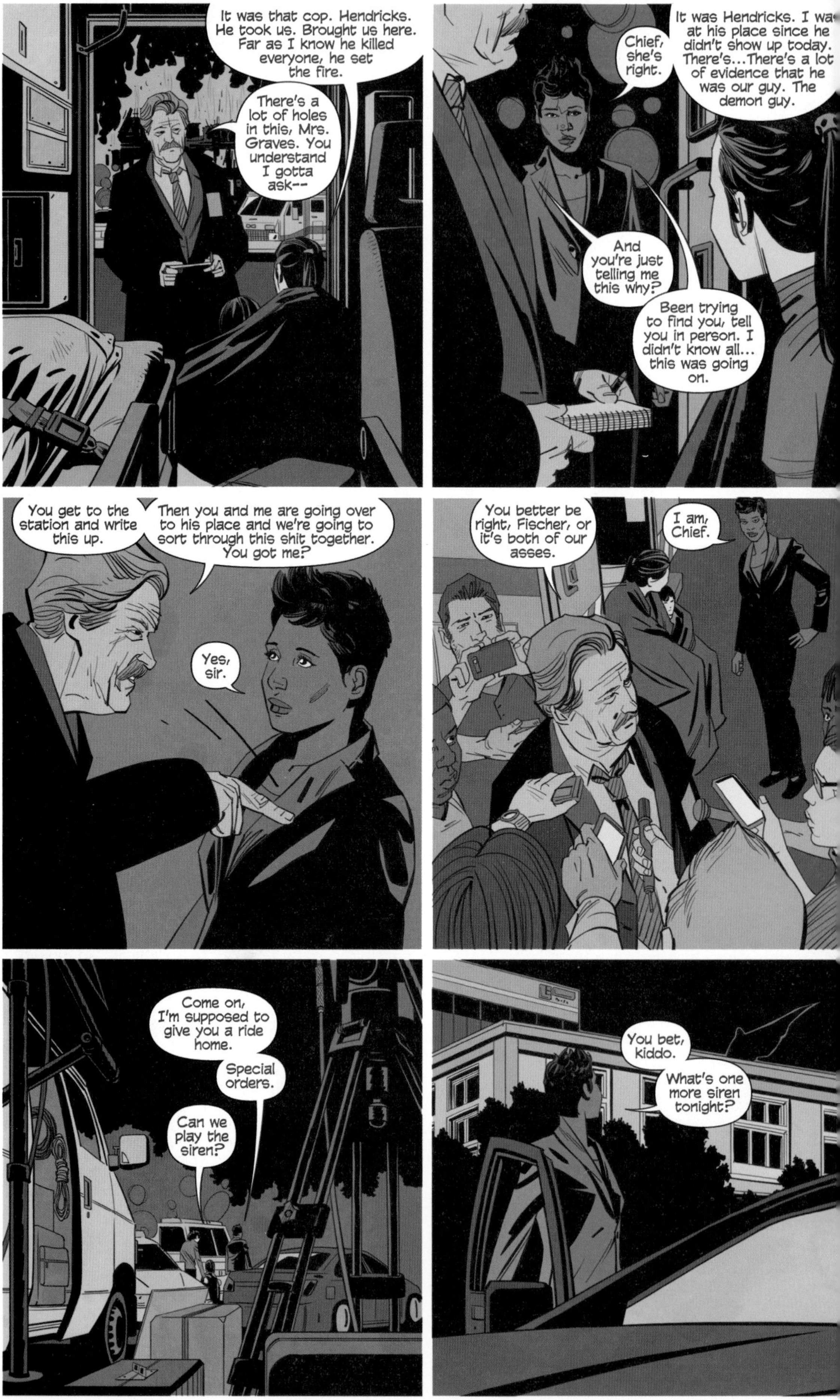
It was that cop. Hendricks. He took us. Brought us here. Far as I know he killed everyone, he set the fire.
There's a lot of holes in this, Mrs. Graves. You understand I gotta ask--
Chief, she's right.
It was Hendricks. I was at his place since he didn't show up today. There's...There's a lot of evidence that he was our guy. The demon guy.
And you're just telling me this why?
Been trying to find you, tell you in person. I didn't know all... this was going on.
You get to the station and write this up.
Then you and me are going over to his place and we're going to sort through this shit together. You got me?
Yes, sir.
You better be right, Fischer, or it's both of our asses.
I am, Chief.
Come on, I'm supposed to give you a ride home.
Special orders.
Can we play the siren?
You bet, kiddo.
What's one more siren tonight?

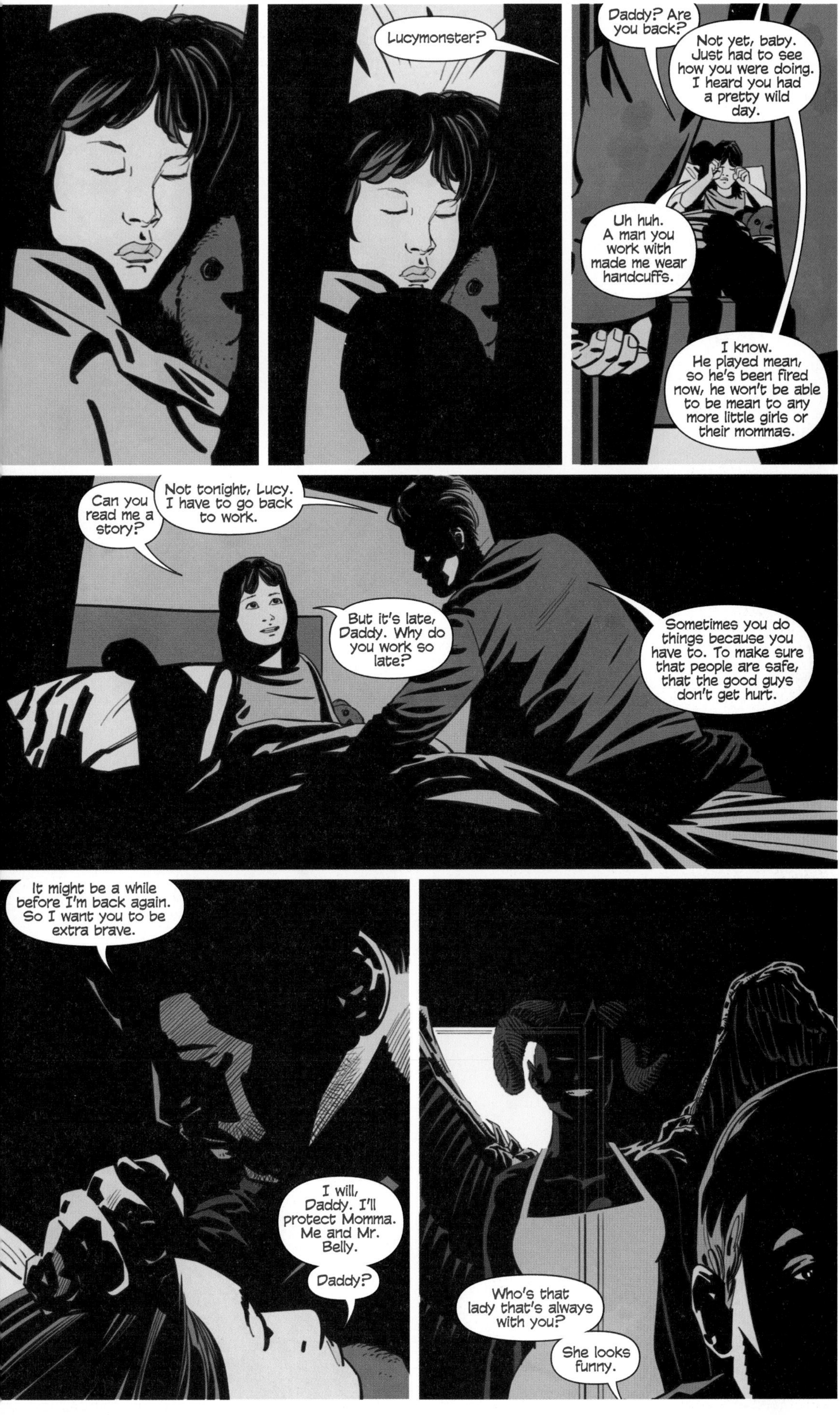
Lucymonster?
Daddy? Are you back?
Not yet, baby. Just had to see how you were doing. I heard you had a pretty wild day.
Uh huh. A man you work with made me wear handcuffs.
I know. He played mean, so he's been fired now, he won't be able to be mean to any more little girls or their mommas.
Can you read me a story?
Not tonight, Lucy. I have to go back to work.
But it's late, Daddy. Why do you work so late?
Sometimes you do things because you have to. To make sure that people are safe, that the good guys don't get hurt.
It might be a while before I'm back again. So I want you to be extra brave.
I will, Daddy. I'll protect Momma. Me and Mr. Belly.
Daddy?
Who's that lady that's always with you?
She looks funny.

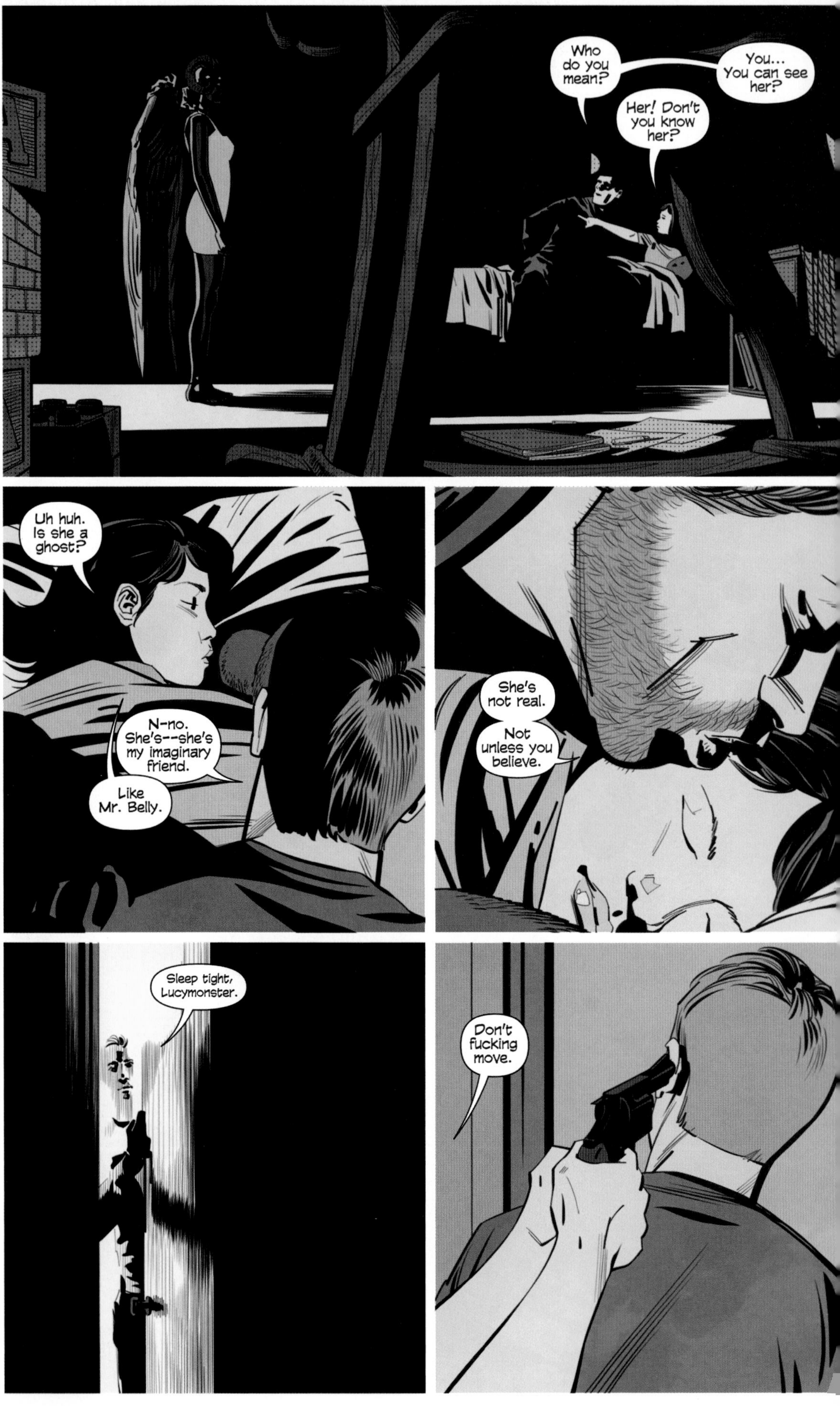
Who do you mean?
You... You can see her?
Her! Don't you know her?
Uh huh. Is she a ghost?
N-no. She's--she's my imaginary friend.
Like Mr. Belly.
She's not real.
Not unless you believe.
Sleep tight, Lucymonster.
Don't fucking move.

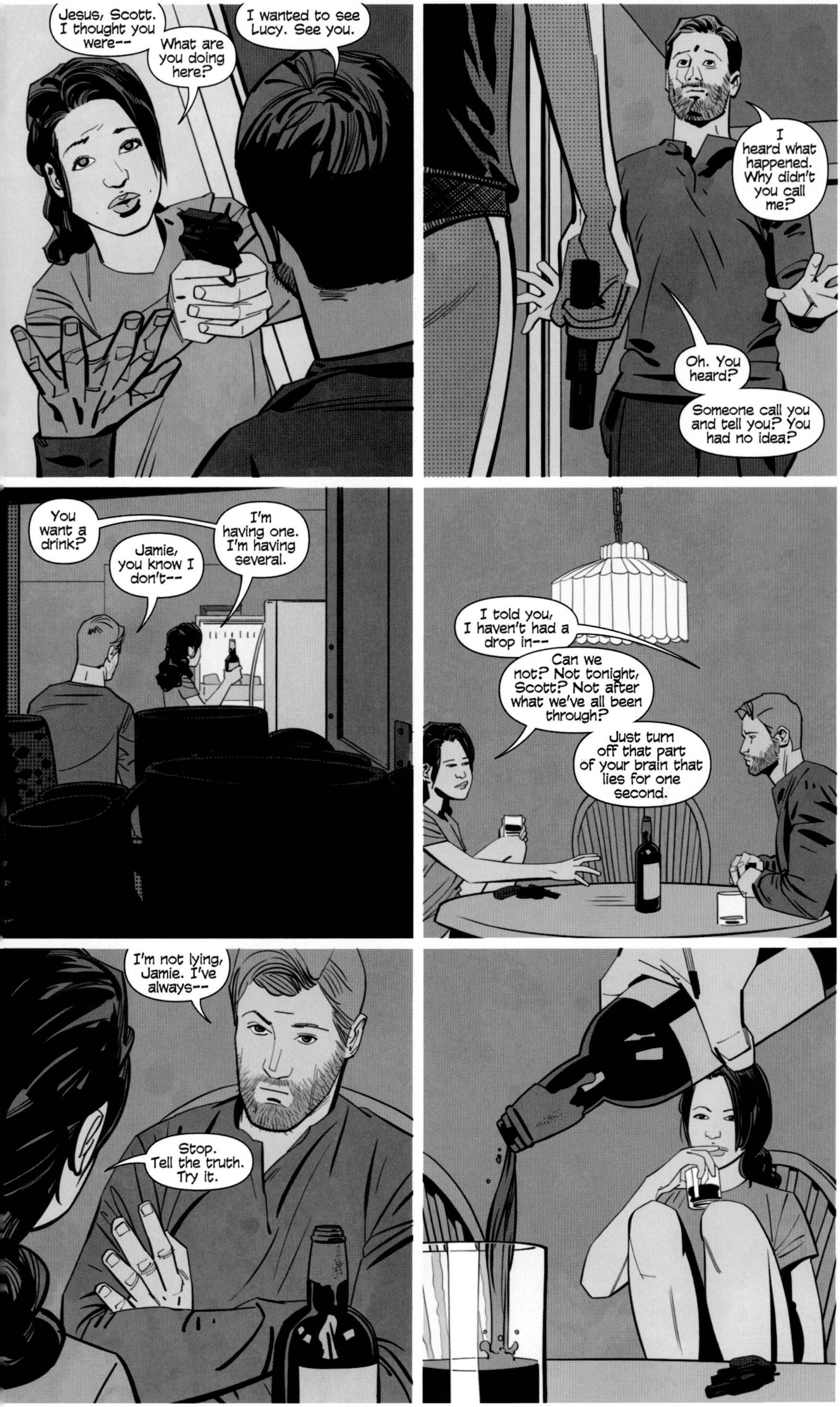
Jesus, Scott. I thought you were--
What are you doing here?
I wanted to see Lucy. See you.
I heard what happened. Why didn't you call me?
Oh. You heard?
Someone call you and tell you? You had no idea?
You want a drink?
Jamie, you know I don't--
I'm having one. I'm having several.
I told you, I haven't had a drop in--
Can we not? Not tonight, Scott? Not after what we've all been through?
Just turn off that part of your brain that lies for one second.
I'm not lying, Jamie. I've always--
Stop. Tell the truth. Try it.

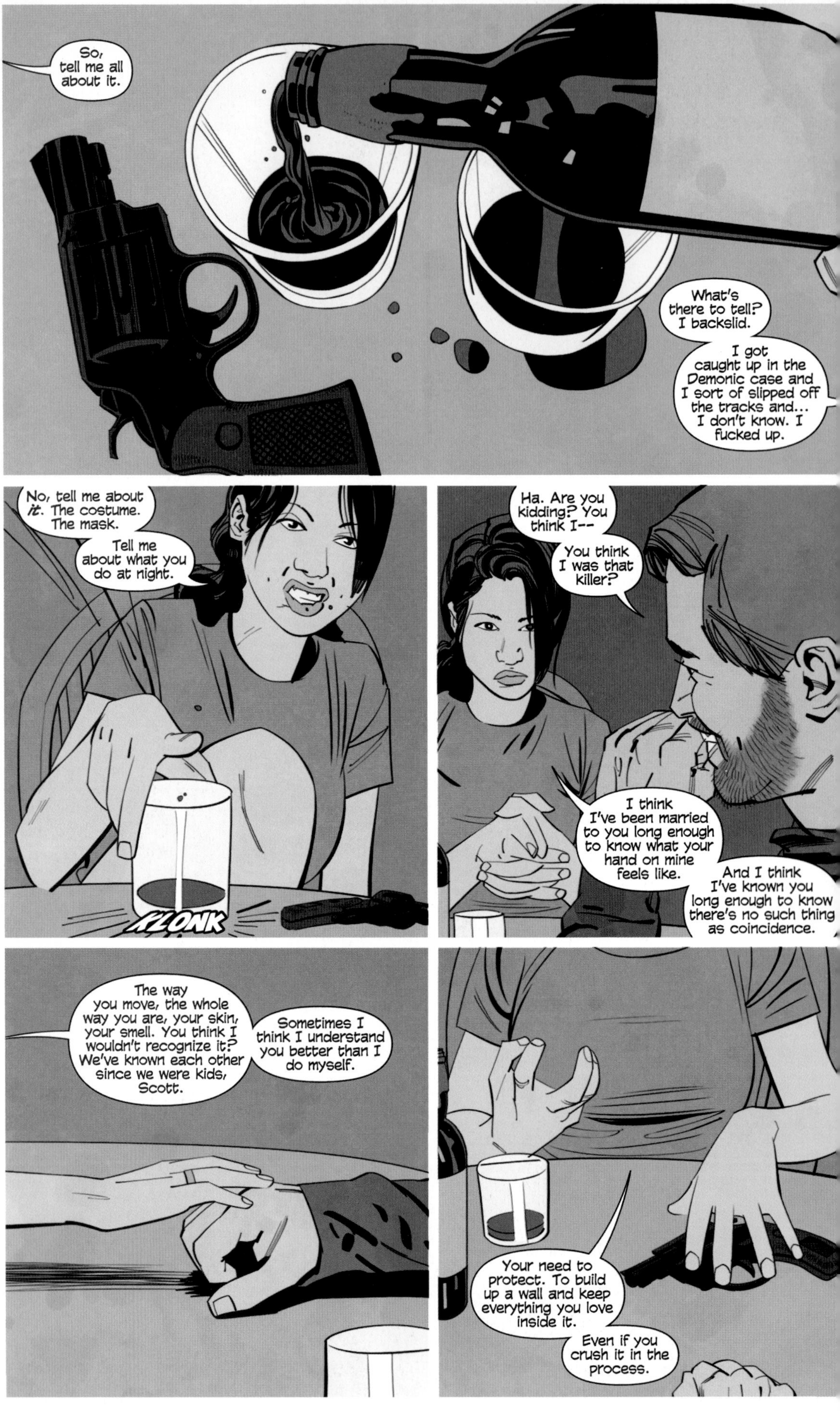
So, tell me all about it.
What's there to tell? I backslid.
I got caught up in the Demonic case and I sort of slipped off the tracks and... I don't know. I fucked up.
No, tell me about *it*. The costume. The mask.
Tell me about what you do at night.
KLONK
Ha. Are you kidding? You think I--
You think I was that killer?
I think I've been married to you long enough to know what your hand on mine feels like.
And I think I've known you long enough to know there's no such thing as coincidence.
The way you move, the whole way you are, your skin, your smell. You think I wouldn't recognize it? We've known each other since we were kids, Scott.
Sometimes I think I understand you better than I do myself.
Your need to protect. To build up a wall and keep everything you love inside it.
Even if you crush it in the process.

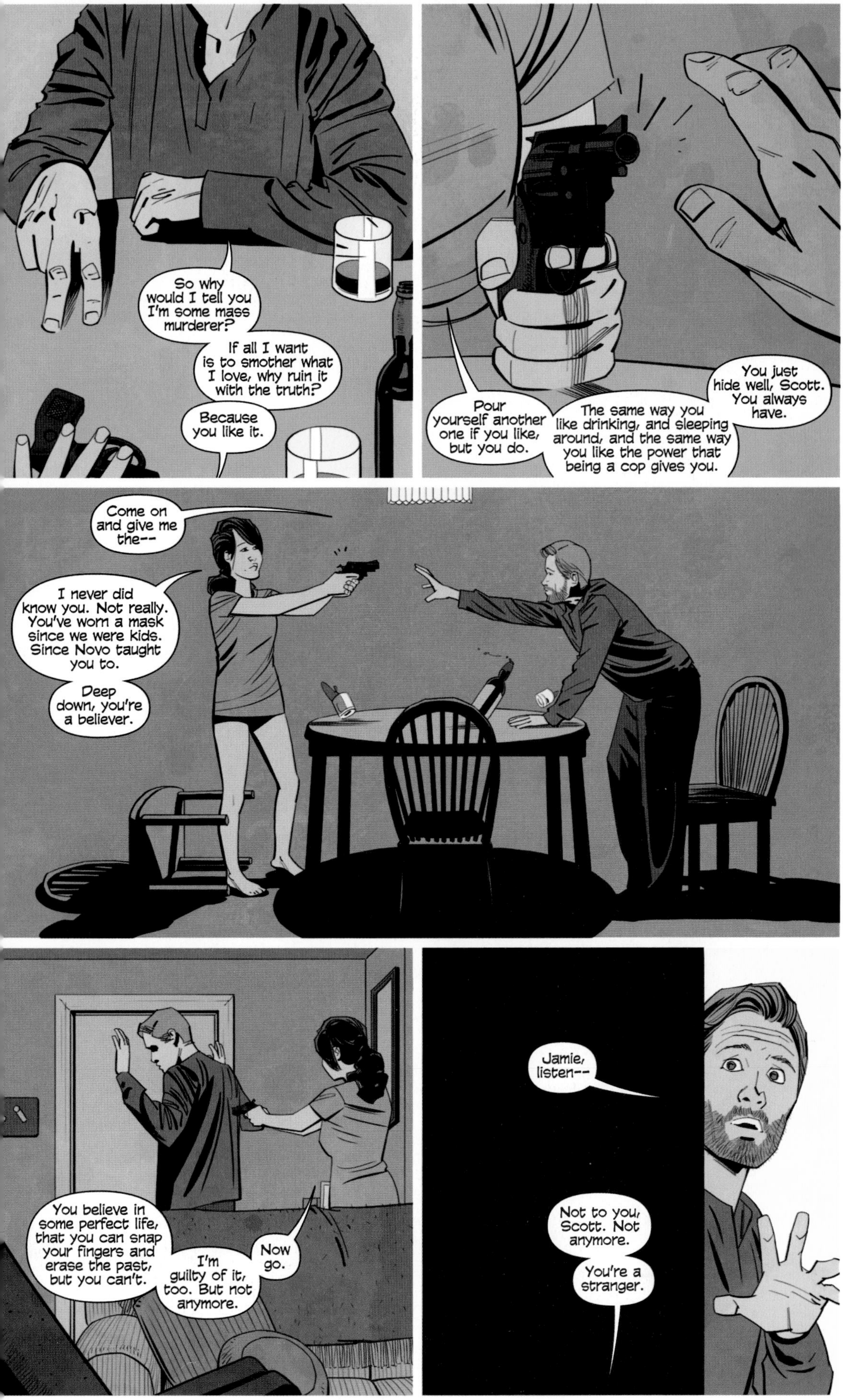
So why would I tell you I'm some mass murderer?
If all I want is to smother what I love, why ruin it with the truth?
Because you like it.
Pour yourself another one if you like, but you do.
The same way you like drinking, and sleeping around, and the same way you like the power that being a cop gives you.
You just hide well, Scott. You always have.
Come on and give me the--
I never did know you. Not really. You've worn a mask since we were kids. Since Novo taught you to.
Deep down, you're a believer.
You believe in some perfect life, that you can snap your fingers and erase the past, but you can't.
I'm guilty of it, too. But not anymore.
Now go.
Jamie, listen--
Not to you, Scott. Not anymore.
You're a stranger.

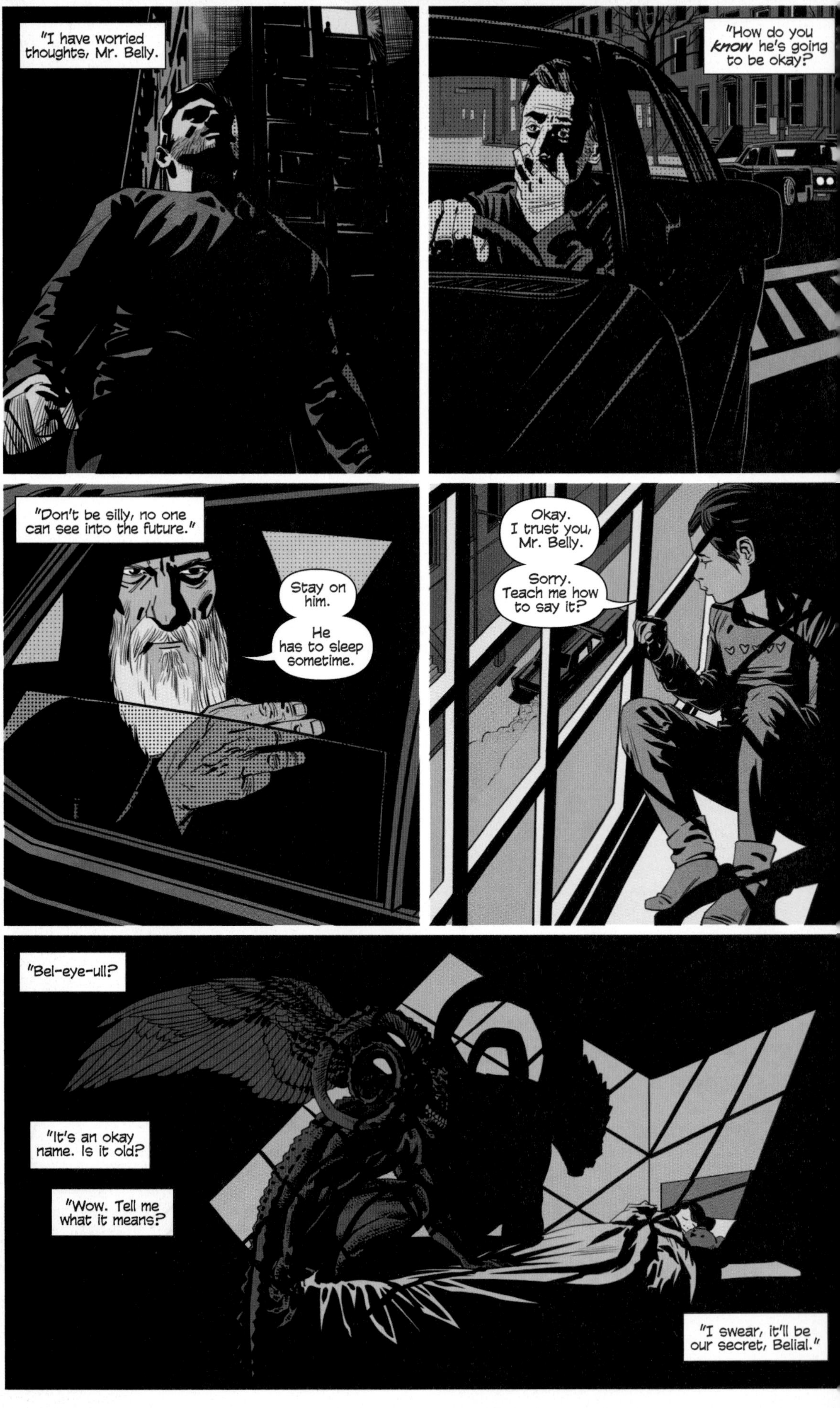
"I have worried thoughts, Mr. Belly.
"How do you *know* he's going to be okay?
"Don't be silly, no one can see into the future."
Stay on him.
He has to sleep sometime.
Okay. I trust you, Mr. Belly.
Sorry. Teach me how to say it?
"Bel-eye-ull?
"It's an okay name. Is it old?
"Wow. Tell me what it means?
"I swear, it'll be our secret, Belial."

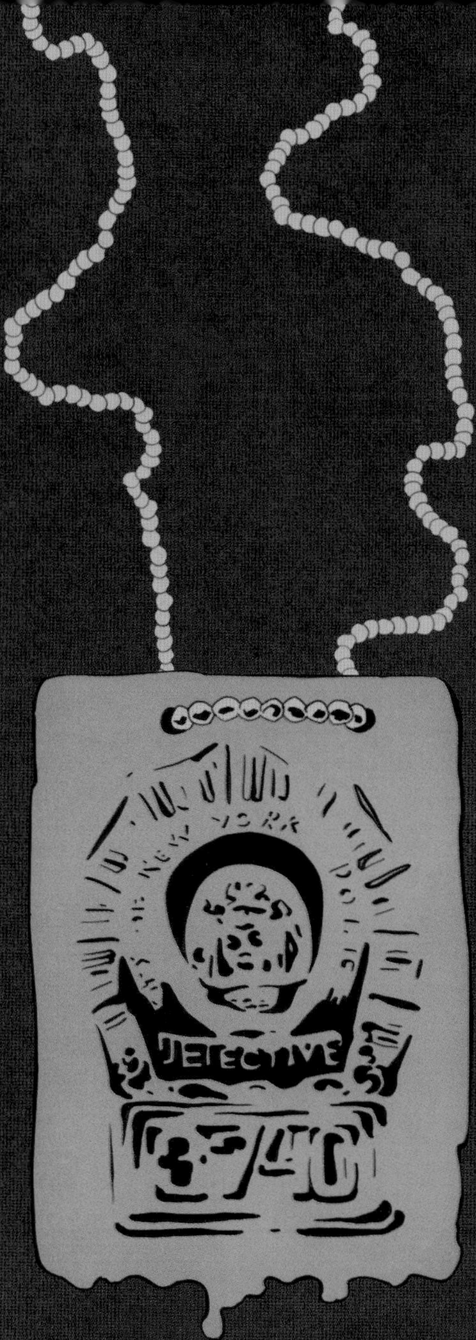
NEW YORK
DETECTIVE

THE END

FOR MORE TALES FROM **ROBERT KIRKMAN** AND **SKYBOUND**

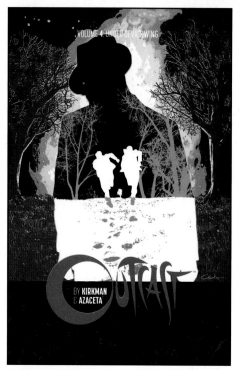

VOLUME 4: UNDER DEVIL'S WING
OUTCAST
BY KIRKMAN & AZACETA

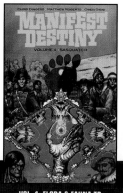

VOL. 1: A DARKNESS SURROUNDS HIM TP
ISBN: 978-1-63215-053-0
$9.99

VOL. 2: A VAST AND UNENDING RUIN TP
ISBN: 978-1-63215-448-4
$14.99

VOL. 3: THIS LITTLE LIGHT TP
ISBN: 978-1-63215-693-8
$14.99

VOL. 4: UNDER DEVIL'S WING TP
ISBN: 978-1-5343-0050-7
$14.99

BIRTHRIGHT
WILLIAMSON BRESSAN LUCAS
VOLUME FOUR
FAMILY HISTORY

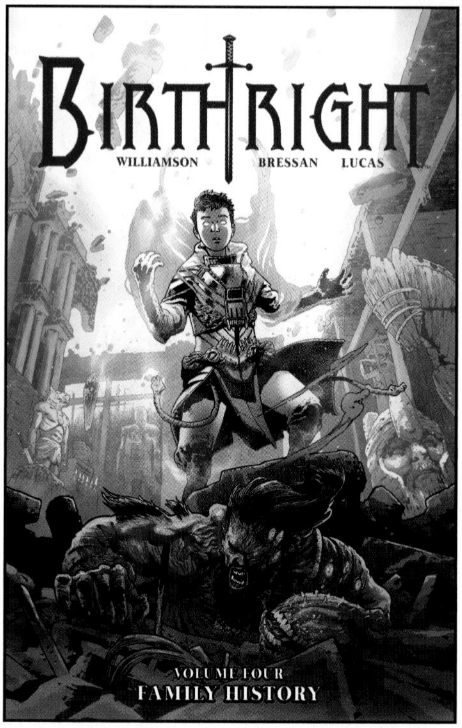

VOL. 1: HOMECOMING TP
ISBN: 978-1-63215-231-2
$9.99

VOL. 2: CALL TO ADVENTURE TP
ISBN: 978-1-63215-446-0
$12.99

VOL. 3: ALLIES AND ENEMIES TP
ISBN: 978-1-63215-683-9
$12.99

VOL. 4: FAMILY HISTORY TP
ISBN: 978-1-63215-871-0
$12.99

BRANDON THOMAS JUAN GEDEON FRANK MARTIN
HORIZON
VOLUME 01 REPRISAL

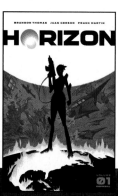

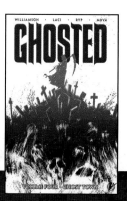

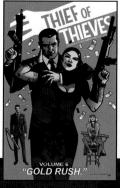

VOL. 1: REPRISAL TP
ISBN: 978-1-5343-0047-7
$9.99

WILLIAMSON · LACI · RVP · MRVA
GHOSTED
VOLUME FOUR · GHOST TOWN

VOL. 1: HAUNTED HEIST TP
ISBN: 978-1-60706-836-5
$9.99

... THE DEAD TP
...215-046-2
...9

... WISH TP
...215-051-6

... OWN TP
...15-317-3

9-12-17
MNEK-2-5-18
0 1

CHRIS DINGESS · MATTHEW ROBERTS · OWEN GIENI
MANIFEST DESTINY
VOLUME 4 · SASQUATCH

VOL. 1: FLORA & FAUNA TP
ISBN: 978-1-60706-982-9
$9.99

VOL. 2: AMPHIBIA & INSECTA TP
ISBN: 978-1-63215-052-3
$14.99

VOL. 3: CHIROPTERA & CARNIFORMAVES TP
ISBN: 978-1-63215-397-5
$14.99

VOL. 4: SASQUATCH TP
ISBN: 978-1-63215-890-1
$14.99

THIEF OF THIEVES
VOLUME 6
"GOLD RUSH."

VOL. 1: "I QUIT."
ISBN: 978-1-60706-592-0
$14.99

VOL. 2: "HELP ME."
ISBN: 978-1-60706-676-7
$14.99

VOL. 3: "VENICE."
ISBN: 978-1-60706-844-0
$14.99

VOL. 4: "THE HIT LIST."
ISBN: 978-1-63215-037-0
$14.99

VOL. 5: "TAKE ME."
ISBN: 978-1-63215-401-9
$14.99

VOL. 6: "GOLD RUSH."
ISBN: 978-1-53430-037-8
$14.99